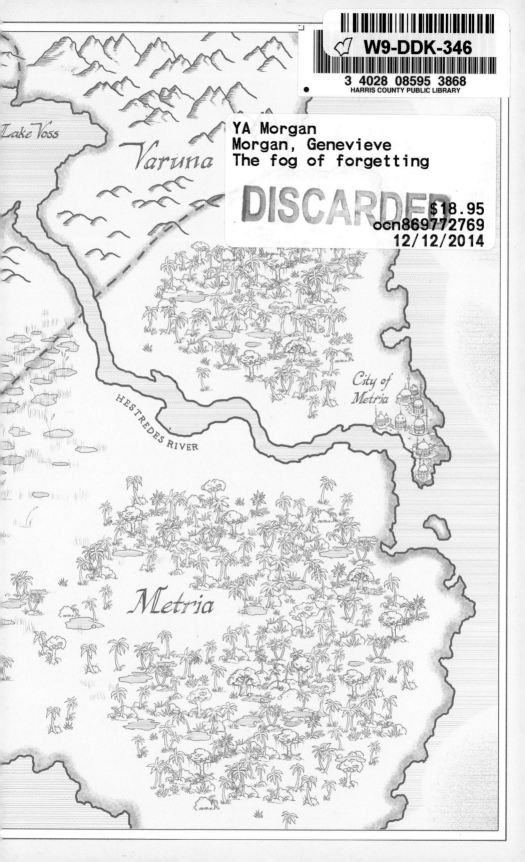

Lake Voss

Varuna

City of
Metria

HESTREDES RIVER

Metria

THE FOG OF
FORGETTING

THE FIVE STONES TRILOGY — BOOK 1

THE FOG OF FORGETTING

G.A. MORGAN

ISLANDPORT PRESS

 ISLANDPORT PRESS

Islandport Press
PO Box 10
247 Portland Street
Yarmouth, ME 04096
Islandportpress.com
books@islandportpress.com

Copyright © 2014 by G. A. Morgan

ISBN 978-1-939017-23-9
Library of Congress Control Number: 2013901201

Printed in the USA by Versa Press

10 9 8 7 6 5 4 3 2 1

Dean L. Lunt, publisher
Cover and book design by Tom Morgan, Blue Design, www.bluedes.com
Endpaper map illustration by Alex Ryan
Cover and backcover artwork by Ernie D'Elia

*For the children on Kinfolk Lane—then and now—
but especially Graham and Wyeth.*

Other young adult titles from Islandport Press:

Uncertain Glory
by Lea Wait

Billy Boy: The Sunday Soldier of the 17th Maine
by Jean Flahive

Cooper and Packrat: Mystery on Pine Lake
by Tamra Wight

Mercy: The Last New England Vampire
by Sarah L. Thomson

THE FOG OF FORGETTING

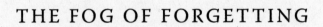

THE ISLE OF AYDA

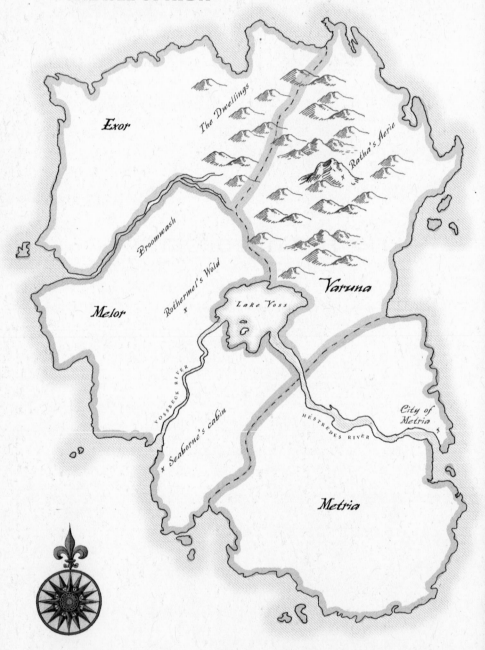

Exor

The Dwellings

Ratha's Aerie

Broomwash

Rothermel's Wold

Melor

Lake Voss

Varuna

VOSSBECK RIVER

Seaborne's cabin

HESTREDES RIVER

City of Metria

Metria

NORTH ATLANTIC

Contents

We shall not cease from exploration
And the end of all our exploring
Will be to arrive where we started
And know the place for the first time.

T. S. ELIOT

THE ATLANTIC OCEAN, 1806

Cannon shot—at least a 24-pounder—jarred the boy awake at the same moment a blistering starburst of tar and timber ripped through the hull above the officer's cot. The ship lurched sharply to port; the boy hurtled out of the shallow box that served as his bed onto the sawdust-covered floor. He pulled down his nightshirt and tried to grab whatever clothes he could reach from the pile at the bottom of the box. Another searing explosion sent him ducking for cover. The box flew up and smashed into the cabin wall, breaking into pieces.

His trousers wafted down to him in a haze of sawdust and splinters, backlit by a stream of afternoon sunlight. He jammed his legs into his pants, sat up, and was astonished to see a hole in the hull twice as large as his head—the source of light illuminating the formerly dim interior of the cabin. Outside, the din of war escalated. Thundering blasts from the big guns reverberated through the air, punctuated by the tinnier-sounding report of a pistol volley. His ship, the HMS *Cavalier,* was under attack—broadsided by the look of it. The enemy was getting bolder, taking advantage of the holes in the British blockade. The French emperor, Napoleon, was forcing open engagement for control of the trade routes to his colonies in North America.

The boy was curious. He had never seen a French battleship up close. He jumped on the cot and craned his neck to look out the blast hole. An imposing sight met his gaze: a multistoried hull with a line of cannon mouths pointing directly—or so it seemed—at him. It must be the new class, the boy thought, a Teresaire, equipped with seventy-four cannons. The *Cavalier* had only thirty-two. He dropped back, his heart pounding. Another raking explosion somewhere midship, followed by a boat-wide recoil, shook him to the floor again. He crawled back to his officer's trunk and dug around, trying to figure out what to salvage. He'd been assigned to keep the cot and cabin tidy for his officer but never thought about what the man might like to save if they were boarded or burned.

Three more cannon rounds went off, followed almost immediately by a whining groan and an ominous crack. Rigging clanked and whistled as something big—one of the masts, perhaps—slammed into the sea. The ship rolled hard to starboard and the boy was hurled into the wall, chased by the cot, trunk, and anything else not moored by floor anchors. He hit and slid to the ground. The rest of the contents of the cabin followed, pinning him painfully against the wall. The sound of the ocean grew louder in his ear. The boy closed his eyes and thought of his mother, the day the captain had come for him to set sail. She argued against it. Her son was too young to be pressed into service, but Father made his mark on the paper and it was official. He was to be a cot boy in the Royal Navy. The family would receive fair trade: a monthly wage and a lifetime annuity should the boy die at sea. The boy snuffled, wiping his nose on what he thought might be the corner of a bedsheet, but he couldn't stop the tears from leaking out his eyes. At least his eight years on Earth would not be for nothing; his family would never starve. A whimper escaped him.

"Is that you, boy? I've been looking for you! Keep blubbering so I can find you in this mess."

The cot was roughly yanked aside and a pair of strong hands grabbed him by the shoulders. He saw blue coat sleeves, and the knuckles on the hands were bruised and cut. The officer was bareheaded; he looked much younger without his hat. He patted the boy.

"Well, lad, we're done in, but I'm thinking Old Boney shouldn't have our necks to stretch. What do you think?"

The boy gave him a quick nod. The officer lifted him off his feet and wedged him under an arm; the brass-and-leather pommel of the officer's cutlass dug into his hip. He noticed that the sword was still in its steel scabbard.

"Both masts gone . . . ship scuttled . . . They'll set her alight for sure. Those hellions would rather roast then play fair. I'll be damned before I swab decks for a bunch of—"

The officer's tirade was replaced by grunts as he carried the boy up the ladder, through the shattered belly of the ship, to the deck. Warm liquid seeped from the officer's side as he moved. The boy touched it and saw blood.

On deck, the sun shimmered, oblong and orange, as it flattened against the horizon. A yellow haze of smoke hid them from view. The white flag of *parlé* flapped overhead: The surrender of the ship was being negotiated. Shouts of protest rose up above the murk, then the sound of scuffling. A pistol shot fired, then another, followed by a loud *splash*.

"That's the kind of amnesty you'll receive from that lot," the officer grumbled. "A quick *merci*, thank you very much, and then a gunshot to the head—here, boy, keep your head down—that smoke may save our biscuit."

He was fumbling with one of the stays that fastened a lifeboat to the side of the ship. Mercifully, it had remained untouched through the attack—not one of the ship's mates had tried to escape. A sudden sense of shame fell over the boy. Should they not face the same outcome as the others? Or at least try to save a few? He cast his eyes around wildly, hoping to catch sight of one of the other cot boys. He was not the only one aboard. The line suddenly gave way and the lifeboat's bow swung sharply from the ship hull.

"Blast it!" the officer swore, flinging an arm over the side to intercept the small craft before it crashed back into the ship. "Hang on!"

He leapt over the side and tossed the boy into the boat; the force of their joint landing snapped the remaining stays. The lifeboat torpedoed, stern first, past the smoking, shredded hull of the *Cavalier*, landing with a smack on the surface of the water. The boy bit his tongue and tasted blood. The officer winced in pain. A raspberry-colored bloom spread along the front of his tunic, staining his coat and sleeves. He was shivering. The boy looked away from the wounded man and out across the empty carpet of water. A thick, gray mist muddied the horizon, creeping toward them in long, wispy fingers, as if it sensed they were there and was reaching for them across the seas.

Fog.

Fear swept over the boy like a bucket of cold water being thrown in his face. Soon it would overtake them and they would be lost. He would never see his home again.

The officer groaned loudly, raised himself up on his good elbow, and bellowed.

"For all that you hold holy, lad, quit your gaping and ROW!"

Chapter 1

THE ATLANTIC COAST,
PRESENT DAY

Chase Thompson was dreaming he was on the porch at Summerledge, looking out over the rocks toward the ocean. He saw something floating out there, bigger than a buoy but too small to be a boat. An overwhelming urge to see what it was took hold of him. He took a few steps and, as happens in dreams, launched himself off the porch and into the air. Below him, the pitched roof of Summerledge and humps of granite dropped away. Out of the corner of his eye, he glimpsed the arc of Secret Beach, the Dellemere cottage, and a ways beyond, the cluster of houses that indicated the village of Fells Harbor. He caught an air current and swooped out over the sea, soaring happily across the green-blue carpet of water until a flash of orange caught his eye. He dove down to get a closer look. It was a life jacket, bubbling around someone floating facedown in the water. He hovered over it. Swells rose and fell, rhythmically; the body floated up to meet him, and then slowly . . . slowly . . . began to roll over.

He bolted awake, heart thumping, and got his bearings. No ocean. No body. He was safe in the backseat of his family's car in the driveway at 320 Elm Ridge Road. School had finally been let out and it was time for his family's annual drive up the coast to Summerledge. His mother, Grace, was fastening the last duffel bag to the collection of luggage and sports equipment already strapped to the roof. A jumble of bikes protruded from the rear, and the inside of the car was packed with bags of groceries.

He ran a hand through his brown, rangey bangs and pulled up his hoodie in an effort to ignore the disgusted look of two ladies who were standing at the bay window of the house across the street. Teddy, Chase's six-year-old brother, came rocketing out the front door looking like a cross between a crazed hobo and the son of Aquaman. He wore a swimsuit, a scruffy baseball shirt stained down the front with what *might* be hot chocolate, swim goggles, and orange-and-blue flippers on his feet. A sticky, red goo was smeared across his face, which he rubbed into his mother's pant leg. She swooped down and strapped him—blond, kicking, and wildly smacking his flippers—into his booster seat. Chase sighed. He knew what the neighbors were saying—everyone in his family knew. Their car, their yard, his brothers, heck, their whole life, was an eyesore on the tidy cul-de-sac.

"*Chathe!*" Teddy sang out, whacking his flippers against the back of the driver's seat. Despite a year of speech therapy, Teddy's S's were still coming out of his mouth sounding like "th's."

"Chasssse—with an *Sssss,*" Chase said back at him, hissing. "Like Sssssnake."

"*Thhh*nake," Teddy repeated, unfazed, lifting one smudged eye piece of his swim goggles. "TTTTTTTTHNAKE!" He yelled louder, flippers whacking. "CHATHE! THHNAKE!"

"Okay, Tedders, whatever—it's a free country." Chase took a peek at the snotty neighbors in the window and smirked. They were wearing matching tracksuits and ponytails. "At least for some people."

"We're going to Thummerledge today," said Teddy happily.

Chase reached over and bumped his knuckles to his brother's sticky little fist, then reached in the front pocket of his sweatshirt for his cell phone—one of the crummy free ones you get when you sign a contract, but it stored music and he could text. Problem was, Chase didn't have anyone to text except for Knox, his other little brother.

His mother bent down and eyed him through the half-open window. She was thin and tired-looking, with brownish hair scrunched into a knot at her neck.

"Do you have your inhaler?" she asked.

Chase yanked the green nylon cord out from under his sweatshirt and wiggled his asthma inhaler at her, then pulled his hood farther up over his eyes and shoved the seat. It rewarded him by groaning pathetically. The neighbors were right: This car *was* a bucket of bolts. He'd been driving around in it since he was a baby thirteen years ago, and it was scrap metal then.

"Can we go already, Mom?"

"As soon as Dad and Knox are ready," she said with a tight little smile, settling herself in the driver's seat.

Chase worked his thumbs on the phone's keyboard, typing: GET OUT HERE, then he popped his earbuds in his ears and scrolled through the list of songs he'd downloaded earlier. He'd discovered just how useful earbuds could be at his new school. Nobody tried to talk to you, but everybody felt free to talk *about* you when they thought you couldn't hear them. Every rotten word, like *freak, loser,* and *in for it.*

His mom had told him things would get better—were getting better—because of their dad's new job, but Chase knew that if school hadn't finally ended and if they weren't driving up to Summerledge *today,* things would definitely, positively, be getting worse. But Chase couldn't tell his mom that. His parents had their own problems. They fought all the time. About the new job. About money. About Knox's grades. For all he knew, they fought about him when he wasn't around. The only thing they didn't fight about was Teddy, and that was because Teddy was still pretty much a baby.

Chase glanced out the car window at the scrubby shrubs leashed down by collars and wires that were staked into the center of the paved cul-de-sac. He figured he could probably uproot all of them with one well-aimed kick.

"Hey, Mom, you ever wonder why they call this place Sherwood Forest? There's nothing that even comes close to a tree around here."

Grace made an unintelligible sound.

"Did you e-mail the Neighborhood Association and explain that humans *are* actually mammals?"

"Chase, stop," she sighed. It was an old argument. Roger, their dog, had to be left behind in Indiana when they moved to Massachusetts because Sherwood Forest had a "No Mammals" pet policy.

"Idiots," Chase coughed into his hand and turned his music up. In his opinion, the only good thing about the move was Sherwood Forest's freshly paved, skateboard-ready road, and that was only because skateboarding was the closest he had gotten all year to flying the heck out of this place—that is, until today.

Knox barreled out the front door carrying a plastic box holding their turtle, Bob, in one hand, and a lacrosse stick and a beat-up guitar case in the other. Knox was twelve, and shorter and stockier than Chase. He had sandy hair cut into a spiky fringe and was the only Thompson brother to inherit their dad's dimples and freckles. He had his mother's wide, blue eyes, like both Chase and Teddy, only one of his was underscored by a knuckle-sized bruise on the left cheekbone.

Chase saw the bruise—sore and glaring at him—as Knox crossed over to the car. He looked away, embarrassed, remembering how Knox had come across two guys from the JV soccer team cornering him in the stairwell on the day before school ended. He had been wheezing so loudly that Knox heard him from the landing, and launched himself at one of the guys. Everyone (except him) had ended up bloody and in the principal's office. The incident would have meant suspension, for sure, if the principal hadn't been as sick of the whole school business as everyone else. Instead, Knox was told to write an essay on the impact of nonviolent protests on history—and he was still mad about it. According to him, if anyone was writing an essay over the summer, that person was Chase. It wasn't *his* fault his older brother was a tool.

Knox shoved his guitar and lacrosse stick in the last sliver of air in the back and dumped Bob on Chase's lap, half on purpose, sloshing turtle water everywhere. He chucked himself into the middle seat, splashing more water onto Chase's jeans.

"Thanks a lot," said Chase, annoyed.

"What are you complaining about? You need a bath anyway." Knox grabbed the aquarium and made a face, then turned to Teddy, who was busy finger-painting the window with peanut butter from his snack.

"Thatta boy, Ted." He looked around the cramped car and made a *ka-che* whip-cracking noise. "Giddy-up, Mom!"

Grace rolled her shoulders back, her hands at 9 and 3 on the steering wheel.

"Just waiting for Dad."

"We'll have to go back to school by the time he gets here," said Knox. "He's packing files and crap."

"He is not," she said, widening her eyes. "And don't say crap."

"He is so."

She sighed, unbuckled her seat belt, and got out of the car. She returned with her husband, Jim, in tow: a tall, angular man who looked like he worked all day under fluorescent lights. He was staring down at his cell phone. Chase could see the bald spot on the top of his dad's head, like an egg in a brown nest.

Grace got back in the driver's seat and strapped in. Jim stalled at the passenger door, scrolling his index finger up and down on the cell-phone screen. Knox pushed through the gap in the front seats and laid on the horn. His dad recoiled as though he'd been shot, then opened the door. His nose crinkled instantly.

"What in God's name is that *smell?*"

"Chase," grinned Knox, dimples flashing.

"Shut UP!" Chase replied. "You're so not funny."

"At least I'm not a loser like you."

"I'm warning you, Knox. SHUT UP!"

"Aren't we touchy, Chathey-Wathey." Knox stuck out his lower lip and made a fake pouty face.

Chase shifted sideways, ignoring his brother.

"None of you are losers," said their father distractedly, looking back down at his phone screen. Grace lowered her window and glanced behind her. Her head snapped around when she heard buttons being pressed.

"Really, Jim?" she asked, gritting her teeth. "I thought you agreed: No calls! We're on vacation. I want us to talk to *each other.* You only have a week up there, which reminds me—" She held her hand out backwards toward the backseat. Chase and Knox reluctantly relinquished their phones. She held the same hand out to her husband. He clutched his cell phone defensively to his chest.

"I have to check in with the lab," he said, trying to sound breezy. She rolled her eyes. He sighed, "I'm the *boss,* Grace; it's part of my job."

"Besides, Mom—nobody talks anymore," said Knox. "That's why they invented texting."

Jim turned around and winked at Knox. Grace cranked the ignition a little too hard.

"I'm looking forward to being together, Grace," Jim said hastily. "I really am. I just wish things at work were a little more settled."

"Are they ever going to be settled?" she replied. "I mean, do you think, in your estimation, there will EVER be a time when we can go on vacation without your cell phone? Jim, it's Summerledge!"

"Aaah, yes, *Summerledge,*" he echoed, voice lowered in mock awe. "The Baker ancestral seat." He closed his eyes and loudly listed off complaints: the scraping and painting that the old wooden house would need in the coming week, the chilly fog that crept along the shore and stayed for days, the endless amount of firewood that needed to be carried from the shed. Then, he sighed.

"Vacation my ass."

"Dad! You thaid ath!" squealed Teddy.

"Don't be stupid," snapped Chase, eyeing his mom for signs of sudden rage explosion.

"You're thtupid, Chathe," said Teddy.

"Don't say stupid," scolded Grace.

"Actually, he said *thtupid,* not stupid," said Knox. "Besides, you guys need to get back to fighting."

"We're not fighting!" both parents shouted in unison.

"*Pickle Jinxth!*" shrieked Teddy. "Now you can't talk until I thay your name, and if you do, your name ith the firtht word you thay."

Grace put her head in her hands and said, "Boys, *enough.*"

"Ha, ha—your name is 'Boyth Enough' now, Mom. That'th funny, Boyth Enough."

"Oh. My. God. Can we just go, *puh-lease,*" groaned Chase.

Grace put the car in gear and drove slowly around the cul-de-sac, collecting herself just in time to wave to her neighbors.

"Nasty old bats," muttered Knox, leaning over Chase to leer and wave. Taken aback, one of them mechanically bent her fingers down. "That's it, wave back, you trolls."

Their mother sighed loudly.

"What? It's true!" cried Knox. "They're always staring at us and sniffing—and the blonde one's ponytail is pulled too tight. It makes her eyes all bulgy. She went mental this winter when I hit her car with a snowball. A *snowball*. You would have thought it was sniper fire. She said she was going to call the police."

Grace half-smiled despite herself and flicked a glance through the mirror at her sons: Chase was adjusting his earbuds, pulling on his hood. Knox's knee bounced up and down, making the water in the aquarium slosh. Teddy's goggle strap was snarled in his curly hair and he'd gone back to licking peanut butter off his window. Her gaze lingered for a moment, protectively, then she stomped on the accelerator. Soon they would be at Summerledge, and in the two months there the boys would forget this past year and everything would be different when school started again. After all, didn't she know better than anyone how a single summer could change everything?

✛   ✛   ✛

Grace's grandfather, Henry Baker, built Summerledge in 1925 as a wedding present for his new wife, Ruth. He returned from fighting in the Great War with a limp, damaged lungs, and a deep longing for a quiet life by the sea where he would never again hear the sound of gunfire. He found it in a parcel of shorefront not far from the village of Fells Harbor, and quickly got to work. When he was finished, the house had three floors, a center chimney, and an iron widow's walk that wrapped around the roof. With the sound of surf in his ears, he walked the length of the long driveway and drove a post into the ground where he installed a shiny metal mailbox and painted the name *Summerledge* on it in green.

After Grace's mother was born, he added a shed, a telephone, and indoor plumbing, but not much else.

As a child, Grace spent eight precious summers at Summerledge with her older brother, Edward and their grandparents. Almost as soon as they could walk, her grandfather taught them both to sail in the small wooden sailboat he refinished with his own hands. By age twelve, Edward was a good enough sailor to take the boat out by himself, often staying out all day to explore the outer islands. He told Grace he would take her with him when she was older—but then came the summer that changed everything: the summer Edward took the sailboat out and never came back.

After that, Grace was taken inland for good, far away from the ocean's glare and the fog that boats—and brothers—got lost in. There she stayed, for more than twenty years, until the day she got a letter in the mail deeding Summerledge and all its belongings to her. That was fifteen years ago, and the Thompsons had been making the drive up to Maine every summer since.

✛   ✛   ✛

Halfway into *this* year's drive, the Thompsons' car hit a small bump in the road. A squealing shudder ripped through the interior. Grace peered nervously out her side mirror.

"You did tie the bikes on tightly, Jim? I mean, with the strap?" she asked her husband.

He gave her an exasperated look.

"I think I can be trusted to pack the bikes, don't you? It's not rocket science."

"Uh . . . Mom?" Knox interrupted, leaning forward to get her attention.

A dull drilling sound from outside the car was picking up volume.

"Just a minute, honey, I want to say something important to Dad—Jim?—*Jim!*" she repeated, louder.

"Hmm?" Jim mumbled, his mind miles away, back at the lab, among racks of test tubes and petri dishes holding exotic strains of bacteria.

"*Mom!*" yelled Knox.

She ignored him, still focused on her husband. "Jim, honey, I—I want you to know that I'm really glad you're coming for the whole week. I know you have a lot of work."

"I'm looking forward to it—" His ear twitched back at the sound of metal groaning. "Grace, this car *really* needs some attention."

"The *car* needs attention?" she repeated, her temper rising again.

"Mom!" Knox yelled, trying one more time and elbowing Chase in the ribs.

"What'd ya do that for?" Chase snapped, removing his earbuds. Knox pointed. One of the ties holding the bikes on board was loose and flapping against the back of the car, its metal end rapping loudly.

"It'th LOUD in here!" Teddy cried, holding his hands up to his ears.

The sudden sound of metal screaming drowned out everything else; the car lurched and, with a *wump-wump-wump—crash,* the bike rack and all the bikes separated from the tail end and fell onto the highway. Cars veered like bowling pins around the flying projectiles of spinning wheels and handlebars.

"Hey, Mom, check it out—that guy's flipping you off," said Chase.

A red sedan bolted by them, its passenger shaking an upturned middle finger out the window. Knox snorted with laughter. Grace navigated the car to the shoulder.

"You three listen to me, right now—not another word. Dad and I have to work this out."

Jim collapsed his face into his hands and muttered a list of what sounded like some very bad swear words.

"Dad?" Knox pointed incredulously at his father's bent head. "What's he gonna do? Call 911?"

"Knox, I mean it: Not. Another. Word." She opened the car door and got out. Jim groaned and followed her.

"I'm going too," said Knox. He unbuckled, handed Bob to Chase, and scrambled over Teddy's car seat.

"Not me," said Chase, making a sour face at the turtle. "If he's stupid enough not to tie the bikes on right—"

"Don't call your father stupid!" Grace barked from outside the car.

The sun was setting when the Thompsons drove down the main street of Fells Harbor, exhausted and three bikes lighter. They passed the post office, library, and a small assortment of shops: a grocery, a hardware store, a marine supply company, and a drugstore called Flo's. As they headed northeast, they went by a cottage belonging to one of their nearest neighbors: Captain Nate. The house faced out to sea but for two windows flanking the front door. A wall of lobster traps divided the driveway from a small, well-kept lawn, and a steady stream of smoke rose from the chimney. Captain Nate was a lobster fisherman and a local legend for his knowledge of all things boat-related, and for his universal dislike of small talk, small children, and trespassers.

Chase rolled down his window, putting his chin against the edge of the glass. The car veered past the house. A flicker of movement caught his eye. He thought he saw the dark shape of Captain Nate standing alone on his dock, watching the water.

"It smells so good here," he announced, to no one in particular.

"Doesn't it, honey?" his mother replied, her own voice soft.

Chase glanced at her and saw that her window was down too, her light brown hair spinning wildly from its bun. She looked happy. His dad was sound asleep, head tilted back against the seat, small moon-shaped dents on his nose from his glasses.

"I'm so glad you like it here," said Grace.

They reached their rusty mailbox and turned right, heading down the long driveway. The sun had sunk low and it was hard to make out familiar shapes in the twilight. Knox peered past Chase, out the window, looking for his tree fort in the gloom.

"I think I see it!" he said excitedly, pointing to a barely visible outline of a platform and rail. "It made it through the winter."

Their dad was awake now, staring out the windshield with unfocused eyes. Quiet billowed through the windows with the scent of the ocean. Each person became lost in their own private memories when, like a dream, the house suddenly appeared around a bend in the driveway. Its silhouette stood erect against the empty horizon—silent and motionless—waiting for them, as it had been all winter.

The car pulled into its space by the shed and Grace turned off the engine. The boys sat up, listening intently to the crash of waves striking the ledge and watching the first bright pinpricks of stars poke through the darkening sky. Beyond the house lay the sea and shining gray mounds of granite that slumped into the depths like whale backs and gave the house its name.

"We're here!" cried Teddy.

"Finally," said Chase.

Chapter 2

UNEXPECTED VISITORS

Chase blinked awake the next morning, blinded for a minute by sunlight. He and Knox bunked together in their mother's old, yellow room at Summerledge. Teddy slept in a smaller room across the hall, just off his parents' corner bedroom. The house had one other bedroom: their uncle Edward's room. No one went in there unless they had guests.

Chase sat up and stretched. The air was cool and smelled like aged wood and ocean salt, with a hint of mildew. The smell of summer. *This* was the moment he'd been waiting for all year. No school. No homework. No teachers telling you what to do all day. And, best of all, no one around to make life miserable—just endless empty hours. He leaned across the space between the twin beds and poked at the Knox-shaped lump in the sleeping bag. It collapsed under his finger, empty. Chase pogo-ed over to the window in his sleeping bag. He shaded his eyes against the glare and watched a small silhouette standing on the outermost ledge, fist in the air, as the tide surged against the rocks, catapulting spray.

"*Wa-hoo!*"

Chase opened the window to yell down to Knox, but the surf was too loud, so he hastily pulled on his shorts, T-shirt, and hoodie and went down the stairs. The kitchen was warm and smelled like coffee; a small fire crackled in the woodstove, and boxes of cereal and bowls were already laid out on the square wooden kitchen table.

Chase paused to put his inhaler around his neck. He took a breath, testing. His lungs were clear for now, but asthma was always there, beneath the surface of his skin, ready to choke him. He'd avoided a full-on attack at school, and complete and utter social doom, by being very careful all year long. Maybe now that he was at Summerledge, the beast in his lungs would relax and he could think about other things.

He went outside, slamming the screen door behind him, and slowly rounded the house. Gulls swooped overhead, calling out to one another. The pitted backs of the granite ledge were strung thick with seaweed and mussels; a dark waterline cut across the rock's face. Out to sea, lobster boats steamed along the horizon, the sound of their engines droning loudly in the clear morning air. When Chase caught up with Knox, still at the farthest edge, his brother's face was wet, his dimples deep in his cheeks from smiling so hard.

"Hey!" yelled Chase over the pound of the waves.

"I saw something out here!" Knox yelled back. "I was looking out the window and saw something cross the yard."

"What?"

Knox shrugged. Another burst of sea spray showered them.

"I dunno, maybe a fox or something. It was gone when I got down here." He looked sideways at Chase. "Wanna have a screaming contest?" It used to be their favorite game.

"That's lame," said Chase, but he was smiling now, too. The movement felt strange; his ears felt heavy, like they'd gained weight over the past year from not smiling for such a long time. Knox shrugged again and circled his mouth with his hands.

"I HATE MATH FACTS! AND MRS. COSGROVE'S WEIRD NECK MOLE WITH THE HAIR GROWING OUT OF IT. AND WORD STUDY!" He lowered his hands for a minute, then screamed, "CARLY STUART IS A CRYBABY! JOE MCNALLY CHEATS AT FOUR SQUARE! TREVOR WILSON'S FARTS STINK LIKE HOT DOGS!"

Chase grinned. He was enjoying his brother's company at the moment. "Anything else?"

Knox shook his head, slowly, happily. "No—but it feels good. Try it." He gave Chase another sideways glance.

"No doubt," said Chase, avoiding eye contact. Knox's shiner was a sickly green this morning. "Maybe later."

Knox chewed on the ribbed collar of his T-shirt for a minute, then he leaned in toward Chase. "You know—"

"I don't want to talk about it." Chase stepped away quickly, moving back toward the house. Knox followed him.

To their right lay a rocky, northeasterly stretch of beach. The geography of Summerledge was too rugged for a dock, so the Thompsons used the old sailboat mooring for their small Whaler, which wasn't in the water yet.

"Lots of traps out there," said Knox, with a nod toward the cluster of bobbing, striped buoys less than a hundred feet from shore. "Maybe Mom will let me put some in this year."

Chase snorted. Knox had only learned to drive the Whaler last summer—now he was the big expert. The salty fisherman. He was about to say something to that effect when he caught sight of the shiner again.

"I doubt it. You know what a freak she is about the water."

Knox's shoulders sagged. It was true. The Thompsons didn't set foot on a boat unless the weather forecast called for sparkling clear days. No way would their mom let Knox go out every day to collect traps. There might be fog, and she was deathly—and nonnegotiably—afraid of fog.

"Yeah," Knox sighed.

Chase gave him a halfhearted punch, trying to be nice. The truth was that the sight of Knox had been making him mad all week—by all rights, the shiner should have been his, not Knox's—but that wasn't why he couldn't talk about it. The real reason was that all week he'd been trying to figure out if he would have done the same thing if he'd been in Knox's position. He wasn't sure. What kind of person would let some kid beat up his little brother? He didn't want to be that kind of person. But maybe he was, and Knox wasn't, and that made it hard to look at him.

"It's low tide," Chase said, instead. "We could check out Secret Beach."

Knox flashed his smile and took off toward the driveway.

Secret Beach wasn't really much of a secret, but it had been called that for as long as anyone could remember. The sandy quarter-mile arch was slotted between two shelves of granite just south of Summerledge. The Thompsons accessed it by a hidden path off the driveway. Because of the currents, Secret Beach was a daily receptacle for every imaginable bit of flotsam and jetsam thrown overboard: sea glass, buoys, coils of colorful, burnt rope, plastic containers, driftwood, banged-up metal traps, old rubber boots. It was like having a treasure chest outside your front door that magically refilled every day.

Chase watched Knox sprint toward the opening in the woods. He swallowed some air deep into his lungs. Testing. It would feel good to be able to run—especially since his skateboard was useless on grass. Now was as good a time as any to find out if the beast would let him. He picked up his pace. At the head of the path, he stopped, huffing and puffing, and took a hit from his inhaler.

"WHEEZER!" Knox yelled, jumping out of the tree fort and landing right behind Chase.

"Are you trying to kill me?" Chase gasped, startled. "I'm not supposed to run, remember?"

"Yeah, whatever," said Knox.

They jostled each other all the way down the path, leaving the shade of the woods where it narrowed as they cut through a stretch of long dune grass, slanting sharply downhill and onto the speckled reaches of the beach. At the other end, they could see the sharp-pitched roof and boxy outline of the cottage that belonged to their nearest neighbor: old Fanny Dellemere. The boys threaded their way through the grass, past the lip of heaped rocks, and out onto the beach. They heard the slight tinkling of water receding over pebbles as the tide ebbed and looked up into the misty glare of the surf. Two narrow figures were stooped at the water's edge.

Blinking in disbelief, Knox whispered, "Oh no!" He poked Chase hard in the ribs. "Girls!"

"Let's just go back," Chase groaned, deflated and annoyed. He didn't want to deal with any other kids. He'd had enough of them all year. They made a move to turn back when the taller of the two figures looked up and waved vigorously; she shook the other, shorter girl by the shoulder. A wave came crashing in and rolled over the tops of the girls' feet. They shrieked and ran up the beach, toward the boys.

"Are you the Thompsons?" yelled the taller girl.

She looked a little younger than Chase, but just as tall and angular. By the fit of her cut-off shorts and stretched-out sweater, she hadn't had time to buy clothes to match her new height. Both girls had round faces, long, curly, chestnut-colored hair, and golden-brown skin. The younger girl's forehead was framed by squared-off bangs, and her smile was missing a tooth. She wore a red windbreaker, rolled-up jeans, and pink high-tops. When the girls got close enough to talk instead of yell, Chase could see that the older girl had enormous brown eyes surrounded by a thick fringe of lashes.

"Umm, two of them . . . We have a little brother. I mean, besides Mom and Dad," answered Knox.

The older girl was silent, studying them. Chase did the same, noticing through his own bangs that she had a long, straight nose which, combined with her large eyes, gave her a serious, almost sad, expression. The younger girl stood on one foot, scratching a mosquito bite on her calf with her pink sneaker.

Finally, the older girl cocked her head in Knox's direction. "You must be Knox."

He nodded. If the girl noticed Knox's bruise, she didn't show it.

"So you must be Chase—" she flicked her eyes at Chase. "And Teddy is the other brother, right?" She had an accent that made her words sound clipped, stressing the D's and T's.

"Yup—how did you know?" asked Knox.

"My grandmother told me," she said matter-of-factly, and extended her hand. Knox took it like it was a used tissue, clearly weirded-out to be shaking hands with another kid.

"Nice to meet you," she said politely. "My name is Evelyn Boudreaux. This is my little sister, Frankie," she said, gesturing to her right. "I'm thirteen and she's nine. How old are you?" She held her hand out to Chase. He hadn't spoken yet. While Evelyn was asking her questions, he was examining the granite shelf to his left, wondering if he could just start climbing and get away before he had to say anything.

"I'm twelve," Knox replied, shoving Chase lightly.

"And you?" Evelyn asked again, this time looking directly at Chase, her hand still extended. When he didn't answer, Evelyn dropped her hand and raised an eyebrow at Knox. "Does he talk?" The way she said it was different than the kids at school. Nicer. As if she didn't care what the answer was.

"I'm almost fourteen," Chase mumbled.

Evelyn acknowledged the answer by saying, "Look what we found."

She held out a small, whitish-gray disc no bigger than a quarter. It was etched with a star pattern and had five small slits along the bottom. She turned the sand dollar over in her palm.

"We've been here almost every day and this is the first time I've seen one. Are they common here?"

Chase tensed. Every day? Who were these girls? This was *their* beach. Plus, they had never found sand dollars on Secret Beach before. It seemed totally unfair that the first one would be found by strangers.

"*We* live here," Knox said, his hackles up. "At Summerledge."

Evelyn nodded, flipping the sand dollar over and over in her palm with a thoughtful expression. "We live here too."

"No you don't!" said Chase. "We've never seen you here before."

"That's because we moved here this winter. Over there." Evelyn pointed toward the spit of land where the Dellemere cottage was located.

"That's Mrs. Dellemere's place," said Knox, confused. "She never said anything about having kids."

"We're not her *kids*," Evelyn replied, emphasizing the last word to draw attention to the obvious, the "duh" implied.

"She's sort of our grandmother," Frankie piped up. Her voice was high and soft, the kind you had to lean in close to hear. A gust of wind puffed her bangs and showed the whole of her round face. Her eyes were the same deep brown as her sister's, but smaller and slightly almond-shaped. Her chin was squarer than her sister's, and when she smiled, her missing tooth made her look younger than her nine years.

"She was a friend of our father's," Evelyn corrected, kicking at the sand. "She knew us when we were little. We only saw her once or twice before—" Her voice broke off. She frowned. "—Before we came here to live with her."

"Why don't you live with your parents?" asked Chase, his curiosity getting the better of his shyness.

It was Evelyn's turn not to answer. She gave him a blank stare, then threw the sand dollar on the ground; before Chase could react, she turned and ran off toward the cottage. Frankie bent down to pick up the sand dollar. It was cracked in half. She shook the broken halves, pouring sand and shell particles into her palm.

"*Colombes de la paix.*"

"Columns de la *what?*" said Knox.

Frankie touched the particles with her fingertip and massaged the empty spot along her gum with her tongue.

"Doves of peace. See, there are five of them." Her finger nudged each one. "Always five. They are a sign of friendship." She reached out and grabbed Knox's hand, placing the shell particles into his upturned palm and closing his fingers around them.

"Our parents are dead—we live here now," she added, simply, and turned to follow her sister up the beach.

Chase and Knox stood frozen, unsure how to react. Leaving felt wrong, but following the girls was clearly not an option. The whole morning thus far had been strange and disorienting, like coming into your bedroom and finding the furniture rearranged; yet Chase had to admit that having the two girls here was also somewhat . . . *cool.* And to find out they were orphans—it was like a story in a book.

"Should we go back?" Knox asked finally, once the girls had disappeared over the far ledge.

"Okay," Chase said, shrugging. Secret Beach seemed less interesting now anyway.

The sun was strong overhead as they scaled the path through the grass. It was a relief to get into the shade of the trees by the driveway, the smell of pine sap hitting their nostrils with each step. The surrounding forest was old and uncut; the tops of the trees lush and evergreen, the bottoms gray and brittle.

Knox broke off a low branch with a loud crack and swung it around his head, swiping at other branches and granite outcroppings along the way. He stopped in front of a rock pile and lopped the top off of a fir sapling growing by the side of the path. Bored of waiting for Chase to catch up, he scaled the rock pile, crawling on all fours around a jumble of moss-covered granite. On the other side of the pile, three large boulders joined to form a deep cavity, tall and wide enough for a grown man to sit up in. He peered in and sniffed.

"This summer, I'm going all the way in," he yelled to Chase over his shoulder.

"Yeah, right. You say that every year," scoffed Chase, who was climbing up behind him.

"No, I mean it, I'm doing it." Knox sat back on his heels, picked up a small pinecone, and threw it into the cave as hard as he could. Then he leaned in, listening for some kind of response, and recoiled, almost toppling backwards off the ledge.

"There's a breeze! It's coming from inside the cave!"

Chase stuck his head in the entrance. "I don't feel it."

Knox shivered despite the sun shining through the trees.

"That cave leads somewhere, I know it. Something's in there. Maybe it's what I saw this morning. Some kind of animal."

"Maybe—or maybe it's a zombie lair!" said Chase, lowering his voice to a growl. "They could be watching us right now! Tonight they'll break in and tear our heads off and suck out our eyeballs!"

"Ha ha ha," Knox replied, trying to sound like he didn't care. He chewed nervously on his T-shirt and backed slowly away from the cave, then jumped off the rock pile.

"Race ya!" he shouted, and sprinted up the driveway.

"Jeez, Knox, I was only joking!" groaned Chase, trotting behind.

Knox slammed into the kitchen. Chase caught the screen door before it closed and followed him in. Their dad stood at the sink looking thoughtfully out a side window, holding a mug to his lips. Teddy was on the floor by the stove. In the center of the room, their mother sat at the breakfast table. Across from her was a tall, white-haired older woman in a yellow slicker—their neighbor, Fanny Dellemere.

"Did you have a nice walk, boys?" Mrs. Dellemere asked without turning around. "Perhaps you ran into something—or someone—unexpected?" She turned and winked at them.

Chase and Knox knew three things about old Mrs. Dellemere: She was a widow, she lived alone (or at least she had—until now), and she had the coolest collection of stuff they'd ever seen. The walls of her cottage were covered with shells, sea glass, dried moss, sun-bleached rodent skulls, old snakeskins, and a huge variety of preserved butterflies and dragonflies. Best of all, one entire wall was filled with shelves of lucky stones: smooth gray-and-black rocks circled by a white ring that you could either wish on and throw back in the ocean or keep in your pocket and rub for good luck.

Their mother's eyes flashed the "be polite" signal.

"Fanny was just telling me about the girls. She thought you two might have met them at the beach."

"Oh yeah—Evelyn and Frankie," said Knox.

"They seem . . . uh . . . nice," Chase mumbled, not knowing whether his mother knew about the whole orphan thing yet.

"We'll have to have them over," said Grace.

Mrs. Dellemere gave their mom a quick pat on the forearm. "I'm sure they would love that, Grace. It's boring for them to be cooped up with an old woman all day. They haven't quite adjusted to the climate here—and I'm afraid the town hasn't quite adjusted to them."

"Why?" asked Chase, curiosity piqued all over again.

Mrs. Dellemere turned around in her chair to face them. "I don't know how much they told you, but they've lost both their parents. Their mother died when Frances was a baby."

The boys exchanged quick looks. *Frances?* No wonder she wanted to be called Frankie.

Grace made a sympathetic noise.

Mrs. Dellemere hesitated, then said by way of explanation, "The girls are from Haiti, from Port-au-Prince."

"Good Lord!" cried Grace. "Were they—I mean, are they—?"

Mrs. Dellemere nodded. "I found them in an orphanage, after."

The gears in Chase's head were clicking. Haiti. The earthquake.

"Their father was born in Canada, but he went to Haiti many years ago. He was a doctor; he met their mother there." Mrs. Dellemere sighed. "The girls and their father were asleep when the first tremor hit. The apartment building collapsed and the girls were trapped. Rescuers pulled them out, but their father—" She shook her head.

Grace reached across the table. "Fanny, I'm so sorry."

Mrs. Dellemere patted her hand. "He was a good friend."

Teddy, oblivious, howled for someone to pour him his cereal. The somber mood in the kitchen lifted a little. Mrs. Dellemere ruffled Teddy's blond mop of hair.

"Well, Grace, the girls are probably wondering where I'm off to." She stood up, and it was as if an ancient, yellow-slickered tree had suddenly sprouted in the kitchen, tall and thick and weathered, with long white hair looped loosely on top. As she passed Chase and Knox standing by the stove, she paused and peered down at them from her great height. Despite her age, her eyes were still bright, the whites clear and strong.

"When those girls lost everything, I decided to take them in. I wasn't sure I wanted to—I like being on my own—but I knew in my heart it was the right thing to do. And you know, now I can't imagine living here without them." With surprising delicacy, she lifted Chase's inhaler by its nylon cord and examined it and his flushed face, then replaced it gently.

"Never mind, lad; haste is overrated." She pinched his shoulder, gave a little backwards wave, and stalked out of the kitchen, rattling the dishes in the cupboard. At the screen door, she thundered, "Nice to see you, Jim! Mind your family while you're here."

The screen door slammed after her like a shot. Jim dropped his coffee mug into the sink. The room suddenly felt small and empty.

"That woman is a tour de force," said Grace admiringly.

"Also known as a battle-ax." Jim winked naughtily at Knox.

"I expect you boys to do whatever you can to make those poor girls feel welcome here. You know what it's like to be new. And after what they've been through! I can't imagine," said Grace.

Chase stifled a groan. He knew he was being selfish, but this was Summerledge. He wasn't in the mood to share it with strangers, even if they seemed nice.

"In fact," his mother went on, "after we go to town I want you to walk over there and personally invite them over for lunch."

This time, it was Knox's turn to groan.

Chapter 3

FOG

Summerledge was a minefield of handyman projects—just as Jim Thompson suspected. The toilet wouldn't flush right; the lawnmower blades were rusty and dull; and the grass was in desperate need of mowing. The house, barn, and little dinghy, *Germ,* all needed paint. Not that Chase or Knox were at all confident that their dad could fix these things—but getting the supplies while they were in town seemed like a step in the right direction. Plus, their parents were planning on stopping by Captain Nate's place to ask him to put the boat on the mooring.

The sun fell brightly on the battered old car as it sped down the little road to Fells Harbor. Chase and Knox took turns pointing out changes they noticed from last summer. Teddy was stripped down to a bathing suit, still wearing his goggles, and ready to go to the beach.

"Dad!" yelled Knox. "Stop! There's town—you drove right past it!"

"Right you are," Jim chortled, visibly startled out of a daydream. He swerved to the side of the two-lane road and did a U-turn. They parked the car outside of the hardware store and the three boys tumbled out of the backseat.

"Keep an eye on Teddy, please," Grace called, heading toward the post office to open the mailbox.

The boys crossed the street to the drugstore. When the door to Flo's swung open, Chase, Knox, and Teddy instinctively breathed in the familiar smell, exactly the same every year: roasted marshmallows, vanilla, and

Coppertone. An old-fashioned soda counter with a big mirror took
up the entire right-hand side of the store. To one side was the fountain
menu—written in flowery, pink script—with twelve different flavors of
ice cream. Pictures of Fells Harbor residents plastered the other side in a
collage: babies, dogs, birthday parties, and some ancient-looking black-
and-white photographs of people standing beside horses-and-buggies.

"I want candy!" shouted Teddy, fishing in his pocket for the dollar
Grace had stuffed there and waving it at Chase. "How much can I get?"

"Wait a second," he replied, then lifted Teddy up to the counter so
he could see the pictures.

It was tradition to start off the summer by looking for the picture of
their mother on the mirror. They found it quickly: a gap-toothed, pigtailed
Grace Baker in a yellow T-shirt, sharing a sundae with her older brother.
Their uncle Edward was Knox's age in the picture, with wavy blond hair
and big teeth. He was licking his spoon and mugging for the camera; Grace
was laughing as though he were the funniest kid in the world.

Knox turned away first and headed for the toy aisle. Seeing the picture
of their lost uncle gave him the same spooky, sad feeling he got from
walking in a graveyard, and—between the new girls and the cave—he'd
had enough spookiness for one day.

✛   ✛   ✛

A half-hour later, their dad came to fetch them. Knox had bought a cap
gun, Teddy was sucking on a miniature baby bottle filled with candied
sugar, and Chase had his nose in a spy novel. On the quick drive home,
Jim pulled over at Captain Nate's house. Grace undid and redid her
scrunched-up bun—a nervous habit.

"I'll go," said Jim.

His wife gave him a quick, grateful smile. Captain Nate made her feel
uncomfortable ever since the day she'd been sent to ask him to help look
for her brother.

Chase squirmed lower in his seat.

"That guy freaks me out."

"Maybe he's a vampire," said Knox. "Maybe if he comes out by day he'll explode."

Teddy removed the plastic baby bottle from his mouth long enough to mumble something that sounded like "Bigfoot."

"He just likes to be left alone," their mom explained, but she shivered a little despite the bright sunlight beaming through the windows.

"Everything's shipshape," Jim announced, whistling happily as he got back in the car. "He'll come around later this afternoon if the weather holds."

But the weather didn't hold. By noon, the sunny day had become an overcast one, and a bank of fog was visible on the horizon; by two o'clock the temperature had dropped ten degrees, and thick mist unrolled across the point like a heavy, woolly blanket. The boys put on fleece jackets and went to bring in more wood for the woodstove. They didn't have to be asked twice: Their mom got edgy in the fog.

They headed to the shed, where the wood was stacked. Ropes of fog drifted in front of them, gauzy tendrils hanging in the cool air.

"Look, cotton candy!" Teddy hooted, running ahead and taking big bites of air.

"Don't get too far ahead," said Knox, his voice heavy with sarcasm. "You might get lost and we'd never find you, just like Uncle Edward!"

"Shut up," Chase snapped at him. He didn't like to admit it, but the fog made him jumpy too. He turned by the corner of the shed and saw a shadow move across the driveway. He stopped suddenly and almost yelled. Knox walked right into him.

"What the heck?"

"Shhh! I see something," whispered Chase, gesturing with his chin. "Over there."

Knox squinted. Something dark was moving across the driveway, about a hundred feet away. He stepped back in alarm.

"I told you something was in that cave!"

A dangerous, panicky feeling rose up in Chase's chest. His lungs constricted. That thing looked bigger than a fox. There were supposed to be bears up here. If that thing was a bear, Teddy would look like a snack-size Snickers. Chase's chest began to whistle. He sucked at his inhaler.

"Get Teddy!"

"Where is he?"

"Out there," Chase gasped between hits.

"I'm not going out there! TEDDY!" Knox bellowed, slamming himself flat against the side of the shed. He pulled the cap gun out of his pocket and raised it like he'd seen guys do in the movies. "COME HERE!"

"What are we going to do?" asked Chase. His breath was raspy. He took another puff.

Knox waved the cap gun in the air. "If it comes closer I'll scare it off with this! TEDDY! Where is that kid?" His hair was wet with drops of condensed fog.

Chase backed himself up against the shed alongside Knox. He hated to admit it, but Knox might be right. If it was an animal, the cap gun might work. The brothers crept slowly along the side of the building, listening for all they were worth. Whatever it was, it was getting closer.

Knox pulled the trigger; the caps exploded next to Chase's ear.

"HOLY CRAP, KNOX!" Chase yelled, painfully cupping his ear. He flung open the shed door and threw himself inside. Knox lurched on top of him and they fell, sprawling, to the ground. They slammed the door and sat with their backs against it, chests heaving.

"What about Teddy?" Chase panted, feeling that familiar skunky feeling—the one that told him he was a coward.

"I don't hear any screaming or flesh-ripping, so he's probably fine," joked Knox.

"Great, really great."

"You go out and get him if you're so worried."

Chase sat silently for a moment, considering the facts. Safe behind the door, their fear outside seemed a little premature. Plus, the inhaler had worked and his lungs were relaxing.

"We don't even know what that was; it could have been Dad for all we know."

"That was definitely not Dad."

"Then we have to go get Teddy. He's only six!"

"Be my guest," Knox said. "Why don't you do something yourself for a change."

A bomb detonated in Chase's brain. He leapt on Knox, shoving him hard. Knox retaliated by landing an expertly aimed fist into the small of Chase's back. Chase managed to hit Knox's thigh. Knox grabbed Chase's knees and pushed, knocking him flat, and then pounced. He was shorter, but almost as heavy as his brother. Chase thrashed beneath him, trying to turn over or toss him off. Knox held both his arms down, taunting.

"You fight like a wuss, Chase. It's no wonder those guys wanted to beat you up."

Chase spit at him; the gooey wad of saliva dropped back on his own cheek. Knox laughed. The door to the shed opened with a creak and they froze.

"Chase? Knox?" called Evelyn's voice. "I found your brother."

She pushed the door open wider, letting in thin strips of fog and a rush of cooler air. Frankie and Teddy stood right behind her. Teddy took one look at his brothers and launched himself on top of them. Chase shoved him off and wiped his cheek. He was embarrassed to be caught losing a fight to his younger brother—by Evelyn and Frankie, no less. Knox punched Teddy in the arm.

"I told you not to run ahead."

"He didn't go far. I found him right by the road." Evelyn shrugged, looking at Chase. "Our grandmother said you wanted us to come over?" A half-question.

Chase glanced at her. In the low light of the shed, Evelyn's brown eyes were very dark and shiny. Her face was framed by strands of damp hair, and her coppery brown skin was bright, even in the dimness. She wore a knitted navy blue sweater with frayed holes at the elbows and faded jeans. Frankie had on a rain slicker and a pair of brown corduroys that were a size too big. Her pink high-tops stuck out beneath her pant cuffs. Both girls looked cold.

"My mom wanted to meet you," said Knox, standing up, putting on his cool-guy voice. He flicked his fingers through his hair, making the fringe stand up. "We were just getting wood for a fire."

He moved to the woodpile and grabbed at a few logs, trying to lift them as if they weighed nothing at all.

"We can help," said Evelyn, walking stiffly over to the pile and extending her arms to be filled. "Do you play cards?" she asked, directing the question at Chase.

Chase jumped up, brushing himself off.

"You're from Haiti?" he blurted stupidly.

"We are," Evelyn replied. Her tone was blunt, but she kept her eyes on him.

"What do you think of it here?" he asked, placing a log into Evelyn's outstretched arms.

"It's cold—and we don't have any friends," Frankie interrupted.

"That's okay; neither does Chase," said Knox.

Chase rolled his eyes. "You're so not funny, Knox."

Evelyn shrugged. "We haven't met many other kids until you, that is true. But then, we don't go to school. Our grandmother teaches us everything, so we don't see many other people, you know? It's really different where we come from." She lowered her enormous dark eyes briefly and then raised them again, meeting Chase's.

He felt something small and fluttery take flight in his chest, but this feeling didn't tighten like an asthma attack. It simply hovered and flew off.

"But I—it's not bad—I mean, we like it here," she continued, warming a little. "My grandmother is very kind. People are happy. There's no fighting, no guns."

Knox whipped out his toy. "I have one. It's just a cap gun; it doesn't shoot bullets. It's more like a firecracker." He passed it to Frankie who passed it to Evelyn. She gave it a once-over and then handed it back with a funny expression on her face.

"What?" asked Knox.

Evelyn shrugged again. "In Haiti, guns are not toys."

Knox put the cap gun back in his jacket pocket, chagrined. There was an awkward silence.

"But it is useful, no?" Evelyn added, quickly. "Especially in the fog? That's how we found you."

Outside, Grace was calling the boys' names from the back door. Knox cracked the door and peered out. The fog hung thick and close, obscuring any landmark. Chase glanced at Evelyn from under his bangs.

"Just so you know, my mother gets a little crazy in the fog. Don't take it personally."

Evelyn gave him a quick nod of understanding. Chase felt a change in the air between them, a relaxation. Evelyn didn't need to be told about families that had a hole where a person was supposed to be.

Chapter 4

BOAT RIDE

The fog lingered for two more days, socking them in completely. Foghorns blew continuously across the harbor, and the air was damp and chilly around the clock. Normally, this would have been a less-than-stellar start to the summer, but the mood around Summerledge was bright due to the constant back-and-forth between its inhabitants and those of the Dellemere cottage. Teddy, in particular, made no bones about following Evelyn and Frankie around wherever they went. Once, when the curtain of fog drew back slightly, Knox called out that the motorboat had appeared on the mooring and the dinghy, freshly painted, was lying upturned on the beach like a giant shell. Their father could not stop wondering aloud about Captain Nate's ability to maneuver seacraft in pea-soup fog.

On the fourth day, the sun rose over the point with dazzling clarity, painting the rocks and ledges in unfamiliar light. After so much fog, Chase and Knox walked around blinking their eyes like newborn kittens. The talk at breakfast was about where they would take the boat for the long-awaited picnic. A handful of shrubby, pine-strewn islands lay scattered to the east: Carp, Hutchin's, Goat (Little and Big), and the Ducks were the closest to pick from. Teddy, who couldn't care less where they went, was pumping his hands in the air to an imaginary beat. He'd given up the goggles and flippers for small, stiff braids that stuck out of his head like quills, set off by a gift from Frankie: a handmade necklace made of mussel shells. He sang loudly between bites:

You can be at the party gettin' loothe
But you can catch a bullet in your bubblegoothe.

"Come again, Ted?" their dad asked, looking up from yesterday's paper. "A bubblegoose?"

Chase smirked into his scrambled eggs.

"It means your butt, Dad," said Knox.

"Hmmm," said Jim, frowning.

"It's a song, by a singer from Haiti."

"Where on earth would you boys learn that?" Jim asked, looking at Teddy.

"Frankie," mumbled Teddy.

Jim raised his eyebrow, still perplexed.

"Evelyn and Frankie? The girls next door?" Chase reminded him.

Silence.

"Because they're—you know—*from there?*" Chase added, as if he were talking to a two year old.

Jim nodded, but it was clear from his expression that this was the first time he had actually digested this fact.

"Haiti, huh?" he mumbled.

"Really, Dad?" Chase groaned. "You know, there's this planet called Earth, it rotates in space, and we all live on it—"

"Yeah, Dad, seriously, phone home sometimes." Knox rolled his eyes. "And people think *I* have ADD."

"That reminds me," Grace interrupted, trying to change the subject. "I'd like to invite Evelyn and Frankie on the picnic—what do you think?"

A chorus of "yesses" chimed in from around the table, shut down by their dad's frantic karate-chop waving.

"No. I'm only here for a few more days, and I want family time. Just Team Thompson today."

"You gotta be kidding me, Dad!" Knox erupted. "Team Thompson? Last time I checked, you were at work when they picked our team!" He looked at Chase for backup.

Chase shrugged. Knox should know by now that parents, by definition, were hypocritical, telling you one thing—like to stop watching TV— then doing the complete opposite themselves.

Their dad frowned. " Now, boys—"

Just then, the phone in the living room rang out, a shrill, old-fashioned ring, saving them from a lecture. Jim got up to answer it. When he came back, his eyes skipped off his wife's and onto the floor.

"Bad news from the lab, I'm afraid. There's been a containment breach. Two of the lab assistants are infected, and all our procedures have to be examined. The place is in an uproar. I have to go back immediately."

"What!" roared Knox. "You just got here!"

"I'm sorry, Knox—" his dad started to say.

"Team Thompson—what a joke." Knox cut him off and stormed outside, making sure to slam the screen door extra hard.

✛   ✛   ✛

An hour later, Chase found Knox in his fort and gave him an update: No picnic. Mom had to drive Dad to the airport, two and a half hours away. He and Knox were to go over to Mrs. Dellemere's and ask if Teddy could stay there with her for the rest of the day.

"She doesn't trust us to babysit?" Knox asked grumpily. "Figures."

"And we're supposed to stay over there, too," Chase added.

"You gotta be kidding me! She thinks *we* need babysitting? Our parents stink." He kicked the side of the fort in frustration. "I can't believe we're not going out on the boat! I'm so sick of Dad and his stupid work. I hope he never comes back!" Knox jumped down from the fort and tore down the path toward Secret Beach.

"Knox, wait up!" yelled Chase. He thought about going after him but decided against it. Instead, he headed back to the house, stopping at the shed when he heard the screen door slam again. It was his mother, moving fast, her mouth set in a tight line. She held Teddy's hand and was carrying a bag full of sweaters and books.

"I've called Fanny and she's expecting you. Evelyn and Frankie are planning something fun for you all to do."

"But what about the boat, Mom? It's a great day to go out," asked Chase, not trying very hard to hide his disappointment. And it was, too. Crystal clear.

His mom sized him up. Her eyes were red and puffy. "I don't want any of you on the water without me," she answered. "We'll go tomorrow if it's nice."

Chase didn't respond.

Grace handed him the bag and let go of Teddy's hand. "Look, honey, I'm not happy about it either, but there's nothing we can do. If Dad has to go back, he has to go back. You're old enough to understand that when you grow up, you don't always get to do what you want."

Chase bit his tongue. He couldn't help feeling that his dad was actually getting *exactly* what he wanted, but he knew better than to say it.

His mother opened the car door. "Now go in and say good-bye. You won't see him for a month. Where's Knox?"

"He ran off. He's really mad."

"I know how he feels." She got into the driver's seat and slammed the door.

✛ ✛ ✛

Mrs. Dellemere was in the garden behind her house when Chase brought Teddy around.

"Is Knox here?" he gasped. He was short of breath after helping Teddy up the rocks.

"Haven't seen him," Mrs. Dellemere replied, taking in Chase's heaving chest. She wore a wide-brimmed straw hat and a brown rubber apron over her jeans; she was making some sort of chest-high tepee structure with twine and sticks.

"Here," she said to Teddy, "hand me the twine. These buggers are hard to tie on. I'm thinking of planting some squash today, Edward—what do you think?"

Chase nipped Teddy on the shoulder. "That's you," he said, then turned back to Mrs. Dellemere. "He doesn't know his name is Edward. He's always been called Teddy."

Mrs. Dellemere's hat nodded with her head. "Why, of course he is. But I'm not one for nicknames, considering I've always been called Fanny for no particular reason at all. So I shall call young master Edward by his full name. It is a good, strong name, honoring an adventurous young man."

Chase was floored. He hadn't thought of it before, but of course, Mrs. Dellemere must have known his uncle when he was alive. She smiled conspiratorially.

"He looked quite a bit like you."

Frankie appeared at the back door. "Gran Fanny, are they coming in?"

Chase raised an eyebrow. "Gran Fanny?"

"What did I tell you about nicknames?" laughed Mrs. Dellemere. "But those girls can call me anything they want. Go on in now, they're waiting for you."

Teddy and Chase followed Frankie into the kitchen and through to the large wood-paneled front room with its amazing collection of treasures. Bright spots of green and blue darted around the room as sunlight bounced off the hundreds of bottles filled with sea glass. Chase looked beyond the wall of lucky stones to see Evelyn sitting on the porch, her knees drawn up to her chin. He swallowed and tried to sound nonchalant.

"Hey—uh, Evelyn, have you seen Knox? He ran off when my dad left."

"Yes, he came by here and told me and Frankie what happened, but then he went back down to the beach. You must have just missed him."

Chase was vaguely annoyed that Knox had already been there. "Yeah, well, now Dad's gone for a month and Mom is going nuclear."

Evelyn shrugged. She didn't have to say it; Chase knew what she was thinking: At least they still had a dad. And a mom. He walked to the edge of the porch and looked out at the water. To the far left their Whaler bobbed lightly on its mooring next to—the dinghy? He shaded his eyes to get a clearer look, and sure enough, as the boat drifted to the right, he could see the stern of the dinghy rafted alongside the Whaler. Had his parents changed their minds? Maybe his dad had gotten another call? Or maybe it was Captain Nate? But the figure on the boat wasn't big enough to be Captain Nate, or his parents. Chase swore out loud.

"What?" asked Evelyn.

"Knox! He's out on our boat! Mom is going to eat him alive! We aren't supposed to be on the boat without her. I gotta go get him."

Evelyn slammed her feet down on the porch. "I'll go, too." They took the front steps two at a time.

Frankie called from somewhere inside, "Where are you going?"

"To get Knox!" yelled Evelyn.

"Wait for me!"

"And me," cried Teddy.

"We'll be right back. Stay here," Chase hollered back at his brother.

Evelyn, Frankie, and Chase sprinted across the beach and over the ledge, not bothering to take the path through the woods. They rounded the house and picked their way over the rocks just as the boat's outboard motor roared to life. Chase couldn't believe it. It was just like Knox to think he could take the boat out by himself. This stunt would mean grounding and a summer of chores for sure.

Frankie waved and called from the shore, catching Knox's attention. He maneuvered the boat closer to them and slowed. Chase splashed through the shallow water and grabbed the metal railing that ran along the bow.

"Knox! You idiot. Mom's going to kill you!" he shouted.

"Anyone up for a picnic?" Knox grinned, flashing his dimples.

Evelyn and Frankie climbed aboard the boat, looking thrilled.

Chase glared at him. "You can't be serious."

"Aw, c'mon, Chase. Just because Dad left doesn't mean we should have to sit around all day when it's nice out. Besides, Mom won't be back for hours."

Chase surveyed the clear horizon, the green mounds of the surrounding islands set in the glittering bay. He was tempted. Knox sensed his advantage.

"We don't have to go out for long; we can just take her around the cove. We'll stay in sight of the house the whole time. C'mon! You know you want to."

Chase weighed the pros and cons: This was beyond breaking the rules. But if they stayed right in front of the house, what could go wrong?

"It'll be more fun with you, Chase," added Evelyn. She grinned at him: a sudden, toothy smile that made her nose turn up and the sides of her eyes crinkle. Chase felt that same fluttery feeling in his chest. He'd never seen her smile before.

"Okay," he agreed reluctantly, "but it better be quick." He set his foot over the gunwale, then withdrew it quickly when he heard footsteps clattering over the rocks behind him: Teddy, his face crumpled in tears and a bloody scrape across his shin. Both girls jumped up.

"What about Teddy?" Frankie asked. "Can't he come?"

Knox shrugged.

Chase couldn't think of a good reason why not, and it did seem cruel to leave him alone on the beach. He lifted Teddy into the boat and climbed in.

"Let's get going before anyone notices," he said, helping Teddy with his life jacket.

They steered away from Summerledge and out the Western Way, a broad channel carved by glaciers between Fells Harbor and the neighboring islands. Wispy clouds laddered the blue sky. The wind was chilly coming off the water, despite the sun overhead.

"Where do you want to go?" asked Chase.

Knox's answer was to push the throttle forward.

Chase looked back to shore at Summerledge and the silhouette of the Dellemere cottage as they passed it, and then the gentle arc of the harbor to the right. Captain Nate's dock nosed out at the center like an arm; his lobster boat, the *Mary Louise,* floated quietly on her mooring. He caught a shudder of movement on Captain Nate's dock, out of the corner of his eye, and called out to Knox.

"I think someone saw us leave—maybe Captain Nate!"

Knox scowled. "So what? He probably thinks we're out with Mom and Dad." He pointed the bow toward open sea. The boat sped across the light chop.

"LET'S GO BACK!" Chase shouted over the wind.

"NO!" Knox yelled back, his eyes flashing. "This is fun! Hey, Evelyn, Frankie—you guys having fun?"

Evelyn turned to face them. She was beaming.

Chase sat down in the stern. Knox laughed and pushed the throttle forward again. He was clearly feeling good.

"We'll just go for a spin," he yelled over his shoulder.

Chase didn't fully catch on until Knox pulled into the cove at Big Duck.
"Aw, Knox. Come ON!"

"Who's up for a swim?" asked Knox, ignoring him.

"I am!" said Teddy

"Me too," said Frankie.

"Me three, I guess," shrugged Evelyn. "But I think you all are crazy to
swim in water this cold."

"How 'bout you, Chasey?" Knox challenged. "Are you ready for this—or
do you still want to be a good little boy and head home?"

Blood rushed to Chase's face. He felt everyone's eyes on him, especially
Evelyn's. Why did Knox always have to be such a show-off? He acted as
if everything was a competition and somewhere some giant, invisible
scoreboard was keeping track of his wins. It was so irritating—and stupid,
since most of the time nobody but Knox cared. Most of the time, Chase
wasn't even *playing*. But not this time. This time, he'd show Evelyn who
could be more fun.

"Grab the anchor," he said.

‡ ‡ ‡

Chase was dreaming again: *that* dream. The nameless body floated
face down in the water; a halo of brown hair undulating like kelp around
the head, its orange life-jacket bulging like a misshapen pumpkin. The
waves pulsed. And just like before, the body began to roll. This time,
he saw a flash of pale skin through the wet strands of hair. One more
swell and he would be able to see the whole face. His heart constricted
with fear. The swell rose–

"Chase, wake up!" Knox's voice yanked him back into consciousness.

Chase sat up and blinked hard, trying to clear the sick feeling left over
from the dream. He gave a quick, relieved look around the boat. Frankie
lay on the bow, shivering. Evelyn and Teddy were huddled with their knees
under their shirts. Knox was at the console, restlessly fiddling with an
antenna. Loose, hazy clouds scudded overhead, and parts of the shoreline
were now in shadow. The wind was blowing onshore. Chase estimated
they'd been swimming in the cove for about an hour before he'd dozed off.

"Time to go?" asked Knox.

"Whatever," Chase replied, trying to sound breezy. He wasn't about to let Knox know how much he wanted to get back on dry land.

"Okay, then, let's go." Knox turned on the ignition and revved the engine. "Wanna drive?"

Chase considered his brother through his bangs for a moment, looking for signs of mockery, but there weren't any. Knox was being serious—for once.

"Yeah, okay," Chase answered, and took the wheel.

Knox hauled up the anchor. Chase gently eased the throttle forward. The boat puttered its way past the spits of granite, out of the cove. When they hit open water, Chase's heart sank and the sick feeling came back twice as hard. A wide bank of fog sat on the horizon to the east. Fingers of mist were twining into the crevices between the islands, heading straight toward them. The fog was moving in—slowly—but with purpose.

"You're going to have to gun it," cried Knox.

"I know!" Chase snapped. The beast stirred in his chest and his lungs constricted in a spasm. He fumbled around his T-shirt for his inhaler, but it was gone—cord and all. He groped wildy around the console to see if it had dropped somewhere, but it wasn't there. Chase gulped in air, trying to inflate his lungs. His eyes strayed to the wall of mist closing in on his right, and then to Evelyn, Frankie, and Teddy in the bow. The dream replayed in his mind: the floating body turning slowly over as a wave surged beneath it. Was it one of them? Chase forced himself to look away, over the water and toward the mainland, where patches of sunshine still could lead them home. Fog was trouble; but if they went full speed, they might outrun it—and his asthma. He leaned hard on the throttle.

They had to outrun it.

Chapter 5

ADRIFT

The sound of waves splashing against the silent hull of the boat woke Evelyn first. She rubbed her eyes and sat upright, struggling to see through the heavy mist. Frankie lay crumpled on the deck of the boat, her head wedged against the seat, Teddy beside her. Chase was slumped across the wheel and Knox lay sideways across the aft bench, nestled amidst a pile of extra life preservers. She slowly made her way around the boat to see if everyone was still breathing. Satisfied that they were, she moved a life preserver out of the way and sat down next to Knox to think. She waved her hands, fanning at the fog in front of her face, but it was hopeless. She couldn't see a thing. Another swell slapped up against the hull. Her heart gave a panicked little leap. Everything was quiet. Too quiet. Then she realized why. No engine.

"Knox!" she yelled, shaking his shoulder. Her voice was strange and high-pitched to her own ears. "Wake up!"

He didn't move.

She shook him harder. "Wake up! Guys! We're drifting!" She yanked one of the life jackets supporting Knox's head out from beneath him. His forehead slammed into the hard wood of the bench. "Get up, Knox!"

"Ten more minutes . . . lemme sleep ten more minutes," he murmured. His face was lined with deep impressions from the webbing of the life jacket.

Evelyn whacked him on the head.

"No! You and Chase have to wake up! We're in the fog and the boat isn't working." She watched as his awareness swam slowly to the surface. The moment it broke through, Knox's eyes flew open. He stood up shakily.

"Where are we?"

"How should I know? We all fell asleep or got knocked out or something, and now the engine's stopped!"

Knox took two steps over to the console and tried to wake up Chase with a shove; then he felt for the key.

"That's weird," he muttered. "The ignition is still on but the engine isn't working. There must be a break in the line somewhere." He groped blindly along the console. The fog swirled around the bow and thickened.

"Evelyn!" he shouted, and pointed at the bow. "Get up there and watch for rocks!"

Evelyn looked confused.

Knox stumbled to the side and grabbed the boat hook that was stowed under the gunwale. "Here, take this—you can fend off with it—just in case."

Chase was slowly resurfacing now, his shoulders rising as his breath deepened. He looked around groggily.

"What's up?"

"*Fog*, Chase, and there's something wrong with the engine line."

Chase shook his head to clear it. He was struggling with the same fuzzy blankness Knox and Evelyn had both experienced, like swimming through yogurt.

"Chase—do something–NOW!" cried Knox.

Chase stood up. The fog seemed to have lifted slightly, but it was still impossible to see beyond a few feet. A breeze blew at his back. Beneath him, the boat rocked gently, and what little water he could see was pitch black. He couldn't hear much of anything, strangely—no foghorns or gulls—but as he started to really wake up, he understood: They had to get moving. At this rate they would either drift out to sea or flounder on a ledge, and, he groaned inwardly, they had Teddy on board! How could he have been so stupid?

Recriminations rose in Chase's chest. He wanted to yell at Knox but there wasn't time. He knew from all the stories he'd been told about the fog that it was stealthy, dangerous; it sucked you in and kept you traveling in circles. They could be lost in it for days if they didn't run aground first. They had no food or water, no warm clothing. They wouldn't last days.

Chase moved to the engine and started fiddling with the gas pump. He felt the gas tanks. They were two-thirds full. He lifted the plastic cover off the engine and was looking for loose wires when he heard a shout. It was Evelyn.

"Something's out there!" she yelled. "I see a shadow—it's darker over there. I think we're near shore!"

Knox scrambled to the bow. Frankie and Teddy were stirring. Evelyn lay sprawled on her stomach, holding the boat hook in front of the bow. Goose bumps on her legs stood out from cold, or fear, or both.

"Do you see it?" she panted.

They could just make out a shift in the fog, a bluish arm of darker fog, maybe a quarter of a mile away. It was hard to tell. Knox stared closely at the water boiling around the bow. The wind was picking up, blowing them onshore, but even so, their speed was too great, too purposeful to just be drifting. A strong current tugged them into the dark pocket, reeling them in like a fish on a line.

"Chase, we have a serious problem!" he shouted, sprinting back to the console and cranking the ignition again and again.

Chase looked helplessly between the engine and the ominous shadow getting larger by the second.

"Everyone, put on a life jacket!" he ordered, and pulled an orange life vest over his head.

"Chathe?" Teddy's small voice quavered through the fog.

Chase's fear was churning wildly now. He took a deep breath to calm himself—surprised that the beast in his chest was sleeping. There was no time to consider why. He exhaled and a mental image of Captain Nate floated in his mind's eye. He almost laughed out loud in relief. Captain Nate had seen them leave! The *Mary Louise* was probably out looking for them now. And nobody could get through fog like Captain Nate. They just had to hold on until they were rescued. The question was, hold on to what?

"We're speeding up!" Knox yelled.

Chase put his hand into the water and felt the strong pull against his palm. He considered trying to row the boat out of the current, but a quick glance around told him they'd left the oars in the dinghy on the mooring. A careless mistake. He squinted through the mist. What had been a shadow was solidifying into a massive, rutted cliff rising up a hundred feet or more—higher than they could see, and approaching incredibly fast. The surf pounded against it, shooting spray, and the boat heaved up and down on the swells. Several large, black holes along the bottom edge of the cliff sucked in great blasts of seawater. Chase's bubble of hope deflated. There was no time to be rescued. They were fish bait. He made his way over to Teddy and piled extra life preservers around him to protect him from the impact. Chase huddled beside him, bracing himself as best he could. The boat heaved and a rain of sea spray pelted their faces.

"I'm so sorry, Ted," he gulped.

Teddy looked up at him, wide-eyed with fear.

Chase looped a hand into the belt of Teddy's life jacket, trying to force the images from his dream out of his head. The boat surged forward toward the wall of rock with a sickening jolt. Waves smashed over the bow. Knox scrambled to hold on to the metal railing as freezing cold water rained down on him. Evelyn and Frankie clung to each other, heads bent, huddled on the deck. The fog thickened. The sound of water churning against jagged rock filled the air.

We're all dead, thought Chase. *Just like Uncle Edward.* He shut his eyes. He didn't want to see what happened next.

"Chase!" Knox shouted. "Look!"

Chase raised his head and squinted through the mist. It took him a moment, but then he spotted it, too, shimmering like a mirage: a string of what looked to be white lights, evenly spaced, meandering along a deep indentation in the cliffs. Lights! Lights meant people!

The wind dropped, then suddenly shifted direction, blowing them offshore and ever-so-slightly away from the cliff. The fog lifted enough to reveal a shallow beach between two large outposts of rock.

"Listen!" Evelyn called out. The surf was quieting, the crashing and pounding becoming more rhythmic and gentle.

"Maybe we've hit the tide right," yelled Chase, thinking about the moment when the tide turned over and the currents were still. The locals in Fells Harbor called it Neptune's Nap; it only lasted a minute or two, but it might be long enough for them to scramble out of the boat and onto dry land. His eyes quickly roamed the beach, looking for any signs of life.

The cliff loomed above them to the left, and the black holes at eye level continued to suck in water, pulling them closer; but, curiously, the boat now seemed to be resisting. It bucked and shimmied violently against the current.

"Something *reeaallly* strange is happening!" Knox yelled. The boat lurched again and swerved, tacking right.

"We're headed straight for the beach!" cried Evelyn, amazed.

Chase stood up, perplexed. It was true: The same current that had them on a collision course was now steering them alongside the foot of the cliff, almost as if it sensed their danger. *But that's impossible*, Chase thought to himself.

Possible or not, in minutes, they found themselves within a foot of a beach covered with smooth rocks glowing white in the gray mist.

Knox jumped out with the bowline, whooping with relief. The others followed and a sense of lightness took the place of the fear.

Teddy picked up one of the large, shining rocks.

"Look! A dinothaur egg!" he cried. He whacked it against another rock, trying to crack it.

"No! Teddy, don't!" said Evelyn.

Chase understood. For some reason it felt wrong to abuse these rocks. They looked tender, if a rock could be such a thing.

"What should we do with the boat?" asked Knox.

"Let's drag it up as far as we can and then tie the line around a rock or something," said Chase, thinking of how they stored the dinghy back home.

They pulled the boat clear of the tide by a few feet and sat down.

"What about those?" asked Frankie. She pointed to the outline of white lights. "It looks like a path. Somebody must live here."

Evelyn craned her head forward, examining the lights.

"Frankie's right; let's see if we can find them."

Chase's thoughts jumped one on top of the other in rapid fire, weighing their options: They could sit on the beach and wait for the fog to clear. They could separate, leaving one group on the beach to watch the boat and one to explore. Or they could all go up the path. There must be electricity and people here if there were lights, and a telephone, maybe even a restaurant or a market. They hadn't eaten since breakfast. He eyed the path: Evelyn was right, they should go look for help . . . but something was stopping him from leaving the beach. A dark, inky feeling.

"I think we should stay here."

"Chase," Evelyn countered in a measured tone. "We have no idea how big this island is. It might be small, maybe even walkable. I think we should try to see what's up there."

Knox grinned. "I'm ready."

"We should stay with the boat," argued Chase.

Evelyn's eyes flashed. "I don't need your permission!"

Knox chimed in. "Yeah, Chase, you're not the boss of us."

Chase crossed his arms over his chest. "If Evelyn wants to go, I can't stop her, but I'm your older brother, and what I say goes when it comes to you and Teddy."

"Says who?" challenged Knox.

"Says Mom and Dad."

"They're not here, and last time I looked I think it was *you* who needed *my* help." Knox puffed out his chest in the way that meant he was looking for a fight.

"I'm not fighting you, Knox," Chase growled.

"Yeah, that's not really what you do, is it, Chase?" Knox pointed to the bruise on his face, or, more accurately, where the bruise once was, since it now appeared totally, mysteriously, healed.

"You are such a pain," said Chase, trying to shut down any further argument.

"Yeah, well at least I'm not a wuss. What's the matter, Chase? Afraid some of your JV soccer friends are hiding up there?" taunted Knox.

Chase lunged at his brother, knocking him to the ground.

"You're gonna get it now, Knox! You and your *C'mon, it'll be fine.*"

Knox grunted with the impact and grabbed a chunk of Chase's hair.

THE FOG OF FORGETTING

"Why don't you start gagging and choking now and calling for Mom? Poor Chasey-Wasey and his widdle asthma!"

Knox flipped Chase off him, pinning him down—but not for long. Before Knox knew it, he was on the bottom again. They flailed around on the rocks, rolling back and forth. Frankie marched past the two wrestling boys, hands on her hips.

"Why do boys always fight? It is so boring."

"Shall we go then, Franks?" asked Evelyn.

Frankie nodded.

"We'll see you later," Evelyn called over her shoulder, heading for the path.

Chase and Knox stopped, mid-fight, and watched them go. Soon the girls' heads were barely visible over the frown of the cliff.

"It doesn't change anything, you know," Chase grunted. "It's your stupid fault we're lost in the first place. You're such an idiot."

Knox's face fell. He pushed Chase off and pulled his knees to his chin. Chase got back into the boat and rooted around the console, coming up with a small, portable horn and a radio. Teddy took the horn. Chase sat with the radio, trying to get it to turn on. Knox chewed his collar, looking torn between following Evelyn and Frankie up the cliff and going back to thrashing Chase. Half an hour passed in total silence, disturbed only by occasional blasts from the horn.

"Chathe, Knoxth, look at me!" Teddy called out. He was wearing as many life preservers as he could fit over his head and around his middle. Knox exploded with laughter. Teddy laughed, too, then pointed past him, into the fog.

"Who'th that?"

A dark silhouette was threading its way toward them through the mist; it looked too big to be Frankie or Evelyn.

"Search me," whispered Knox. "Who do you think it is?"

"Someone who lives here, genius," snorted Chase.

The figure crooked his elbow and raised its hand hip height, hesitated, then lifted it and waved.

"I heard the horn," a man shouted. In moments, he materialized in front of them. Chase had to rub his eyes to make sure he was seeing clearly. The man was tall, broad-shouldered, and shirtless, with brown knots of hair that fell to his shoulders and graying fuzz on his weathered chin. A green cloth was wrapped several times around his waist, and a thick leather harness was slung across his chest, from which hung several tools at odd angles, as well as a small ax and a slingshot. At his side was a squared metal blade—a machete—hanging off a woven leather belt. The man did not smile, but bent his arm up again in greeting, bringing it chest-high this time, fingers splayed and the palm facing them.

"I am Seaborne," he said, and nodded to the boat. "I see you lads have run aground."

Knox looked at Seaborne's upraised hand, then at Chase, and then back at Seaborne, palm still raised. Knox hesitated, then gave it a high five. The man, Seaborne, made a wry face and lowered his hand.

"I'm Knox, and these are my brothers, Chase and Teddy. Our boat got lost in the fog," Knox explained.

"Did it, now? I wonder."

Chase swallowed. He looked up into Seaborne's face. His eyes were light green, almost gray in the overcast, and he looked to be about their father's age, maybe a little older.

"Sorry. We can call someone to come get us if you have a phone."

Seaborne suddenly smiled—a warm, encouraging smile. His eyes strayed to the boat and Teddy encased in life jackets. He cocked his head at the sight but remained silent.

"Where are we?" asked Chase.

Seaborne rubbed the seam of his harness with his thumb and looked out at the fog sitting on the horizon.

"That is not the easiest question to answer, but I can tell you this: You are on the southwestern shore of the island of Ayda, in the land of Melor."

Chase shifted uneasily. He'd never heard of an island called Ayda anywhere near Fells Harbor. He took a half-step back toward Teddy, his eyes never leaving the machete. This was one of those freaky moments with strangers that parents warn you about, but they had no choice. They *had* to talk to this guy. Maybe he was friendly-crazy, not psycho-crazy.

"Uh, we're not planning on staying. Our parents will be looking for us. We'll be off your property as soon as we can call them."

Again, Seaborne's eyes strayed toward the horizon, or what would have been the horizon, were it not engulfed by fog.

"You will find it is not so easy to find Ayda, nor leave once you have strayed onto her shores." Then, as if coming back to himself, he gestured at their boat "But perhaps your story will have a different ending than mine. We shall see. Now, let me examine your vessel." He strode past Chase, Knox, and Teddy, toward the boat. As he passed, they saw a long, steel scabbard strapped to his back, and what looked to be an enormous sword with a leather pommel.

"Do you see that?" gurgled Knox.

"A machete *and* a sword! Great. That's perfect. SO glad I came out on the boat, Knox," whispered Chase. He began mentally ticking off options again. They should probably run for it, as bad a runner as he was. He scanned the beach; it was hemmed in on three sides by cliff and the fourth by water and fog. The only way out was up the steep cliffside. They'd never be able to climb fast enough. The panic he'd felt earlier in the boat began to bubble up again, but before it boiled over, Knox had shoved a rock into his hand. Teddy had a small rock, too.

"Aim for his head. If we knock him out, we may have enough time to get away," said Knox, holding a rock of his own. "On my count—"

"What if we miss?" whispered Chase.

"Don't miss!"

They ratcheted back their arms. Seaborne, oblivious to them, was squatted down with his nose an inch from the fiberglass hull, muttering to himself.

"One . . . two . . . THREE!" Knox hissed.

The boys chucked the rocks as hard as they could. Teddy's landed short, but Chase's and Knox's sailed through the air, right on target. Just before the moment of impact, Seaborne stood and caught a rock in each hand, as easily as if he were playing catch.

"Well, at least we didn't miss," groaned Knox.

Seaborne placed the rocks on the ground and was on the boys in three strides, his expression dark and scowling.

"I—I," Knox stammered.

Seaborne held up a hand, cutting him off.

"The first thing you must learn in Ayda is who your enemies are. The second—never underestimate them." Seaborne's fingers traced the wooden hilt of the machete at his hip as he considered the boys, eyes roaming between them. Teddy whimpered. Knox stuffed the collar of his T-shirt into his mouth. Chase held his breath. After several exruciating seconds, Seaborne sighed and dropped his hand.

"I am not the enemy, lads."

Chase exhaled.

"Thorry, Mr. Theaborne," said Teddy, still wrapped in life preservers. The edges of Seaborne's mouth twitched up.

"And that is lucky for you with such an ill-considered attempt. Rocks are unreliable weapons. Should you ever need to use them again, wield them with your hands—like a club." He demonstrated by chopping his hand at Chase's temple, playfully. Chase winced, then took a surprisingly deep breath. His brain had shut down but for three words: Get. Help. Now.

"Umm, Mr. Seaborne, uh, we'd just as soon get going. So would you mind, I mean—please—could we use a phone?"

Seaborne paced back toward the boat and climbed over the transom.

"If I knew what a phone was, I would be more than happy to get you one."

Knox spit out his collar.

"A TELE-phone. The thing you use to call people? To talk from a distance?" He pantomimed holding an imaginary reciever up to his ear and pushing some imaginary buttons.

Seaborne shrugged, not even curious.

"I'm hungry!" said Teddy

"Are you, small one?" asked Seaborne. "Well, I may not have a telephone, but I do have food and drink. I'll be finished in just a moment." Then he began asking questions.

Chase and Knox answered as best they could, with some help from Teddy, but their story felt loose in their heads, like rocks rattling in a tin can. When they got around to describing Evelyn and Frankie's departure from the beach, Seaborne grew agitated.

"They left how long ago?" he demanded.

"I don't know," Chase replied. "Maybe an hour?"

Seaborne shook his head in dismay. "It's not safe for any of you to wander—"

"Why?"

"It is too dangerous."

"Why? What's out there?" Chase asked again, eyes once again on the machete.

Seaborne didn't answer.

"So, uh, Seaborne, *where* is Ayda exactly?" asked Knox, trying a different tack.

"I don't know."

"Oh-kay." Knox exhaled dramatically, rolling his eyes at Chase, "let me get this straight. You don't know where you live?"

Seaborne gave him a sharp look.

"I have told you where I live. What I cannot tell you is where, *exactly,* the island of Ayda is. I came here a long time ago—when I was a boy not much older than that one there." He nodded to Teddy. "There may be a map somewhere that can tell you where Ayda lies in relation to everything that is known to you, but I have never seen it. Nor do I now remember clearly anything else that was once known to me." He ran his finger along the gunwale of the boat and chucked his chin toward the sea. "It is the fog. It makes you forget."

Knox mouthed the word *cuckoo* to Chase.

Chase rubbed his eyes again, getting impatient.

"So, you came here when you were a kid?"

"Yes; not here, precisely, but to Ayda. I came ashore east of here, in the neighboring land of Metria."

"And you stayed? By yourself? What about your family? Your friends?"

A shadow crossed over Seaborne's face, and he frowned. "I have told you, I do not remember much of anyone who once mattered to me," he said.

"I don't want to forget Mommy and Daddy!" yelled Teddy.

"Shhh, Teddy, he's only joking," said Chase, but he had the sinking feeling that Seaborne was being completely serious. "Do you have a boat?" he tried again, desperate.

"I did. Once."

"Where is it?"

"At the bottom of the sea."

Chase smacked his own forehead in frustration. Compared to this guy, he was a born conversationalist.

"I can't believe this fog," said Knox, staring at the line where the horizon should have been. "When's it gonna burn off?"

"It never burns off," answered Seaborne, climbing out of the boat. He had gathered everything he could from the Whaler: boat hook, cushions, radio—even the old pair of sunglasses from the cubby in the console—and used the bowline to tie it all in a tidy bundle, a network of veins flexing across his muscled forearms. He lifted it to his shoulder. "The fog is always there. I've never seen it change, except when it crowds in at dusk."

"But if it never burns off, how does anyone go back and forth?" gulped Chase.

"They don't. Not usually. You are the first people from beyond the fog I've seen since I came here myself." He smiled again, that sudden, warm smile that seemed so out of place with the rest of him. "It's nice to have company of my own kind."

Seaborne walked past them, toward the white lights on the cliff, glowing dimly in the haze. He began to climb, scaling the cliff as easily as if he were crossing the street.

"Coming?" he called down.

Chase and Knox exchanged glances. What else could they do? They let Teddy go first, still wrapped in life preservers, and moving slowly. Seaborne was waiting for them at the top, the bundle of possessions at his feet. Chase saw it and mentally kicked himself for making no objection to him stripping the boat. Another careless mistake. He bent over to catch his breath, more out of habit than necessity.

"Who else lives here?" he asked.

"Ayda has many inhabitants," said Seaborne.

Chase lifted his head. *Progress.* "Where do *they* live?"

"Well, some of them live here, in Melor. Others live in other lands."

Chase exhaled loudly. Not much progress. At this rate, Teddy would be a teenager before they got any real answers.

Knox was fiddling with a stone he'd brought with him from the beach. He held it a minute, then pitched it over the cliff. Teddy watched it fly until it disappeared and landed with a distant *thwack*.

Seaborne grimaced and picked up the bundle. "You're very sure of yourself, aren't you, lad?"

Knox tried to come up with a smart reply, but came up short.

Seaborne considered the three boys for a moment. "There are forces at work in Ayda that are not always visible to the eye—or particularly friendly. Take nothing for granted," he said seriously.

A shiver went down Chase's spine. Was it his imagination, or was the fog getting thicker? He turned away from the cliff's edge. The white lights led inland and disappeared in the murk several hundred feet down the path. The air was thick and quiet, as if the fog had absorbed all the normal sounds and smells of the forest. For the third time that day, he felt afraid.

"It is a mystery, to be sure, your presence here," Seaborne continued, looking directly at Chase. "Boats do not idly wash up on Ayda's shore. Indeed, it is hardly possible—" He broke off and dove ahead into the woods, stopping once more to watch as Teddy tried to dig his way out of his life-preserver suit. His mouth twitched again.

"'Tis a strange costume young ones now wear beyond the fog."

Teddy froze.

Seaborne stooped down to help him out of the last life preserver.

"Tell me, little man, would you like to see my home?"

Teddy nodded, the little braids in his hair standing straight up.

Seaborne's laugh rang out in the gloom.

"Good! I am glad."

Chapter 6

THE HOUNDS OF MELOR

This place looks just like Fells Harbor, only the trees are bigger," Knox insisted. He was trying to convince Chase that they were safe on one of the outer islands. "Look at how tall those suckers are." He pointed with his thumb to a massive tree trunk the size of a boulder.

Chase gave his brother a tight smile. Maybe Knox was right. Maybe they weren't far from Summerledge . . . but something in his gut told him otherwise. Mist was clinging to the ground and snaking around their ankles and between the trees, hungrily moving inland. Only the regular spacing of the white lights along the path kept them from being completely lost—swallowed up by the fog. As it was, they couldn't see Seaborne and the sword strapped to his back anymore.

"Stick close, Teddy," Chase said nervously.

"D'ya think he's ditching us?" whispered Knox. "He's crackers, but he's better than no one."

Before Chase could reply, Seaborne's voice boomed out of the mist.

"Would you lads tighten line and heave to?"

They picked up the pace and rounded a steep C-shaped curve that led across a footbridge, which spanned a broad stream and took them into a clearing. At its center stood a small cabin that looked airlifted from a fairy tale. It had log walls and a pitched roof blanketed in thick layers of dried moss and grass. One end of the cabin was taken up completely by a stone chimney. At the other end, a large, slow-turning waterwheel churned in the stream. Seaborne stood at the door of the cabin, on a low, flat rock that served as his stoop; to his right was a small window cut into the wall. He lifted the door open on its leather hinges and went inside.

"Cool!" crowed Teddy, racing ahead.

"Whoa," said Knox. "Where's the witch?"

"Who needs a witch, when you have *him*," said Chase, eyes darting around the clearing. "Do you think Evelyn and Frankie came here?"

The small lamps lighting the path were flickering weakly now, like wicks drowning in melted wax. The one directly beside them sputtered, flared, then died. As eerie as the light had been, the forest was blacker and seemed damper without it.

"Are you coming in or not?" asked Seaborne, poking his grizzled head out the door.

Chase and Knox exchanged looks of resignation. Teddy was already inside. Reluctantly, they picked up their feet and followed.

The interior of the cabin was dim and musty. The sound of falling water from the churning waterwheel filled the air. A quick inspection revealed that there were no telephones, lights, or indoor plumbing. The fireplace took up most of the wall on the left, and a metal arm stuck out from the rocks that made up the hearth. Across from the door was a bed set sideways against the wall. Next to the bed there were a number of pegs in the wall on which hung shapeless lumps of clothing.

Seaborne removed his harness, knife belt, and sword and stowed them at the door. Then, he pulled an intact clamshell from deep beneath the folds of cloth around his waist. Stooping by the fireplace, he gently opened the shell and took out a still-glowing coal and placed it on the tinder that lay there. He carefully blew on the spark until it caught and blazed brightly. The fire crackled, flames throwing a dancing orange glow against the wall of the cabin. The damp air retreated.

"How'd you do that?" Knox asked, impressed.

Seaborne handed him the clamshell. Inside, other orange-tinged coals smoldered on a nest of fresh seaweed.

"'Tis called an ember chamber. Saves the effort of starting from scratch each time." He took back the shell and leaned in toward the fire, staring into the flames. The combination of the sound from the waterwheel together with the light of the fire made the cabin feel cozy—homey, even. Teddy's stomach growled loudly.

Seaborne lifted his head. "Ah yes, I'd promised the little one some supper. I'll fetch us something to eat."

"We need to go look for the girls," Chase cut in, noticing that it was getting very dark outside.

Seaborne frowned, strapping on his harness with rough movements. "They'll be safe enough tonight. There's no point trying to look for them now. It will have to wait until morning." He pulled open the door. "I'll be back shortly—don't leave the cabin." He stepped out into the night, machete in hand, and shut the door firmly on its hinges.

"That guy is certifiable," Knox said, "and what's with the skirt?" His eyes roamed around the small room. "But so far, so good, I guess—though I feel bad about Evelyn and Frankie. I wonder where they went. Do you think maybe he knows, but he doesn't want to say? Maybe he has them locked up somewhere and he's lying about it. Maybe we're next."

"Shut up, Knox," hissed Chase, chucking his chin in Teddy's direction.

Chase's thoughts were swimming around in his head. All he wanted was to collapse on the bed, but Knox was right. They couldn't just abandon Evelyn and Frankie in the dark for the entire night without at least trying to look for them. He took a deep breath and forced himself to go outside. He strained to see through the lengthening shadows falling across the clearing. To his surprise, Seaborne was crouched by the stream. Chase approached him.

"What do you mean, Evelyn and Frankie are safe enough?"

"I mean exactly that. It is too late in the day to begin a search."

"Are they in danger?"

Seaborne was quiet for a moment, then answered. "No more than you were when you first landed, and, perhaps, no more than you will be in the future. It is difficult to say."

Chase noted the deepening gloom of the forest, held momentarily at bay by the last rays of light in the sky and the orange glow radiating from the door of the cabin.

"Well, that's reassuring," he said, scornfully. He was getting tired of Seaborne's evasive answers. "Look, we really need to find Evelyn and Frankie and find a phone. Our mother is going to lose her mind. Her older brother got lost in the fog and never came back." Chase kicked at the dirt. "Listen, you gotta believe me—my mom is freaking out! She probably has the Coast Guard and the Navy and the Marines out there right now. We just need to call someone or send up a signal or something. There's got to be *someone* around here who will help us."

Seaborne looked up from his crouch with a strange, vacant expression. "Not won't. *Can't.*"

"Why? Why can't you help us?" Chase demanded, his voice rising higher. "Why are you here? And where is everyone else? What have you done with the girls?" He was half-wheezing, half-shouting now, the beast in his chest roaring to life—finally. His lungs tightened, his heart knocked against his ribs. He felt dizzy and hot. There wasn't much time before it took over. He had to make Seaborne understand . . . what? That they needed to get home? That he was having trouble keeping his thoughts in one place? That he was tired of being scared? He shook his head, closing his eyes, trying to clear his mind. When he opened them again, everything seemed to pulsate and move in the darkness. He sucked in air, but it was like breathing through a straw. An image of his missing inhaler came to mind. It usually hung on the doorknob of his room at home. *Home.* He tried to picture Summerledge. His parents. But it was as if the only thing that was real was here, now: Seaborne. The rustle of branches. The smell of pine. The chug of the waterwheel. Chase's body pitched forward.

"We have to get out of here," he whimpered.

He was aware of hands catching him, arms cradling him. His head lolled back and he saw the first glimmer of the evening's stars above the clearing. Then everything went black.

✛   ✛   ✛

When Chase came around, he was lying on Seaborne's bed. Knox and Teddy were ogling him from the side.

"What happened?" he asked groggily.

Knox grinned. "You passed out. Seaborne brought you back around by holding this under your nose!" He held out a handful of bright green leaves topped with yellow flowers. They smelled strongly of cat urine.

"Ugh," said Chase, wrinkling his nose.

"Yeah, I know, but it worked." Knox took a whiff and made a face; he went to the window and chucked them outside.

"I helped, too!" said Teddy. "I wath pinching you!" He grabbed the skin on Chase's forearm and gave it a big nip.

"Ow, Tedders! Stop it!" Chase sat up. His stomach gave a lurch but his lungs were clear. "Where's Seaborne?" he asked, a little sheepishly. He had never fainted before during an asthma attack, but then again, he'd always had his inhaler.

"I don't know," Knox replied, sitting on the bed. "He carried you back in here, went out and got the stinkweed, told me to shove it under your nose, and then left again, saying the usual."

"The usual?"

"You know," Knox scrunched up his brow. " 'Don't leave the cabin. Don't go outside.' What is *up* with this place? All this doom and gloom is freaking me out, and you getting carried in here all blue didn't help." He looked anxiously at Chase. "What are we going to do when that guy walks back in here?" Knox nodded toward the door. "He could be out there getting a pot to boil us in. And check this out: I think he's military."

Knox plucked a piece of clothing off a peg by the bed and brought it over to Chase. It was a long, old-fashioned blue jacket, threadbare and moldy, with a few remaining gold-metal buttons and arms that were stained brown, but even in its decayed state it looked official.

"Plus, he's got that sword." Knox prowled the small confines of the room, chewing on his collar. "We're sitting ducks in here! I say we make a break for it. Whatever's out there, I'd rather take our chances."

"And go where?" Chase asked, swinging his legs onto the floor. He was feeling better. "We don't have flashlights or anything."

Knox rolled his eyes. "No flashlights? Okay, Mom."

"I think if he wanted to kill us, he would have done it by now."

"You're right about that, lad." Seaborne's voice boomed through the window, startling them. He opened the door and tossed a pair of skinned rabbits on the floor. "Put these on the fire—I have another errand to run. Stay put." He closed the door again.

Stunned into silence, Knox did as he was told, threading the rabbits as best he could onto the iron spit and sliding them over the fire. Soon, a rich, meaty aroma filled the room.

"Well, at least we have food," said Knox.

"And a bed!" said Teddy, who was dangling upside down from the edge of the low mattress.

"And a—" Chase was about to add *fire,* when a loud snort interrupted him. It came from outside, and was quickly followed by another great snuffling noise through the crack where the door didn't quite meet the floor.

"Oh man," cried Knox, hurling himself against the opposite wall. "What's that?"

"I don't know, but whatever it is, it sounds big."

The sniffing got louder and more persistent, this time punctuated by a menacing growl. Chase's heart pounded in his ears.

"Knox," he whispered, "we should hold the door shut."

They tiptoed across the floor toward the door. Teddy followed.

"Get back on the bed, Teddy," hissed Chase.

Teddy leapt back on the bed. The sound stopped abruptly.

"I wish I had my cap gun," Knox whispered.

Thhwunk! The door slammed open, almost ripped off its hinges, and an impossibly large, mud-colored beast bounded into the cabin, knocking Knox and Chase to the floor. Two black eyes shone in the firelight above a square, wiry snout and a wide mouth that was dripping with saliva. Its fur was matted and greasy and its eyes were locked on the two boys lying spread-eagled on the ground.

"What does rabies look like?" asked Knox.

"Pretty much like that, I think," answered Chase.

A low, throaty growl rumbled up from the beast.

"We have to lure it away from Teddy," whispered Chase. He rolled over onto his hands and knees and began to crawl slowly backwards toward the open door behind them, making clucking noises.

"They're not ducks!" Knox protested in a hoarse whisper.

The animal responded by leaning back in a crouch, ready to spring.

Knox scuttled crab-like toward the door and accidentally smacked Chase hard in the cheek with his foot. They both tumbled backwards in a heap on the doorstep. Chase poked his head across the threshold.

"Don't move, Ted. STAY ON THE BED."

"Okay," came his brother's weak reply.

"Now what do we do?" muttered Chase. His heart was pounding in his chest, but oddly, his lungs felt clear. For now. Just then, another growl came rumbling across the footbridge, higher-pitched and, if possible, even more hair-raising.

"Seaborne?" Knox squeaked.

Chase's eyes adjusted until he could just make out another large beast sitting patiently at the footbridge, waiting, as though it had all the time in the world.

"Great," Knox groaned. "It has an evil twin."

Chase whipped his head back and forth between the cabin and the footbridge, looking for an escape route.

"They must have smelled the rabbit."

Knox grimaced, "Yeah, well, who's the rabbit now?"

"You probably don't taste as good," a voice sang out from somewhere in the gloam, then a peal of giggles followed by the sound of light footsteps. Evelyn and Frankie emerged from the woods with Seaborne in tow. The giant creature in the cabin bounded out through the door and leapt lightly over Chase and Knox, clearing their heads by a good margin.

Frankie reached out to pat the back of the larger, darker animal, which stood even with her shoulder. Its fur was chocolate-colored and matted with small twigs and dust.

"This one is Axl, and that one," she pointed to the lighter-colored, ever-so-slightly smaller animal sitting calmly on the footbridge, "is her brother, Tar."

"They're . . . *dogs?*" Chase asked, unconvinced.

"They're *friendly?*" added Knox.

"When they want to be," answered Seaborne, coming up beside Tar. He laid his palm on the back of Tar's broad skull. "Dogs they may be, of a sort, but not just. These creatures are the great warrior hounds of Melor. Rothermel has sent them to keep watch over you. They were escorting your friends to the cabin when I joined them. A fortunate event, considering it cut my travel in half."

Teddy came out of the cabin and edged up to Tar, reaching out his hand. Tar sniffed it, then licked it.

"Where did you go?" he asked Seaborne.

"To get your friends and ease your worry. They were safe, but I knew by this boy's concern," he tossed his chin in Chase's direction, "that you would not believe me until you saw them with your own eyes."

Evelyn shot Chase a curious look. "You were worried?"

Chase felt his cheeks flush. "Maybe a little."

"That's kind." She crossed the footbridge to give Chase's hand a quick squeeze. "Thank you."

His face turned red.

"You needn't have been, though," said Evelyn. "We only walked a few miles before we ran into some people—" She corrected herself. "I mean, Melorians."

"Melorians?" Knox asked incredulously. He shot a quick apologetic glance at Seaborne. "Sorry—it's just that it all sounds crazy."

"Everything here is so strange," Evelyn said slowly, puzzled. "It all looks the same on the outside, but it's, I don't know—a feeling more than anything else—as if everything is less real and more real at the same time. Like I've been here before, or dreamed it." She shook her head at the impossibility.

"*Déja vu,*" said Frankie, winding her fingers through Tar's bristly fur. "When old soul and new soul touch." Her eyes met Evelyn's.

"*Oui, ma petite, déja vu,*" replied Evelyn softly.

A shift in the wind lifted the branches of the trees and scattered enough low-lying fog to see the new moon rise over the clearing, furred and muddied. They watched in silence as it came to rest in a hammock of uppermost tree limbs. Teddy opened his mouth in an enormous yawn.

"Speaking of dreams," Seaborne said, breaking the spell. He lifted Teddy and trundled him into the cabin. The others followed him inside. Seaborne produced a mysterious cache of blankets and fur skins and spread them out before the fire, laying a few on the bed. He carved the roasted rabbit flesh into two wooden bowls and pushed one into Teddy's hands, the other into Evelyn's, and gestured for them to be passed around. The bowls made a few rounds before they were emptied. Seaborne ate nothing.

"Now, sleep," he said, and nodded to Chase and Knox. "Stretch out beside the hounds in front of the fire. They have kept me warm in far colder places. The girls and Teddy will have the bed."

Chase settled himself beside the great, heaving mass of Axl. Knox threw himself on the ground on the other side. A log in the hearth slipped, crackling loudly. Axl jerked and growled. Chase patted Axl's shoulder.

"It's just the fire, girl."

"Chathe?" Teddy's voice whispered into the room.

"Yeah, Teddy?" he whispered back.

"I can't thleep."

"Try."

"I can't." A strangled little sob came out of Teddy's throat. "I want to thee—"

Chase steeled himself, knowing what was coming.

"I want to thee Mommy!" Teddy screeched.

"Shh, Teddy, it's time to sleep," said Knox.

"I want to go home," he sobbed.

Chase sat up, trying to think of what else to say.

"I bet the entire Coast Guard will be waiting for us down at the beach tomorrow, Teddy. We'll be back in our own beds by tomorrow night. You'll see."

Seaborne stirred uneasily in his corner.

Teddy continued to cry, his shuddery sobs flooding the shadowy corners of the cabin.

"Don't worry, Teddy," soothed Evelyn. Her voice sounded low and soft with sleep. "I promise you'll see your mommy again." Then, she began to hum a slow, quiet song.

Teddy's cries grew gentler; he was listening.

Chase lay back down, feeling grateful for Evelyn. Axl groaned and stretched her long legs. He snuggled into her flank, his head, rising and falling with the hound's deep breaths, grew sleepy. One last, terrible thought drifted across his mind before he dropped off: How could Evelyn make a promise like that when she knew, firsthand, that it was entirely possible they might not ever see their parents again?

Chapter 7

MELORIANS

Seaborne was the first one up in the morning. Chase, eyes half-opened, watched him stretch in the pearly morning light coming through the small window. A bird sang into the stillness. Seaborne paused to listen for a moment, then strapped on his harness, machete, sword, and belt and strode outside. Axl and Tar followed at his heels.

Chase extended his legs into the space the hounds left behind and, for a minute, in the peaceful predawn dusk of the cabin, forgot about the seriousness of their dilemma. Then, like a light switch being flicked on, the urgency of getting home came rushing back all at once. He had the impulse to shake Knox, still curled up asleep next to him, but checked it when he saw how small and cold his brother looked. How young he was. Chase stood up impatiently. How could he have been so stupid? How could he have allowed Knox to take them all out on the boat? He hadn't put up much resistance at all considering he was older and knew better—and now, here they were, in this *situation*. A totally mind-bending, survivalist-cult freak show. Chase went out the door after Seaborne, resolved to finish what he had started the night before.

Outside, he stopped at the stream to drink and splash some cold water on his face. Mist still lay heavy on the ground, casting a haze across the forest path. The surrounding thicket of low-lying branches felt close and impenetrable. A cold shiver ran down his spine. Anything—or anyone—could be out there, watching.

Chase wiped the water from his face with his sleeve, licking drips from the edge of his mouth. He rolled over and saw Evelyn watching him from the doorway. Her face was puffy with sleep and her hair was curled in tiny ringlets from the moisture in the air. Chase sat up and said hello with an awkward wave.

"Good morning," she said pleasantly.

"Umm—I was just getting a drink," he explained, realizing too late how idiotic that sounded. What else would he be doing?

She shrugged her shoulders without taking her eyes off of him. He ran his damp hand through his bangs, acutely aware of how ridiculous he must look. Wet face, stained shirt. But then again, she wasn't looking so tidy either. Her shirt was torn at the sleeve and her white shorts were more coffee-colored now. She pulled on her ratty blue sweater and walked over to the stream.

Chase tried to think of something else to say. "It looks like it might be a pretty nice day once this fog clears."

Evelyn stared at him. "Haven't you been listening? The fog *never* clears; it's always there. We were told it was put there on purpose—for protection." She emphasized the middle part of the last word, her accent making it sound even more important.

Chase shook his head. "That's impossible!" This he knew. No fog lasts forever; eventually the sun gets hot enough to burn it off or the wind blows it away. "Besides, protection against what?"

Evelyn knelt down next to him to drink from the stream. When she finished, she stood up and looked him in the eye.

"From outsiders—strangers—people like us."

Chase rubbed his eyes with his knuckles. "You're telling me that the fog is man-made?" He struggled to imagine a fog machine big enough to enclose an entire island with fog. Even if such a machine existed, how would it work? Even synthetic fog couldn't just sit in one place forever.

"I don't believe it," he argued.

Evelyn shrugged again. "Well, that's what we were told by the people who live here."

Clearly Evelyn didn't subscribe to logic. Chase wondered what else she'd heard and accepted without question.

"Where are we then?" he challenged. "And why didn't the fog keep *us* out?"

"They call it Ayda. And no one seems to have any idea why we were 'allowed'—as they say—through the fog. They were confused—actually, they were afraid."

Chase was astonished at how well Evelyn's story matched up with Seaborne's. He thought for a moment.

"Are the others like him?" Chase nodded toward Seaborne's cabin. "With the clothes and the knives and the—?" He scrunched up his forehead and gave Evelyn a grim look.

She nodded back. "But different, too. They have darker skin and hair and eyes. More like Frankie and me. Seaborne looks more like you."

A little thrill went through Chase.

"Did they say if it ever happened before?"

Evelyn stepped down onto the path and stretched her arms over her head. Her brown hair was matted in the back from sleeping on it.

"Yes, it's happened—" she furrowed her brow. "I think it must have happened to Seaborne, and to others, possibly." Her voice trailed off.

"So you think Seaborne came here by mistake? Shipwrecked?"

"Or lost, like us."

"And never found?"

"Or decided he didn't want to be," Evelyn concluded. "Either way, he's still here."

Chase fell silent, trying to imagine what his lost uncle might look like now. Maybe Seaborne was him, gone crazy as a castaway! Then he remembered the military coat and the sword. His uncle didn't have anything like that. Also, Seaborne looked older than his uncle would be. Not ancient or anything, but definitely older. His heart sank. It didn't seem likely.

The wrenching cry of a gull flying overhead made them both look up. Dawn was giving way to an overcast sky, dark gray and brooding—as if a storm was on its way.

"I don't like the looks of that," Evelyn muttered.

Almost as soon as the words were out of her mouth, a seam in the gray mantle broke open and a bright sheet of sunlight poured into the clearing. The branches of the trees seemed to pull back, and the stream leapt and burbled with renewed vigor. A sharp crack came from the forest as Axl and Tar bounded into view. They loped past Chase and Evelyn and into the cabin. Chase heard a loud squeal and a gruff "Get off," and guessed that one or both dogs were now on top of Knox. In minutes, Knox, Teddy, and Frankie were herded out the front door. From the woods, Seaborne's scruffy figure emerged, followed by six people walking in single file.

"Melorians," breathed Evelyn.

Axl and Tar frolicked around the newcomers, rubbing into their hips, leaping happily into the air.

"Old friends, old friends, we are happy to see you, too," said a deep voice that came from a tall man, in line directly behind Seaborne.

Chase blinked a few times in disbelief as the Melorians came fully into view. The leader wore a leather vest over a tunic and leggings made from animal skins. He carried an enormous crossbow over one shoulder. The rest of the party, two women and three men, were dressed similarly and wore hooded green ponchos that hid their faces. Like Seaborne, the men were armed with a host of weapons and tools hung on harnesses across their chests. Two of them carried large, conical grass baskets on their backs. The women were smaller, and each bore a bow and quiver of arrows. Knife hilts poked out from beneath their ponchos.

"They have a lot of weapons," Chase whispered to Evelyn.

"Behave yourself then," she whispered back.

The Melorians set their baskets down and the men removed their hoods. Shining black hair fell past their shoulders, framing wide brown faces with dark eyes and thick, black brows. Knox gaped at the leader's crossbow. It was easily as big as Teddy, and probably weighed more, with a shaft the width of his own forearm. It was a weapon that would stop a buffalo with a single bolt. Knox looked over at the huge forms of Axl and Tar.

"How big do the animals get here?" he gulped, coming closer.

The leader crooked his elbow and raised his hand, palm out, as Seaborne had done when they first met him on the beach. His voice was low, but it carried across the clearing.

"I am Tinator, a captain in the Melorian army." He nodded to the women first. "This is my wife, Mara, and my daughter, Calla. These men," he gestured to the three other men, "are my guards. We have been sent to lend you aid."

The Melorians stood perfectly erect and still, their faces taut and unsmiling. The children stared openly. Tinator's wife, the woman called Mara, wore a hood that heavily shadowed her face. Evelyn could just make out a pair of brown eyes, a generous mouth, and a square, firmly set chin. Mara responded to her inquisitiveness by kneeling and emptying the contents of the basket she was carrying. She pulled out an assortment of brown pelts, green cloth, and leather coverings.

"Do they have food?" Teddy asked in a loud whisper.

The other Melorian woman, Calla, laughed, a fresh clear trill that melded quickly with the burble of the stream.

"The little one is hungry!" she said, half-teasing.

"'Tis a constant problem with that one," said Seaborne.

"I'm not little!" Teddy protested.

Calla knelt down and peered into Teddy's face. "I can see that now," she said kindly.

"How old are *you?*" he asked.

Calla looked bewildered, clearly troubled by how to answer. Seaborne came to her rescue.

"Old enough for you to mind her, little one."

Calla laughed. "I am of full age, child. My daylights have spoken."

Teddy shrugged. "Oh—well, I'm thix. That'th big."

"He means six," mumbled Knox, "he has trouble with S's."

Calla nodded appreciatively. "Well, six is big and strong enough to help me," she laughed, and unpacked her basket, extracting a soft woven blanket. Calla motioned to Teddy to grab the other end and spread it on the ground. She reached back into the basket and produced several loaves of bread, clay jars containing what appeared to be honey, and hollowed-out gourds filled with berries. One of the men reached under his tunic and brought out two more large gourds. He gestured roughly to Knox.

"Drink."

Knox took the gourd and sniffed it.

"It's all right, lad," said Seaborne.

He tipped the gourd toward his lips and took a tiny sip. When he brought it down, he had a thin white film on his upper lip.

"Milk!" Knox crowed.

Calla pulled down her hood and smiled. She had brown eyes like her mother, a long oval face, and waist-length hair pulled loosely into a braid.

"There must be cows somewhere," said Evelyn.

"Yes," said Calla, with pride. "In Melor we have cows and chickens, and sheep, and goats, and pigs, among many other creatures who give their gifts to us." She patted the blanket, inviting everyone to sit down.

Chase sat across from Calla, wondering how old she really was. He guessed college age, like twenty or something. When her eyes caught his, he saw they were flecked with gold.

"Eat now, for there is much work to be done," Tinator commanded. "You are to be guests in our lands; as such, Rothermel has charged us with your protection. You will stay here—in the service of the outlier, Seaborne—until we can be sure that your arrival here is accidental."

"Who the heck is Rothermel?" asked Knox, before stuffing a handful of berries into his mouth. He swallowed quickly and added, "And what else would it be? We didn't come here on purpose."

Tinator said nothing, but a look passed between him and Mara. She turned away and busied herself laying out the contents of her basket. She moved efficiently, assembling a small pile of garments alongside each of them. The boys were given fur-trimmed shirts, open at the neck, and leather vests to wear over loose woven pants. Evelyn and Frankie received longer tunics, leggings, and light leather corslets. Finally, Mara laid out five of the green hooded ponchos that the Melorians wore, which turned out to be thickly lined with fur. She had brought a number of boot-like moccasins, similar to Seaborne's, but after inspecting their feet, she put them back into her basket.

"I don't think she's ever seen sneakers before," Frankie whispered.

Evelyn took a long glug of milk and replied, "Definitely not pink high-tops like yours."

Knox pet the fur on the collar of the shirt beside him. "Excuse me, uh, Mara?" he stammered, tripping over his effort to sound polite. "I was just thinking—with all the layers and everything." His face flushed and his freckles stood out. "That hood must be really hot."

By way of an answer, Mara lifted her hands and brought her hood down. Frankie yelped. Alongside Mara's left cheek, running down the side of her face, under her chin, and along her neck and shoulder was a ropey white scar, as if the skin in that spot had been turned inside out and the muscle and tendons were now on the outside. Her mouth was full and untouched, her dark eyes were flecked with gold like those of her daughter. She did not flinch when they looked at her.

"I'm sorry," Knox mumbled, averting his eyes. "I didn't know."

"Of course you didn't," replied Mara graciously. "However, it is not to hide wounds that we wear our hoods, but to ward off receiving them. It is tradition in Melor."

"Why?" asked Frankie.

Mara brought her fingertips to her neck and gently traced a ridge of her scar. "For privacy—and for protection. Those who walk unnoticed walk in safety." She bent down in one fluid motion and picked up the poncho next to Evelyn. She looked pointedly at the children. "You must always wear this when you leave the clearing, with the hood raised." Her eyes flashed over to where her daughter and the group of men were talking. "With your hood, you may travel within Melor without drawing attention. There are . . . some," again she glanced at Calla, "who assume that proficiency with a bow or knife is all that is needed. But it is not so."

Evelyn asked hoarsely, "What's out there? Animals?"

Mara shook her head. "Animals do not wound for sport or for pleasure, but so they may eat." She gritted her teeth and turned her head. Viewed from the right, her skin was burnished and smooth, sloping without imperfection from the strong jut of her cheekbone. "What you see is the work of men. Exorians. It was a warning."

Knox shook his head, trying to understand. "A warning? Exorians?"

Mara sighed and pulled her hood back up over her head, contemplating the group of strange children clustered around her. Evelyn took the poncho from Mara's hand and pulled it quickly over her head. It was soft and smelled of pine and a sweetness she guessed came from the grass the basket was woven from.

"A warning that fire does not discriminate," answered Mara, with a bitter smile. "It consumes all things, no matter how fast, or skilled, or precious." She gently raised Evelyn's hood, her fingers lightly, briefly, grazing the skin at Evelyn's temples. Before Evelyn could stop herself, her own hand returned the gesture, rising up to touch the angry ridges along Mara's jawline.

Mara removed her hand, squeezing it lightly before she dropped it, and stepped away.

"Dress yourselves now; Calla and I are to take you into the forest. There is much for you to learn if you are to live among us. Five mouths need food."

Evelyn's dark eyes followed Mara's retreating back, the pupils constricted with anger.

"It's a burn! Somebody burned her!"

"Why would anyone do that?" Frankie asked.

Evelyn snatched another poncho off the ground and shook it at her sister. "I don't know, but you'd better put this on." She whirled around to the boys. "And you," she snapped, her voice tight, almost crying. "Get dressed!"

"Jeez, don't blame us—" Knox started, but the fierce expression on Evelyn's face stopped him cold.

Chapter 8

THE FIRST LESSON

Wh]at a fine bunch of Melorians you make!" Seaborne boomed, making his way toward them with Tinator.

Knox gave up trying to tie a long leather band around his waist and grinned. Seaborne took it from him and belted it, leaving two equal ends that he crisscrossed over Knox's chest and back and fastened onto the belt. He rocked back on his heels.

"That'll do." He did the same for the others and laughed when he saw Teddy, whose poncho dragged on the ground. "We'll have to shorten that dress you're wearing, lad; you won't run very fast in that." He ruffled Teddy's hair.

Teddy leaned heavily into his leg. Surprised, Seaborne patted his back awkwardly and mumbled, "If you give it to me now, I'll fix it up for you myself."

Tinator laid down his massive crossbow to inspect them, adjusting one thing or another with firm, swift movements. When he was finished, he stepped back. Mara collected their old, discarded clothing and put it in a basket. The children studied themselves and each other in amazement. They *did* look like Melorians, only smaller.

"And now, your weapons," said Tinator.

Knox caught Chase's eye and mouthed, *Weapons?*

Tinator motioned to one of his guards, who brought over a wadded pelt. Wrapped inside was a collection of small hunting knives and throwing axes, all made by hand, and a number of slingshots carved from a dark wood and slung with leather. He gave Evelyn and Frankie each a slingshot and a knife, the blades of which appeared to be freshly sharpened and attached by sinew to handles of worn animal bone. Evelyn curled her fingers around her knife and touched the blade with her index finger. A sliver of crimson oozed to her fingertip.

"Ow!" she yelped, sticking her finger in her mouth.

Calla took the knife from her. She examined it carefully, holding it so that the bright blade caught the sun and glistened.

"This is an excellent weapon. Very light—very precise. It was mine once."

"Really?" said Evelyn, feeling proud.

Calla gave it back, handle first. "Mind it well."

"What about mine?" asked Frankie, holding her weapon up.

Calla went through the same motions, handing it back with a smile.

"A blade will find its mark if your heart is true; isn't that right, Father?"

Tinator gave a curt nod. "A weapon is a tool; the intent of its owner wields the real power."

"Your first lesson!" said Calla, with an impish wink.

Knox was presented with three short knives and two throwing axes. His eyes strayed longingly toward the crossbow lying on the ground, but he managed to say "Thank you." Teddy was given a slingshot with a soft leather bag filled with perfectly round rocks. When it was Chase's turn, Tinator moved to another basket and withdrew a long sword in a worn leather scabbard. The blade was cast in two metals, one dark, one light, and hammered in a pattern that shimmered like the skin of a reptile. Tinator handed the sword to Chase.

"This is a Metrian-forged blade. It has served its former masters well—may it do the same for you."

Chase's arm sank with the weight of the sword. He didn't dare pull it out of the scabbard, worried he might stab himself. The two younger boys eyed Chase's sword and looked at one another. Knox's face flushed with envy. Teddy tugged on Tinator's sleeve.

"I want that," he whined, pointing at Chase's weapon.

"Do you now?" replied Tinator, unsmiling. He gestured to Chase. "Boy—here, let your brother have the sword."

"That's not fair!" cried Knox. "He's too little. I should get the sword! I'm stronger than both of them!"

Tinator squatted, surveying the three Thompson boys with a keen eye. He ignored Knox's outburst.

"Boy, give the little one, Teddy, your sword," he said again, quietly.

Chase shook his head, appalled. "No way! Teddy will kill himself with this thing. Besides, you gave it to me." He was secretly thrilled that Tinator had chosen him to carry the sword, out of all of them.

Seaborne cuffed Chase on the shoulder. "Mind yourself. Do as Tinator says."

"That's crazy!" Chase objected. "He's too little. He won't even be able to hold it!"

"Do it now, or I'll make you," growled Seaborne. "You will not disrespect Tinator in my presence and call yourself my friend."

Chase gaped at him for a moment, then handed Teddy the sword. Teddy's knees buckled under its weight.

"I told you he couldn't lift it," said Chase. "This is stupid."

Tinator was unfazed. He moved into the center of the clearing and drew a shining broadsword from the sheath at his hip. It had a thick, bronze handle and two thin tubes of bronze that spiraled around his wrist. With his arm extended down, the sword's tip just grazed the ground.

"Come, youngest boy, time to fight," he said, grimacing. His cheekbones jutted like carved stone above the burnished planes of his cheeks.

Teddy's eyes darted to Seaborne, searching for some clue as to what he should do. Seaborne and the Melorians stood silent, unmoving. Evelyn put her hands on her hips, her face full of emotion, and moved protectively in front of Teddy.

"He can't fight a grown man; it's ridiculous—" she began. "I won't allow it."

Mara laid a gentle hand on her arm. "It is what he asked for," she said, silencing her.

Teddy hesitated. It was hard for him to hold the sword in both arms, let alone try and take it out of the sheath and wield it. He dropped one arm and the sword clattered to the ground.

"I don't know how," he sobbed. He hid his face in Evelyn's poncho.

"Don't worry, Ted. You don't have to." Evelyn glared at Tinator, whose lips had become a tight line. She picked up the sword. "I don't know about this island," she said, "but on the island where I was born, men do not pick fights with babies. If you must fight someone, fight me."

Tinator crossed the few yards between them and snatched the weapon from her. He threw it on the ground.

"In Melor, you will learn to fight your own battles—of which there will be plenty. Do not ask for more." He turned on Teddy and Knox.

"Wanting what one sees, without thought to one's ability to bear the gift when it is received, is a dangerous form of blindness. You should know who you are—what strengths you possess—before you make your claims." Then, he scowled at Chase. "You, eldest, have been given this weapon out of necessity only—not merit. Time will tell if you deserve the honor." Tinator turned his back and strode quickly back to the center of the clearing. He balanced his sword between two hands, turning it over and over, as if he was testing, weighing it, his mind pacing the alternatives.

"Duon, get me the leash," he ordered, and turned to the group assembled before him. One of the Melorian men sprang to his basket and returned with a woven piece of leather about four feet long.

"Tie them together," said Tinator, indicating Knox and Chase.

Chase's heart pounded furiously. *What the hell was this?*

The man called Duon approached them with the length of leather. Chase thought about running, but the strong hand of Seaborne turned him around so that he was back-to-back with Knox. Duon tied one end of the leash around each of their ankles. When he finished, they faced one another, utterly bewildered.

"Is this some kind of game?" whispered Knox.

"Shhh!" hissed Seaborne.

"The contest will begin now," said Tinator. "The one who draws first blood shall win the right to wield the sword. The youngest has forfeited his chance."

Chase and Knox stared at him, their mouths open, uncomprehending.

"I think he wants you to fight," cried Evelyn. "Don't do it!"

Knox cocked an eyebrow at Chase. "That's what he *wants*? Does he know we fight all the time?"

It was true, Chase thought. They did fight all the time, but now, standing here with full permission to hit Knox until he bled, Chase didn't want to fight him at all.

"Knox can have the sword if he wants it so bad," he said.

"No!" Tinator thundered. He shoved the boys toward one another roughly. "You will fight for it or I shall set you both loose into the forest and you will learn how to fight with your lives."

"I don't think he's kidding around," said Knox. He gave Chase a weak smile. "Now's your chance, Chase. Let's see what you got." He threw a halfhearted punch at Chase's bicep.

Chase stared at Knox, then at Tinator, then down at the leash tied to his ankle. His brain was having trouble registering that this was actually happening.

"Harder!" Tinator growled.

Knox hit him again. Chase did not respond. He was not going to fight back. He wasn't going to give these people the satisfaction. He took a step back.

"Fight him!" Tinator cried, shoving Chase into Knox. "Your younger brother thinks he's better than you. You heard him just now—isn't that so, Knox? You do not respect your kin. You think your older brother is weak. Do you not?" He taunted and pushed Chase into Knox again. This time, Knox shoved back, more angry at Tinator than his brother. Chase brought an arm up to protect himself. Knox stepped back.

"Do you or do you not want the sword?" Tinator seethed. "'Tis a simple question!" He leaned into Knox's ear. "If you want the sword, claim it—or are you too afraid?"

Knox's body went stiff with anger. His hand curled into a fist.

"Yes–" Tinator nodded.

"I'M NOT AFRAID!" yelled Knox. He punched Chase square in the jaw, harder than he had ever hit him before, opening his brother's lip. Chase grunted in surprise. Knox didn't care: It was as if all the resentment and frustration he had ever had with Chase came pouring out in one furious burst. He hit him again and then again, pounding Chase's face with his fist before Chase had time to react. A geyser of blood erupted from Chase's nose.

"THTOP IT, KNOXTH!" screamed Teddy. He dove at Knox's knees, trying to tackle him.

Knox, startled by Teddy, grabbed his fist in his other hand, to hold it back from hitting Chase again. Chase held his hand to his mouth and bent his head so his bangs hid his face. Blood poured over his fingers and dropped heavily on the ground.

"God, Knox, why'd you do that? I already told you, you can have the stupid sword."

"You're a jerk, Knoxth! I hate you!" Teddy shouted. He pummeled Knox's back with his little fists, swinging wildly, and sobbed.

"I hate this plathe! I want to go home! I want to go home, Chathe!"

Chase kneeled and hugged Teddy to him, smearing dark blood across the little boy's blond curls.

"It's okay, Tedders. I'm okay," he murmured, but feeling like he was most definitely not okay.

Knox stared blankly at his brothers, as if he did not fully understand how all this had happened. He looked at the one hand still holding on to the other tightly curled fist, then up at the Melorians.

Tinator was watching him with a smug, satisfied expression. Knox whipped one of the small knives from his harness and bent down to cut the leather cord connecting him to Chase; then he turned to face Tinator.

The Melorian leaned casually on his broadsword, his mouth set in a grim line, his thick eyebrows drawn like a shelf over his brow. Power began to flow from him like a tide they could all feel and nearly see: electrifying and golden. It shimmered out across the clearing and into the trees like an invisible sea of energy.

Knox picked up the discarded sword from the ground.

"You want a fight? Let's fight!" he snarled, squaring up against Tinator.

"KNOX—NO!" yelled Chase through his cupped, bloody hands. "Don't be an idiot; he'll kill you!"

Knox dropped the scabbard and brought the sword in front of his face. He heard a loud thrumming in his ears; blood pumped through his veins. Everything else had been swept away by the current of energy between himself and Tinator. Knox saw only his opponent, felt only the sword—light and agile in his hands—as if he had always known how to

wield it. He rushed straight at the grown man. With a long swipe, Tinator brought his blade down hard to Knox's left. Knox easily blocked the
thrust with the flat edge of his sword. A sharp clanging echoed across
the clearing. Knox was bleeding now, too; he had bitten his lip with the
recoil from the first parry. Tinator advanced on him and Knox retreated
in a moment of sheer panic.

"Do not show your fear!" he heard Calla cry from somewhere behind
him.

Knox took a deep breath and circled around, leaping to the side and
swinging his sword to the right, just in time to ward off another of Tinator's blows. Tinator advanced. Knox windshield-wipered his blade with
both hands, blocking each of Tinator's thrusts. Feeling more confident,
he stepped closer and jabbed at Tinator's chest. Tinator swiped his blade
away easily, then sprang, sweeping the air between them in a blaze of
flashing metal. Chase would never be able to understand or describe how,
but Knox was managing—barely—to defend himself. Tinator advanced,
clobbering him with broad sweeps of his sword. Knox fell backwards a
few steps, panting.

"Anytime you want this to end, lower your sword," Tinator barked.

Knox replied with a clumsy feint. The sword was getting heavier. He
stumbled and ducked under a halfhearted swipe at his head. In desperation, Knox put both hands on the sword hilt, circled, and leapt, raking
his blade at Tinator's knees. Tinator hopped over the blade and retreated
a small distance. He put his sword tip to the ground and casually leaned
on the handle.

Knox locked eyes with him. The electrifying current seemed to have
burned out. He was gulping at air, his muscles twitching with the effort
it had cost to fight against his much older and better-trained opponent.

"Don't give up!" Calla's voice called to him again.

"Don't listen to her, boy," Tinator taunted. "Why *not* give up?"

Knox felt himself shrink under Tinator's stare, but he lifted his sword
defiantly in another challenge.

Tinator swung his head back and forth, as if there was no point in it.
Knox was reminded of a large branch swaying in the wind.

"I've seen your kind before," said Tinator. "Bold but careless. Is there anyone else who wants to show me what I already know to be true?" He calmly sheathed his sword, dismissing him.

Knox's face burned with humiliation. If there was one thing he knew about himself, it was that he wasn't afraid of a fight. Why couldn't Tinator see that? He centered his weight, surprised at how much heavier the sword felt now. A strange feeling took hold of him, similiar to how he felt when he hit Chase, as if he was watching his own body but not controlling it. Before he knew it, he was sprinting toward Tinator, sword raised. He swung hard. Tinator repelled the stroke with a small knife, already drawn in anticipation of his attack. Knox's sword glanced off the knife, but not before it sliced into the unprotected crook of Tinator's elbow, opening a deep gash. At the sight of blood seeping to the surface, Knox dropped the sword.

"I—I'm sorry—I didn't mean–" he choked, confused.

Tinator covered the gash with his hand. "Of course you meant it—did you not heed your first lesson? Intent is the greatest weapon of all." He closed his eyes, keeping one hand firmly cupped over the wound. After a few moments, he dropped his hand, stowed his hunting knife, and flexed his arm. The bloodstain and the tear in his shirt were still there, but the gash had sealed itself.

Knox rubbed his eyes with his fists.

Seaborne sauntered over to him and smiled. "You did well."

"Did you see that?" asked Knox. "The blood. The cut! It was deep. Now it's gone!"

"The daylights are strong here. The vessel is not easily wounded," Seaborne replied, as though everything that had happened in the last twenty minutes was the most natural thing in the world.

Chapter 9

DAYLIGHTS

Whether the heck are are you talking about?" asked Knox, shaking his head at Seaborne. "Everybody on this island is certifiable, and now I'm going crazy, too."

Seaborne surveyed him quietly for a minute, then said, "Tinator's daylights are very strong."

Knox thought maybe—somehow—he'd been hit in the head because Seaborne wasn't making any sense. Seaborne put a hand on his shoulder and pointed him toward the stream.

"Drink."

Knox did as he was told. The water was cool and delicious. After a few palmfuls, he felt revived and turned back to face Seaborne.

"What were you saying?"

"I was saying that Tinator's daylights are very strong. I'm not surprised you felt them."

Knox pulled the collar of his tunic to his mouth in his usual habit, but spit it out when he tasted fur. "I felt *something* out there, that's for sure—but *daylights*? What the heck are they?"

"The daylights make us who we are. They are the essence of the divided *atar,* the great life force that resides in all living things and connects all life forms to others, including you and Tinator and everything around you." Seaborne squatted beside Knox.

"The daylights are in the trees and in this stream that bathes their roots and in the sun that warms them and in the wind that spreads their seed. In us, the daylights influence every choice and desire. All creatures on Ayda feel their daylights intensely; it is how they learn where they belong and to which Keeper they owe their allegiance."

"Keeper?"

Seaborne cocked his head. "Before, you asked about Rothermel. He is the Keeper of Melor and the protector of all who feel their daylights most distinctly among green, growing things."

Knox pondered this for a minute, then asked, "Do I have daylights?"

"Of course, but until now you have been unaware of them. Such is the way with outliers. Your daylights will gain in strength the longer you are here. And if you are lucky, someday soon, they will speak to you clearly and you will hear them."

"So you're telling me that it was my daylights that helped me fight?" Knox questioned.

Seaborne nodded. "Tinator is descended from the first Aydans. He is very powerful and can summon his daylights at will—bring them to the surface, if you like—so that your daylights would respond in turn and you might sense them with ease."

"Whoa," said Knox, reliving the current of energy that had swept over him. He looked sideways at Seaborne. "How powerful are you?"

"Not so. I was not born on Ayda. It took me many years to learn to draw upon my daylights, to hear their calling. As I told you, I came ashore to the east, in Metria, and for a long time I tried to deny my daylights and make those lands my home. I loved it very much, and the Keeper of Metria, who is called Rysta, raised me as her own." Seaborne's forehead crumpled in thought. "But it was not to be. My daylights speak loudest and clearest to me in Melor. I am a Melorian at heart."

Knox gave Seaborne a quizzical look. "What do you think I am?"

"I do not know, lad; it is too soon to say. By the time you are full-grown, you will know where you belong. There are four realms in Ayda: Melor, Metria, Varuna, and Exor. All who live within a land are there because their daylights insist upon it and they, in turn, are subject to its Keeper."

Seaborne glanced up suddenly, shading his eyes from the sun that continued to burn away at the cloudy sky. He stood up.

"Come now, the others will want to know you are all right."

"How old were you when you found out you were a Melorian?" asked Knox, standing up, too.

Seaborne looked puzzled, as though Knox had just asked him when he learned to fly.

"I have no earthly idea."

"Well, how old are you now? We'll count back. You don't look older than, I don't know, fifty?"

Seaborne's laughed. "Ahh, lad, you still see Ayda with eyes from beyond the fog. The daylights are stronger here so the body does not sicken or age as quickly as it does there. I am certain I am far older than fifty."

Knox stopped. "How old do you think you are then?"

Seaborne paused in thought, counting on his fingers.

"I cannot say, truly—I was put on a ship as a cot boy during an age when men battled at sea, that much I remember. I can still see her name on the stern, written in gold: the HMS *Cavalier*. She did not deserve her fate, I will tell you that much; but then, not many do."

Knox thought back to a time when battles were fought at sea, before airplanes and missiles. He snorted.

"That's ridiculous! You're saying you're two hundred years old! Nobody lives that long." He couldn't wait to tell Chase.

Seaborne looked at him sideways, saying nothing.

Knox bit his lip. "Is that how you got the sword?"

Seaborne's expression tightened. "From my officer, the one I served—but that is not important. The daylights are what is important."

They walked a few steps together in silence.

"So let me get this right," Knox blurted. "On Ayda the daylights are like superpowers or something. They make everyone immortal?" His voice rose in excitement. "And I have some?"

"I'm not explaining this well," sighed Seaborne. "*We* are not immortal—the daylights are. They give one's vessel strength and guidance, but they do not abide in one form forever. The daylights return eventually to their source and are reborn in another form. I will die one day, as everything dies, when my daylights fragment."

"So they're recyclable. Is that what you're saying? But not for a long, long time?" asked Knox.

Seaborne frowned. "Re-cycla-ble? I do not know this word."

"Forget it, it's okay. It's new—well, at least it would be to you, since you're, like, uh, really, very, extremely old," stammered Knox, backing away and almost falling in his hurry to get back to the others.

Seaborne called after him, "I'm not that old!"

Knox sprinted across the clearing.

"Evelyn, let me see your cut!"

She removed the leaf pressed against her cut and lifted her finger. The skin was untouched; no visible cut at all.

Knox whirled around to Chase, who was still cupping his hand over his lip and nose.

"Chase! Your lip! Let me see it!"

Chase was in no mood to do anything for Knox, but his brother's wild expression made him curious, so he brought his hand down. His nose had stopped bleeding, and now his split lip had reknit with fresh, pink skin.

"Holy crap! They're working!" Knox jigged around on one foot. "The daylights are working! We're going to live forever!"

Chase and Evelyn exchanged looks.

"What are you saying, Knox?" Evelyn asked gently, as if she were talking to a lunatic.

Knox repeated everything Seaborne had told him.

"What a bunch of crap. No way," scoffed Chase. He twirled one of Teddy's braids with his fingers.

Evelyn and Frankie remained silent.

Knox shrugged. "Look at how fast you and Evelyn healed . . . and my black eye. You said it was gone! And *something* helped me to fight Tinator."

"You were cool, Knoxth," said Teddy.

Knox gently fist-bumped his little brother and mumbled in Chase's direction, "Yeah, uh, I'm sorry about before. Don't hate me, Teddy—okay?"

Teddy nodded.

"It *was* brave, Knox—very stupid, as usual, but, brave," admitted Chase.

"Brave, maybe, but needless," said Seaborne, catching up to Knox. "Tinator was already aware of your strength—and your courage."

"Sure he is—now!" crowed Knox.

Seaborne caught him by the elbow. "Mind yourself, lad. Perhaps one day you will become a great warrior like Tinator, or a great hunter, like Duon, but do not fool yourself. The daylights do not always have a choice when to fragment—sometimes that choice is made by another. Tinator could have killed you today with a flick of his wrist. Everything that occurred here today was by his design."

"What about his arm?" Knox pointed out.

Seaborne sighed, exasperated. "If you persist in only looking at what is on the surface and not *seeing,* you will never find your way."

"And where would that be?" Knox asked rudely. "Home?"

Seaborne frowned. "To the place you are meant to be, lad. That should be home enough for anyone."

＋　　＋　　＋

Back at the cabin, Tinator motioned to Chase to follow him out of earshot of the others. There, Tinator handed him the sword.

"I thought Knox won it. He drew first blood," said Chase. He tried to sound like he didn't care.

"There are many different kinds of strength," Tinator replied. "Such a blade as this is safest in the hands of one more reluctant to use it. Drawing blood is easy; deciding when it is necessary is not."

Chase studied Tinator out of the corner of his eye, not sure he could trust this sudden kindness. His black hair showed no signs of gray, but his dark brown face was as worn as the tree trunks surrounding the clearing, and his high forehead was rutted by deep horizontal lines. Despite what Seaborne said, Tinator definitely appeared older than the other Melorians.

"So I should have the sword, but I shouldn't use it," said Chase.

Tinator caught his eye and said gently, "Perhaps you'll be lucky enough never to have to."

Chase did another double take. Maybe Seaborne was telling the truth, and the whole thing this morning really had been an act. He felt the reassuring heat of the sun on his back and lifted his eyes. The sky was a deep indigo blue above the tall tops of the trees. No clouds. No fog—at least as far as he could see. He decided to push this nicer Tinator with a question.

"Is it true that no one ever leaves Ayda?"

Tinator was silent.

"What about my parents, and Evelyn and Frankie's grandmother? How would you feel if Calla just dis—"

"Do not speak of such things!" Tinator cut him off, roaring back into his old, ferocious self. "Do not call misfortune upon my family!" He spit and ground the spittle into the earth under his moccasin. "May your words fall into the earth like rain and never be heard again!" He then stepped uncomfortably close to Chase. The top of Chase's head came up to Tinator's shoulder—a difference in size that seemed to have an effect on the older man. He turned away, studying the ground.

Chase waited and watched, wondering if Tinator expected the grass to answer. When Tinator faced him again, his expression was unyielding.

"Hear this, eldest. All that you once knew is forever divided from you. You will never return from whence you came, nor will your people find you. You are beyond their reach. Your survival here depends on how well you and your kin accept this fact. You must learn our ways if you wish to keep your family protected. Ayda lives under a shadow of menace. Nowhere is this felt more keenly than in Melor. Our enemies in Exor do not hesitate to reach across our border and take what they want, including children. You must be vigilant. What matters now is not the past; it is how you behave in the present." He turned on his heel. "Enough talk—you have work to do to earn your keep."

Chase followed him slowly back across the clearing. A puff of wind scattered his bangs, raking the grass and bringing with it the sweet smell of pine and earth. He inhaled deeply, then looked down at his outfit and the heavy sword at his hip. It was as if they were all in some kind of make-believe game gone dreadfully wrong—the kind of game he and Knox used to play, where they imagined they were pirates or knights and had to rescue one of their stuffed animals. But this was *real*. He really did have a sword at his hip. Knox had already been in a duel. If this was a game, it was deadly serious. He didn't know whether to laugh or start bawling.

Chapter 10

CAPTURE

From the bulk of their supplies, it looked as if the Melorians intended to stay at the clearing for some time, but Seaborne cautioned the children not to assume anything. He explained that when a Melorian set out on a trip or a hunt, he or she packed all that was essential on their backs and parted with no words of leaving or return.

"They do not believe in endings," he replied, when they asked why.

Days and nights at the cabin soon slipped into a rhythm that made it hard to keep track of how much time had passed since their first day on Ayda. Time, in general, was not something the Melorians seemed to think much about, except to take care not to be in the forest alone after sunset.

The outliers were taught how to weave a hammock, to hunt and clean small game, and to communicate from a distance through hand and secret voice signals. Tinator and Duon and the other Melorian men, who were identified as Duor and Sarn, often went deep into the woods to hunt while the women stayed closer to camp. Evelyn, Frankie, and the boys were divided between them. Seaborne did not hunt with the others, preferring to stay by the shore and fish. Each afternoon, one of the Melorian warriors returned to the clearing to give weapons instruction with Calla, an expert in hand-to-hand combat.

"Be smart," she told them. "Don't lower your guard—especially if you're alone or traveling in the north, near the Exorian border. The enemy is stealthy. You must know how to identify their tracks and fight back.

Never hesitate. *Ever.* If you are attacked, use whatever you can to defend yourself. Arrows can be used as spears, knife hilts as bludgeons, fingers and fingernails can gouge and scrape. Use everything you have available to you."

"What do Exorians look like?" asked Frankie.

Calla looked up at Duor. He shook his head.

"Never mind," she said quickly. "You'll know one if you ever have the misfortune to see one." Calla had Evelyn hold up her knife.

"A knife is a silent and stealthy weapon, an assassin's weapon. It can be thrown, but you will have more accuracy if you allow your attacker to get very close"—she stood only two inches from Evelyn, her chin even with Evelyn's forehead—"before you strike!" She jabbed her arm hard into Evelyn's solar plexus and twisted her fist.

"Ooomph," grunted Evelyn.

"If I had been armed, it would have hurt less but been much more deadly—and do not make that mistake: Exorians are always armed." She smiled and pulled back her fist, her voice rising to address the group.

"Melorians must always be prepared to feed and defend themselves. When you are well-versed with the weapons you've been given, I shall show you how to use larger blades." Her eyes twinkled beneath her hood. She drew two great knives from beneath the hem of her poncho, long and curved, and swept them in a rapid arc around her head, then released them. They flew through the air and struck the side of the cabin with such force that the blades stuck deep into the wood.

Knox's mouth fell open. He took his axes from his harness and held them by their handles.

"You gotta show me how to do that!"

Calla winked at him. "Practice."

That night, Evelyn and Frankie lay huddled next to each other in the small bed, Teddy snoring on the other side.

"Do you think they get attacked a lot?" Frankie whispered into the darkness.

Evelyn shivered in response and turned over, pressing her back into the familiar, warm figure of her sister. "I don't know. I hope not," she said.

"No wonder they hate Exorians." Frankie yawned and rolled over.

Evelyn stared into the shadowy black of the room, listening to the breathing of the two younger children. Pale moonglow from the waxing moon shone on the floor through the open window. Evelyn closed her eyes and saw Calla's slender fingers wrapped around her knives, circling them over her head; then, she saw Mara's face and remembered the way Mara's cool fingers had brushed against her face when she pulled up her hood: firmly, protectively—motherly. Evelyn's heart constricted with a longing that she had not allowed herself to feel for a long time. She rubbed the spot on her chest and clenched her teeth, hard, to make it stop.

It wouldn't do to get attached to these people, she told herself. It wasn't worth it. The only thing that came from loving people was losing them and then having to carry the weight of their ghosts forever. She had Frankie, and that was enough to look out for. Evelyn rolled to her side and threw a protective arm around her sister, determined to graduate to larger blades as soon as possible.

☩   ☩   ☩

In the morning, Calla showed Teddy how to use flat rocks to dig a deep, V-shaped trench set back from the clearing; such a large group needed a latrine.

"You can't dig it too close to the stream or the river or it will poison the drinking water," she explained. "And you must dig it at least three feet down, then throw in pine needles and leaves. Every few days, you throw in more." She grunted as she pushed a large mound of black earth to the side of the trench, molding it into a loose ridge on one side. "When you leave, fill it in, like this." She kicked the ridge with her foot, emptying the dirt back into the trench. "Then, you walk over the area several times and cover it with branches. This is important whenever you leave your scent in the forest. Otherwise you'll leave a trail an enemy can follow." She sat back on her haunches. A dirty streak of mud smudged her cheek.

"Here, take this," she said, handing him a large, flat rock.

Seaborne was leaning quietly against a deeply rutted tree stump. Tar panted happily by his side. Teddy gestured wildly at him with the rock.

"I'm making a toilet!"

Seaborne winked at him. "A useful thing, to be sure." His eyes rested on Calla for a moment, or what he could see of her shadowed face under her hood. He reached over and gently wiped the mud from her cheek with the back of his hand.

"There, now, you won't go back to your mother looking like you've been making mudcakes."

"But that's exactly what I have been doing!" she joked.

The corners of Seaborne's mouth lifted. The morning was warm. The fog had retreated farther than usual and the blue sky was brilliant against the trees. They could see Mara's head bent over some work through the scrim of tree branches. Seaborne made a quick visual inspection of the nearby area and put his hand on Tar's blocky shoulders.

"Calla, there's plenty to be done. Your father tells me you will depart 'ere the full moon, and I could use your help training Knox on the bow. Tar can stay with the little one. He'll be safe enough."

Calla's shoulders tensed. She picked up the quiver and bow lying on the ground. She looked around apprehensively.

"I'm not sure," she said in a low voice. "I think one of us should stay."

Tar gave a deep *woof* and a low growl. He shook his head violently and, in one giant leap, landed on all four paws right behind Teddy.

Calla laughed. "All right, Tar, all right."

Tar barked a quick reply, circled Teddy once, and sat back down.

"I guess I know when I'm not needed," laughed Calla. She slung the quiver and bow on her back and nodded to Seaborne. "I'm all yours."

Seaborne's smile broadened.

"But just in case—Teddy," she cried, "don't go anywhere without Tar. When you're finished, he'll walk you back to the clearing. I'll come check on you in a little while. Tar, watch him!" The dog cocked his ear and wagged his tail. Teddy nodded and went back to digging.

Seaborne whispered loudly to Calla, "Don't worry, Tar can see and hear any danger a mile off, plenty of time for us to get here."

Tar agreed with another loud *woof.*

"You're right, " Calla answered. "And there is a lot to do before we go." They walked back to the clearing single-file without breaking a single branch.

Calla and Seaborne worked with Knox until he was able to line an arrow in the bow, pull back the string, and loose the arrow without it wobbling in the air. Duon showed him how to whittle a stick into a straight shaft, notch the ends, and fletch it. By the time his lesson was finished, the sun was almost directly overhead in the sky. Tinator, Duor, and Sarn had left at dawn, taking Axl with them. Chase was helping Evelyn piece together several small skins Mara had given her, and one that she had prepared on her own into a shirt to give to Seaborne. She was so immersed in her work that she didn't hear Frankie creep up behind her. Frankie clapped her hands on her sister's shoulder.

"*Gotcha!*"

Evelyn shrieked and threw the skins in the air. One landed on Chase's head. Knox doubled over, laughing so hard he snapped his new arrow shaft in half. Calla, Seaborne, and Duon joined in. Mara heard them and lifted her eyes from her own work. The small smile she wore under her hood quickly faded.

"Where is the little one?" she asked. "Was he with you, Calla?"

Calla retraced her steps to the edge of the clearing and called for Teddy. There was no reply.

"Oh, no!" she cried, her eyes scanning the woods.

Seaborne was already running in that direction. He swept by her.

"It's my fault!" he yelled. "I told you he would be safe—Tar! Where are you?"

The Melorians scattered. Duon and Calla sprinted to Seaborne's side so quickly that before Knox took five steps, they had disappeared completely into the forest.

Chase followed them, shouting, "Knox, check the beach!"

Knox breathed a sigh of relief. The beach! Of course Teddy would go there. He loved those rocks. Knox took off down the path. Mara rounded the back of the cabin, shouting Teddy's name. Evelyn and Frankie stood rooted to the spot, unsure of what to do.

"I'll check the cabin," said Evelyn, in a dreadful voice. "Maybe he got tired and went inside."

Frankie nodded. Around her voices called out for Teddy and Tar. She knew she should do something. Voices like that had called her name before:

scared, hoping for a sign. She wanted to tell Evelyn to look under the bed. That's where she had hid. She wanted to go look herself, but it was as if her muscles were no longer obeying her brain. It was a feeling she'd felt once before; the time the earth had moved and turned everything she'd thought was solid into dust, including her father. There was a rustling behind her. The hair on her arms stood up and she felt tiny pinpricks of pain like little electric shocks all over her body. She tasted a metallic tang at the edges of her tongue and her mouth went completely dry.

"Evelyn!" she called out.

The outline of the cabin stood black against the clear sky. The sun, at its height overhead, beat down on her, as dazzling and hot as any sun she had ever felt. Frankie shut her eyes against it; she felt sick and nearly vomited. When she opened them again, the clearing had disappeared into a white blaze of light: There was movement, then a green flash—a halo around the sun—and then nothing.

✢ ✢ ✢

"I found him! I found him! He was at the beach!" Knox shot onto the path, red-faced and dripping with sweat after running with Teddy up the cliff. His heart was pounding like rapid gunfire in his chest.

"Teddy, you scared the daylights out of me!" cried Chase, tearing out of the forest to meet them.

Knox cackled, on the brink of hysterics.

"*Daylights*, Chase—get it? He scared the *daylights* out of you! I never got it before!"

The Melorians and Seaborne appeared out of nowhere and assembled silently behind the boys.

"He is found," Calla muttered, subdued, walking away toward the cabin. She would not look at Seaborne or her mother. Seaborne grabbed Teddy from Knox and held him at arm's length, high off the ground.

"Why didn't you stay put as you were told!" he cried. "You nearly were the end of me!" He grabbed the little boy to his chest and held him, his face creased with worry.

"The child must never be left alone again," said Mara plainly.

"But he wasn't alone," said Seaborne. "We left him with Tar. I'd bet my life on Tar defending any one of us. Where is that blasted hound anyway?"

Teddy looked up at the circle of faces towering above him.

"He thmelled thomething," he said.

Calla looked puzzled. She touched Seaborne on the arm and she and Duon retreated back into the forest. Seaborne frowned, putting his hand to his machete.

"He smelled something? What do you mean?"

"I don't know," Teddy said. "I wath digging and then Tar thniffed the air and leaped over me and ran away. I wanted to know where he wath going."

Seaborne crossed his arms. "Tar would never leave his post, unless—" His hand strayed toward his shoulder, toward the long sword strapped in its scabbard.

"Unless what?" asked Knox.

"Unless he sensed a greater danger, something—" Seaborne was cut off by the sound of Evelyn shouting.

"What now?" cried Mara.

At the cabin, Evelyn knelt beside a burnt circle of grass.

"She's gone. She's gone!" she moaned. "Frankie's gone."

Mara looked at Seaborne. "Get the children into the cabin."

"No!" shouted Knox. He turned to run after Calla and Duon but Seaborne stopped him, lifting him up with one arm. He crossed the clearing to the cabin, shoved the door open, and heaved the boy onto the floor.

"Now is not the time, Knox. You've been given weapons for a reason. You must stay here and guard the others, especially Teddy! The smaller ones are most vulnerable." Seaborne came back to Chase, Teddy, and Mara, who was kneeling over Evelyn. Slowly, Mara helped her up and half-carried her across to the cabin. Teddy followed closely behind. Seaborne stared at Chase, looking into his eyes with a ferocity that scared him more than anything else that had happened so far.

"I will not lie to you, boy. All your strength and courage are required at this moment. The enemy is afoot; he is near and may strike again. If he does, you must draw on the skills you have learned. Heed your daylights." And with that he was gone, running down the path toward the beach.

Chase followed him with his eyes until he was out of sight, then turned to face what lay waiting for him in the cabin. Everything had happened so fast. The weight of the sword around his waist made him limp a little as he walked. Mara emerged on the doorstep. Her hood was pulled far over her forehead, her expression buried in shadow.

"The girl, Evelyn, is asleep. I have given her a calming draught. You must stay inside the cabin, but be alert—keep your sword unsheathed and, above all, do not light any fires!"

"Where are you going?" asked Chase, wishing his voice didn't sound quite so young and nervous.

"My heart tells me that the enemy has struck at more than one today." She swept silently into the forest, the sharp tip of a knife glinting below her poncho.

Chase entered the cabin and closed the door. Evelyn's sleeping form lay on the bed under the covers. Knox sat at the hearth, fastening feathers to the tails of a bundle of newly hewn arrow shafts. His mouth was set in a grim line as he stacked the arrows on the floor one by one. Teddy watched him silently from the foot of the bed. Chase drew his sword and leaned his back against the wall between the window and the door. His ears were tingling with the effort of listening for movement outside.

Knox looked at Teddy, then Chase, and then, meaningfully, across at Evelyn, sleeping on the bed.

"We have to get her back," he growled, then returned to his work, sharpening his knives on the small whetstone at his feet, as though he'd been doing it all his life.

✝   ✝   ✝

What seemed like hours passed in silence. Teddy fell asleep on the bed at Evelyn's feet. Chase's back and legs were aching from standing at attention by the window for so long. Knox had turned from arrow-making to throwing his knives against the wall. A dull *thwack* greeted each meeting of knife and wood, accompanied by a curse. He paced back and forth between throws, complaining in hoarse whispers to Chase.

Chase was silent but positioned his body to watch the window and bar the door against Knox escaping as well as he could manage. He looked out the window for what felt like the millionth time that day. The sun was westering, bringing on the customary afternoon chill, and the trees cast long shadows into the clearing. Chase looked longingly at the fireplace, wishing for the warmth and security a fire would provide.

"Don't even think about it!" Knox hissed, guessing his brother's thoughts.

Chase returned to his vigil by the window. His eyes were tired and sore and his head hurt from trying to figure out what had happened. From his vantage point, he could see the charred circle of grass and ground. It looked like a lightning strike—but Frankie had disappeared in broad daylight under an almost cloudless sky. A small rustle of movement at the periphery of the clearing caught his eye.

"Knox!" he whispered. "Get over here!"

Knox was there in an instant, an arrow already nocked in his bow. For several heart-pounding seconds they stared out the small aperture, straining to make out anything unusual. A shrill whistle sounded from the wood, bird-like, which was quickly followed by another matching trill in a lower register.

Chase slumped his head on the windowsill in relief. Knox lowered his bow. It was the all-clear signal. The Melorians entered the clearing as they always did—emerging from the lip of the woods in single file—only this time Sarn was carrying the crossbow. Tinator bore a large, misshapen burden around his shoulders. At his side, Axl worried the edge of his tunic. Seaborne, Mara, and Calla followed. Duon and Duor stayed behind to patrol the edge of the clearing. Tinator knelt down when he reached the grass and transferred Tar's heavy body to the ground.

"Oh no!" cried Knox, racing out of the cabin. He crashed to his knees alongside the massive hound. "Is he dead?"

"Not quite," replied Tinator, putting his ear to the dog's furry rib cage. "He has been sorely abused."

Tinator stroked the large head with one hand as the other explored Tar's spine and forelegs, checking for wounds. Great gashes that looked like claw marks had been opened around his neck and haunches. All over

his body, chunks of fur and skin were missing. Axl licked frantically at
Tar's mouth.

"What happened to him?"

"*Tehuantl*," Tinator grunted. "They are an ancient race not often seen
in Melor—but then, they are not the only strange creatures to stray into
our lands these days." He looked pointedly at Knox.

Calla took over guarding the door of the cabin so that Chase could
join his brother. The grass was stained red with Tar's blood and the poor
dog's flank was ripped open, exposing strips of pulsating pink-and-white
tissue that lay beneath his skin. Chase looked away, nauseated.

With Mara's help, Tinator gently turned Tar over and combed through
the matted hair at the juncture of his hind leg and underbelly. There, barely
visible, was a two-inch wound, crusted over with dried blood. Around
the wound, Tar's matted fur was stained a darker color.

"His wounds are already closing, but there is something poisonous left
inside that has left him helpless," said Tinator. "Some dark Exorian art
forged to defeat the healing power of the daylights." He looked at Mara
for answers.

"We will have to cut it out," she said simply, drawing her knife.

"*THTOP!*" came a shriek from the cabin. Calla was wrestling with
Teddy at the door.

"He's hurt, Ted! Mara needs to operate on him," Chase yelled back,
quickly.

"Wait!" Teddy freed himself and bolted into the group.

"C'mon, Tedders, you don't want to see this, " Knox said, his voice thick.

Seaborne disagreed, shaking his head.

"The little one should see if he wants to; so should you all. We have
warned you of the dangers of the enemy—now you must learn for yourself.
No one is safe." He stroked Tar's head, adding, "Not even a mighty hound
of Melor."

"He will need to be held down," Mara advised, tightening her grip on
the knife.

Tinator leaned in close to Tar's enormous head. Seaborne moved to
hold his body, but Knox pushed his hand away.

"I want to do it."

Mara poised the dagger over the wound and sliced into Tar's flank. The dog screamed and pawed the ground violently, trying to escape. Knox, Tinator, and Seaborne bore down on him to combine their weight. Chase was still unable to look. Mara worked quickly, exploring tentatively at first, then more desperately.

Tar's breath grew jagged. His eyelids fluttered. Axl whimpered and then howled, a long, drawn-out cry that flushed birds from the tree limbs.

"You're hurting him!" sobbed Teddy.

Knox began to cry openly, too, not bothering to wipe away the tears.

"Here." Mara motioned to Chase with her free hand. "Hold this open."

Chase knelt by her side to take the hilt of the knife, which now served to keep the skin pulled apart. Tar's wound was doubled now; blood geysered from the opening. Chase's stomach revolted and he almost dropped the knife.

"Hold it steady, now," hissed Mara.

Axl let out another sorrowful howl; Teddy sobbed louder. Chase gritted his teeth and clenched his fist harder around the hilt of the knife. Mara plunged her fingers into the gaping wound. Tar screamed again, then whimpered; then he stopped struggling and lay deathly quiet. After several intolerable seconds, Mara exhaled.

"I have it," she said, and slowly drew out a long, gray splinter from Tar's side. She placed it gingerly in the pocket of her poncho. Once it was safely stowed, she moved faster than Chase had ever seen anyone move, grabbing the knife and roughly pushing him away. Tinator knelt beside her. They covered the bleeding wound with their hands. Mara began a low chant in an unintelligible language, which Tinator joined. Waves of heat radiated from their bodies.

Teddy and Knox lay flat on the ground, their heads buried against Tar's head, both sobbing. Tar's eyes were closed and his tongue lolled at the side of his mouth. He didn't appear to be breathing. Chase crawled over to his brothers and pressed his face into the cool ground next to Teddy. A sudden thought made him sit bolt upright.

Tar had been guarding Teddy.

Chase hung his head, ashamed of how he had almost lost his grip on the knife. What if whatever that thing was inside Tar had been meant for Teddy?

Mara and Tinator stopped chanting and removed their hands. Tar's breath deepened; his eyelids quivered, then opened, pale pink rims, almost black irises. Axl gave a great bark and barreled through, frantically licking the deep slash made by Mara's dagger and the wounds made by the *tehuantl,* which, as Tinator had said, were already sealing themselves. Several tense minutes passed before Tar rolled gingerly onto his stomach, panting.

Tinator stroked his side. "Now, now, my friend. You are strong, but you must rest—and drink." He cradled the hound's massive head with his hands and bowed his own forehead to meet it. "I will fetch you water."

Tar tossed his head back and licked Tinator's hand, his tail wagging limply. Tar was weak, but he was alive.

When Tinator returned with water from the stream, he sighed deeply, then spoke.

"I know not what these events mean, but they do not bode well for your safety. This cabin is no longer secure, if ever it was. We have drawn the fire of the Exorians, and I"—he swallowed—"I am no longer confident that I have the ability to protect you."

His eyes darted around the clearing and landed on Mara's poncho. He lifted it delicately and folded it several times into a thick bundle around the deadly sliver.

"The enemy's weapons and reach have grown more deadly. We must take this to Rothermel. He will learn of all that has happened here today. Once the girl has risen and Tar can walk, we will depart."

"What about Frankie?" asked Knox. "She has to be around here somewhere! We can't just let her get ripped apart like Tar!"

Tinator's face blackened. "Never before have the enemy's forces dared to strike, unprovoked, with so many warriors at hand. My hope is that they have some use for the girl. If that is so, she will be kept alive. Most are."

"*Most?* There are others?" Chase was horrified.

"The enemy cares little for sustaining the daylights of his own people," replied Tinator. "Exorians are powerful, but short-lived. The imbalance of their daylights consumes their vessels, so the enemy must find his . . .

reinforcements elsewhere. He hunts often in Melor. But why he has chosen the young girl, and gone to such lengths to get her—" Tinator shook his head. "I do not know."

Chase and Knox unhooked and rolled their hammocks. Seaborne brought them each a basket to carry their few belongings—along with Evelyn's and Teddy's—on their backs. Knox gathered the arrows he'd made and restocked his quiver; he slung it and the bow over his shoulder and attached his knives to his harness, stuffing one into his tube sock, which was now brown with dirt. He pulled the pant leg down, straightened, and grabbed his basket.

"You really do look like a Melorian," said Chase.

Knox examined the knives in his harness.

"Well, I guess I'm feeling like one," he said. "And now I want to find Frankie."

Chapter 11

A LEGEND REVEALED

They left the cabin at first light, after only a few hours of sleep, filing through the woods in Melorian fashion on a path few would be able to discern without knowing it was there. Tinator led, armed with his crossbow; Evelyn stumbled behind him, eyes cast down, not caring where she was going. She hadn't uttered a word since Frankie's disappearance, and she walked hunched over, as if her shoulders had curved inward overnight.

Mara followed closely behind Evelyn, steering her now and then with a light touch on her elbow. Her poncho was stowed carefully in the bottom of her basket, wrapped around the poisoned sliver. Without her hood, her scar was vivid across the left side of her face, spilling down her neck in raised, ropey channels like the melted wax of a candle. Behind her walked Teddy, then Seaborne, followed by Chase, Calla, Knox, and Sarn. Duon and Duor had gone ahead to scout. Axl brought up the rear, moving slowly to keep pace with a limping Tar.

They proceeded battle-ready; this would mean long marches with few stops, nights on the ground, and no fires whatsoever. Everyone was to have their hoods up, their weapons close and ready to deploy at Tinator's signal. When Teddy grew tired, Seaborne carried him. In this manner, Tinator hoped to reach the inner sanctuary of Melor, a place the Melorians called the Wold, in two days. As they walked inland, to the north, the forest grew denser and more dimly lit, with only small patches of sun filtering through the canopy. Pine needles carpeted the ground, muffling their footsteps, and hillocks of moss sprouted here and there in varying shades of electric green.

Knox took close note of everything, looking for landmarks and unusual markings so that he would remember their path if they needed to travel it again. It seemed important, though he couldn't exactly say why. Every now and then, his eyes strayed ahead toward his brothers and to the back of Evelyn's hood.

Evelyn marched without registering anything but the searing pain in her chest. For as long as she could remember she had carried a weight there, something vague and heavy but fragile enough to break into sharp, tearing little pieces that pierced her from the inside. She curved herself around the pain, trying not to jostle the pieces and embed them further. Her mouth shaped a silent prayer as she walked, her lips moving without sound.

If she's dead, let me die.

And why not? The Haitian gods of death, the Ghede, had been stalking her since she was a baby. They had taken everything from her: her parents, her home, her country. And now they had followed her here. *Please. Please,* she begged silently, hoping they would listen. *Please don't take Frankie, too.* A silent wail rose from deep inside her and threatened to escape. She clamped her lips down.

"She may yet be found," said Mara reassuringly, from behind.

Evelyn was sick of trying to figure out how the Melorians knew what they did. There were people like them in Haiti: holy men and women who read people's thoughts as if they were spelled out on their chests. She wondered if Mara could see inside her heart, and if so, would it look as black as it felt.

It was near dark when Tinator called for a halt to their march. Through the shadowy lacework of branches overhead, the setting sun tinged the edges of the few, forlorn clouds with a brilliant pink. Birds trilled a warning at their passage, but otherwise, the company laid their burdens to the ground in complete silence. Mara parceled out small bars of dried fruit and grain and a strip of dried meat each. They ate quickly and hungrily.

Evelyn alone refused food, staring unseeingly into the darkness. Mara settled herself beside her, saying nothing, lying so that their backs touched.

The warm pressure startled Evelyn. The Melorians rarely touched one another—or any of them—unless it was necessary. Mara was giving her a great gift, Evelyn realized, and with the realization came the grief that Evelyn had been trying to keep at bay through the long day. Her mouth opened wide and a high keening poured out, shaking her body. Mara lay unmoving as a tree trunk, allowing her back to absorb the impact of Evelyn's shuddering sobs.

"Don't cry, Evelyn. Don't cry, *please,*" Knox pleaded in a stricken whisper. "We'll find her. We'll get her back."

"Shhh, let her cry, lad," said Seaborne. "Sometimes the best dressing for a wound is salt water."

Chase crossed his arms over his head and buried his head in the crook of his elbows. The sound of Evelyn crying was worse than anything they had experienced so far.

"What do the Exorians want with Frankie, anyway? Why did they attack us, and what the heck is a *tehuantl?*" He cried out. His voice cracked the stillness of the evening like a shot, but Chase didn't care.

Seaborne gave him a piteous look. Tinator shifted uneasily on his haunches and sighed heavily. When he next spoke, his voice sounded old and tired.

"You have suffered a loss we Melorians know too well. I have been loathe to reveal too much to you before, but it is time you understood our enemy. You deserve to know how it came to be that we are at war with the Exorians, since you, too, now have your own grievance to right. But before you understand the power of the enemy, you must learn about your own powers and of the making of the *atar* at the beginning of things. It is a story every Melorian child knows. I shall tell it to you now, for it may give you hope." Tinator sat cross-legged on the ground, his back erect, his crossbow leaning against his knee. He spoke softly.

"Before dawn, before time and weather, before the arc of life began its ascent, the great Weaver, of many names and many forms, both male and female, known and unknown, grew cold and weary in the darkness of eternity. Wishing for warmth and companionship, the Weaver set this desire against the limitless void, like flint against stone. Sparks flew from the darkness and from these sparks grew the soul of all being: the divine fire, the *atar,* which is the energy that binds all living creatures to one another and to the Weaver, the creator of all.

"The full force of the *atar* cannot be seen or described in human terms—it cannot be fathomed or contained. Even in the beginning the *atar* shifted and warped so that life as we know it was slow to take hold. No sooner would the Weaver shape a vessel than the potency of the *atar* would consume it. There was no constancy and the world was slow to take form. Desiring this new creation to thrive, the Weaver divided the *atar* into four lesser qualities that were more easily contained. They are the foundation of all life." A gentle breeze stirred the underbrush. Tinator paused for a moment, then continued.

"On Ayda, we call these four qualities *daylights.* One feels them most readily when the wind blows, the earth moves, the rain falls, and the sun rises. What is less understood is how these qualities move *within* us and other vessels." Tinator cast his eyes around the huddled group.

"In an animal, indeed, in us, the balance of daylights is more equal than in, say, a tree or a brook, yet all living things have a stronger quality of daylight that defines their destiny. It is how a blade of grass becomes a blade of grass, or how an Aydan knows to which land he or she belongs. I am a Melorian because the strength of my daylights is fed by the earth and the trees. You may find your own daylights call you elsewhere and bind you to your own Keeper."

"Seaborne told me about the Keepers," said Knox. "Aren't they like your chief or something?"

Tinator shifted, unsure whether or not he should continue. He questioned Mara with a glance; she assented, nodding for him to go on.

"On Ayda, we are blessed to be home to the four stones of power: Each stone contains one of the essential qualities of the daylights so that the full power of the *atar* remains divided and contained. The people and the lands of Ayda are named for their stone: Melor, Metria, Varuna, and Exor. In turn, our lands and each stone is protected by a Keeper. It is the sacred duty of the Keepers to steward the daylights under their protection and ensure the balance between the four, because life thrives only when the daylights work together as the Weaver intended—here," Tinator swept his arm to encompass the forest, "—and here." He brought his hand to his heart. "I am a Melorian, thus I am bound by my essential nature to the stone of Melor, my Melorian kin, and our stone's Keeper, Rothermel. He is charged with the preservation of the stone of Melor and all those who hear its call."

Chase had remained silent throughout Tinator's explanation, trying to make sense of it. Now he felt compelled to ask more questions.

"If Rothermel is the Keeper of Melor, who and where are the others?"

"Rothermel has two sisters: Rysta is the Keeper of Metria, the water stone, who refreshes the memories of the world. Ratha is the Keeper of the stone of Varuna. She governs the air and wind and sees that none fall into torpor and stagnation."

"And Exor?"

Tinator grimaced visibly in the dim light.

"The fire stone of Exor was once kept by their brother, Ranu, steward of the Exorian lands and all who inhabit them. His task was to warm and comfort the Earth and its people so they might shine undimmed, but his daylights were fragmented long ago. He fell at the hands of the enemy during the Great Battle, and his lands, people, and the stone of Exor were stolen. They now belong to Dankar, scourge of Melor. It is he who took the little girl, he who has caused your grief."

"But why?" croaked Evelyn, out of the gloom, her voice raw from crying.

"It is enough to tell you that there was once one other stone on Ayda—the most powerful of all: the Fifth Stone, which was the heartstone that bound the essences of the other four and governed the full force of the *atar*."

"What do you mean *bound the essences of the other four?*" asked Chase. All this talk of stones and special powers was making him wonder all over again if the Melorians had a screw loose.

By way of an answer, Tinator raised the thumb and forefinger on each of his hands and, as he did, named them out loud.

"Melor, Metria, Varuna, Exor: the four stones of Ayda. Separately, each has limited power, but if I connect them—" he pressed the thumb and forefinger of one hand to the thumb and forefinger of the other hand to form a diamond shape, "their qualities form a complete circuit—very strong, but also limited." He broke the shape and then pressed it back together to underscore his words.

"What you do not see resides in the space between: the *atar,* the limitless energy that is contained in the Fifth Stone, which was born from the spark of creation at the beginning of things."

Chase unconsciously mimicked Tinator, pressing together his thumbs and forefingers, thinking out loud.

"So there's this cosmic energy, or whatever, that is keeping everything together. And then there are these other qualities, the daylights, and the Keepers watch over it all, including us, to make sure it's all humming along. But where does this guy Dankar come in?"

Tinator turned a heavy eye toward him.

"Dankar's desire to possess all of the stones has plagued us and brought enmity to Melor; for he would have dominion over everything and everyone."

"But what about the Fifth Stone? Can't it stop him?" Evelyn whispered.

"The Fifth Stone has passed beyond knowledge," Tinator replied sadly. "It was lost to Ayda during the Great Battle, perhaps gone beyond this world's grasp forever."

"So you're saying it doesn't really exist," Chase interuppted.

"No, I did not say that. I, for one, do not believe the power of the Fifth Stone is so easily forsaken, wherever it now resides. The Weaver has given us many reminders that the five stones are inseparable and not easily divided, including the shape of our vessel." Tinator placed a hand on each of his thighs, then on his forearms, and then drew a line from his head to his heart. "The Four and the One, bound together. So it is with all things."

Teddy held one of his hands up, palm facing out, in the customary Melorian greeting. He wiggled his fingers and thumb.

"Four and one."

Tinator pressed his own fingertips to Teddy's and bowed his head.

"The power of the five stones is all around us. It *is* us," he explained. "And that is why we must not despair. One day the Fifth Stone will return to Ayda to defeat Dankar. One day our people shall be reunited, and we will have peace."

Chapter 12

SKY CROSSING

They were up and marching again at daylight. The ground rose gently as the morning wore on; soon they could hear the sound of water rushing over rocks in the distance. By midday, Tinator called for a halt atop a vast granite shelf that wrapped around a rising shoulder of earth and then dropped off precariously. A great curtain of water, at least a hundred feet across, fell straight down from a dizzying height above them. Chase stooped by the edge of the shelf and threw a small rock down into the gulch, watching it drop into misty haze.

"How far down does it go?" he asked.

"Far and deep," answered Tinator, elusive as usual. "We call the river that feeds it the Vossbeck; it is one of the two great rivers that flow from Lake Voss, which marks the northern border of Melor. These falls are known as the Veil of the Vossbeck." He turned his ear toward the roar of tumbling water. "We are now at the threshold of the Wold, the stronghold of the Melorian people. It is well-protected: None may enter without Rothermel's permission."

Knox peered over the shelf edge and said, "I'm assuming we have permission."

Seaborne gave him a nudge backwards from the edge.

"We'll find out soon enough, won't we?"

Tinator took the lead once again, walking at an easy pace, the line of his shoulders now more relaxed. The sense of imminent danger lessened and the morning grew bright and warm. Chase daydreamed as he walked, trying to picture the Wold. The Melorians had said very little about it, but from their descriptions it sounded like a real village with farms and houses and people. If it weren't for the forlorn way Evelyn's hood pouched over her head, or for the fact that whoever took Frankie might be coming for them next, he might have been excited.

"Chase, do you see anything?" whispered Knox, appearing suddenly at his elbow.

"Like what?"

"Dunno; a hidden guy or a weapon or something? Seaborne said this area is well-protected, but I don't see anything or anyone."

"You never see a Melorian in the forest unless he or she wants to be seen," Calla interjected. "You should know that by—"

Tinator stopped abruptly, cutting her off. He lifted his hand to indicate silence and cocked his head to the side to listen. Instinctively, Seaborne lifted Teddy onto his back. A loud, sharp whistle rang out to the south of them—a signal of danger from either Duon or Duor. Tinator circled back around to the rear at a dead run, gesturing for Sarn and Axl to accompany him. Mara would not allow Tar to follow. Moments later, strangled-sounding screams echoed through the trees, loud enough to be heard over the distant yet still roaring sound of the waterfall.

"Oh man," groaned Knox, "is that what I think it is?"

"Run!" Calla yelled in response, knives drawn.

"Follow me," cried Seaborne. He tightened his hold on Teddy and bolted into the dense forest. Knox took off, followed by Chase, who shoved Evelyn, waking her from her trance. They ran blindly, all thoughts of staying in formation waylaid by the urgency in Seaborne's voice. Shouts of warning echoed around them. Mara and Calla stayed behind to join Tinator and his guard. Tar sprinted into the woods. Another scream rang through the air, closer this time.

"Move! Faster!" yelled Seaborne.

Chase was running hard. He'd run farther and faster than he thought possible, but his lungs were straining and he was going to have to stop. He threw a look over his shoulder and saw a flash of movement in the bushes not far away. Whatever it was, it would be on him in no time. He struggled for breath, his legs weak. He knew he needed to run, but his lungs wouldn't let him. He made a quick decision, slowed, and pulled out his sword. Then he turned around. Branches and leaves shuddered in the distance. Something was approaching. Chase raised his sword.

"What do you think you're doing?" cried Evelyn as she reeled back beside him.

"I—I can't breathe . . . can't run," he panted.

She looked straight in his eyes for a moment, then calmly pulled out her knife.

"I'm not running either. If these things hurt Frankie, I'm going to kill them." Her voice was strange and remote, her eyes glittered beneath the hood. "I hope you learned how to use that," she nodded toward the sword.

Chase looked down at his hands. "Umm, sort of."

Sunlight flickered through the forest canopy; the leaves of the dense brush ahead of them shook as if a wind was blowing, but the air remained still, and deadly quiet. Chase's heart pounded so loudly he wondered if Evelyn could hear it. The bush shook again. Something was crawling toward them.

"Remember, we have to let it come close," Evelyn whispered.

Chase swallowed.

All at once the forest erupted in shredded leaves and screaming snarls that seemed to come from everywhere. Tinator burst into view in a dead sprint, his crossbow lowered. Mara, Calla, and Sarn emerged, fanning out in a protective net. Calla stopped when she saw the two eldest children. She shook her head in disbelief.

"Do the two of you think you can fend off a pack of *tehuantl* with a knife and a sword? They'll have your throats out before you take a stroke. Put the blades away. You must climb!"

The Melorians herded Chase and Evelyn to the foot of a distant tree and formed a semicircle around them, weapons facing out. A hand descended from one of the lower branches. Evelyn grabbed it and was pulled to safety. Chase went next, coming face-to-face with Seaborne. Knox and Teddy peered down from a branch above them.

A deep, menacing bark in the distance preceded another roar: very close this time. The Melorians circled the tree.

"Why do I get the feeling *tehuantl* can climb trees?" croaked Knox.

"Jump into and climb," whispered Seaborne. "Not much they can't do, actually."

"Great—jumping, climbing, man-eating machines."

"Not machines," said Seaborne. "*Cats.*"

As if they'd been conjured by Seaborne's words, three enormous jet-black panthers suddenly leapt from the underbrush and landed, spitting and snarling, just yards from the tree. Their ears were flattened above their narrowed eye sockets, which revealed only a sliver of deep yellow that flashed like gold against their sleek, dark fur. They whipped long tails back and forth, sizing up the Melorians on the ground.

"Holy crap, look at them!" Knox exclaimed.

"They're beautiful," breathed Evelyn.

"That's one word for them," said Seaborne.

No one moved. The *tehuantl* paced a few feet away from the Melorians, muscles undulating like waves under their glossy fur.

"Why don't they shoot?" Chase whispered to Seaborne.

"The *tehuantl* were once a great race, like the hounds of Melor—it is grievous to harm them, even now when their daylights have been corrupted by the enemy," Seaborne whispered back. "Tinator will not strike unless he must."

Tinator seemed transfixed by the animals' fluid movements, his eyes keeping pace as the *tehuantl* circled the tree, their heads even with Mara and Calla's shoulders. Yet the arm holding the crossbow did not flex. Chase remembered what Tinator had told him the first day they met: *Drawing blood is easy; deciding when it is necessary is not.*

A low, threatening growl rose from the largest cat's throat. Its lips curled back, showing long, pointed fangs and a thin froth of spittle. It stopped directly in front of Tinator and their eyes locked. The cat shifted its weight onto its haunches, ready to pounce. The two others did the same. Tinator pulled back the bow string. All three cats leapt into the air simultaneouly. Tinator released a bolt just as a sudden volley of arrows rained down from above.

The *tehuantl* fell back, hissing and snarling in pain, arrows embedded deep in their flanks. Tinator's long feathered bolt jutted from the chest of the largest *tehuantl.* It screamed and batted at the shaft with an enormous, clawed paw, then stumbled off into the forest. The remaining two creatures hissed and paced a few more times, then slunk away after their leader. After several tense moments, Tinator finally lowered his crossbow and lifted himself up into the tree.

"You shot that one straight in the chest!" cried Knox, eyes agog.

Tinator wore a troubled expression. "The daylights of the ancient breeds are hearty. They do not fragment so easily, yet my blow may have been the killing kind. I am sorry for it, but there was no other way." He sighed and chucked his crossbow more firmly on his shoulder, then asked Chase, "What are you waiting for?"

Chase made a move to swing down.

"No," said Tinator, and pointed toward the sky with his thumb. Chase looked up. Above were thick branches circling higher and higher around the trunk like a ladder. Seaborne and Teddy were already climbing hand over hand, to the top. "Follow them."

Within minutes, the entire company had risen high enough for the ground to disappear completely. About two-thirds of the way up, they came to a wide platform built around the tree, accessed by a small hatch and a wooden ladder. Chase followed Knox and Evelyn through the hatch where they found Seaborne and Teddy, along with three stern-looking strangers—Melorians by their dress—with helmets, longbows, and breastplates strapped over their tunics. Tinator held up his hand once everyone had gained the platform.

"We are crossing into the Wold, heartland of Melor and home to its Keeper. For this reason, crossings to the Wold are secret, guarded with vigilance—as you have already witnessed—by those bound to protect it or die." He nodded to the three well-armed Melorians.

"Once you have crossed, you may not leave the Wold without permission from Rothermel. Should you try, you will either be killed or cast into the cold waters of the Vossbeck. You have seen what lies waiting for you in the forest. Do not hold the trust Rothermel has placed in you lightly."

One of the guards handed Tinator a thick coil of rope tied with many knots and loops. It attached to another loop and ran across a wooden pulley that rolled back and forth across two taut ropes, which were completely hidden by the greens and browns of the forest canopy.

Sarn stepped up first. He placed each foot in a loop and put his arms through two higher loops, then wrapped his fists around the main shaft of rope. He jumped lightly off the platform and shot through the trees and past the waterfall, the pulley whizzing through the air above him.

"Melor is so cool!" Knox exclaimed.

"Except for all the things trying to kill us," countered Chase.

The pulley came back into view, empty. Calla grabbed Evelyn's arm. From somewhere behind them, one of the Melorian warriors produced a thick plank of wood with two holes bored at each end. Calla quickly tied it, like a swing seat, onto the rope. She climbed through and leaned against the plank, motioning to Evelyn to do the same.

"Hang on!" she yelled, and yanked the rope. They swung out over the treetops, twisting with the momentum and gaining breathtaking speed as they flew out over the shade of the forest. On their right, passing so quickly that Evelyn barely had time to register it, the Veil of the Vossbeck fell into the sparkling depths of the ravine. The pulley screamed as the swing ran swiftly into the cool of the forest on the other side. Another broad platform had been built amidst a stand of close-growing trees. Sarn was waiting on it, accompanied by an array of Melorian guards. As Calla and Evelyn came near, the swing slowed, so that by the time they reached the platform it was at a complete standstill. They hopped off lightly. Calla tugged at the rope. It retreated, jerking with each invisible pull of the wire at the other end.

Two by two they crossed the waterfall.

"So that's how you move around!" said Knox, grinning. He and Tinator were the last to land on the platform.

Calla nodded. "We also have bridges, but the nearest one is another day's march. Only Melorians know the whereabouts of sky crossings." She looked past Knox at her father, who was already in deep discussion with one of the guards. When Tinator turned back to the group, his eyes lingered on Evelyn.

"Rothermel awaits us," he announced grimly.

Chapter 13

PRISONER

Frankie came to with a blinding headache. Her temples throbbed in time with a strumming pulse of green, which was all she could see behind her closed eyelids. She opened her eyes, but her vision did not return. Cold seeped through the back of her poncho; she was lying on something hard and smooth, almost wet. She reached out tentatively to feel around her in the darkness. The air smelled dank and earthy. She sat up and hit her head on something hard. She reeled back in pain, eyes smarting, and tried to remember the last thing that had happened to her. Teddy was missing. The outline of the cabin against the sky. Then a dazzling light and a green flash. Maybe she had been hit by something and knocked out and the others thought she was dead. Maybe they had buried her alive!

"Help! Evelyn—Chase! I'm not dead!" It hurt her head to yell so loudly, but she had to get their attention.

She heard footsteps approaching. She yelled louder. A great scraping sound could be heard, followed by a piercing column of light and a *whoosh* of fresh air. Frankie covered her eyes against the sudden glare.

"I'm alive, I'm not dead!" she called out in relief, looking through her fingers.

It was hard for her to make out anything in the bright light, just moving shadows. An arm reached into the space, groped around for a moment, then caught her and pulled her roughly out onto the forest floor. She lay facedown for a minute, reassured by the clean smell of the moss and pine.

She rolled over expecting to see Seaborne or Evelyn. Instead, a blurry, round face of an unfamiliar man swam into sight. She tried to focus her eyes, instinctively reaching for her knife under the poncho.

"You won't find it there," the man said.

Frankie blinked. Her head was still pounding.

"Sit up; you'll feel better."

"Where am I?" Frankie asked, doing as he said. Immediately, she felt some of the pressure drain from her head and she opened her eyes. The man came into focus more clearly. It was impossible to say how old he was, since every adult she had met on Ayda seemed roughly the same age, but she thought he looked younger than Seaborne. He was very tanned, almost burnt. His head was shaved bald and his eyes were a dark and unsettled blue beneath sand-colored eyebrows. He studied her for a moment and swung his arm up as if to strike her. She cowered.

He jerked the hood of her poncho up. "You'd do well to keep covered up when the others return. You'll be the worse for it if you don't," the strange man warned. "Dankar wants you alive; that's why I'm here. But there's only so much I can do. Exorians aren't exactly reliable when it comes to Melorians."

Frankie shivered. Dankar? She'd never heard that name, but by the biting way the man said it, he didn't sound very nice. She glanced around at the forest, its dappled light and green canopy familiar and home-like to her now.

"I'm not really a Melorian," she whispered, feeling a little guilty. "I'm just dressed like one."

"I know that," the man replied. His eyes took on a strange light. "You are an outlier. You come from beyond the fog."

She nodded. "Where is everyone? Where's Evelyn?"

The strange man blinked and stood up. He was not as tall as a Melorian, and was dressed only in long, tan-colored shorts.

"We're still in the forest. We hid you until it was safe to move."

Frankie looked over her shoulder at her hiding place. Above her loomed a wide rock shelf; at the foot was a small hole carved into the surface leading to a larger cave. From the look of it, she had been put there and the opening covered by another rock and some branches, that now lay scattered about. The man spoke again, startling her.

"The others will be back soon and we'll have to get moving. You'd better drink this." The man held out a glass vial of a clear liquid.

Frankie felt a trickle of fear. She tried to think. Where was she? How far from the cabin?

"Go on, drink it."

She eyed him warily, not moving.

"Don't be difficult," he sighed, shaking the vial at her. "Would I go to all this trouble to hide you if I intended to poison you?" He took a sip and then rubbed his bare stomach theatrically. "Mmmm." He pushed the vial at her. It looked like water.

Frankie was suddenly aware of how thirsty she was. Her throat burned. She took the vial from him and took a sip; the liquid tasted sweet and tart, like lemonade. She tipped her head back and guzzled the whole thing. The pain in her throat and her head went away instantly. She gave the empty vial back to the man and studied him from behind her eyelashes. He had an odd way about him; his appearance was off-putting, but his manner seemed somehow normal and familiar; more so even than the Melorians, or Seaborne, for that matter. Her fear subsided a bit and she decided to ask him some questions.

"What's your name?"

"That is no concern of yours," he answered gruffly. "All you need to know is that you are now the property of Dankar and will do as he commands."

"Dankar?" Frankie questioned.

"The lord and ruler of Exor," the man replied, matter-of-factly. He moved to a tree and gave her a queer smile; then, he picked up a large, fierce-looking spear and leaned on it. "Dankar has a fondness for travelers. He is anxious for news from your lands. I hope, for your sake, that you will provide it for him."

"What news could I give him?" Frankie asked, shrinking back against the rock ledge. "Nobody tells me anything. I'm only nine."

The man stared at her; he tightened his lips. "Well, you'd better think of something." He fiddled with his spear, impatient, then growled to himself. "They must be done with them by now. There weren't that many. I wonder what's keeping them?"

Frankie's chest tightened. "What do you mean, *done with them?*"

The man turned on her, his blue eyes darkening: "Done with the Melorians. Once they have been fragmented, we will take you and your companions to Dankar. He is waiting for you all."

Frankie's eyes blazed. "Fragmented?"

"Never mind." The man shifted his eyes away from hers.

"You mean you're going to hurt them, don't you?" cried Frankie, trying to stand but wobbling a little. She put her hands on her hips. "You won't. They are great warriors, and Tinator will protect them!"

"Like he protected you?" The man laughed. "I don't think so. You will see your little cohort of friends again, I assure you of that." He stopped and pondered Frankie with the same strange gleam. "That is, if they don't anger the Exorians." He took his spear and thrust it deep into the heart of the tree. Above them, the branches groaned in the wind. "Rothermel will not be able to keep you to himself this time."

A shout and a rustle brought her captor to attention. Out of the forest undergrowth a group of three men emerged carrying long spears like the one the man had stabbed into the tree. Frankie gasped in dismay. They wore the same long, tan shorts as her captor, but the visible skin on their faces and torsos was tough and cracked and covered in dark, sore-looking mottled patches, like scales; one of them looked directly at her, showing bloodshot eyes that blinked heavily beneath swollen eyelids. The hide-like skin covered his lips, making his mouth barely distinguishable until he opened it to breathe and revealed a healthy, pink tongue. The contrast was frightening.

Frankie retreated further into her hood and kept her eyes on her captor. He had skin, lips, and eyes that looked human. He seemed to be in charge of the other ones, the ones he called Exorians. Maybe the other man wasn't an Exorian? Either way, he had told her the Exorians were the enemy of the Melorians and wanted to kill them. She needed to warn Evelyn and the others. Frankie explored the area with her eyes, looking for some way to escape, but before she could come up with a plan, the man yanked his spear out of the tree and crossed over to her.

"Get up," he said. "Time to move."

"Where are we going? You said my sister and my friends would be here."

"We're headed north. We will catch up to them then."

Frankie stood, her legs shaking. She felt very small and very alone. The man stared at her impatiently. She glanced over at the three Exorians, with their grotesque, baked skin. Like reptiles. Her lip quivered.

"Please don't take me to Dankar, *please,*" she begged. "Take me back to my sister. I don't know anything. She knows more than I do. Everybody knows more than I do. I—I'm afraid!" Hot tears welled up in her eyes and brimmed over. She tried to wipe them off quickly so he wouldn't see, but the man slapped her hand away. He stared at her, then bent closer with his finger extended and caught a tear as it dropped off her chin. He studied the tip of his finger for several moments. When he looked up, she saw a strange, distant look in his eyes.

"Do not waste your body water," he said, more gently than before. "You will need it later." He turned to go, then half-turned back to add, "You are very young. If you become tired, you may rest. Your sister has also moved north. You will see her soon."

Frankie rubbed her face with her palms. She felt a little better.

"Can I walk with you, at least, not with . . . *them?*" she asked, indicating the three Exorians who stood several yards away. The man said nothing but nodded once. The Exorians moved to the front and used their spears to savagely beat a path through the woods. Frankie and the strange, nameless man followed.

Chapter 14

ROTHERMEL

Evelyn and the boys soon found themselves standing in a dappled forest, even more vibrant and bright than the one they had just left on the other bank of the Vossbeck. Sunbeams shone through the canopy in columns of bright light. Dense thatch collared the taller trees and whorled purple flowers grew in tight bouquets at their feet.

Knox's ears twitched with the sound of small game moving, sudden rushes of leaves, a broken twig. It was as if every living thing in the forest was speaking to him at once: tuttering and twittering and calling. Even the wind moving through the trees and the sun coming down in great shafts suddenly seemed to make sounds, brushing and whirring and beating. He clamped his hands over his ears, but he couldn't muffle the noise. It was as loud inside his own body as it was outside. Every small motion or reflex drew his attention, even the sound of his own eyelids grazing the surface of his eyes. He couldn't shut anything out. The effect was dizzying. The ground bucked and sank beneath him; his knees gave out. He shut his eyes and held himself still, thinking he might be sick if he moved any more. The sounds within him began to blend with those of the forest until there was no division between the two. Knox wondered if he would ever be able to move again, or if he would want to. A light hand on his shoulder quieted the noise and, in its place, he heard a low, steady voice.

"Your daylights are tuned to the earth, Knox. They speak loudly when their Keeper is near. They will soften now."

Knox lowered his hands from his ears. His eyes opened to meet the gaze of a man kneeling in front of him—the oldest person he had met on Ayda by far. The man's eyes were a vivid green and set deep beneath an imposing ridge of ash-colored eyebrows. His skin was the familiar deep brown of a Melorian, but it was marked by thick lines that crenellated the corners of his eyes and mouth. When he removed his hand from Knox's shoulder, Knox missed the weight of it immediately.

"Is he okay?" Knox heard Chase ask. His brother's face floated into view.

"He is fine," the man replied. "It would appear your brother is a Melorian in the making."

"What happened?" asked Chase, looking at Knox.

Knox suddenly felt embarrassed. He wanted to tell Chase about the sounds and the feeling he had of being part of the forest, but couldn't. He shrugged.

"I dunno, I just felt kind of sick."

The man peered into Knox's face once more, then stood up. He was staggeringly tall and dressed like all Melorian warriors except for the addition of a thick metal belt circling his waist that was buckled by a large sand-colored stone set into a silver oval. The man held a faded leather helmet in one hand. He was otherwise unarmed.

"I am Rothermel, Keeper of the forest of Melor and all the beings therein. Welcome to the Wold." The man lifted his hand in what was now the familiar open-palm greeting. Each child lightly touched their fingertips to his. Rothermel's green eyes held their gaze for several moments. When he reached Evelyn his forehead creased and a shadow fell across his expression. He spoke directly to her.

"Your loss saddens me. Come, you will tell me of it."

Rothermel led the company, grown larger now by several more fully armed Melorians, through a wide arch cut into the brush and into a round dell encircled by flowering branches. In the center rose a pitted hump of granite onto which Rothermel lowered himself.

"Sit, please. Nothing will harm you here," he assured them.

Evelyn and the boys sank to the ground; the Melorians massed behind them, standing. Tinator stepped out and quickly relayed everything that had happened to them, including Frankie's disappearance, Tar's injuries, and their flight from the *tehuantl*. Rothermel kept his head bowed, listening closely. As Tinator finished, the Keeper sat motionless for several long minutes, during which Evelyn thought her heart might explode. When she was about to cry out, Rothermel raised his head and met her tense gaze.

"The course of events since the arrival of these outliers fills me with misgiving. The eyes of my sister's spies tell me that a band of Exorians was seen several days ago moving swiftly southeast from the Broomwash into the northern borders of Melor. It appears that Dankar was aware of the presence of these children almost from the day of their arrival—if not before—and set his plans into motion with haste."

Mara stood, hands clasped at her waist. She presented a slim, solemn figure, her scar a sickening reminder of what the enemy was capable of.

"Good Keeper," she began, "I have spent each footstep of our journey pondering one question. I cannot think what value a small girl might offer to Dankar, unless to be groomed as a slave-bride. The girl, Frankie, is young, barely out of babyhood. If this is his intent, then Dankar has fallen even deeper into blackness."

"I cannot pretend to know Dankar's thoughts," Rothermel replied. "I can only judge his actions, past and present. Not so long ago by our measure, another boat was cast mysteriously on our shores, in Metria. In it was a wounded man and a boy escaping a war on the seas beyond the fog. The man and boy did much as you have done, leaving their boat and walking inland to find aid. Before help was found, they were set upon by Exorians. The man was killed, but—strangely—the Exorians kept the boy alive. En route to Exor, the kidnappers and their captive were overtaken by a large guard of Metrians and the boy was saved. That boy is the man, Seaborne, who stands with you today."

Four pairs of eyes swiveled to look at Seaborne.

Seaborne made a face. "Now you know my fog story."

"Two questions remain that have puzzled us since," Rothermel continued. "Why was Seaborne's boat able to penetrate the fog, and how did the Exorians have knowledge of it? As you can see, these are the same questions we now face. To my mind, only a few answers exist. The first is the most likely: Dankar has found a way to bring outliers to our shores for a reason we have not yet discovered. His experience with Seaborne has shown him that we will protect them, especially when they are young and defenseless. Perhaps he thinks I will challenge him directly for the freedom of your sister as my sister did for Seaborne in Metria."

"Won't you?" blurted Evelyn.

"I know it is what you would have me do," Rothermel said after a long silence. "But the truth is, I do not know if I am strong enough to win, and to lose would be perilous to the stone of Melor and all those bound to it. If I should fail and the stone of Melor fall into Dankar's hands, my people and lands would be enslaved—or worse."

"Worse?" interrupted Knox, uncomprehending.

"My sisters might be compelled to come to my aid and all of Ayda—" Rothermel shook his head; his voice trailed off into a whisper. "It could be the end."

"The end of *what?*" asked Evelyn.

Rothermel's gaze traveled past her head, seeing deep into the forest beyond.

"The end of Melor, most certainly, but also of Ayda, and perhaps even beyond that; it would not be wrong to think it could be the end of all things, for Ayda is true home to the five great stones. All things that occur beyond the fog are reflections of what happens here. Like mighty pebbles dropped in a pool, the stones send ripples out to the far reaches of our shared world. They echo and resound in every living thing. Dankar does not grasp the true meaning of this. He seeks only power and control for himself, alone; but the stones' real value lies in their ability to balance one another. It is only by working together that they may preserve life."

"But I don't understand! What does Frankie have to do with all of this?" Evelyn pressed her fists into her temples, trying to stay calm.

"It is likely that the Usurper sent a raiding party after all of you, but was thwarted by the presence of so many Melorian warriors—and of those, so many descended from the ancients." Rothermel traced the seam of his helmet with a weathered thumb. "It would be like Dankar to try, then, to pick you off, starting with the younger and most vulnerable among you. He would know it would roil my blood. He plays a dangerous game. He wishes to stir the daylights of my people, as one would stir the embers of a dying flame."

"Pick us off?" repeated Evelyn, horrified.

"I do not think he intends to kill you, if that is any comfort, nor do I think he chose the girl-child for a specific reason, except that she had the least protection. It is likely he would have done the same with any of you, had he been given the chance."

Rothermel glanced sorrowfully at Evelyn.

"After the Great Battle and the loss of the Fifth Stone, life on Ayda has continued for one reason: There are three of us and only one of him. It is a fragile state. Dankar must never be allowed to possess another stone—and for this reason alone I would not risk open war. Not even for the sake of your sister."

"How can you do nothing? She's just a little girl, and she's all alone!" A sob caught in Evelyn's throat.

Mara grabbed Evelyn by the elbow, silencing her.

Rothermel donned his helmet. "The fire stone of Exor and those under its sway are very strong. It saddens me to hear of the cooperation of the *tehuantl,* for they are a noble breed. Dankar must be gaining strength. We will remove further into the Wold. When, and if, the girl is seen by any of the scouts I have dispatched, we may then construct a plan for her rescue."

Chase and Knox came closer to Evelyn. Her face was haggard.

"I'm going after her myself if they won't," she whispered.

Chase frowned. "We don't know where she is."

"You don't understand; I *have* to," said Evelyn. She covered her face with her hands, whispering. "My father told me to take care of her. It was the last thing he ever said to me."

Knox swiped clumsily at Evelyn's arm, in an attempt to be comforting. "We'll figure something out."

"Figure what out?" asked Calla, who had crept up silently beside them. "You would all do well not to think yourselves wiser than Rothermel. What has happened is terrible, but he has seen worse. He does not treat this disappearance lightly, nor does he think of himself in this matter—only of his duty and his charge," she chided them, looking straight at Chase. "As the eldest, it might serve you well to do the same."

✛   ✛   ✛

They followed Rothermel and the Melorians out of the dell and headed northwest, or as Rothermel had said, deeper into the Wold. Teddy walked with Seaborne, a few paces behind. The forest around them appeared to be growing younger. The immense trees and broad-reaching limbs thinned, and they were now in the midst of chest-high yellow-flowered brush and smaller birch and elder saplings. The ground felt spongy underfoot, and, in places, muddy. Amidst the grass, Knox saw patches of deeper green, low-lying foliage and small clusters of bright blue berries. He stooped down to pick some, turning around to show Evelyn.

"Blueberries?" she asked.

"Looks like it to me," Knox replied.

"Show Chase."

Chase was right behind her and took the berries from Knox. He sniffed them, gave them back to Knox, and shrugged. "They seem all right—but don't eat them until you know for sure." Calla's comment about being the eldest was still ringing in his ears.

Knox gave him a wry grin. "Only one way to know for sure!" He tossed one of the berries up into the air and moved under it, his mouth open and waiting. A strong hand shoved him to the side. The berry fell harmlessly to the ground.

"We do not pick, hunt, or eat anything that lives here."

Knox, embarrassed, asked roughly, "Why not? The birds are eating them."

Tinator answered without breaking his stride. "This part of the forest and that which we are about to enter mark the site of a battle. It was here that many ancients met their death in the Great Battle. In honor of their memory, Rothermel has granted perpetual springtime to this glen. All that live and grow here may do so unmolested. No unnatural or untimely death may seek them. Should one challenge this decree, they do so at their own peril. Eating those berries would only sicken your heart and cast your mind permanently into shadow."

Knox looked down at the rest of the berries in his hand and threw them into the bushes. Evelyn pushed past him. Within minutes, the landscape changed again. This time, it felt as if they were entering a forest so very old it was already a memory of itself. Across a wide, broad plain, rows of gnarled trees, bare but for coats of gray, dripping moss, rose against the sky. Knee-deep grass grew in hillocks and the air was dense and stank like rotting vegetation; it penetrated their clothing, driving a swampy blackness straight into the depths of their chests.

"What is this place?" Evelyn cried out in distress, rubbing the spot over her heart.

This time, Calla answered. "This is the deathfield. It stands to remind us of what we have lost and what we have yet to lose should Dankar ever gain the stone of Melor."

Evelyn stumbled. Chase caught her arm as she tripped. She looked up at him, her brown eyes black with grief. He tried to think of something to say but came up blank.

Seaborne stopped beside them, carrying a sleeping Teddy on his back. "Best not to linger here," he prodded. "Carry on."

✢   ✢   ✢

Nightfall found the Melorians, the boys, and Evelyn traveling along a wide dirt road cut through sparse woodlands and rolling hills of increasingly cultivated land. To the northeast, a snowcapped mountain range filled the horizon. As the sun passed into the west, the mountains turned a light, then deeper shade of purple. A cluster of round, thatched houses came into view, tucked deftly into low-lying hills. Thin streams of smoke rose from the chimneys. Knox saw a flock of sheep dotting a distant meadow. In between stands of trees, large rectangles of tilled earth, orchards, and undulating crops of grain waved at them as they passed. Rothermel sent a few Melorians to gather food from the nearest houses to supplement their store. He led the rest off the main road, through a thicket of trees, and into the protected meadow of a valley, which lay hidden between two forested hills and abutted a small, reed-filled pond at its far end. This deep into the safety of the Wold, they would build an open fire and cook their first hot meal in days.

"It's very strange," Chase said aloud, warming his hands at the edge of the blazing fire.

"What?" Evelyn replied. She was sitting a few feet off. Mara hovered behind her at a comfortably close distance, as she had ever since they'd left Seaborne's cabin. Chase nodded to the fire.

"That something that feels so good can be so bad."

Evelyn put her face between her knees, feeling the heat creep over the top of her head. The sharp thing in her chest was jabbing at her, threatening to shred her insides apart. She prayed that Frankie was feeling the good part.

Chapter 15

FARTHER IN

Frankie kept her eyes fixed on the path, stumbling behind the strange man, resting only to eat and drink. She did not see what the Exorian soldiers ate, but took what was offered to her: an orange and another fruit that reminded her of a tomato, and some flat, bland-tasting bread. She ate hesitantly at first, but with more gusto as the day and night went by. The march seemed unending. She stopped asking where they were going, or when they would get there, since the only answers she received were curt, one-word replies.

The first day, the woods they traveled through were familiar enough that her fear began to lift. The man, whom she had taken to calling Louis in her head (a name she remembered from a history book), hinted at the fact that she would see Evelyn and the Thompson boys soon.

Frankie had no idea in what direction they were heading. At one point they crossed a wide river mouth on wooden rafts that the Exorians had stashed in the forest, and then it seemed to her that they turned away from the sea. The forest slowly flattened, and the tree cover became increasingly sparse, interspersed with large, grassy meadows. The air around her was gold in the late afternoon light, and her surroundings felt somehow comforting. She allowed herself to hum under her breath as she walked, one of the songs her father had sung to her when she was a baby. The man—"Louis"—walked behind her. He stopped her, abruptly grabbing her shoulder.

"What are you doing?" he demanded.

"I'm humming," replied Frankie, surprised.

"Stop it."

"Why? What's wrong with humming?"

"In Exor, such things are forbidden."

Frankie shook her head, perplexed. "You're not allowed to hum in Exor? Why? What's wrong with humming?"

"It is a useless distraction."

Frankie shrugged. "I like it." She hummed a little louder.

The man whirled her around to face him.

"What you like doesn't matter. There is no purpose to it. In Exor, everything must have a purpose."

"People too?"

"Yes."

"What's your purpose?"

"To serve Dankar."

"Humming stops you from serving Dankar? That doesn't make any sense. Lots of people hum when they're doing other stuff."

The man's eyes widened. Frankie couldn't be sure, but she thought his mouth twitched upward. He dismissed her with a wave and indicated for her to get moving. After a moment, he spoke again.

"It doesn't matter whether it makes sense, only that it is forbidden. Exorians are not allowed to make music."

"That's the stupidest thing I've ever heard," said Frankie. "What else aren't you allowed to do?"

The man hesitated, then answered by rote. "All Exorians must put Dankar's wishes and work above their own, and hold no one more dear than he."

Frankie mouthed the words to herself.

"Exor must be very boring," she said. "I don't know who Dankar is, but he sounds mean and selfish. His rules don't apply to me. I'm not an Exorian."

The man she called Louis half-smiled again. "I guess that's true—for the present. Go ahead. Hum while you can." He pushed past her, and she followed, humming loudly.

After a few minutes, Louis stopped again. "What is it you hum?"

"It's a song called 'Frère Jacques'—it's French." She sang the words, ending with a loud chorus of *"Din-Dan-Don!"*

"Shhh," ordered Louis, casting a look at the mottled backs of the Exorians marching a little ways ahead. He raised an eyebrow. "French?"

"Yes, French. Not everyone speaks English, you know."

"So, you speak French, too?" Louis asked.

"I used to. In Haiti—where I lived before. My father was from Canada. They speak French there, too. And in France, they speak French, obviously."

"Walk." Louis prodded Frankie with his finger. "We speak with one tongue on Ayda. I do not understand how it would be to live amongst those who spoke another."

"It's like a code. Once you know what the words mean, it's the same. Here, I'll teach you." She pointed to a tree in the distance. "Tree ... *l'arbre.*" Then to the sky. "Sky ... *le ciel.*" She pointed to Louis. "Man: *l'homme.*" Then to her pink-clad feet, "Feet: *les pieds.*"

Louis was silent, thinking.

"Tell me what the song says," he said.

Frankie was happy to oblige now that he was being nicer to her. She felt sort of sorry for him, not being able to sing or hum or anything. They passed the last hour of daylight with Frankie telling Louis as many French words as she could think of. She walked ahead of him, so she couldn't see his expression, but he didn't ask her to stop. When they halted for the night, he gave her an extra orange to eat. She felt confident enough to ask him a few more questions.

"Are we near my sister? Will I see her soon?"

"Soon enough," Louis answered, but with less coldness than before. "First there is a task for the warriors to complete."

That night the light shone dimly from a waxing moon above the barest outline of a mountain range lying inland. Frankie was given strict instructions to keep quiet and stay hidden. She slept for a few hours underneath the stooped branches of a small bush, wrapped in her poncho, but was awakened by a sudden awareness of a shift in her surroundings. She knelt and pushed away the leaves to get a better view. What she saw drained any remaining warmth from her bones.

A large group of Exorian warriors, many more than the three that had accompanied them, were amassed in front of Louis. All were armed with broad, spiked shields and tall spears. Two giant black cats threaded their way through the warriors' legs, tongues panting through their open jaws.

Louis had his head bent toward one of the warriors, listening intently to whatever was being said. By the look of it, some kind of report. Frankie knew, instinctively, that whatever it was, it had to do with Evelyn and the boys. The Melorians must be close. Her heart leapt at the idea. She had to warn them! Maybe she could use a Melorian whistle signal—if she could escape.

Frankie crept across the grass without a sound. She was grateful for the camouflage of her poncho. When she was close enough to Louis to hear his voice, she stopped and moved to the side, hoping he would not look in her direction. The Exorians brought the hilts of their spears down hard on the ground and yelled as one. The tips of their spears burst into flame simultaneously and their eyes flickered orange. The panthers screamed and leapt to the front, baring their teeth. Frankie fell back in fear. When the last whoop of the cry had grown quiet, Louis stepped into the band of light created by the torches. The Exorians turned toward him with their blank, orange eyes and ruined skin. Louis raised his arms over his head in salute.

"In the name of Dankar, Keeper of the stone of Exor, go now and do what you must to bring the outlier children to me—unharmed," he cried. "Many daylights will be freed tonight—but do not be afraid, brothers—the day we have long awaited approaches." Louis's voice grew louder; he walked a few steps back and forth.

"The outliers are to be brought to Dankar. Those who do not heed his bidding shall know the measure of his wrath." He paused to let this sink in, then repeated: "Deliver them alive and unharmed. Kill the rest." He looked at the panthers. "And the dogs."

The Exorians lowered their spears, thudding the ends on the ground, chanting "Ex-or! Ex-or!"

Frankie covered her ears. One of the warriors caught the movement; his head snapped toward her hiding place. The chanting ceased abruptly. Fifty or more pairs of blazing eyes were glued to her. Frankie's heart stopped. The chanting began again, spears pounding faster and faster. Louis whipped around in alarm.

"Get back!" he yelled.

Frankie quickly retreated into the shadows.

Louis's voice rose high above the chanting. "Melorian daylights await the release of your torches." He paced in front of the place where Frankie had lain. "Go! Free the daylights of your brothers and sisters, chained and misled by the lies of Rothermel. Bring the others to me!"

The Exorians shouted in unison and took off in a sprint. They made a burning line as they spread out across the forest floor. Frankie lay flat on the ground, her blood pounding in her ears. After several minutes, she heard Louis calling.

"I know you are here," he said. His voice was back to normal.

She did not reply.

"Ahh." He was directly above her. She sighed into the ground and rolled over, looking up into his face.

"That was foolish," he said flatly

"What are those . . . those *things* going to do?" Frankie squeaked. "You talked about freeing daylights and bringing outliers here. You sent them—" She shuddered. "You sent them after my sister?" A surge of rage passed through her, raising her to her feet. "And I . . . I was beginning to think you were nice!" She felt the blood rush to her face, waves of heat radiating from beneath her hood. She wished she had her knife. She wouldn't think twice about driving it straight into Louis's heart, if he even had one.

"STAY AWAY FROM ME!" she screamed, running away from him as fast as she could, trying to follow the line she remembered the Exorians taking, but it was dark and she had no idea where she was going. Branches whipped at her face and her calves as she ran, her legs pumping through the brush. She would find her sister and the boys. She would warn the Melorians. She just had to run a little faster. Her foot snagged on a root and her legs suddenly buckled under her. She pitched forward, tumbling blindly down a steep incline. On instinct, she twisted her body as she rolled to take the force of the impact on her side; her hips and elbows smashed painfully into rocks that lay half-buried in the hill. Finally, she came to a stop, slamming her head hard into the trunk of a tree. For a minute, the night seemed to grow bright with stars; then everything faded into an all-too familiar blackness.

Chapter 16

FLIGHT

Chase had only just fallen asleep when Seaborne was yelling in his ear. "Get up, boy, now, and man your weapons!"

He tumbled out of his hammock, landing facedown on the ground and struggling to remember where he was. When he raised his head, the campsite was in complete confusion. His first thought was that the fire had not been properly put out, because an explosion of flames as tall as the treetops reached into the air. He could feel the heat on his face even though he was at least fifty feet away. Above the roar of the blaze, he heard the clash of metal against metal.

"Holy crap!" Knox exclaimed, standing above Chase, his eyes wild. He was strapping on his harness. "Look at them!"

A deadly skirmish played out before them, backlit by the fire. Chase could just make out black huddles of quick-moving shapes. Two figures broke free and moved closer. One was a Melorian warrior judging by the man's height and his helmet. The other, shorter and heavier, held back the rain of blows from the Melorian's sword. He wore no armor, but wielded a long, pointed shield in one hand and a burning spear in the other. The Melorian redoubled his efforts, but his opponent held his ground, raising the shield and advancing with the burning spear tip. Chase watched helplessly as the flames made contact with the Melorian's tunic. It burst into flame as if it had been dipped in oil. The Melorian screamed and clawed at the leather straps of his breastplate. He dropped to the ground and rolled. The attacker raised his shield high, ready to strike a killing blow. Chase closed his eyes; he couldn't bear to watch. An arrow whistled behind his right ear with a high-pitched *twang*. His eyes shot open. The attacker stumbled and dropped his shield, an arrow shaft sticking out of his shoulder. Calla came abreast of the boys, her bow raised.

"An Exorian raiding party!" she yelled. "Gather the others and take them around to the pond."

Before he could reply, Seaborne whirled out of the flames, his long sword gleaming in the firelight. He looked at Knox, then pulled Chase to his feet.

"Skirt the edges of the fighting, the long way. Keep to the trees. Around there—" Seaborne gesticulated wildly to the forested hem of the meadow to the east.

In a flash, Chase saw the trouble they were in. The Exorians had blocked the only retreat from the V of the valley. The hills were too thick with trees to make an escape, and the pond lay as a barrier at the other end. The only way out was to push the Exorians back toward the main road—and they would not go easy. He'd fallen asleep in what he thought was a safe refuge and awoken to a death trap.

"Mara will take Evelyn. She will wait for you until the others are safe." Seaborne shot a long look at Calla. "If you know what's good for you, you'll go with them."

Calla shook her head.

"Well, come on then, if you must. And strike hard—the devils have skin like leather." He sprinted into the fray, Calla hot on his heels.

Knox grabbed Chase's shoulder. "C'mon, let's go!" he shouted.

Chase yanked on his brother's tunic with his free hand. "No!" He had to yell at the top of his lungs to be heard over the hissing and popping of the fire. "We're going to do what Seaborne said! We have to get Teddy and go to the pond."

Knox stared at him, not believing his ears. "You've got to be kidding! Why did they train us to use these weapons if not to fight! You do what you want, but I'm not running away!" Knox tore himself away and leapt into the skirmish.

"KNOX!" Chase screamed.

"What'th happening?" asked Teddy, his face dusky with sleep. "Where'th Theaborne?"

Chase grabbed him by the hand. Holding his sword with his right hand and Teddy with his left, he took off running as fast as he could, keeping to the shadows beyond the large circle of firelight. The heat was intense. His nostrils and lungs burned with smoke and filaments of burning ash. Through streaming eyes and breaks in the flame, he could see fighting, but not Knox.

He was breathing in great raspy breaths now, his lungs constricting with the thick veil of smoke hovering at eye level. How long before the beast took over? He was stronger on Ayda, he'd walked far enough to prove that, but the combination of smoke, fear, and running might be too much for his lungs to handle. Chase maneuvered farther away from the fire, trying to find cleaner air. To his horror, sparks streamed from the meadow where most of the fighting was taking place and into the forest canopy, landing on the tops of trees and instantly setting them ablaze. Soon they'd be in the middle of an inferno. Anyone who wasn't killed would be cooked alive. Chase's lungs whistled. He couldn't catch his breath. They'd never make it. He dropped Teddy's hand.

"Tedders, you've got to run on your own now, okay?" Chase wheezed. "I'll be right behind you—run through the trees, straight to the pond. Don't stop. Don't look back. Just run. Fast as you can, okay? GO!"

Teddy nodded and made a wild dash, head down. Chase was winded and clumsy running with the sword, but he tried to keep pace beside his little brother. He could see the pond's edge shining in the refracted light of the raging fire, only a couple of hundred feet away. A few more seconds and they'd be there.

Out of nowhere, a shadow stepped into their path, dark and menacing but for the fire burning at the end of its long spear. Chase looked up into the hideous face of the Exorian, and felt whatever wisp of breath left inside his lungs evaporate. The Exorian's face, neck, and torso were scarred in dense, thick patches that looked impenetrable. Flames flickered in his eyes. He held his shield close to his body, his right hand extended with the burning spear.

Chase instinctively pulled Teddy behind him. The roar of the fire was deafening. The Exorian moved closer. In a moment, he would be close enough to touch Chase with the torch and it would all be over. He would die and Teddy would be taken to Exor to be made a slave—or killed. He wobbled and fell to his knees. The Exorian's grotesque lips turned up slightly at the edges, anticipating an easy victory.

Chase waited for the touch of flame, the searing pain, but was surprised to feel, instead, a cold wind coming from some unknown origin, soothing the back of his neck. It defied the heat and enveloped his chest, rising toward his mouth. For a moment, he could inhale deeply. The air that filled his lungs was pure and sweet. It tasted like new snow. He filled his lungs and felt his head clear. His fingers found the hilt of his sword, and he remembered that he was not helpless. He had been trained for this. He stood up, squared his shoulders, and drew the sword, grasping it with both hands. The Exorian frowned.

"Leave us ALONE!" Chase roared.

The Exorian lifted his spear and swung it at Chase, who—much to his own surprise—blocked it. His arm shook with a deep reverberation that meant his sword had hit metal. He recovered, advanced, and jabbed blindly with his blade, hoping to hit skin. He missed and the sword tip thudded against the thick hull of the shield. The Exorian stepped back. Encouraged, Chase lunged again and again, shouting.

"Run, Teddy, run to the pond! GO!"

Chase warded off another lunge by the flaming spear. Teddy sprinted to Chase's right, skirting the Exorian's shield, and headed straight for the pond. The Exorian did not follow, much to Chase's relief. Now all Chase had to do was distract him until Teddy was safely at the pond's edge. Mara would be there to protect him. Chase's arm muscles burned, his legs felt heavy, his reflexes slowed. He was coated with sweat—but he was breathing! With a step back, he turned to the side, barely avoiding the tip of the burning spear. He knew from watching the other skirmish that this was part of the Exorian's strategy: to wear him out and then set him on fire.

The Exorian glared at him. Chase took another step backwards and stumbled. The Exorian saw his chance and moved forward, the ball of flame at the end of the torch seeming to grow. It filled Chase's field of vision, erasing everything else. It blazed hotter and brighter; in moments it would be on his skin. Then suddenly, only inches away, it went out, like a snuffed candle. Chase gaped in amazement as the man before him fell to his knees and dropped the heavy shield. He toppled forward, facedown, one throwing ax protruding from the back of his head, and another from his thick, scaly back—deadly accurate.

"All right?" Knox barked. With quick, practiced jerks, he withdrew his axes from the lifeless body.

Chase was on all fours, gulping in the searing air.

"It's hard to breathe with all this smoke," said Knox, worried.

"You just killed that guy," panted Chase,

"Yeah, well, it was either that or you were going to get barbecued."

Chase glanced up. The trees were burning. "We all are."

"Get to the pond. It'll be okay."

"What about you?" Chase asked, a little wary. Knox seemed strange to him all of a sudden, somehow distant and powerful. "Come with me!" he implored. "These guys aren't kidding around!"

"I'll be there soon!" Knox said. "Tinator told us to keep them busy and away from Rothermel!"

Rothermel! How could Chase have forgotten? They couldn't let the Exorians find Rothermel.

"Where is he?"

Knox nodded toward the pond. "Over there, doing some kind of rain dance or something."

Chase squinted through the waves of heat. A small cluster of people were grouped at the shore, none tall enough to be Rothermel. Then Chase saw the darker outline of a figure wading out waist-high into the center of the pond. As if on cue, thunder burst over their heads.

Knox gave a huge whoop and sprinted back into the fight. Another clap of thunder brought on a downpour, and a cheer rose up. Rain streamed down, as if someone had tipped a pitcher from the sky. Chase opened his mouth and drank it in, then groped his way to the edge of the pond where he found Mara, Seaborne, Evelyn, and Teddy. Two Melorian guards stood a few feet away, their crossbows raised, water drumming down on the shafts. From this vantage point, Chase could see more of the battle:

Fire hissed through the curtain of rain, and great clouds of steam rose as if the surface of the earth had cracked open to release some kind of internal pressure. Above, it seemed like the trees were lifting the tips of their burning branches up to meet the rain.

Chase looked over his shoulder at Rothermel. The Keeper was standing at the center of the pond, his back toward them, large ripples spreading out in concentric waves around him. A sheet of water fell from the back of his helmet. His hands were splayed above the surface. A small scream from Evelyn whipped Chase's head back around. Three Exorians were running toward them, bereft of their massive shields, their spears no longer tipped with flame, but still deadly. The Melorian guards met them with a fierce counterattack. Calla and Mara raised their bows.

"You must go now, children. Follow Seaborne," Mara commanded.

"What about Knox?" yelled Chase.

"Tinator will bring him to you."

Chase shook his head. "I'm not leaving without Knox."

"Do as you're told," Calla hissed.

He decided that now was not the time to argue.

Evelyn, Chase, and Teddy jogged behind Seaborne as he skirted the far edge of the pond and headed into the charred forest; up, away from the fighting. Seaborne moved quickly, clearing a path through the dense underbrush with his blade, as though he knew exactly where they were headed. Within minutes the fugitives reached an open plateau and began to run in earnest. Before them lay a rolling plain of grassy hills, shining gray in the moonlight. Seaborne lifted Teddy onto his back and shouted to Evelyn and Chase.

"We're in the open now. Stay together!" He picked up the pace. They tunneled noiselessly through the knee-high grass. The noise of the battle receded, until it could no longer be heard. Finally Seaborne halted, breathing hard under Teddy's extra weight.

"We . . . can . . . rest . . . for . . . a . . . minute . . . now." He motioned for them to drop. They fell to the ground gratefully. Chase drew in deep lungfuls of air.

"Where are we going?" gasped Evelyn.

"We'll take the long way to the Wold—the main road is too risky. Dankar must be tracking us. I don't know about you, but I'd rather not run into another pack of those uglies."

"But Frankie might be with them!" she argued. "We have to find out."

"If Frankie is with them, Rothermel will find her." Seaborne was thoughtful for a moment. "I don't think they knew Rothermel was with us, or they wouldn't have attacked us with so few. We can be grateful for that."

"That was just a *few?* There must have been thirty of them, at least!" cried Chase.

Seaborne grinned a tight little smile. "You'd need a great many more to take down a Keeper."

"Seaborne," Evelyn asked, "how did Rothermel get it to rain?"

"He asked his sister, Rysta, that's how," replied Seaborne, proudly.

"How did he do that?"

"The Keepers don't communicate directly very often, but when they do—it's something, don't you think?" He smiled again. "I don't know much about it, but it can happen. They do speak—well, I think it's more like their stones speak to each other."

Evelyn was concentrating hard on her sneakers, her brow furrowed. "If they—the stones—can talk to each other," she said slowly, "how come they can't talk to the Keeper of the Fifth Stone, or, even . . . Dankar?"

"Why would they want to talk to him?" Chase interrupted.

Evelyn's dark eyes flashed. "Because then we could find out about Frankie!"

Seaborne considered her for a moment. "I'm afraid it doesn't work that way. The stones don't actually talk like you and I do; it's closer to—well, it's more like a signal. Besides, I don't think Dankar can be summoned or called in the same way, and even if he could, it wouldn't be to our benefit, or your sister's. The devil only has it one way: his own. And as for the Fifth Stone, I believe it's well beyond any entreaties from the likes of us."

Evelyn sighed in resignation and looked up.

"Look!" She pointed to the sky. "A shooting star!"

Her finger tracked a trail of light traversing the sky. It fell for several seconds, leaving a long, glittering tail. It was followed by another, then another, and then another in rapid succession.

"Tho many," whispered Teddy. "I can't wish on them all."

Seaborne leapt up, alarmed. The falling stars appeared to be getting closer, their light flashing like lightning across their upturned faces.

"That's because they're not stars! Come. We've got to move."

They took off again, but before they had traveled very far, one of the stars landed in front of them and exploded. A great flash of light and heat seared across their path. The grass in front of them caught fire. There was another explosion, and another flash, and another. In seconds, they were surrounded by a ring of burning grass. They had not escaped the Exorians after all.

"We'll have to run for it!" shouted Seaborne. "Pull your hoods down over your faces and cover your mouths!"

"I can't!" screamed Evelyn. Her face contorted in terror, watching the flames lick higher and higher into the sky, devouring the grass. "It's too big! We'll never make it!"

"You have to try!" cried Seaborne. "Follow me!" But before he could move, dark shadows flickered in the flames, and with a great screaming yowl, a pair of *tehuantl* burst through the wall of fire, unharmed by the spitting heat. They were followed by a band of fully armed Exorians, their thick skin untouched by the flames.

The *tehuantl* closed in on the escapees. Arrows whizzed through the air, shot from the crossbows of the Melorians who'd given chase and were now held at bay on the other side by the fire. Seaborne gave Evelyn and Chase a look of warning and leapt in front of them with a shout. His sword flashed, sending a shiver through the Exorians. The *tehuantl* pounced. Seaborne swung his blade. The creatures snarled and retreated, pacing the ring of flame, guarding the perimeter to prevent any Melorians from breaking through or any of the children from escaping. The Exorians fell on Seaborne.

Evelyn pulled the knife from beneath her poncho. Chase grabbed his own blade. Teddy raised his slingshot. They advanced. In response, the Exorians made a wall with their shields, isolating Seaborne from the three.

Seaborne bore down on the Exorians with a fury, forcing them to raise their spears. Chase and Evelyn took advantage of the opening; Evelyn sunk her knife into the shoulder of the nearest Exorian. He grimaced and grabbed for her wildly. She ducked out of reach, pulling the blade out of his shoulder as she went.

Chase hacked away at whatever unprotected legs and torsos he could find, maneuvering around the shields. He glanced quickly over his shoulder and saw Teddy on one knee, slingshot loaded and aimed at the head of a nearby Exorian. Evelyn was on the ground, cornered by an Exorian, the tip of her knife broken. She stabbed madly at her attacker's bare feet with the jagged tip of her weapon. The Exorian roared in pain and slammed his shield into the side of Evelyn's head. She fell to the ground, unconscious. The man dropped the shield and lifted her prone figure onto his shoulder.

Chase's blood ran cold. Both he and Seaborne were too far away to reach her.

"Teddy!" Chase yelled, pointing to the Exorian carrying Evelyn. "TAKE HIM OUT!"

Teddy nodded and reloaded his slingshot. He pulled the band as far back as it would go and released a rock the size of a small apple. To Chase's surprise, it found its mark, hitting the Exorian squarely in the temple. He crumpled to the ground.

"Nice one!" Chase hollered.

"Keep them coming, Teddy, my lad!" Seaborne yelled. "We need all the help we can get!"

With a hair-raising growl, Axl and Tar shot through the wall of fire, their hackles singed and standing up like manes down their backs. The *tehuantl* hissed and leapt into the air. The dogs charged. A furious screaming exploded the air. The flames parted again and into the circle sprang a larger hound, tawny brown with a gray ridge of bristled fur. Behind it poured the remaining Melorians, including Tinator, Mara, Calla, and Knox. The great, tawny hound clamped his jaws down on one of the cats and hurled it, lifeless, to the ground. Axl and Tar joined forces to dispatch the other. Knox fought his way over to Chase and Teddy, and together they dragged the still-unconscious Evelyn to relative safety at the edge of the melee.

"What do we do now?" asked Knox, staring at the impassable wall of fire surrounding them. His face was black with sweat and soot. Evelyn's head bobbed against his shoulder. Chase tried to shield Teddy from the heat.

"We can't run through it—not like this. They won't make it." Chase nodded toward Evelyn and Teddy.

Knox gritted his teeth. "Do you think they'll make it if we don't?"

In answer, the ground beneath them groaned ominously, then rumbled and shook. The air shuddered and the earth around them ripped apart with a great crack. Knox shoved Evelyn to safety; Teddy and Chase fell backwards. The crack lengthened and widened until it encircled the flames, and then, in one great heave, it swallowed the ring of flames and resealed as quickly as it had opened. The remaining Exorians changed tactics and sped toward them, spears blazing in the sudden darkness. Tinator stepped from the shadows to intercept them. With one graceful gesture he released a bolt from his crossbow; an Exorian fell. Two more took his place. He lowered the crossbow, his last bolt spent, and, before he could reach for his sword, the Exorians pressed their advantage.

Knox stumbled to help him, exhausted and also defenseless, having lost his knives and axes in the last battle. He tore the shaft of Tinator's crossbow bolt out of the fallen Exorian and stabbed it into the back of another. Tinator swung his crossbow blindly like a club, then lost his balance, sinking beneath his attackers.

"Tinator!" Knox called out.

Chase squinted in the dim light. The Exorians had Tinator on the ground. The Melorians, distracted by their own fight, were too far away to see the danger. Evelyn and Teddy lay in the grass at Chase's feet. Knox lay sprawled several yards away. He couldn't drag Knox to safety and get to Tinator in time. He would have to choose between them. Through the gaps between the Exorians' legs, Chase saw Tinator raise his head. Their eyes met.

"I'm sorry," Chase mouthed.

Tinator blinked in understanding.

"Not me, not me!" Knox shouted as Chase heaved him over to Teddy and Evelyn. "They'll kill him! Chase!" Knox gave a desperate look over his shoulder toward Tinator.

Chase dropped Knox next to Teddy and grimaced, doubled over in pain. His lungs were burning: each breath felt like tiny razors piercing his chest. His legs were shaking.

Knox pulled himself up, and clawed at Chase's arm. "You have to help him, Chase! He can't fight them alone."

A memory stirred at the edge of Chase's brain, more like the echo of a memory than the real thing—as if Chase had heard the story from someone else: A school stairwell, lit by a deceptively rosy light. The light of summer, rising. Two boys had cornered him, backpacks thrown on the floor, shoving him against the wall. Threats. His lungs whistled loudly in the cavernous air. Then, out of nowhere, a shadow blocked the light and the boys were on the ground. It was Knox, come to save him.

Now, he knew, it was his turn.

Chase tightened his grip on his sword and turned to face the Exorians. In the light cast by their torch spears, he saw that Tinator lay prone, convulsed in pain. A spear had found its mark. The Exorians were circled around the fallen Melorian, spears down, allowing the poison to do the fighting for them. Their confidence made Chase forget how tired he was.

He yelled and ran toward them in a fury. They turned almost lazily to repel him, just as the hounds of Melor sprang from the shadows. In minutes, the fight was truly over. All of the Exorians were dead.

Chase let his sword fall to the ground.

Chapter 17

THE LEAVING

Bodies of fallen warriors lay scattered in the moonlight at the center of the charred circle. Melorian and Exorian blood pooled together and sank into the ground. Evelyn sat up, sporting an egg-size welt on her forehead. Tinator lay sprawled, bloodied and unresponsive, the tip of an Exorian spear embedded in his ribs. He did not move. Mara and Calla and a small group of Melorians gathered around him.

"He will heal, right, Mother?" Calla pleaded. "He is strong."

"Yes, Calla, his daylights are strong," Mara replied. "I will tend him. See to the others."

Calla helped Chase and Knox to their feet. Evelyn and Teddy joined them at Tinator's side. Axl and Tar made their way through the assembled group, friendly dogs once more, followed by Rothermel, who stooped to examine Tinator. The dying man's breath came in shallow, short gasps.

"Tinator's daylights have been loosened by battle and the poisoned tip of the spear," said Rothermel, frowning. "We must remove the tip quickly if he is to have any chance of recovering. We will make camp here and care for him. And Seaborne."

"Seaborne?" Evelyn asked groggily. "What happened to Seaborne?"

"He is also injured, though not as grievously." With a deep sigh, he surveyed the grass plain and looked to the east.

"Dankar seems intent on your capture and willing enough to follow you to the gates of my own halls. Your presence here is a danger to my people.

You must go to Metria, to Rysta, my sister. The stone of Metria is most feared by Dankar. He will not risk such boldness beyond her borders."

The Keeper bent and spoke something low into Axl's ear; with a deep bark, the hound sprinted away. All eyes returned to Tinator. Rothermel placed his large hand on the warrior's forehead, waxy and pale, and covered his eyes with his palm. When he lifted his hand, Tinator's breath deepened. He appeared to be sleeping.

"How do you do that?" exclaimed Knox.

Rothermel made several swift, precise movements and removed the spear tip from Tinator's side. He held his hand against Tinator's wound and answered, "I am his Keeper; I may influence his daylights."

"And make him live?" pleaded Knox.

Rothermel shook his head. "I have used the power of Melor to allow a healing sleep for Tinator, but I may not use it to overcome the guidance of his heart, nor to make him do something unnatural to his being—and I cannot keep him from dying if his injuries are too great for his vessel to bear. "

Mara dabbed at Tinator's wound with a tincture and dried moss. He opened his eyes and raised his arm, grimacing with the pain the effort caused him. He ran his fingers across her scar.

"Wife," he whispered. "Do not be afraid."

Knox picked up Tinator's crossbow and lay it at his side. His eyes traveled from Tinator's face across the shadowy battlefield, taking in the wounded and dead Melorians.

"We did this," he said, in a terrible voice. "If we hadn't come here, none of this would have happened. I'm sorry."

Tinator grazed the boy's fingers with his own. "Heed what I told you about the Fifth Stone. Fight for Melor, and do not give up hope."

"Look, his daylights have stopped the blood, " Calla murmured, pointing to a dried brown rivulet of blood on Tinator's side. "He is strong."

"There is no one stronger," said Seaborne, who had been carried off the battlefield to a makeshift sickbed beside Tinator's. His face was battered and bruised and his hands were bandaged, but his eyes were soft and he was smiling. At Calla.

Knox sat beside him and gave him a wan half-smile. "So, that's your secret."

Seaborne winked at him. "If you tell anyone, I'll make these Exorians look like a training exercise."

"Does she know?"

"I think so," said Seaborne. "Maybe. But she is young yet. Her love is strongest for her father." One by one, the other children made their way over to Seaborne, clustering around him as if he could protect them from what was happening to Tinator.

"Are you okay, Theaborne?" asked Teddy.

Seaborne lifted up a bandaged hand and patted Teddy's arm, a little wistfully. He glanced again at Calla, her head bent low to catch any words from her father's stricken lips. His face fell.

"Battle robs us all," he whispered.

Tinator writhed in pain and let out a groan. Rothermel held his palm to Tinator's chest for several moments, then addressed Mara, his expression grave.

"It is up to him now. Either his daylights will remain in the vessel we know as Tinator, or they will fragment. Either way, he will not be lost. You know this. He will always be among us, if not in this form, then another."

"I prefer this form," Mara answered, her voice breaking.

"It is one of the finest I have known," agreed Rothermel, "and I have known legion."

A snort and a burst of warm breath smelling like fresh grain and sweetgrass announced the sudden arrival of four horses, tall and muscular and dark as the night from which they appeared. Rothermel met them with affection, speaking low and stroking the muzzle of the largest horse. It whinnied happily. He turned to face Evelyn and the boys.

"My friends have agreed to take you to the eastern boundary of Melor, to the northern banks of the great Hestredes. You will find my sister's people waiting for you there."

"What?" cried Knox, disbelieving.

"What about Frankie?" Evelyn demanded.

"And Dankar?" said Chase.

"I don't want to go!" squealed Teddy.

"Quiet." The Keeper's voice was low and unyielding, resonating in their bones and rolling across them like the tremor they had felt before when the earth split open. "You will go to Metria and do as Rysta bids you. Much has been ventured on your account" —his eyes flitted across to Tinator— "and much lost. You will not stray, nor lead your companions, be they two-footed or four-, into further danger. The enemy is after you. Of that there is no longer any doubt. I do not wish for you to find out why. However"—he turned to Evelyn—"should you want to find your sister, you need only disobey me. Dankar will find you readily enough, and you will join her—and her fate. If that is your heart's counsel, I will not restrain you; it is your choice, but yours alone. Please do not take the others with you against their wishes."

"It is their wish, isn't it?" Evelyn turned to the boys.

Knox looked at the ground. "Yeah—we need to find Frankie. She must be here somewhere."

Chase cut in. "Knox, Evelyn! You saw them, right—the Exorians? We have to leave before they kill everyone in Melor to get to us. *Everyone.*" He paused to let his words sink in. "We can't let that happen."

Evelyn took a few paces away and looked out over the battlefield. The Melorians were gathering their dead, Duon among them. She watched as the fallen were rolled into their hammocks and placed side by side in the pale moonlight. She had seen death lain out like this before. She put her hands to her face.

"I have told you that Rysta is most feared by Dankar," said Rothermel. "There is no greater challenge to the power of Exor than the stone of Metria. Melor is a fading power, almost spent. I am now only capable of protecting what is left. You must seek further guidance and aid from my sister." He stepped back. "I believe we have overcome the greatest danger, but I send you forth with a friend, just in case."

Calla crossed over to them, her face flushed and angry. She twirled her hand on one of the horse's manes and effortlessly hoisted herself onto its bare back.

"Let's go," she snapped.

"You're coming?" cried Teddy, with relief.

"And she's not too happy about it, obviously," mumbled Knox beneath his breath.

Calla maneuvered her horse next to Seaborne and reached down to grab Teddy and settle him safely in front of her. She turned her horse and stared impatiently at the other three children.

"What are you waiting for?"

"Knox and I don't know how to ride," Chase admitted sheepishly.

Calla snorted. "Fortunately for you, the horses do. Get on."

Rothermel whistled softly. Axl and Tar sprang to his side.

"You two shall go as well, and return with Calla. No Melorian will travel alone this night." He closed his eyes and laid a hand on Calla's horse. "May the blessing of Melor be with you," he said, "and may your daylights protect you. Let nothing stay your course."

Above, the sky was lightening from deep blue to a shade of indigo. All that remained of the rainstorm were a few spools of thready clouds, unwinding across the almost-full moon. Calla manuvered her horse east, toward the mountains; it whinnied and reared, its forelegs pawing the air. Calla's steady figure, a shadow against the purple sky, urged it forward. Before Chase, Knox, or Evelyn could say a word, their horses followed Calla's in a smooth, swift gallop. Hills of grass fell beneath their hooves. They rode hard, without hesitation, toward the rising sun. They did not pause to look back—not even when cries of mourning at the passing of Tinator were carried to them on the wind.

Chapter 18

THE BROOMWASH

Whee Frankie came around, it was with the familiar sensation of a bad headache. She was lying on a makeshift cot. Her poncho had been removed and was folded neatly under her head. A solitary torch burned a ways off. Her body ached all over. She groaned out loud. A movement in her peripheral vision turned out to be Louis, moving quickly to her side. He didn't say anything, but knelt beside her and looked into her eyes. The gaze that met her own was more worried than she would have guessed. A throb of anger returned. Not knowing what to do, she put her hands to her face and sobbed.

"Why do you want to kill them?"

"Didn't you hear me?" asked Louis. "I specifically told them *not* to harm your sister or your friends. Dankar doesn't want to hurt you or them. He wants to *help* you."

Frankie raised her face from her hands, trying to read Louis's stare in the blurry light of the torch.

"Help us?" she asked. "How does attacking the Melorians help us?"

Louis sat down by her side, clasping and unclasping his hands.

"The Melorians have been at war with the people of Exor for as long as I have known. It is the way of this land. And tonight, more Exorian blood may have been spilled than any other. You've been unconscious for a while, and yet not a single one of my brothers has returned from the foray."

Frankie glanced sideways at Louis. "How can Dankar help us?" she asked again.

Louis sighed. "Tell me what the Melorians told you when you came to this place. What did they say when you asked them to help you find your way home."

Frankie scowled, trying to remember. Then, haltingly, she said, "They—well, actually, Seaborne, he's a friend. He lives in the cabin where you, uh, took me. He told us we couldn't. That it was impossible. The fog makes it impossible for anyone to leave Ayda."

Louis grimaced. "That's exactly what I was told. We are all prisoners here, unable to pierce the blanket of fog that encircles this place—yet what is fog but water and air? And who has influence over water and air but the Keepers of the stones that rule those daylights? We are kept here because the Keepers *want* us here, not because it's impossible to leave."

Frankie shook her head. "That's not the way he made it sound—"

"Bah!" Louis interrupted. "Rothermel has been telling these lies to his people for so long that they no longer know truth from tales. Tell me! What makes fog disappear?"

Frankie thought for a moment. "Sun—" she replied. "It burns fog away."

"And who controls the fire daylights?"

"D-D-D-Dankar," Frankie stammered.

Louis nodded, letting the idea sink in.

"So you're saying that Dankar is trying to burn the fog away?"

He nodded again.

"And that he wants to get us all out of Melor so that when the fog has lifted he can take us back—home?"

Louis nodded. "He cannot banish the fog until he has power over the other Keepers and their stones. So, it is to this end that we fight the injustice of those who seek to keep us here, hidden forever. He sent me to rescue you from your captors. I am to bring you and the others to Exor, where you will stay until the day of your, of *our*, liberation."

Frankie listened closely. Louis's words dropped into her ears and floated in her brain. She was having trouble connecting what she heard and what she knew of the Melorians, yet some of it did make sense. And what Louis said about the fog; could it be true? Had they been lied to? But what about the Exorians? Those lizard-like faces. Their repulsive skin—like blisters that had been caked over with blood and hardened to scales.

"The Exorians. They don't seem like rescuers. The Melorians are afraid of them. I am, too."

Louis weighed his answer. "Exorian warrors are highly honored for their devotion to Dankar. They can be careless; at times, impulsive. They believe that nothing and no one—including themselves—are more important than their duty to Dankar and the stone of Exor. They do not question. In exchange, they receive a great gift."

Frankie stared at him blankly.

Louis spoke to her slowly, as if to underline the importance of what he was saying.

"Once an Exorian becomes a warrior, he is no longer alone. He becomes part of a brotherhood, bound by a single vision. The warriors think as one, act as one, live as one—for Dankar and his dream of freedom for Ayda. Their will is his to command."

Frankie's expression froze. "*Bokor,*" she whispered. She pulled up her hood as if it would hide her. Her shoulders slumped.

"More French?" asked Louis, amused.

"I know this magic from my country. It is dark voodoo to take a person's will and control it." She shuddered. "Dankar is a black sorcerer, a *bokor.* Those men are shadows, slaves to him."

"You misunderstand," Louis argued. "It is a great achievement to become a warrior in Exor. You make it sound like a curse."

"*Wanga,*" Frankie hissed. "It is a curse. If you accept it, you are doomed from the moment it is laid upon you, and your soul will drain from you until you have no life of your own. My father told me of these things."

Louis shook his head. "You're wrong. It's an honor, a gift. Think about it. To be free from fear and confusion, from . . ." He struggled to find the right word. "From wanting—" His face contorted, his voice dropped to a growl. "And missing what you can't ever have again, everything that's been lost." He gave Frankie a terrible look. "Wouldn't you give anything to be free of those feelings?"

Frankie didn't know how to answer. "I want lots of things." she said, finally. "For instance, I want to see my sister."

Louis shook his head. "That is not what I meant. I'm speaking of greater longings—for things that can never be, that have passed beyond reach forever." His voice sounded so hollow that Frankie's eyes darted to his face in alarm. She recognized what she saw there; she'd seen it on Evelyn's face a hundred times the past year.

Louis was homesick.

"What is it?" asked Frankie. "What do you miss?"

Louis would not answer.

✞   ✞   ✞

Day broke and there was still no sign of Evelyn, Chase, Knox, or Teddy, nor any returning Exorians. Frankie dozed off. The sound of grunting woke her up. It was Louis, struggling to carve a message on the trunk of a tree with the edge of his spear.

"Get what you need to eat quickly. We're leaving," he announced.

"But what about the others?"

"Change . . . of . . . plans," said Louis, breathing heavily from his efforts.

"I don't want to go anywhere without my sister. You told me they were being rescued. You told me they were coming with us." A lump rose in Frankie's throat.

"I'm not happy about it either," said Louis. He whipped the spear tip back into the tree in a fury. "Why would I be? Stuck alone in enemy territory, a four-day march across the Broomwash and the Exorian plateau would be enough, but no! I have to keep you alive as well." He made the word *you* sound particularly hateful.

Frankie willed herself not to cry. She was pretty sure it would only make him more angry.

"Where are they?"

Louis threw the spear on the ground. "I dunno. Dead probably—"

Frankie's gut-wrenching howl cut him off.

"I don't mean your people, I mean . . . mine," he added quickly, but it didn't help. Frankie kept wailing. Louis marched over and shook her roughly.

"Stop making all this noise! The Melorians might hear you!" he growled.

"Good!" she cried.

Louis sighed, then pulled her to her feet and brushed the twigs and leaves off her back. She was surprised to feel his palm give her two short pats between the shoulder blades, then he spoke to her in a normal tone.

"I'm sure your sister's fine—and your friends. The Exorians haven't come back because they failed. The Melorians must have escaped, which means they took your sister and the others with them. So now we've lost our escort and the Melorians are itching for a fight. We have to move fast. I want to make the Broomwash by nightfall."

"What's a Broomwash?"

"The Exorian border. Keep your eyes out for water and food to gather. There's not much to be had between the Broomwash and the Dwellings."

Frankie stared at him blankly.

"The Dwellings," he repeated, as if this was self-explanatory. "Where the Exorians live. That's where Dankar is waiting for us, where I live."

"Dankar is waiting for us?" she repeated stupidly.

"Yes." Louis looked down at his feet. With an ominous frown, he lifted his flask and took several deep swallows.

Frankie was suddenly too afraid to ask any more questions.

Chapter 19

CALLA'S FAREWELL

The horses ran without tiring, their hooves beating a steady rhythm on the ground. The cadence and ceaseless movement made it hard for Evelyn to stay awake. She was so tired. They had ridden for hours, always keeping the mountains on their left. Earlier, their hooves had thundered across a wooden bridge, jarring her to her senses, but returned to the quiet, steady gait moments later.

As the sun rose, the children instinctively lifted their faces to meet it. Warmth spread through their sore bones and their spirits lifted. The horses caught new wind and broke into a fresh gallop. The land beneath them began to change; grassy hills grew larger, the valleys between them deeper. Calla slowed the horses to a walk. She turned up one of the hills. When they reached the summit, she dismounted. The children dropped off their horses, rubbing their backsides. Calla stood apart from them, surveying the landscape.

"Look—the Voss." She pointed to a large lake shining like an oblong coin at the foot of the mountains, some distance to the north. "The Vossbeck flows southwest from the lake into my country. The Hestredes flows southeast into Metria. You can just see the head of it there." Again she pointed, this time to a silver thread of water, barely visible, snaking through a valley to the right. "That is where we are headed. We shall be there soon."

"Can we rest a little first?" asked Evelyn, as she sprawled on the ground. "I can't ride anymore." The horses were grazing happily on the grass. Axl and Tar rolled on their backs. The sun was warm, tempered by a gentle breeze coming off the mountains. Chase felt his muscles relax. He looked anxiously at Calla, then at Knox, who hadn't said a word since they left the Melorians. Nobody mentioned Tinator, but his death lay between them like a heavy cloud.

"The horses will need water soon," said Calla. "We cannot stop long."

Chase cleared his throat. "Umm, Calla," he began. "I'm really sorry about—"

Calla did not stay to listen. She walked purposefully to the horses and began to swipe the sweaty foam from their backs with the edge of her hand.

Chase threw himself down next to Knox and put his chin in his elbow. "I can't believe he's dead," he muttered.

Knox didn't know what to say. How could he explain to Chase what this meant to him? If Tinator could die, that meant they all could—and it was his fault. He'd as good as murdered Tinator. It didn't matter how brave he'd been or how hard he'd fought. If he hadn't brought them all to this place—even if it was by mistake—Tinator would still be alive. Knox lay back and smelled the green smell of grass warming in the sun. His heart beat a heavy thud and the dull buzzing of small insects filled his ears. He closed his eyes. His body was battle-sore and his throat ached with things he wished he had told Tinator. How much he had learned from him. How much he respected him. The buzzing grew louder and solidified into a chord of sound. Knox listened, thinking that if electricity had a sound it would be this. Suddenly, as clear as a bell tolling, he heard Tinator's deep voice say his name, as if he were sitting next to him. Knox sat up with a jolt. He looked around to see if anyone else had heard it. No one else had moved. They all seemed to be asleep, except for Calla, who was leaning against her horse, looking out over the horizon. Knox shook his head to clear it. Maybe he'd just fallen asleep and dreamed it. But the voice felt so near, so real. Calla must have seen him move out of the corner of her eye, because she too, stirred.

"Everybody up!" she said. "We have another few hours to ride."

They mounted their horses, walking down the slope of the hill at a gentle pace. Calla did not want the horses to run after eating, and the danger of the enemy was now lessened significantly. The rolling green hillsides flattened out. The grasses grew taller and more reed-like as the ground underneath the horses' hooves softened. Soon they found themselves traveling along the edge of a marshy estuary. Rivulets and small ponds of water stretched out before them. Great, swooping birds the color of glass flew up at their approach, angling quickly into the sky, then returning back to earth. Bright purple, orange, and green dragonflies skimmed the surface of the water. The horses seemed to know their way and picked out a firm path to follow through the marshland. The children sat lazily astride the horses' backs, lulled by the soft, warm air and the ever-present drone of insect life buzzing around them. Calla raised her right hand and halted them.

"This is the borderland between Melor and Metria," she said. "In a few hundred yards, we will have left my country, but see how it changes little. Ayda never used to be a country of borders. When the power of the stones is unfettered and true, there are no seams between the daylights—they work in chorus for the beauty of all." She scowled. "This is not the case in the northernmost region of my home, where my country meets Exor. The Broomwash it is called now, since all things green and tender have perished—swept away by Dankar's ire. It is a brown, forsaken land. Pray you do not find yourself there someday."

Evelyn spurred her horse closer to Calla.

"What do Metrians look like?" she asked.

Calla shrugged. "Much like everyone else, I suppose, but it can be hard to tell. I have seen them only a few times in my life, travelers and messengers. Those I saw wore richly colored layers, but once I saw the hilt of a sword and the flash of other metal under their robes—so I know that some of them travel armed." She was thoughtful for a moment.

"They wrap many long, beautiful scarves around themselves for protection from the sun. I have only seen them given as gifts of favor. My fath—" She paused and swallowed, the word stuck in her throat. "My father has several in our home. They are a wonder to hold: so light and delicate, but very strong. I tried one on once. I did not want to take it off—such a delight after the weight of this." Calla pulled at the edges of her thick hood in irritation, then stopped as if she'd thought better of it.

"But Metria is a different land than Melor in many ways. It is very hot in the south—too hot for those used to the cool of the forest. The vegetation there grows without bounds. One leaf can measure the length of a man's arm, or so I am told." She smiled vaguely to herself.

"Seaborne once lived in the great city of Metria. He has told me much of it. The sand on its shores is pink as the inside of the newest shell and softer than the most tender grass. They live in houses that have no angles and rise up from the ground like the cap of a mushroom. Their windows are open always to the warm air and the sea breeze and their roofs are blue and gold; from a distance, the city of Metria looks like a great wave from the deepest sea rolling east, glittering in the sun."

"Go on," Evelyn urged.

"Seaborne says Metrians travel by water. In the city, white bridges span avenues where boats navigate the rivertides. There are many high watchtowers, and beneath the city lie secret pathways to deep caverns, covered by water and known only to the families of ancient Metrians. In times of danger, the watchmen will sound the tower bells. The people then swim to safety in the caverns. I—I would like to see it for myself one day."

"Is that where we are going?" Evelyn asked. "To the city of Metria?"

"I do not know. Perhaps. I have been told to take you to the enterlude of the Hestredes, in the north. That is all. Rysta and her people shall lead you thenceforth."

Evelyn felt a slight surge of panic. "So you aren't coming with us?"

Calla slowed her horse until it walked evenly alongside Evelyn. "It is confusing to me that you still do not understand the ways of Ayda, despite what you have seen. Did I not just show you that there are no beginnings and endings here? Does the earth weep as the river, flushed with the winter's thaw, moves through it? Does the tree mourn when it loses its leaves? No. It knows that new leaves are borne from that loss. All that is comes from what was. The power of the daylights washes in and around us all, binding us as one. Even if our bodies were to part, I have not left you. The daylights that reside in me, reside in you; what parts of them hearken to Rothermel and the power of the stone of Melor will always unite us. There can be no sadness in that." She pulled Teddy's body closer to hers, a heaviness in her voice competing with the conviction of her words.

Evelyn dropped back. In hushed tones, she repeated everything Calla had told her about Metria to Chase and Knox. The horses swerved right and began following a steadier path. The sun passed its midpoint and was now behind them, bearing down on their backs. They passed through the marshland and found themselves once again in green country, on solid land. Through the shrubby trees on their left, a small silver pond stretched out invitingly. Knox began to talk loudly about stopping for another break, and possibly, a swim.

"Those are your water daylights speaking," said Calla. "Already the power of Melor is fading and your heart hears the call of Rysta's stone."

"Rysta's stone or not, " Knox yelled, "I'm HOT!"

Before them lay a hill of some size, freckled with stone outcroppings and short, leafy trees. They rode through the shade of a deep ravine and along a dry riverbed. The horses' hooves clacked loudly on the loose stones as they walked. The air was rife with the sound of flowing water. Within minutes, the riverbed grew muddy and pitted with bracken. The horses stuck to the sides, climbing out onto the drier edges. They emerged as a group onto a flat, grassy plain that opened onto the widest river the children had ever seen.

The water moved rapidly, sun glittering across its rippled surface, and a fresh breeze bathed their hot faces. But this was not the only surprise. At least twenty small boats with brightly painted red-and-white sails were clustered in the middle of the river, some sailing back and forth lightly. A larger ship with two white, square sails was tied to a long ramp that jutted out into the river from their side of the shore. Dories lay beached alongside the ramp. Knox, Chase, and Evelyn stared at the sight, then at each other. *Boats! Boats that worked!*

Calla checked her horse and brought them all around in a circle. She spoke firmly.

"I am here to entrust you to the care of Rysta, great Keeper of the water stone of Metria. You have come here by the leave and will of Rothermel. You will honor him by behaving in a way befitting a Melorian." She dropped her voice an octave and growled, "Don't embarrass me!"

They had gone almost halfway to the shore when they were met by what appeared to be a large party of guards coming toward them on foot.

Calla dismounted and motioned for the children to do the same. As the guard approached, she bowed her head and raised her right palm, fingers gently splayed. The children mimicked her, following her lead.

The Metrians wore cloth boots and leggings. A flowing bluish-purple skirt with gold embroidery fell to their knees, swaying under a layer of light chain mail. They were as tall as Melorians, made taller by the domed, metal helmets they wore on their heads. Light brown hair flowed beneath the helmets to their shoulders. Curved, pearl-hilted swords were strapped to their skirts.

"Welcome to Metria," said a man's voice, slowly, rolling the R. The man who spoke raised his palm in greeting. Calla grazed his fingertips with her own.

"We have traveled through the night after a long battle—" she began.

The leader stopped her. "Our Keeper has received word of your journey. She has given instructions: You are to follow me. She will greet you after you have eaten and rested, as she is eager to hear your story from your own lips. We will see to your horses, and to the hounds of Melor." He nodded respectfully to Axl and Tar. "We are honored to receive them."

"Thank you," said Calla. "I am grateful to you and to the sister of Rothermel, but I must return to my mother as soon as the horses have rested. I do not require anything for my return journey. It may be far for these outliers to travel from Melor to Metria, but not for me, nor for the horses and hounds of Melor. I will take my leave as soon as they are settled."

Teddy grabbed at Calla's hand with an anguished cry. Calla rebuffed him, pulling her hand out of his reach. The man registered the exchange silently, then nodded once.

"As you wish."

The Metrian guard began marching toward the river. Reluctantly, the children followed. Calla hung back, walking slowly, leading the horses. About halfway to the river, she stopped and squatted on the ground. The horses bent to graze. Axl and Tar sat beside her.

"I go no further. Your fate lies with the Metrians now," she said, turning her face away from the children with the pretense of watching a broad-winged bird hover over the river.

"What?" asked Knox. "You're stopping here?"

"Yes."

They gathered around her, protesting noisily .

Calla looked at them coldly without answering. Her slingshot hung at her belt beside its satchel of carefully picked rocks; her bow and quiver were hitched up on her shoulder; the tips of her two hunting knives pointed to the ground by the soft, brown suede of her boots. At that moment she was more like an imaginary creature—half-fiercesome warrior, half-shrouded maiden of the wood—than the Calla they knew.

"But what about the domed houses and the white bridges?" pleaded Evelyn. "You told me you wanted to see Metria." A strange desperate pain took hold of her; the broken thing inside her chest drove itself in deeper.

"Come with uth, Calla!" cried Teddy. He threw himself on the ground beside her and crossed his arms. "I'm not going if you're not going."

The spell broke. Calla cracked the smallest of grins and ruffled his hair. She was back to being her usual self.

"Yes, I'm afraid you are. You will not dishonor my father and my kinsmen and the Great Keeper of Melor by being disobedient. You have been trained as a Melorian, you must act like one, even when I am not there to watch over you."

The guard ahead stopped, waiting for them. Chase pulled Teddy to his feet. Calla stood, too, fussing over each of them in turn, correcting the way Knox had stowed his knives, smoothing Evelyn's hood, lacing Teddy's boot, and finally, adjusting Chase's sword hilt on his belt. No words were exchanged, but the older children seemed to know, in the way Melorians had known things about them without asking, that this was the only good-bye they would have.

"Will you be all right?" asked Evelyn.

Calla assented with a nod and turned to her horse, watching them from the corner of her eye as she pretended to work a burr out of the horse's mane. She saw them clad in the clothes she and her mother had prepared, carrying weapons made by her father, and walking toward the Metrian guard in the long, silent ground-covering strides of a Melorian. She did not turn to face them as they descended to the shore; nor when they walked out onto the makeshift pier to the ship; nor when they gained the ship's deck; nor when each of the small heads looked over in her direction. But she saw them.

She mounted, clucked to the other horses to follow, and rode away. Within minutes, she had reentered the dry riverbed. Axl and Tar howled long, baying cries that echoed up and across the striated walls of the canyon. The sun glinted sharply across the bleached stones lining the riverbed, burning her eyes and making them leak water.

Chapter 20

METRIA

That night, Evelyn, Chase, Knox, and Teddy slept in a cabin in the bow of a ship, which was outfitted with matching berths covered with soft sheets and blankets. The boat rocked back and forth lightly with the river's subtle swell, and they slept deeply until pale pink morning light filtered through the cabin and woke Evelyn. She sat up and smacked her head on the bottom of Knox's bunk overhead.

"Wake up, everyone," she said, reeling a little and rubbing her forehead from the impact.

"Calla!" Teddy yelled. "She'th waiting for uth!"

"No, she's not Tedders," Knox said sadly. "She had to—uh—get back to her mom."

"She didn't thay good-bye!" Teddy sniffed. "And I didn't get to thay good-bye to Axthl and Tar!"

Knox shrugged. "They don't say good-bye in Melor, remember, Ted? They just go."

"But what about Theaborne? And Mara?" Teddy's lower lip quivered.

"I don't know," Knox said to the ceiling. He rubbed the hilt of one of his throwing knives. "I'm sick of all the things I don't know."

Evelyn twisted her legs over the side of her berth and stood up. Her head was even with Knox's, who was lying flat on his pillow.

"So am I. We're just being sent around to whoever will have us. I know a little something about that, and it hardly *ever* works out." She chewed on her lip for a moment and added, "Rothermel says his sister is Dankar's biggest threat. We should try to see her as soon as possible and figure out how to find Frankie. After that, we'll ask her if we can borrow one of these boats to go home. It's about time we started taking control of our own lives, not leaving them up to everybody else."

Chase rolled over in his bunk on the other side of cabin, listening, feeling a shift almost back to normal. Evelyn was sounding a lot more like her old self, which was a relief.

"I wonder what they eat in Metria?" asked Knox, sounding happier. He swung off his bunk and vaulted down over the edge, landing on his feet next to Evelyn.

It wasn't long before they found out. In the adjoining cabin, a long table had been set for them with fruit, fresh juice, eggs, butter, and honey. Sun streamed through four oval portholes recessed along each side of the boat.

"Now *this* is breakfast," Knox said, settling down at once and helping himself to a huge serving of eggs. Chase sat next to him, taking it all in. When he looked up, Evelyn caught his eye.

"It's a lot of food, isn't it?" she said, pulling an orange from one of the piles.

"Enough to feed an army," he said, and pushed his plate away with a hollow feeling in his stomach. He wondered what Seaborne, Calla, and Mara would be eating today.

"Or at least me," said Knox, with his mouth full.

A delicious smell wafted through the cabin quickly followed by a woman in purple robes carrying a tray piled high with freshly baked bread. She had a wide, pale face and blue eyes that peered out from a curtain of sand-colored hair. As she walked, her bare toes poked out from beneath the hem of her robes. She lowered the tray onto the table, smiled, and then retreated out of sight without a word.

"That was weird," said Knox, picking up a piece of warm bread and smelling it appreciatively.

Evelyn shrugged. "She probably thinks *we're* weird."

"Knoxth ith weird," Teddy said.

Chase and Evelyn looked at each other and said in unison, "Definitely."

"Ha-ha, very funny," said Knox, helping himself to seconds. "Just see if I come running the next time you need someone to chuck a knife."

"That won't be necessary here," interrupted an unfamiliar voice. It came from a helmeted figure dressed in chain mail, descending the ladder into their cabin. Standing, the helmet knocked lightly on the ceiling. A swift hand removed it to reveal the oval face and light hair of another Metrian. Like the woman who had served them bread, her eyes were a startling, clear blue.

"I see you have enjoyed your rest, and"—she eyed the table littered with crumbs—"your breakfast. That is good. You have been through a great ordeal and we wish only for your comfort. My name is Hesam. This is my vessel." She raised her palm in the traditional greeting. "Soon I will take you to our Keeper, who wishes to see you with her own eyes. But first, you must—ah—wash."

Evelyn raised her arm to her nose to smell herself, then sniffed at Knox's hair. None of them had bathed since they'd arrived on Ayda, how many weeks ago? The Melorians never washed, and it didn't seem to matter, but it was a different story inside the closed quarters of the ship.

Knox's eyes were fixed on the shiny helmet that Hesam had in her hand—it had a small point at the top that ended in a mushroom-shaped cap. Hesam noticed, and placed it in front of Knox, allowing him to examine it more closely. It was made of hammered bronze and decorated with gold engraving. At the center, a gold medallion embossed like a sand dollar was affixed to the nose guard, and intricate curtains of mail fell loosely from the sides and back.

"They don't have these in Melor," said Knox.

Hesam laughed. "Of course they don't."

"There'th a lot that you don't have, I bet," cried Teddy, defensively. "Like thky crothingth!"

"The gifts of Ayda are many and varied to be sure," agreed Hesam, easily understanding Teddy despite his lisp. "The people of the stone of Melor are much advantaged. There are none braver, nor wiser in the growing, nurturing, and harvesting of living things. But this one," she pointed at Knox, "is right. Nowhere else on Ayda can be found better craftsmanship of such things. In Metria, we take pleasure in taking that which is whole and good and using our arts to make it more beautiful. If you would follow me, you will soon see for yourselves."

Evelyn and the boys rose from the table and politely began to gather their dishes. Hesam stopped them.

"That will be taken care of. On my ship, each person has an assigned duty. If it is not your duty, then you must leave it be, or confusion will ensue. Come with me." She gestured up the ladder.

"I like that," crowed Knox, putting down his plate.

"Just wait until you're on dish duty," replied Evelyn.

On deck, a steady breeze filled the sails as they headed downriver. Evelyn peeked over the edge of the ship; the water flowed deep blue and green and extraordinarily clear. Her eyes swept over the rest of the ship, noting Hesam's impressive armor and that of her crew: the curved swords at their hips, their swift, efficient movements, and the billowing sails that kept the ship moving fast, every minute taking them farther and farther away from Frankie. Evelyn chewed her lip, wishing the water flowing past the ship could give her answers. Where was her sister now? Was she hurt? Afraid? Was she alive? As the ship sped southeast, Evelyn couldn't help feeling that she was headed in the opposite direction of where she should be going.

✛   ✛   ✛

By afternoon, the ship had reached a peninsula of rock where the river split in two. Hesam gave the order to tack right, westward, and they sailed into a broad cove, at the back of which stood the mouth of a cavern. The crew lowered the sails as two small skiffs issued forth, manned by rowers with long oars.

"Ith thith Metria?" asked Teddy, as he climbed down a ladder into one of the skiffs, followed by Evelyn. Chase and Knox lowered themselves into the other. Hesam peered over the rail of her ship.

"All that you see is guarded by the great Keeper Rysta, but this is merely a waystation on your journey. We are to stop here until plans are made for your transport to the city," she answered.

Evelyn frowned. "Why can't you take us all the way there? We need to see Rysta."

"She will see you here. If all is well, you will proceed to the city soon enough."

"What do you mean, if all is well?" asked Chase. "Does Rysta think we've come to cause trouble?"

"My orders were to bring you here, and here I have brought you. That is all I know," answered Hesam, with an air of finality.

"They don't trust us," said Evelyn in a low voice.

"Can you blame them?" replied Chase, thinking of the damage they had left behind them in Melor.

The rowers dipped their oars rhythmically into the green water, smoothly gliding away from Hesam's ship and into the mouth of a tunnel. They emerged from the other side into a small, underground lagoon. Long stalactites of sand-colored stone hung from the roof and light poured through various openings in the rockface, glancing off the water and catching tiny flecks of quartz embedded in the walls. The effect was dazzling—like paddling across a sparkling snow globe. The sound of gently falling water filled the cavern. Chase swiveled his head, looking for the source of the sound.

"Teddy, look!" he gasped, pointing toward the far wall of the cavern. A sheet of water cascaded down from some unseen height, splashing into the lagoon and making a small rainbow. The skiffs pulled up to a shallow beach where several Metrians awaited them. Strong hands grabbed the skiffs and hauled them ashore.

Back on land, Evelyn and the boys followed their hosts deeper into the cavern. It was impossible to know how far underground they were, but there was no lack of light. It came pouring in through small and large apertures bored through the walls of the tunnels, and everywhere the sound of water running, trickling, and rushing surrounded them. After a few more twists and turns, they were shown into a comfortable room outfitted with stacks of pillows and long cushions, a low table, and rows of bright candles nestled into the rock. At the far end of the room stood an open archway partially obscured by mist.

A woman not much taller than Evelyn approached.

"You must come with us," she whispered, gingerly touching Evelyn's shoulder.

"No way, she stays with us," said Chase.

Evelyn gave him a quick, grateful smile.

The woman, flustered, consulted the others. When she returned, she spoke so quietly that Chase had to lean in to hear her words.

"It is for the bath," she explained. "She will return later to the gathering room, unless it is custom in your country for boys and girls to bathe together?"

Chase's lips twitched into a nervous smile. He raised an eyebrow at Evelyn.

"I'll be okay," she assured him, and gave a little wave before disappearing with her guides into the dim light of the tunnel.

The boys' bathroom turned out to be another low-ceilinged room with an enormous steaming pool of water in the center. An open window looked out on the river flowing not a hundred yards away. Their guides withdrew. Teddy and Knox peeled off their soiled Melorian clothing and dropped their weapons to the floor. Chase took his poncho off, but hesitated when it came to removing his sword.

With a loud whoop, Teddy cannonballed into the pool.

"Hurry up, Chase!" cried Knox, jumping in.

Chase unstrapped his belt and untied the drawstring to his leggings. His sword clattered to the ground. He quickly lowered himself into the bath, relaxing as his muscles hit the warm water.

"It's deep!" he said. "And hot!"

A few Metrians returned with a pile of brown sponges and a shell full of sweet-scented soap. They picked up the piles of discarded clothing as well as their weapons.

"Hey, we'll be needing those back!" shouted Chase at the retreating back of the Metrians, but before he could say anything else, a wet sponge hit him full in the face.

"Monkey in the middle!" yelled Teddy.

Knox chucked another sponge at Chase, then dove under, resurfacing next to Teddy.

"Who's the monkey now?" he grinned, hoisting Teddy up and tossing him lightly into the center of the pool. Teddy shrieked happily. Through the window, the afternoon sun slowly melted and the river became a ribbon of gold. As the boys cavorted in and out of the pool, chucking wet sponges at each other, heavy memories of the battle and Tinator's death began to lift. Safe in Metria, in this clean, gold-lit room, the events of the past few days seemed like another life, strangely unreal.

"I loooove Metria," Knox groaned.

"Me too," said Teddy, floating on his back, his arms and legs extended, starfish-like.

"It won't love you if you don't get out of the bath soon!" Evelyn's voice came from the archway. "You've been in there forever. I bet you're prunes."

The boys reluctantly hauled themselves out of the pool. Towels of thin linen, along with an assortment of new, clean clothing in the loose, flowing style of the Metrians had mysteriously appeared in a stack by the door. The boys quickly donned the pajama-like pants, long shirts, and colorful scarves.

"Where do you think they took our weapons?" asked Knox, looking down at his knee-length tunic. Weapons might help counteract the feeling that he was wearing a dress.

"I knew we shouldn't have let them go," replied Chase, frowning. "There's nothing we can do about it now."

In the adjoining room, candles had been lit, and a Metrian woman knelt by the low table, which had been set with fruit and a pitcher of water. Her face was hidden by several folds of a scarf she had wrapped around her head. Was this Rysta, come to visit? The boys hung back, not sure what to do.

"I don't have cooties, you know," the woman said in Evelyn's voice. She stood up and peeled off the scarf. Evelyn's face glowed like new bronze fresh from its scrubbing. Her hair was braided with small seed pearls matching a diadem on her forehead.

"It feels good to be clean, doesn't it?"

"Wow!" said Chase, kneeling across from her. "You look great."

"Like a printheth," Teddy agreed.

Evelyn's color deepened. "You don't look so shabby yourselves, and we all probably smell a whole lot better." She suddenly felt shy in front of them.

"Look at this," Knox said, twirling around in his tunic. "Do you think we'll have to dress like this from now on?"

"I like it better than that poncho," Evelyn admitted. She stood up to show off her new lavender-colored silk pants and a matching shirt embroidered in white. Her feet were laced into thin sandals.

"What are we supposed to do now, I wonder?" asked Knox, his eyes roaming around the cushioned room. He threw himself down on one of the mattresses and yawned. "I guess we hang out here until someone comes to get us."

"Here we are again, waiting," said Evelyn, catching his yawn.

Teddy popped a strawberry in his mouth and yawned, too.

"So far, Metria is pretty plush, though," Knox countered. "No fire-spouting Exorians, lots of food, hot baths." He thumped his fist into a cushion and and closed his eyes.

Chase lowered himself down on a mattress and stared at the flickering shadows cast by the candles set into the wall. His gaze lingered on the yellow tips that burned brightly and added light and comfort to the cavern; yet, at the same time, he knew he could set the whole room on fire with the swipe of his hand. The only difference between the candle flames in Metria and the fire they had escaped in Melor was that here it was contained. Chase lay back, sleepy, wondering how to keep it that way.

Chapter 21

INTO EXOR

Louis and Frankie crossed the Broomwash at dusk. The change in their surroundings was immediate, as if they had crossed an invisible line that separated a cool spring evening and a dry summer day. Heat radiated up from the bare ground, which was cracked and devoid of trees or grass as far as they could see. Frankie gazed across the dust-colored plain.

"Is this the desert?" she asked

Louis made a funny face. "It's becoming one. There used to be watering holes and fields here once, but they've all dried up." He looked around and wiped the sweat off his face with a piece of cloth. "It's always been hot, but it has not always been barren. Your Keeper friends did this."

"Why would they do that?"

Louis gave her a hard look. "Because they can."

Frankie shook her head. It didn't add up. From what the Melorians had told her, she didn't believe that Rothermel would purposefully kill living, growing things. There must be another reason, but the look on Louis's face made her keep her mouth shut, and besides, she was too hot to argue. Sweat dripped down her arms and face.

"It's so hot." She flapped the front of her poncho, trying to cool herself, and whimpered, "I'm boiling."

"Not the worst fate in Exor I can think of," said Louis. "Be patient. You'll be cold by nightfall."

Frankie sulked, dragging her feet. Louis quickened his step and muttered to himself as if he had forgotten she was there.

"There's a bridge a mile or so to the north. We'll cross there. Guards are on watch, and we can send a message ahead. We should be able to get a ride."

Frankie plodded along behind him, looking mostly at the ground; there wasn't anything else to see. When she looked up a while later, Louis had disappeared.

"Louis!" she yelled. "Where are you?" Her words were swallowed by the silence of the lifeless air. "Louis?"

No answer.

She tried to make out footsteps in the hard, dessicated earth, but there were no tracks of any kind. The sun dipped low to the west, huge and brick-colored, and sank fast. Within moments, darkness descended like a lid on a pan. Frankie froze, afraid to go any farther. Her legs trembled beneath her. Night stretched out across the Broomwash with terrifying quiet. Frankie's heart drummed in her chest, the only sound for miles. She sank to the ground.

"Where are you?" she sobbed. "Louis, *please* come back!"

"Hey, hey, what's all this?" said Louis, his voice penetrating the night. He lifted her up and hugged her awkwardly against his hip. "You're crying like you lost your best friend. I told you to save the moisture in your body—and who's Louis?"

"You are. That's what I named you." She buried her head in the thick folds of her poncho. "You left me out here all by myself. I don't like the dark."

"I did no such thing," he chided her gently. "You're just slow."

"I can't walk as fast as you," she sniffed.

"That is true." He held her another minute, patting her back until she stopped trembling, then put his hand on her shoulder.

"What's your real name?" asked Frankie.

"None of your business." He handed her the cloth he had used earlier to wipe his face. She blew her nose and handed it back. He squatted beside her.

"What do you want me to call you, then?" she asked.

"Louis will do."

Frankie smiled and leaned a little into his shoulder, comforted by the solidness of his presence in the enormous blackness all around them.

"Look up," he said, nudging her with his shoulder.

Overhead, millions of stars lay thick across the sky, seemingly so near that Frankie reached up to try and touch one. Her eyes adjusted to their low light and she saw Louis's profile, silhouetted against the night. He was biting his lip, lost in thought.

"My sister does that," she said.

"Does what?"

"Chews her lip when she's thinking."

Louis touched his finger to his lips, surprised.

"I didn't know I did that."

Frankie shrugged. "It's okay. It reminds me of her." She leaned into his shoulder a little more. Louis gently tucked her bangs behind her ears and pulled her hood up.

"Here's what we're going to do," he said, getting to his feet. "I'm going to carry you the rest of the way and over the bridge. When we get across, you can wait with the guards. I'll go ahead and make my report, then I'll come back for you; that way you won't have to walk so far."

"What are the guards like?" she asked, eyeing him nervously. "Are they like you, or are they"—she shuddered—"like them?"

"You'll be fine. Just keep to yourself." He offered her his hand. "Climb aboard."

Frankie pulled herself up and settled on Louis's back, wrapping her arms tightly around his neck. He adjusted her legs around his waist and began walking. Frankie remembered being carried like this by her father. Out of habit, she dug her chin into the soft spot between his shoulders. Louis gasped and stopped dead in his tracks.

"What?" she asked.

"Nothing. You—you just reminded me of someone."

He stood still for a long time, lost in thought.

"Louis, what?" she repeated.

"It's nothing," he answered. "Just a feeling." He tucked Frankie's legs up tightly around his waist, grabbed her calves more securely, and resumed walking.

✛ ✛ ✛

The bridge into Exor was a narrow rock structure and only partially visible in the light of the full moon. It was long and studded with peaks of crumbling rock, as if it were spun from sugar or sand. The bridge stretched over a vast pit of blackness between two canyon walls. From Frankie's perspective, it seemed impossible to cross without falling off one side or the other. She shivered in her poncho, trying to see the other side. The temperature of the air had plunged, as Louis had said it would, but this was more than being cold. She was terrified.

Louis picked her up and took a shaky step onto the bridge, then set her down again, not trusting his balance with the extra weight. He poked his finger between her shoulder blades and nudged her forward.

"Don't look down," he said.

"You're always telling me what to do," grumbled Frankie. "You should meet my sister. You two would like each other."

"Plenty of time for that. Walk."

Frankie edged her way onto the bridge, taking tiny steps and keeping her eyes glued just ahead of her feet. She did not dare lift her head or look to either side into the darkness. Louis followed a step behind, his hand resting lightly against her back. Slowly, carefully, they reached the apex of the bridge and descended. This was trickier; at one point Frankie's ankle rolled over and her weight shifted dangerously to the side. Louis caught her by the scruff of the neck before she fell. When they reached the safety of the other side, her heart was racing.

"Not bad," whispered Louis.

Two young men appeared, both with shaved heads and spears, but with normal skin, not the hideous scales of the Exorian warriors. They wore long pieces of fabric wrapped several times around their waists and their torsos were bare. Frankie breathed a sigh of relief.

The guards at the bridge spoke with Louis, then looked at her. She quickly lowered her head, avoiding eye contact. After a few minutes, they escorted her to a shallow cave dug into the ridge. A fire burned at the edge, brightly illuminating the brown clay walls, on which hung assorted pieces of clothing and bedding. It reminded her vaguely of Melor, in a reassuring way. Louis had her sit by the fire and gave her a cup of water. She drank greedily. From one of the sacks hanging on the wall he pulled out fruit, a strange-looking cracker, and a hearty meat spread. He prepared the food for her and watched as she began to eat. His eyes were expectant, waiting. Frankie took a bite. She grabbed for the water, eyes streaming.

"It's spicy!" she choked.

Louis nodded, then smiled slightly.

"You get used to it." He stood up. "Eat as much as you want. I'll be back by morning. The guards will stay out here. They won't bother you."

"How do you know?" Frankie asked, trying to peer into the dark beyond the fire.

"They are scribes, not warriors, for one thing. And"—he grinned—"I told them Dankar would be coming for you at daybreak, and if he didn't find you here . . . ." Louis let his voice trail off. "I left *that* up to their imaginations."

Frankie watched him leave, trepidation filling her stomach. She pushed the food away, nervous about the morning and missing him. She tried to think about what Louis had said: Dankar wanted to help her. He wanted to reunite her with Evelyn and the boys. She laid her head down on the blanket. It smelled faintly of dried herbs, sweat, and sun—a scent she recognized from that other island, the one where she and Evelyn were born. A log fell into the fire and a plume of sparks rose into the inky sky, melding with the stars.

Maybe Louis was right about Rothermel, thought Frankie. Her father had been killed by moving earth, her island almost swallowed up. Could Keepers do that? She nestled inside her warm poncho, not wanting to believe it—yet Louis was so sure Rothermel was bad. She closed her eyes. Tomorrow she would meet Dankar and find out for herself, but tonight she decided to trust Louis.

Chapter 22

RYSTA'S TALE

Thomeone's coming," whispered Teddy, shaking Chase awake. Chase was instantly alert. He hadn't forgotten the last time he'd been woken from a deep sleep in Ayda. It took him a moment to orient himself in the new surroundings. The candles had long since burnt out and the room was pitch dark except for a silvery glow filtering in from one of the wall apertures. He had no idea how long they'd been sleeping, but he felt refreshed and calm, all battle aches and soreness gone.

A long shadow flitting against the wall proved to be a solitary Metrian holding a candle. She stood expectantly as Chase and Teddy woke the others, then motioned for them to follow. They retraced their steps back to the great cavern where a pair of skiffs bobbed gently on the shore of the lagoon. Two more robed Metrians stood waiting beside them, holding lanterns, which they hung on the prows of the boats.

Evelyn and the boys were silent as the Metrians rowed them swiftly across the lake. The lanterns cast wavering circles of light in the great darkness of the cave. The gentle splash of oars was soon overpowered by the sound of falling water as the skiffs approached the far end of the lagoon. The rowers nosed the skiffs into the cascade and the water parted neatly around them, ushering them into a smaller lagoon completely open to the night sky. Phosphorescent lights shimmered under the water's surface, like waterbound stars, and clung to the oars.

"Look," breathed Teddy, dragging his hand through the iridescent water. "We're twinkling."

The rowers rowed on toward a dense, negative space ahead. In time it revealed itself to be a small island at the center of the lagoon. The skiffs delivered Chase, Knox, Teddy, and Eyelyn to a strip of silver beach and retreated. From the shadows came a tall woman, pale and blonde, wearing a purple-and-silver robe. Her head, feet, and arms were bare and her hair shone with small jewels and fell in gentle waves to where her hands rested at her sides. She considered the four newcomers quietly, then, in a smooth movement, sank to her knees and threw her arms wide. A sudden, inexplicable impulse to run to her, like small children to their mother, washed over them. Teddy obeyed the urge. She rewarded him with a small smile and a warm introduction.

"I am Rysta, Keeper of the stone of Metria and sister to Rothermel. I am sorry if I disturbed you, but I could wait no longer to meet you." Her voice was a low throb that filled every part of their ears. She stood, holding Teddy's hand with one of hers and gestured to Chase, Knox, and Evelyn with the other. When they did not move, she smiled at them again.

"I see you have been long in my brother's country. Trust is a rare gift there—but be assured, I will not hurt you. I know you were once five, now four, and that you have been ill used by the Usurper and his people. I have no wish to add to your distress. I only wish to comfort you and keep you safe so that you may forget your pain. It is the gift of Metria to do so."

Evelyn stirred. "You know about my sister?"

Rysta's brow furrowed, her eyes darkened. "Yes, but I wish to know more. You must tell me everything."

She turned and they followed her soft, barely visible footprints to an enclosure in the sand surrounding a black pool of water. Reflections of stars littered the pool, and a small canopy had been erected beside it. A low, cushioned couch and several rugs and pillows were arrayed under the canopy. Rysta lowered herself gracefully onto the couch, guiding Teddy next to her. She beckoned for the older children to seat themselves around her. Chase was uncomfortably reminded of the first time they had met Rothermel, his piercing green eyes now replaced by the blue-eyed gaze of his sister.

"Please, join me. Let us have some refreshments."

From some undisclosed location behind the canopy, several Metrians emerged. They carried pitchers and dishes of steaming food, which they set on a long, low table at the side of the canopy. It looked tempting, but none of the children could bring themselves to move. A laziness had come over them—not fatigue, exactly, but an unwillingness to exert themselves. It all felt so much like a dream. No one spoke for many minutes.

"Eldest girl," Rysta began, "Evelyn . . . Sit, speak. Tell me about your sister."

"I don't . . . I don't know where to begin," stammered Evelyn. "So much has happened."

Rysta leaned toward her encouragingly; as she did, a brief flash of silver revealed a necklace or chain around her neck.

"I find it is easiest to begin with the nearest memory and work backward. Tell me, what was your journey like from Melor to my home; how did you fare against the Exorians?"

Evelyn began to describe the long, frightening night and their flight from Melor. Both Knox and Teddy interrupted her at points to add in their own stories. Rysta proved to be an appreciative audience. She clapped and laughed and sighed at the right moments. When it came to the injury and death of Tinator, only Chase, who had been silent up to then, had the heart to speak. After a respectful pause, Rysta prompted them once more, taking them back in time to relive the awakening in the fog, their first encounter with the cliffs of Ayda, and the glowing rocks that lit the path to Seaborne's cabin. Rysta was particularly gratified by what she heard of Seaborne.

"So he has flourished in Melor, as his daylights indicated he would. I am glad to hear it."

"Rothermel told us that you saved Seaborne when he first came here. Dankar had kidnapped him, just like Frankie, but you rescued him." Evelyn could not hide the sense of expectation in her voice.

Rysta dipped her hand in the pool.

"It is true. He was a small boy then, caught in a terrible war, as so many are in the lands beyond the fog." The pool at Rysta's feet began to flicker and glow. An image swam to the surface: a small boy and a limping, bleeding man crossing a desolate beach. The man was wearing a long, blue military coat and a blood-stained shirt. His steel sword hung limply in his hand.

"I know that coat!" hooted Teddy. He pointed to the little boy. "Ith that Theaborne?"

Rysta nodded.

Chase leaned in for a closer look. He recognized the sword. It was the one Seaborne wore strapped to his back.

"He was fortunate—as you have been," Rysta continued. "He came through the fog to Metria and lived with me until the call of his daylights could be ignored no longer. He is a creature of the earth, though his heart, I believe, is still moved by the sea. We have not seen one another for a very long time." The image in the pool faded.

"Can't he jutht come vithit?" asked Teddy.

Rysta shook her head. "Travel in Ayda is dangerous, as you well know. Of the many things that were lost with the disappearance of the Fifth Stone, the division of our lands and the eternal separation from my brother and sister are most bitter to me." She leaned forward. "And what of my brother? How does he fare? I am most anxious to hear."

It was Knox's turn to answer. Rysta's smooth brow furrowed and her mouth turned down at the corners when she was told the details of Frankie's capture. Her agitation grew as the children repeated Rothermel's words—his concern for Frankie, and his fear that Dankar's power had grown. When they described Rothermel's weariness, Rysta stood abruptly and paced the edges of the pool. A heavy silence descended. The pool lay smooth and undisturbed, like a mirror of the sky above it. When Rysta looked up, a strange tremor passed over the surface of the water.

"I am distressed to hear this news, and of my brother's failure to try and recover the girl or seek her captors, for in matters such as these, timing is crucial, and the opportune moments have passed. Her captors have had three full moonrises to travel to their lands unmolested. It is my belief that the attack on your camp was a distraction. I agree that the raiding party did not anticipate the presence of a Keeper and therefore came unprepared for the power he called upon. They were vanquished, but not necessarily to the detriment of Dankar's plan. His intent was always to waylay the Melorians in battle and spirit the captive away."

"But why?" asked Evelyn. "What does Dankar want with Frankie?"

Again the pool at Rysta's feet rippled with an unseen breeze.

"It is a mistake to think of Dankar as you would yourself, to attribute to him the same desires or needs that you have," said Rysta. "Dankar is kin to an ancient race, as I am. We have seen the cycling of daylights pass through generations of men and women, and rarely concern ourselves with the fate of just one." Her fingers traveled to the chain at her neck.

"As twisted as Dankar has become, we are perhaps not so far apart as I would like to think. I have spent too much time with the misdeeds of Dankar not to recognize some of my own weakness." Rysta looked over their heads into the depths behind them, as if she might see something, or someone, standing there.

"Tinator told us that Dankar wants all your stones—and the Fifth Stone," Knox informed her. "But Frankie doesn't have it; she doesn't know anything about the five stones. Neither do we."

Rysta pulled her necklace out from beneath her robes. At the end of it hung a perfectly round, grey-blue stone, approximately the size of a small egg, wrapped in a cage of thin white metal wire. It looked like a stone anyone might pick up on the beach, but Rysta held it reverently.

"Ith that your magic thtone? The thtone of Metria?" Teddy asked, eyes wide.

Rysta contemplated him for a moment, then answered.

"No, it is not the stone of Metria. It would be foolish to keep a stone of power on my body, if only that it would be too easily found. This stone that I wear is but a child of the stone of Metria, a shard, imbued with some of her power. The real stone is hidden in a place known only to me."

"It doesn't look like much," mumbled Knox.

Chase had to agree. He hadn't known what to expect from a stone of power, or a piece of a stone of power, but this seemed pretty anticlimactic.

Rysta caressed the stone between her fingertips. "This stone may not look like much, but it is more precious to me than the finest treasure. This stone connects me to the parent stone of Metria, and to the stones of my brother and sister, but like most truths that matter, it does not reveal itself so easily." She replaced the stone beneath the folds of her robe and bent down to trail her fingers through the pool, her eyes lazily following the rippling water. She looked up at the children through her long eyelashes.

"When the path ahead is uncertain, one must look where one has been. So we must go back to move forward. It has always been thus. Time circles upon itself." She withdrew her fingers and shook them, sending small droplets of water raining down onto the pool's surface. Concentric circles spread, moving outward until they overlapped. She fanned her hand over the circles; they continued to grow and spread.

"Your story is like one of these circles. It began as a small drop in the sea of time, but it has grown now to overlap and become one with mine." Rysta raised her head and gazed at Teddy. "My story is an old story. A sad story. I wonder if it is too sad for ones so young to hear."

Evelyn shifted in her seat. "We aren't so young."

Rysta gave Evelyn a sharp, perceptive look.

"Perhaps you are not."

She settled herself on one hip and gazed deeply into the pool for several minutes, lost in thought. Then, she began to speak.

"My history begins with your history, a very long time ago, when the world was young, forged, barely, from the flint of the *atar*, and the daylights ranged across the Earth, unchecked and untamed, bringing form and purpose to the void, and, also, chaos. As time passed and the daylights were tamed into the four qualities that define our world—earth, fire, water, and air—they took on solid shape and matter and their interdependence grew."

Rysta waved a hand over the surface of the pool, which responded by rippling as if stirred by a gentle breeze. The thin bracelets on her arm tinkled. Pale streaks of color shimmered up from the depths. An image of a wild and empty land materialized on the surface. Rysta continued, her eyes fixed and unfocused, as if she had forgotten the children were there. As she spoke, the images in the pool began to flicker and change, one flowing into another almost before she said the words.

"The Earth grew warm and light and a garden grew across the lands, seeded by the wind. Great waters formed in the belly and crevasses of the world. The moon followed the sun and the tides of the oceans beat against the shores, dividing day and night. In these early times, there was no constant, and life was slow to take root. No vessel could contain their daylights for long; then, there was little difference between what we know now as a tree and a man, a wolf, a flower, a fish. The daylights would gather and take shape for a short time, only to fragment and gather again in another form.

"Life had no anchor then. Creatures were as insubstantial as ether, never lingering long enough to flourish and populate the Earth. Men and women died easily, and children were barely brought to suckle before the daylights moved beyond them. Other forms, those in which one quality of daylight existed in far greater measure than the other three, had better success. A hillock, a lake, a tree, or a stone became just that: The daylights which were contained therein grew more solid and settled, content to flourish in their one form. But this was not the case for those creatures that contained a more equal measure of all four daylights. The life of all animals ever since has been hard and short."

Teddy was leaning so far forward over the pool, he almost toppled over. Rysta pulled him back and patted his head.

"And of all the creatures, there was one race who was esteemed most by the great Weaver of life, born out of great love." Rysta paused dramatically and raised an eyebrow. "Who do you think it might be?"

Teddy pointed at his own chest. Rysta laughed.

"Exactly right. Yet, despite this love, the human vessel flourished only briefly before fragmenting. The Weaver despaired of humans ever learning to master their daylights. Have you heard stories of a tribe of immortals, sons of the Weaver, sent to aid the fledgling world?"

The children stared blankly at each other, then back at Rysta. Knox shook his head. The light radiating from the pool suddenly grew blinding. Out of it stepped a ghostly hologram of ten figures, taller than any human beings the children had ever seen. They hovered inches above the water, trailing a spinning nebula of color.

"These beings were the mightiest of all creatures—reflections of the original thought of creation. They were given many names through the ages and walked in many human shapes, but they were not human. They were sent to our world by the Weaver, for they alone knew the nature and the need of the *atar* as none shall or will, and could direct their daylights to shift and change as in the earliest of days. On Ayda, they are called the Watchers." Rysta was silent for a moment. The figures shimmered above the pool in an unearthly glow.

"When the Watchers walked the Earth, there was a time of wisdom and tranquility. The air was filled with the music of the daylights working as one. There were no stones of power, no Keepers, and no need for them, for the Watchers taught men and women the skills to flourish: farming, healing, writing, metalwork, weaving, carpentry, art, music, storytelling. They helped humans tame the nature of their daylights with intelligence; in doing so, they trusted that humankind would respect the daylights all living vessels share."

The glimmer coming off the hologram figures intensified, turning the pool a metallic silver. Rysta's voice grew soft, wistful.

"The Weaver entrusted the Earth to the Watchers, and gave it to them to steward for eternity, so that the daylights could work in harmony and all creatures live in peace. But there was a condition to this trust, a vow never to be broken: The Watchers were to guide and protect humans as parents do their children. Romantic love between the two races was forbidden.

"For an age the Watchers abided by their vow, but after several human lifetimes, they could not help but become attached to their lives on Earth and the world in their care. They eventually broke their vow and married human spouses and, to the sorrow of the world, created families of their own—for their offspring were an abomination." The pool exploded and a bloody red spray flew into the air. The ten ghostly figures disappeared like smoke.

"The children of these forbidden unions grew strong with the blood of their fathers. They lived unnaturally long and powerful lives, but, unlike their fathers, they used their gifts to enslave their human kin and hoard the earth's riches for themselves. Disease, war, and pestilence took over, and once again the lives of your kind were wretched and brief. These cursed children are known on Ayda as the Others: half-Watcher, half-human. They are not immortal, but they do not fade or sicken readily, and have spent the ages in your lands under different disguises. You may find them by the trail of death and human misery they leave in their wake."

Rysta looked pointedly into the eyes of each of the children. "I know this to be true because I am one of them, as is my brother and sister. Our father was a Watcher. His name was Remiel. Our mother was human. Her name was Rachel. They broke the vow that kept the world in peace."

The water in the pool begain to roil beside her.

"And when their betrayal was discovered, there are no words to describe the wrath of the Weaver." An image of a great cliff under a black sky bubbled to the surface of the pool. The same ten tall figures that had risen out of the pool now stood at the edge of the cliff, cowering before a voice that thundered across the enclosure.

"SO I HAVE MADE YOU, SO I SHALL DESTROY YOU!" the voice roared.

Teddy clapped his hands over his ears.

"That day, a choice was given to my father and his kin," said Rysta. "One last chance: Sacrifice themselves and their families, and the human race would live on without them in peace." She waved her hand over the pool once more and it grew still.

Teddy lowered his hands.

"It was a cruel choice," she sighed, "and in the end none save my father leapt from the cliff. None of his brothers would sacrifice their own lives for the sake of all humankind. So it was alone that Remiel and Rachel and their four children jumped into the unknown. We fell for a very long time, longer than the height of the cliff would warrant, anticipating our end the whole way down—but there was no ending, nor slap of earth or water; instead, we landed on the soft back of a winged creature that bore us hence, to Ayda, to the shores of the Voss. We were made to understand that my father's willingness to sacrifice those he held most dear was our salvation. He was forgiven, and Ayda became our home, a place set apart from the rest of the world, where once again the daylights worked together as the Weaver intended.

"Those on the cliff saw only a great frothing of waves and a blinding flash of sun. As the seas calmed and the wind retreated, they congratulated themselves and laughed at their fortune until, one by one, the remaining Watchers were struck down where they stood, their daylights unleashed and their human form turned irreparably to ash. Their children, the Others, were spared, but their daylights grew rigid and unyielding and their powers diminished. Their deceit turned one against another and many of their evil deeds reversed upon them—but not all, sadly. Thus, the history of your world is written by their actions. It is indeed sorrowful."

The room descended into unhappy silence.

"Enough of this talk!" Rysta exclaimed, jumping up and clapping her hands. "I forget you are but children and should not be burdened with the past. Shall we play a game? My attendants are very good at games!" She raised her hands and her bracelets let out a soft, showering trill. Several attendants assembled silently under the canopy. Rysta motioned for a tall, slender woman to step forward.

"Here is my friend Urza. She will assist me." Rysta removed her outer robe, her bracelets, and her necklace and handed them to Urza. "I do not often play this game with strangers, but I think you will enjoy it." She smiled mischievously and proceeded to melt in a quick cascade of water. Teddy gasped. Evelyn shrieked. Knox moved quickly to Urza's side and looked down.

"Pick her up and put her in the pool. She cannot breathe unfettered air for long," said Urza calmly.

Knox bent down and when he stood back up, he held a large rose-scaled fish, gazing at them with a placid blue eye.

"Put her in now, Knox." Urza gestured toward the pool.

Knox released the fish and it disappeared into the depths of the pool.

"Where did she go?" asked Evelyn, searching the surface with her eyes.

The fish leapt out of the pool with a loud *swoosh,* trailing a column of foamy water. Tiny glittering shards churned with the froth, diffuse at first and then spinning together in a solid beam of light. In another instant, Rysta stood before them again, her blonde hair streaming down her back, her pale arms folded lightly across her dress. She was panting with the exertion of the transformation and collapsed. Urza covered her wet robes with the dry one.

"Thank you, Urza," she said, quickly replacing her necklace and bracelets. When she recovered fully, she sat up and laughed brightly at the children's stupefied faces.

Teddy was almost levitating with excitement. "Can I do that?"

Rysta smiled indulgently at him.

"No, little one. All creatures on Ayda will feel the potency of their daylights, but only a Keeper of a stone may transform, and then only when we are in our own lands, near to our stones. Without the Fifth Stone, it is dangerous even for Keepers to allow their daylights so much free rein. It disturbs the balance and makes us weak."

"But—" Teddy insisted. "I want to be a dolphin!" He was hopping up and down, "No, I want to be a turtle! Make me a turtle!"

Chase grabbed Teddy's shoulder. "Shhh," he chided him.

Rysta laughed again. "No, no, let him be. It gladdens my heart to hear him. I am not often with children."

"Don't you have any kidth?" Teddy asked.

Rysta's full-lipped mouth tightened. She shook her head.

"Keepers are solitary; we are not meant to marry or mate. Our vow is to our stone of power and to those to whom it calls."

Evelyn frowned. Rysta leaned over and touched her brow, her fingers sweeping across the skin like mist.

"Do not trouble your heart. One can only miss what one has known. In Metria, we wish only for the return of Ayda as it once was, in the beginning, before the coming of Dankar and the loss of the Fifth Stone. It is this hope that we carry in our hearts."

"Rysta," Chase asked, thoughtfully, "you said it was only *your* family who were brought to Ayda?"

She nodded.

"But you also said Dankar was your cousin, so he must be an Other, too, right? One of the ones left behind?"

Rysta looked at him keenly. "Yes, Chase, you are perceptive. He is one of the original Others, son to my father's brother. Many like him lived on in the world beyond the fog. However, many generatons have passed since then. Their lines are scattered."

"But not Dankar's?"

"No, Dankar came here long ago, even by Ayda's reckoning."

"If he didn't come with you, then how did he get here?"

Rysta turned away abruptly, unaware that at her feet the pool had conjured an image of a young man peering through a telescope over the prow of a low-slung wooden ship. He had the look of someone who had spent his days at sea, but his gray eyes were wide with anticipation, as if whatever vista that lay in the field of his telescope was the fulfillment of a dream.

"Who is *that?*" demanded Evelyn, taken aback by the sudden vision. "Is that Dankar?"

Rysta looked into the pool. When she saw the man, her eyes hardened; the pool began to boil once more, erasing the image.

"He is of no concern to you," she said, raising her voice. Her hair lay flat and streaming against her robes and her necklace shone dully in the dim light. She was, in an instant, something entirely other, something cold and bloodless and removed, as ghostly as the shadows of the Watchers that had climbed from her pool. A lonely, high-pitched chord seemed to rise up from the water, gaining pitch and vibration until it filled the enclosure. Misery washed over the children, sudden and deep, as if a great hole had opened inside them and swallowed every hope they had ever had. The chord screeched louder.

"Stop!" cried Evelyn, plugging her fingers into her ears. "*Please!*"

Teddy began to scream. Chase and Knox sprang up in alarm.

The chord faded. Rysta's cold voice lingered over it.

"The pool sings of my loss," she lamented. "As do the tides and the currents and the streams that search endlessly for its resolution. The rivers bleed with it, and the rain cries it to every corner of the Earth. You outliers think you have met with great misfortune—but not until you have lived with loss as long as I have will you know it for what it truly is. Go now and consider all that I have told you. If you are to be at home on Ayda, you must accustom yourself to grief."

Chapter 23

THE DWELLINGS

Louis kept his promise and returned at sunrise the next day. He wore a scowl but his manner was kind.

"Let's go. Dankar wants to see you." He disappeared for a moment and came back with a long, white cotton tunic, leather sandals, and a piece of orange fabric.

"Put these on—leave the rest." He turned on his heel and descended the small ledge to wait for her.

Frankie did as she was told, carefully folding her Melorian pants and poncho in a neat pile and pulling the thin tunic over her head. It felt delightfully cool. She wrapped the orange fabric around her head, tucking in any loose strands of hair, and tied the ends in a tight knot at the nape of her neck. She then removed her—now well-worn—pink Converse sneakers and laid them on top of the pile of discarded clothes. She put on the sandals and wiggled her free toes, then stretched her arms up and yawned, feeling remarkably happy considering the circumstances. Glancing over the last remnants of her life in Melor, Frankie felt a pang for Evelyn, Calla, and Mara. She was sad to part with the clothing she had worn for so long, but she had to admit, these new clothes were far more comfortable in the heat. She left the cave to join Louis at the foot of the bridge, where he was flanked by two tall, saddled camels.

Frankie pointed to them and laughed. "Are we riding those?"

"Of course," Louis replied easily. "I'm glad to get you out of that Melorian sweatsuit—you smelled like a cow."

With an easy swoop, he picked her up and placed her atop the wooden saddle fastened just behind the camel's hump. The camel's back was broad, so her skinny legs stuck out almost straight from beneath her tunic. She grabbed the semicircular handle to steady herself. The camel arched its neck and bared its teeth, but it suffered her weight without further complaint. Louis swung up gracefully onto the other camel. He nudged its ear with a small reed. It raised its head and lurched forward in a long, loping stride. Frankie's camel followed behind on its own accord.

"I'm afraid your breakfast will have to wait until we reach the Dwellings," he called to her. "It's an hour's ride from here."

Frankie shrugged. Who cared about breakfast when she was riding a camel? She wished Evelyn or her grandmother could see her now! A funny feeling stabbed at her with the thought of her grandmother, but she ignored it and leaned over the handle to sniff the camel's flank. It smelled like mud and hay. The ground below seemed very far away. She clung on tightly and settled her body into the saddle, swaying back and forth with the camel's rhythmic stride. The air felt clean and dry on her skin. Exor wasn't half as bad as she'd expected. Dusty and flat, yes, but not ugly. On the horizon, large domes of sand-colored rock resembling mudcastles broke the otherwise empty plain. If Frankie turned her head to the right, she could just make out the jagged outline of a mountain ridge and what might be ice glinting in the sunlight.

Louis veered toward the cluster of rock humps, urging his camel into a jog. Frankie's followed instinctively. Her weight slipped back and accustomed itself to the new side-to-side movement of the camel's run. The saddle was reasonably comfortable, and she lost any fear of falling and began enjoying the ride, whooping in excitement as the camel's hooves pounded the ground. In minutes, they were in the shadow between the rock pilings. This close up, Frankie could see striations of color and glitter in the rock. The camels slowed.

Louis stopped at the far edge of the rock pilings and indicated that she should do the same. They had reached the edge of the plateau, and below them was a wide canyon and, at the bottom of it, a small, running stream. Frankie's eyes automatically skipped to the patches of green and verdant earth along the banks of the stream—so striking after the dullness of the Broomwash.

"It's beautiful," she breathed.

"It used to be, before the river dried up, or so I'm told," said Louis.

"Is this the Dwellings?" she asked.

"The outskirts." He looked out over the flat plain. "In the days before the fog, there was a big river here. Look—there—you can just see the outline of what it used to be." Louis pointed across to the broad, stepped wall they were standing on, showing her how it descended into the valley and rose again on the opposite side.

Frankie studied the canyon walls and the shallow stream that snaked through the wide sandbed at the bottom of the valley. It didn't seem possible that this trickle of water could ever have been a river swollen to such a height. Louis watched her closely.

"The water comes from the mountains, from Varuna." He gestured to the east. "It once flowed from there all the way through Exor, to the sea." He swept his hand across the plateau in the opposite direction. His voice went hollow and flat. Frankie followed his gaze.

"I'm sorry," she said, not knowing what else to say.

Louis jerked his head around. "It is not for you to be sorry. But perhaps you may understand why the Exorians are at war. It is a hard thing to be denied such a necessity as water." He touched the ear of his camel again with the reed. "Follow me."

The camels plodded down into the valley via a series of switchbacks cut in the canyon wall. Frankie's camel visibly perked up when it smelled the grass growing along the shores of the stream. Louis dismounted and allowed the camels to rest, and eat and drink.

When the camels were finished, they remounted and splashed through the trickling stream, then climbed out of the canyon on the opposite side. The path was smooth and well-traveled. Louis pointed past the far wall of the canyon toward low, dust-colored hills shimmering in the rising heat of the plain, and beyond them, spire-like rock formations that rose high into the sky.

"The Dwellings. The road passes through there," he said, with a nod.

Frankie saw a long dirt road wind its way directly toward the hills. It was lined by small stone pyramids on both sides and dead-ended into thin air at the lip of the canyon wall. Its terminus was flanked by two large stone pillars.

"What are those?" she asked, indicating the pyramids.

"They're lit when Dankar leaves the Dwellings to come to the canyon's edge. It does not happen often."

Frankie tried to envision such a spectacle and wanted to ask why anyone would build a road that led nowhere, but the mention of Dankar made her stomach hurt.

"What does Dankar look like?" she said, trying not to sound worried. "Like you?" she asked hopefully.

"Are you asking if he is an Exorian warrior?"

Frankie swallowed. Her throat was parched. "Why do they look like that anyway?"

Louis slowed his camel to walk beside her. "You mean, their skin?"

Frankie nodded her head. "And their eyes. They're so . . . empty." She patted the hump of her camel with her free hand. "What happened to them?"

"To become a soldier of Dankar, one must face many trials and undergo great pain and sacrifice. It is an honor. The scales on a warror's skin are a sign of his journey—the thicker the skin, the greater the warrior." Louis put his hand to his chest, tracing the outline of a design. "I intend to join them."

"What?" she cried. Her camel's ears twitched; it growled and spat.

Louis looked at her sideways. "Warriors are revered in Exor. All male children aspire to the honor."

"What about the girls?"

"They are appointed other tasks. No one is idle in Exor."

"What about the scribes?"

Louis gave her a funny look. "There is no valor in becoming a scribe. Scribes are men who could not tolerate the initiation into warriorhood. Their daylights are too"—he groped for a word—"unstable."

"What do you have to do to become a warrior?" She couldn't imagine what someone might have to go through to become one of those monsters.

Louis gave her a small smile. "What I am told. *You* are helping me." He tickled his camel's ear, triggering a swift jog. "Bringing you to Dankar was an important test."

Frankie swayed helplessly back and forth on her saddle, shocked; the road below passed too quickly under the camel's long strides. In minutes it took them into a wide courtyard surrounded by thick, misshapen mud walls. Several layers of broad stone steps led to a columned pavilion and the entrance to a palatial building dug into the sand-colored hillside. Frankie felt a chill despite the heat and gripped the pommel of her saddle tightly.

Louis maneuvered his camel back to stand beside her. He nodded at the impressive facade.

"Home," he said, his expression unreadable.

Frankie stared at him, stiff with fear.

He swung off his camel and lifted his arms to help her down.

"C'mon, I won't bite."

She swung one leg over and dropped into his arms. She wrapped her little legs around his middle and clung to him, like a baby being carried.

Louis felt the weight of the small girl in his arms and instinctively tightened his grip. "Don't worry, Frankie," he mumbled. "It's not so bad here once you get used to it."

"How long does that take?"

"Not long," he said evasively, and set her down.

He led the way up the masses of steps, through the columned pavilion and into the palace. They passed through an archway and into an inner courtyard, verdant and warm, with a trickling fountain at its center. The courtyard was walled on all four sides, with narrow, arched windows and wood balustrades looking down from several stories. At each end pointed archways indicated halls that led in opposing directions.

"Wait here," Louis ordered.

"Okay," she said, her eyes climbing the walls of the courtyard nervously, trying to peer through the shade of the archways. For all she knew, Dankar could be watching her right now.

"Louis!" she called out after him.

There was no answer, except for the sound of the fountain. A spongy carpet of small, green tufts grew up between the flat tiles under her feet.

Large trees with heart-shaped leaves and yellow and orange fruit grew in the corners. She thought one tree might be a lemon tree, but the fruits were too large. The water splashing into the basin of the fountain made her realize how thirsty she was. She kneeled before it and held out her cupped hands to catch some to drink.

"There is nothing like cool water when one has traveled a great distance," said a low, silky voice behind her.

Frankie whirled around to face the speaker. A white-robed figure stood next to Louis in one of the archways. He was at least a head taller than Louis and—the most appropriate word Frankie could think of—handsome. Very handsome. His smooth skin glowed in shades of caramel and red as though it had absorbed the sunburnt colors of the Exorian desert. Gold bracelets lined his upper arms and a narrow gold wire encircled his closely shorn head. He crossed the courtyard toward her and she felt a sudden warmth spread across the distance between them, as if the sun were emerging from a cloud. The feeling was so pleasant that she was surprised to find small, hard eyes looking down at her. A trickle of fear, like ice, went down her spine.

"The boy tells me you have been teaching him French," the man said.

"I did, a little. Is that . . . umm . . . allowed?" she mumbled, looking to Louis for reassurance.

The man attempted a smile, baring teeth that were alarmingly white. "Of course; we are always interested in learning new things, shut off as we are—here." He gestured vaguely around the courtyard. "You must speak French to me, too, child; it has been such a long time since I have heard it." He pressed his lips into a semblance of a smile again. "Hmm, let me think now, what is that word . . . the French word . . ." He tapped a long, elegant finger at his temple. "Ah yes, *amie*. That is it, isn't it? *Friend?* You will be my *amie*, I think? And I will be yours. Ah—what a joy to recall another language. It has been too long." Again, he waved his hand dismissively. "It is quite boring here. Everyone says things the same way. Not like"—he shot a pointed look at Frankie—"where you are from."

Frankie shuddered. She was confused. Everything on the surface of this man, with the exception of his eyes, seemed friendly and welcoming, but it felt all wrong. As if he could sense her fear, the man took a few steps away from her, walking back toward Louis; his expression was indistinct in the glare of the open courtyard. His voice, however, continued to seep toward her.

"Now that we are friends, you must tell me your name and I will tell you mine."

Frankie glanced over at Louis again. He nodded for her to answer.

"My name is Frances Martine Boudreaux, but people call me Frankie," she whispered, feeling as if she were about to cry. Her emotions were racketing around her chest, and she did not know which was the right one.

"Frankie? That is a harsh name for a pretty girl such as you—such a delightful girl. And very brave, too, from what I hear. No, *amie,* you need a name that suits you better. As you have become accustomed to yours, I guess I shall call you Frances." The soft syllables of her name slipped through his lips. He came closer again and knelt before her so that their eyes were level. "You know, Frances, I have no children of my own. Your escort, the one you call Louis, has come to look upon me as a sort of uncle, and I hope that someday you, too, will do the same. I have long desired a daughter. A girl of talent and intelligence—and curiosity." The man laid his hand on Frankie's head. "A girl I can trust with my secrets."

The man's praise was burning away at her misgivings. Warmth from his hand spread across her scalp, making its way down the back of her head and across her shoulders. His gold bangles sent shards of light across the courtyard. He held her gaze a moment longer and said quietly, "Frances, I am he whom they call Dankar, Lord of Exor and the Exorian people."

Frankie took a step back, though it was not really a surprise.

Dankar's ears twitched. "I can see that my reputation precedes me. But surely someone as bright as you must know that a person may be considered one way by his enemies and quite another by his friends." He extended his hand. "And I am your friend, Frances, even if you are not mine. I ask you only one thing: Do not judge me by what others have told you. I ask you to stay here in Exor and then judge for yourself—"

"Am I a prisoner?" Frankie interrupted.

A flash of impatience crossed Dankar's gleaming brow, but he regained his composure quickly.

"Prisoner? No, no. Think of yourself as my guest—my most valued guest. It is my hope that once you become accustomed to our ways, you will be happy to accept Exor as your home . . . as . . ." He paused, searching, then smiled, "as, ah, *Louis* has done."

Frankie threw another searching look at Louis, who remained impassively at his post. She had the sensation that a small battle was being waged here, one that she was losing, and yet it did not feel terrible to lose. It felt easy, like changing into a new set of clothes.

Dankar rose to his feet, smiling a peculiar, satisfied half-smile, as if some question had been answered. He dislodged one of the gold bangles from his bicep and slipped it on Frankie's small wrist. It was very loose, but as he slipped it up her arm, the band tightened until it stuck. Frankie's fear and doubt evaporated completely. Instead, she was filled with a warm, relaxing—almost sleepy—delight, like a cat who discovers a patch of sun to rest in.

"A token of my enduring friendship, Frances. Now—won't you join me for breakfast?" Despite the encouraging sensation of the bracelet, Frankie still hesitated.

"What about my sister—and the others?" she asked, feeling slightly dizzy.

Dankar sighed and raised his hands with the palms up, radiant.

"All of this fighting is just a misunderstanding. You know that, don't you? Rothermel and I are *family*. Do you not fight with your sister on occasion? Such is the way in families. There are disagreements."

"You're related to Rothermel?"

Dankar nodded. Beams of hot light bounced off his crown.

"Then why do you fight with the Melorians? Why did you send all those warriors to attack them?"

Dankar patted her shoulder. "Do not trouble yourself with ancient history, dearest, or misunderstandings between adults."

Frankie didn't know what to say. Now that she was here with Dankar, he didn't seem nearly as frightening as she'd imagined he would be. He seemed to care about her—and Louis.

Dankar patted her again, on the head, and led her past where Louis stood in the shade of an archway. He stopped.

"Join us."

Louis bowed his head. "Uncle, I am always eager to do your bidding, but—the initiation—I have been wait—" He was cut off.

"You have performed well. Frances is here, unharmed. You will be rewarded with the honor you so desire. Your initiation shall begin tonight. Should you succeed, we will discuss your wish to enter warrior training."

Frankie stopped in her tracks. She tore her hand away from Dankar's and threw herself at Louis.

"Don't do it! Please don't do it!" she begged.

Strong hands pinched her shoulders and pulled her away.

"Frances, you are new to Exor, but soon enough you will come to see the honor of serving in my house. Your companion has achieved much; should he not be rewarded?"

Frankie searched Louis's face for some sign of understanding. His features were regular and pleasing—and now familiar.

"This is something I *want,* Frankie," he said. "I have wanted it for a long time."

"Why? Why can't you just stay the way you are?"

Louis looked past her. "It's hard to explain; let's just say it's a necessary step."

"But Louis . . . won't it hurt?" She trembled just thinking about what a person would have to do to look like that.

Dankar firmly inserted Frankie's hand back into his and resumed his gait. "Do you think, dear one, that I would allow someone so close to me—someone I have raised since boyhood—to risk his life for no reason? Your companion has long sought this honor. If he completes the warrior training, Louis will be the first of his kind to do so. It will be a great accomplishment! A sign of wondrous things to come." He patted Frankie's arm, leaving a rosy glow where he touched her skin.

She shook her head, not understanding.

Dankar looked quizzically at Louis and then back at Frankie.

"Has he not told you?"

"Told me what?"

Dankar chuckled as if just let in on a highly entertaining joke.

"Louis is one of *you*—an outlier—cast on the shores of Exor some years ago. We three have this ill fortune in common—and one other thing." Dankar's lips parted hungrily, baring his teeth.

"We all want to go back."

Chapter 24

THE FOG OF FORGETTING

In Metria, time unfolded like a long, luxurious dream. Nothing much was expected of Chase, Evelyn, Knox, and Teddy, except that they bathe regularly, eat their meals, and not ask too many questions. The older children had not seen Rysta again since the first night, though Teddy was often called to her side.

"Maybe he can find out where our weapons are," griped Knox. He, Chase, and Evelyn sat at the low table in the gathering room, where they were eating breakfast.

"Have you noticed something different about Teddy since he's been spending so much time with Rysta?" asked Chase, slathering a delicious-smelling sweet bun with butter.

Knox shrugged. "Not really." He peeled a banana and ate half in one bite.

"His lisp is better—it's almost gone. Don't you think that's weird?"

Knox took another bite and chewed and swallowed before answering.

"You mean weirder than landing on a mysterious island in the fog and not being able to leave? Or being hunted by some half-human fire god and his army of demons? Or wait—" He grinned. "How about weirder than hanging out with a guy who was on a ship that sank in a war over two hundred years ago? Like, weirder than that?"

"You know what I mean," said Chase.

"He's probably just outgrowing it."

Chase turned to Evelyn. "What do you think?"

"I think it's both," said Evelyn. "Remember what Seaborne told us? The daylights are stronger on Ayda. Maybe that means that people grow faster and get stronger and other stuff goes away, like lisps and, maybe, other things." She gave him a sideways glance. "Like asthma."

"But if you are perfect like me," Knox cut in, "you just get even more perfect."

Chase rolled his eyes. Evelyn chucked a pillow at him. The morning wore on, as it had every day since they'd arrived in Metria.

✝   ✝   ✝

Knox began to take long excursions into the bay to pass the time. Chase befriended Hesam, the captain of the ship they had met on their first day in Metria. She showed him several intricate, hand-drawn maps of Ayda and the Hestredes, and taught him basic navigation. Evelyn discovered that the anonymity of her Metrian clothes made it easy for her to mingle undetected with Rysta's people and listen in on their conversations. She pieced together much of what she, Chase, Knox, and Teddy had already guessed: They would soon be taken to the city of Metria and kept there for their safety. Once grown, they would be free to settle wherever their daylights dictated. No one could say exactly when that would be; the best Evelyn could make out was that a child in Metria was considered grown when he or she heard the call of their own daylights.

Evelyn wondered if the daylights actually had a sound, or if the call was more like a thought that slowly grew from an idea to a certainty. Whatever it was, she was sure it hadn't happened to her yet. And she was also sure that she had no intention of going anywhere until she had some news of Frankie. Several more days passed pleasantly enough, matched by an equal and growing sense of restlessness that was contagious. Soon this feeling—and their missing weapons—was the only thing Evelyn, Knox, and Chase could talk about.

"I can't stay here another day without doing *something* to find Frankie!" said Evelyn, thoroughly exasperated.

She, Chase, and Knox were perched on top of the cavern's ledge, overlooking the bay that led out to the river. As usual, Teddy was off with Rysta.

"It's comfortable and nice and all, but . . . at this rate we're *never* going to find her."

"I think that's the point," mumbled Chase. He lay facedown on the sand-colored stone, the backs of his calves pink from the sun.

"What d'you mean?" demanded Evelyn.

"It's pretty clear we've been sent here to be kept out of the way. Rysta's going to take us to the city where she can keep an eye on us and Dankar can't possibly reach us."

Evelyn opened and shut her mouth, trying to frame what she wanted to say. She made a sour face. "Does she think I'm just going to forget Frankie? Does she think I'm stupid?" She looked pointedly at Knox for backup. He was wiggling a small pink stone out of the ledge with the toe of his bare foot.

Chase rolled over lazily and shielded his eyes so he could look up at Evelyn.

"She thinks we're kids—which we are—and that you'll get used to it eventually. You heard what she said. She hasn't seen her brother or sister in—who knows around here? Hundreds, thousands of years?"

"Well, then, she doesn't know me very well. I'm not going to get used to it or sit around waiting for some stone to come back before I see my sister again. We need to *do* something."

Knox looked up, his interest piqued. "What kind of something?"

"Well, are we going to go with Rysta like good little boys and girls, or are we going to help Frankie?"

Chase pretended to yawn. He'd been afraid of this since Hesam had shown him a map of Ayda. He began to sketch the island into the dust of the ledge; its outline shaped like an elongated heart. Metria was at the far south. Exor lay in the opposite direction, north and west, and between the two lay a vast lake and an unknown number of towering mountains, not to mention Exorian warriors. It wasn't that he didn't *want* to help Frankie; he did. But how? She was long gone by now, miles and miles away—so he said nothing.

Evelyn slapped her arms to her sides in frustration and glared at them. "*Well?*"

Knox picked up the loosened pebble and rolled it between his fingertips. "I'd help if I knew what to do. I mean, we don't know where she is, where our weapons are—it just seems kind of hopeless. Besides, Rothermel was pretty clear about doing what Rysta says."

"Rothermel was pretty clear," Evelyn taunted. "That's great. That's just great. Now that you believe all this stuff, you think he's some kind of god or something. How do you know they're not all in on it! They don't trust us, Knox, not even your precious Rothermel. We're prisoners here as much as Frankie is . . . wherever she is! *If* she even is," shouted Evelyn. She clenched her fists and jammed them under her armpits. "This is my sister we're talking about! My *sister*. The only family I have left! Remember?"

"Okay, okay, calm down," said Chase. "You're right." He stood up and brushed the sand off his chest. "Let's swim and then find Teddy. Maybe he can talk Rysta into seeing us again."

Teddy's help wasn't necessary. When Evelyn and the boys returned to their rooms, there was a message from Rysta summoning them to join her that evening at her enclosure by the pool. This time, they rowed themselves, no longer needing guides to ferry them about. She was just as they had first seen her: lovely and pale, clad in purple and silver, her hair glittering with jewels. The necklace with the stone lay shining openly on her breast. She greeted them warmly and bid them to join her by the pool, which lay still and calm, reflecting only the flickering candlelight.

"I regret our last parting," she said simply, and bid Evelyn to sit near her.

Teddy sat on her other side, as if it were the most natural place for him to be. Evelyn's eyes fell on the necklace. Rysta noticed and gathered the stone pendant in her fingers, caressing it as she spoke.

"I am not your enemy, children. You should know this, for you have already suffered at the hands of the real enemy."

"Rysta," Evelyn began, wasting no time, "I need to find my sister. Will you help?"

Rysta sighed. "If it were in my power to return your sister to you, I would do so. Alas, I can only see that you remain safe within my own lands. It is not for me to command my people to wage war against Dankar when so many could perish."

Evelyn looked crestfallen.

"Do not underestimate Dankar, child. He possesses craft and patience and something nearly as powerful as a stone of power: hatred. Dankar cares little for the lives of his people; he expends them carelessly, as a tree drops its leaves."

"All the more reason to get my sister away from him!" cried Evelyn.

"Do not think me hard. I know your suffering. Remember, Dankar killed my brother."

Evelyn had forgotten. She buried her head deep in her hands.

"There's something I don't understand," said Chase, eyeing Rysta nervously. "I don't mean any disrespect, but if you—or, umm, your kind—are half-human, then can't Dankar be killed? Why don't you and Rothermel and Ratha get together and take the stone of Exor back? It would be three against one, right?"

Rysta leaned back and contemplated him for a moment, with an odd, soft look, as if he reminded her of someone.

"As one who has endured the Great Battle and the ages hence, I agree with my brother's counsel: To venture open warfare without knowledge of the Fifth Stone is to court a doom that could envelop more than just Ayda."

"So you would rather just—*hide?*" interrupted Knox, not able to contain his disbelief.

Rysta's mouth tightened. "War would seem the obvious thing to one whose sight comes from beyond the fog, but tell me, Knox—if my siblings and I are the only beings able to restrain Dankar, what would happen to the world should one—or all—of us lose? How many of our people would suffer the fate of the Exorians should Dankar possess another stone? And how many of yours, should Dankar use our stones to penetrate the fog? It is an easy thing to demand war when one does not have to sacrifice oneself or one's loved ones to win it." She shook her head. "No. The risk is too great. Until the return of the Fifth Stone, my siblings and I will fight Dankar the way we have always done—by restricting him to his own lands and fighting him on ours should he dare trespass. It is Ayda's burden, and we shall bear it."

"You fought for Seaborne," said Evelyn. "Why won't you do the same for my sister?"

"It was chance that favored Seaborne, and the tide that brought him to my lands, where I could protect him. It is not for me to direct the destiny of the souls who have washed ashore elsewhere. My powers are not so great."

Silence descended with the finality of her words.

Chase stirred, struck by what she had just said. "You said *souls,* plural. How many have there been, besides us?"

"I am certain only of yourselves and Seaborne; however, there was a time, before the fog, when many outliers visited our shores."

"You mean they could come and go?"

"It was long ago, before the Great Battle, when your kind traveled by sea. If by chance a ship landed on Ayda's shores, all aboard were given a choice. They were welcome to stay or free to go, but should they choose to leave, they would never be able to return. No instrument, map, or star would guide them. It was my father's doing."

"Why? I don't get it," said Knox.

"I do," said Chase. "Rysta's father knew what would happen if the Others found out about Ayda—and the Fifth Stone. The place would be wrecked." He looked into the shadows beyond the candlelight, trying to map out what must have happened next, because, obviously, somebody—namely Dankar—*had* found out.

"Many in Ayda are kin to those who remained," Rysta explained. "But those who returned to their homes went back to tell tales of a wondrous land, for there was no fog of forgetting then to erase their memories. They described animals that could understand their thoughts, plentiful food and drink, and a land where people did not wither or sicken. Ayda grew in their imaginations and, as so often happens with memory, they bestowed upon it ever-fairer descriptions. Ayda drifted into legend and story, and many sought her without success. Soon enough, there were few in your lands who paid attention to the ravings of sailors. Talk of this paradise was thought to be a kind of madness, a delusion brought on by too many nights at sea." Rysta's voice lowered.

"But not all stopped listening. There was one in particular who heard these tales often enough through the ages for them to take hold of his thoughts until they could not be unthought. His desire to find and possess the powers that lay in Ayda grew to be a torment to him."

"Dankar," Knox said, with a grimace.

Rysta nodded again. "Yes, Dankar. Once he believed the tales to be true, he began to seek Ayda himself, in earnest, bending whatever skills of his Watcher father that he still possessed. He was clever and patient and—in time—we fell into his trap. His forces beset Ayda armed with brutal instruments unknown to us at that time: swords, maces, lances, and arrows. Many ancients—ancestors to Urza and Tinator, as well as others—fragmented in this first attack, others were cruelly tortured and enslaved, but Dankar could not ferret us all out of our hiding places." She leaned forward, agitated by the memory.

"And we held one important secret that Dankar knew not—at least in the beginning. We had the Fifth Stone; its safety was my father's charge, and foremost in his mind. In Ayda's darkest time, he and my mother traveled high into the mountains of Varuna to hide it." She sighed. "But the fate of the Fifth Stone remains unknown to this day, as does the fate of my father. My mother returned alone from the mountains bearing not the one, but four lesser stones: Exor, Varuna, Melor, and Metria, to which she pledged her children. A great carpet of fog grew up around our shores and Ayda disappeared entirely from the world. Forgotten.

"No longer could strangers journey to our shores as they once had. And the few who did," she nodded to the children, "had no choice in their fate. Ayda became a world unto itself, a world at war, dreaming of another age, and those who pierced the fog to stray upon her shores were destined to remain—including Dankar. For you must understand: The fog is intended to keep him *in* as much as it keeps the rest of the world out." Rysta paused to let this sink in.

"Protected by our stones, my siblings and I gathered what remained of our people to the four corners of Ayda and defended our lands. In this way, by division, my parents hoped to keep the full power of the daylights from falling into Dankar's hands."

"So what happened to the Fifth Stone then?" asked Knox. "Did your father have to break it to make the other stones?"

Rysta looked deeply into her pool. "I do not believe that the Fifth Stone was destroyed in the making of the four, but it—and my father—were never seen on Ayda again."

"What happened to your mother?" whispered Evelyn.

Rysta's voice wavered. "My mother's daylights could not be separated from the Fifth Stone. They lingered for a while, and then, one day, she, too, was gone." She gazed meaningfully at Evelyn.

"So you see, I know much of your despair—for it is also mine. For over five hundred of your years I have lived apart from those I love, hoping beyond reason for some sign of the Fifth Stone and reunion with what is left of my family. I admit, I am weary of the wait—though it is now ours to share." She shifted Teddy off her lap, whispered something in his ear, and rose to leave.

"You should know one last thing," she said, hesitating at the perimeter of the enclosure. "When the Watchers broke their vow, a long age of suffering was visited upon the Earth by their offspring—but it will not be an eternity. The Fifth Stone was created as a promise to the world. As long as it stays out of the hands of those who would do evil with it, Ayda and the daylights will outlast whatever troubles beset an age. We may suffer, but we will never perish completely."

"But—" cried Knox, "what if it's already in the wrong hands?"

"The Fifth Stone is a formidable power; its misuse or destruction would leave a vacuum no living creature could ignore."

"What does *that* mean?" asked Chase. "Does the world implode or something?"

"Not the world, no. Something—else," Rysta answered, tapping the spot above her heart with her open hand.

Chapter 25

THIEVES

Morning was in full flush when Evelyn and the boys emerged back through the wall of water and rowed across the lagoon to their chambers. No one spoke during the voyage, lost as they were in the interweaving strands of Rysta's story. Finally alone, they luxuriated in the expanse of the gathering room. A breeze blew in through the apertures in the ledge, and every now and then they heard the trill of a bird. No one felt the slightest bit sleepy, though they had been awake through the night. Knox paced the room, rehashing what Rysta had told them.

"What did she say to you, anyway, Tedders?"

Teddy smiled. "She told me where I can see the turtles."

Chase patted Teddy on the back, smiling at Teddy's new ability to say S. "She does seem to like you, Ted."

"That's 'cause I'm special!"

Knox wrapped his arms around his front and turned his back to Teddy, pretending he was locked in a passionate embrace. "Oohh, I am so *special,*" he cooed.

Teddy's face flushed. He was about to take a flying leap onto Knox's back, fists flying, when Evelyn intervened.

"Stop it, Knox. Rothermel said as much to you, so I don't know why you're teasing Teddy—all that stuff about you being a true Melorian or whatever. He didn't say anything like that to Chase or me."

Chase walked over to the window and looked out at the river. "Do you think it's true? I mean, all this stuff about the daylights, and how every living thing has all four kinds, but is guided by one?"

Evelyn shrugged. "Why does it matter? It doesn't get us any closer to finding Frankie."

"You weren't listening closely enough, Ev."

Evelyn shot Chase a look that said she would be highly surprised if she missed something he didn't.

"Rysta told us those stories to warn us *against* going after Frankie! Her own brother died fighting Dankar, and he was a Keeper. Her father sacrificed himself to keep the Fifth Stone away from Dankar. She's trying to get us to understand how bad he really is."

Evelyn gave no reply. The only sound that could be heard in the room was the gentle lap of water against rock from outside the window. It was strangely reminiscent of the sound she had first heard when she woke up that day on the boat, engulfed in fog. As she looked around at her comfortable surroundings, it occurred to her that they had come a very far distance—or possibly nowhere at all.

"It makes no sense," she said finally. "If he's so powerful, why does he need Frankie?"

Knox rapped his knuckles on the table absentmindedly.

"Rothermel already told us why Dankar took Frankie, and Rysta's story just proves it."

Chase rolled his eyes. Evelyn stared.

"What do you mean?" she asked.

"I mean, look at what Dankar did—he killed Ranu to get the stone of Exor, and he's been in a stalemate ever since." Knox shot to his feet and began pacing again, his voice rising, warming to his subject. "We know, so he must know, that he can't beat the other Keepers in a pure game of power—it's always a standoff. Or worse. Three against one. So what does he do? *He changes the odds.* He keeps the other three off balance by taking advantage of their weakness—the fact that they *care:* for Ayda, for each other. From what Rothermel and Rysta told us, Dankar knows Keepers actually have a soft spot for humans, and for human children in particular." Knox tossed his head at Teddy, as if to prove his point was self-evident.

"Dankar is a patient guy—Rysta told us that. We aren't the only outliers to wash up here. He didn't get Seaborne, but he knew from that experience that the fog wasn't totally impenetrable. All he had to do was wait and watch for another opportunity. And time is, like, nothing here. Fast-forward two hundred years and you get us. *Five* of us—pay dirt. He knows we're here, but he decides to let us stay in Melor for a while, let the Melorians get attached to us and us to them, and then—*WHAM!* He attacks! If he gets us, instant bargaining power! It's like Rothermel said: Dankar took Frankie so that one or all of the other Keepers would challenge him to an open fight—a fight he thinks he'll win."

Chase and Evelyn exchanged looks, surprised by Knox's newfound powers of perception.

"I can see how some of that could be true, but Rothermel saw through his plan. He won't engage—and neither will his sisters," argued Chase.

"They might not for just Frankie, but what if he had all of us? What if that was what the raid on the campsite was about?"

"If that's his game plan, how come he's not coming after us?"

Knox shrugged. "Because he can't. The stone of Metria is too powerful. That's why Rothermel sent us here."

"It makes sense." Chase nodded, catching Knox's drift.

Knox cocked his head dramatically, hitting his right ear as if he was trying to clear water out of the left.

"Did I actually hear that? Did I just hear Chase say I'm right?"

"But what does that mean for Frankie?" insisted Evelyn, ignoring Knox.

Chase spoke for him, his thoughts one step ahead of his words. "What does Dankar want more than anything? The Fifth Stone. He knows he's not going to get that—it's gone, possibly forever. So, he has to take everything down a notch and get one of the other stones of power, to even out the sides in order to wage any kind of war. Ratha lives far away in the mountains—too cold and far away for Exorians—and Rysta is too powerful for Dankar to fight head-on, so Dankar settles on Rothermel. He lays siege on the Melorians; their lands are easily reached to the south. He harasses them, sends raiding parties and *tehuantl* to attack them, steals their people, burns their villages—he gives Rothermel no rest. He's trying to wear him down, make him desperate."

"Go on," said Knox, his eyes wide.

"But Rothermel won't bite. Dankar is frustrated. And then, as you said, the odds change. We stumble into Melor through the fog. Spies report us and Dankar sees his chance." Chase winced internally, regretting the spectacle they made of themselves that first day—the foghorn blasts and the fighting on the beach.

Evelyn chewed on her lip. "So you think Dankar wants all of us, not just Frankie?"

"I think he wants any outlier he can get—that's why he attacked the campsite. Only he didn't plan on Rothermel actually being with us." Chase saw in his mind's eye the wall of flames licking the night sky, the hulking Exorians striding through the flames. He remembered the tawny hound that leapt through the wall of flame, clearing the way for the Melorians, and was willing to bet money that it had been Rothermel.

Evelyn yanked on one of her long curls in frustration, as if it would help spur her brain into action. Suddenly, her eyes lit up.

"Listen, Dankar took Frankie as bait, but he really wants a stone of power. We can't give him one, even if we could find one, but we could give him something else. You said he'd take any of us, right?" She looked pointedly at Chase and Knox. "Maybe he would make a trade?"

"Are you thinking we should offer Dankar a deal? One of us for your sister?" asked Chase, taken aback.

"I was *thinking* me, but I guess any of us would do," she said.

Knox's knee bobbed up and down in excitement. His face shone as if some inner light had just been kindled. "It's a great idea, Evelyn! We're older and more prepared. We could get behind enemy lines and help the Melorians, spy for them or something."

"Like baseball cards," said Teddy. "Trade Frankie for Knox!"

"NO!" Chase shouted, agitated. "This is the craziest idea I ever heard! We are not going to swap you or me or Evelyn for Frankie. It does nothing to improve the situation. It's idiotic. We don't even know—" He broke off.

"Know *what,* Chase?" Evelyn squared off with him. "Whether or not my sister is alive? Is that what you were going to say?" She threw him a disgusted look and crossed over to an aperture that faced the river. The water moved silkily beneath her, the morning sun lighting up the shallow ripples on its surface. Suddenly, she smacked her forehead and her eyes sharpened.

"Wait, I have a better idea!" she cried, turning toward them again.

"What?" asked Knox, all ears.

"I don't want to tell you now, I just want you to trust me; okay?"

"Not if it means you doing something stupid," said Chase.

"Like going out on your boat?" snapped Evelyn, her eyes sweeping the room. "This is all your fault, and now you won't do anything to help me fix it! It's well and good for you; you are all sitting right here! I wish Frankie and I had never met you that day on the beach. We were doing just fine without you."

Chase was momentarily stunned speechless, then he started shouting. "I can't believe this! You think this is *my* fault? I'm the one who told you not to go out on the boat in the first place! You sided with Knox. If you want to blame anyone, blame yourself—and *him*." Chase pointed a finger at Knox.

"I knew it! I knew you blamed me!" yelled Knox. "All this time you've been bottling it up, just waiting to throw it in my face." He took a step toward Chase.

"Don't fight!" screeched Teddy, bolting between them. He grabbed Knox around the waist, pinning his brother's arms to his sides. "It's Dankar's fault! He took Frankie."

Chase flung himself listlessly onto a cushion, ignoring Knox. Teddy was right. There was no point in fighting, no point in any of this, really. Their future had already been worked out for them. How come Knox and Evelyn couldn't see it? The five of them were just pieces in a gigantic game that the Keepers had been playing for centuries. It was suicide to go up against Dankar when even the Keepers wouldn't do it.

Evelyn huffed out of the chamber.

Knox ran after her.

"Whatever you're thinking, I'm in," he said.

‡ ‡ ‡

Chase, Knox, and Teddy were digging into dinner when Hesam entered the gathering room. Evelyn had not returned all day.

"Rysta has left to make preparations for your departure to the city," Hesam announced. "Before she left, she told me that she had promised to show the young one where the sea turtles rest. They do not often come this far north up the river—only when they sense unsettled seas. Please, follow me."

Outside the cavern, gold tinged the tops of the trees as the sun descended to the west. By themselves in a skiff following in Hesam's wake, the boys watched the deep purple shadows lengthen across the waters of the bay, disturbed only by the dip and pull of Chase's oar stroke. A flock of low-flying birds skimmed the surface ahead of them.

Teddy was at the bow, bare-chested, his skin tanned a deep brown, his blond hair grown past his shoulders. He looked strong and lean and barely recognizable as their baby brother.

Chase rowed with ease, and they crossed the bay quickly to a small sliver of sand, overgrown with tangled roots from the encroaching jungle. Hesam, already on shore, pointed to large mounds massed at the edge, half-in, half-out of the water. The turtles moved slowly, making it easy to walk between them and touch their mottled shells. Every now and then, one would lumber into the water and disappear.

"That one's as big as our skiff," Knox whistled, pointing to a giant greenish-yellow mound. Hesam nodded appreciatively.

"He is very old. The sea turtles of Metria have lived long on Ayda. They carry much wisdom on their backs," she said.

"Yeah, well now they're carrying Teddy, too." Knox laughed, waving at Teddy, who sat astride a slightly smaller and more-delicate-looking shell.

"Get off of it, Ted!" he yelled, and just in time. Without warning, the whole troop of turtles began to move into the water.

"Maybe we scared them," Chase puzzled, trying to figure out why they would all leave in a swarm.

"I don't think so," Hesam murmured, then pointed. "Look."

A huge, silent boat had entered the mouth of the bay, its square sail the color of the moon. Small individual lights flickered from the deck and the berths below. Though the boat moved at a steady clip under full sail, there was no sound of the rigging and no apparent breeze to fill the sail, nor did the boat leave even the most minor ripple in its wake. It looked like an illusion of a boat—yet it was real. The three boys waded into the bay to try and get a better look. There was no movement on board, but as the boat came about and headed straight for the mouth of the cavern, they spotted a shining figure at the bow.

Rysta.

Hesam smiled. "Your transport to the city has arrived."

When they got back to the cavern, Evelyn met them at the beach. She was in a frenzy.

"We're supposed to leave tomorrow at first light!" she panted. "We have to do something now, or we'll never get the chance."

Chase was happy that they had parted from Hesam at the stern of Rysta's boat. Evelyn was acting a little crazy. He touched her shoulder lightly.

"Ev, we never had a chance."

Evelyn shrugged away from his touch.

"Knox, you said if I thought of something, you'd be in. Are you in?"

Knox grinned at her. "What are you thinking?"

"Don't worry about it," she snapped, and bent down to relaunch the skiff. She settled into the little boat and began to row. "Get some supplies and meet me at the outlet to the river."

The three boys watched as Evelyn rowed out of the cavern and toward Rysta's ship. Knox headed down the tunnel toward the gathering room. Chase interrupted him.

"C'mon, Knox, you can't be serious."

Knox spread a scarf out on the table and began piling up fruit and what remained of their dinner, happy to have a sense of purpose again. Chase put his hand on the scarf. Knox slapped it away.

"Knox!" Chase bellowed.

"What? No one's asking you or Teddy to do anything. I told her I was in, and I'm in. I'm bored of Metria," he said, honestly. "I prefer risking it in Melor."

"Are you *that* stupid?"

"Don't say stupid," chided Teddy. Chase gave him a look of exasperation.

"It's not Melor you have to worry about, Knox. It's Exor! You heard Rothermel and Rysta. All we have to do is make one wrong move and we're toast. Game over!"

Knox stopped what he was doing and looked straight into Chase's eyes. "I'm going with Evelyn. You and Teddy can stay here, but I'm going. You can't stop me."

"I'm going, too," said Teddy.

Knox grinned. "Team Thompson."

"Like hell I can't!" Chase yelled. "You're not doing this again, Knox! This time you'll do what I tell you to do!"

Knox knotted the bundle neatly and hoisted it off the table. He stuffed a few blankets in the crook of his arm. He took a step to the right. Chase mirrored him.

"Sure you want to try that?" Knox asked.

Chase didn't budge.

Knox put down his load. His face wore the same expression as when the Exorians first attacked: grim, determined. Chase tried reasoning with him once more.

"Think for a minute. This is too dangerous."

"Sorry," said Knox, deadly calm.

Chase moved to block him.

Knox shook his head. "*Don't.*"

Chase planted his feet and squared his shoulders.

With a lightning-quick jab, Knox drove a fist into Chase's chest, just below the heart. Chase's lungs exploded. He fell to his knees, unable to breathe.

"*Intent is the greatest weapon of all.* A great man once said that," said Knox, brushing past his older brother. "C'mon, Ted, if you're coming."

"Come with us, Chase," Teddy implored.

Chase couldn't answer, still gasping from having the wind knocked out of him. Teddy gave his brother a sad look and followed Knox out into the tunnel.

It took several long seconds before Chase was able to stand up. He ran without thinking, as fast as he could, so angry he could see nothing but a blinding, white light. When he got to the beach, Knox and Teddy were in a skiff halfway across the lagoon. He waded in behind them. Before he knew it, he was swimming, pulling at the water with vicious strokes.

"Knox, STOP!" Chase cried out.

Stop . . . stop . . . stop echoed in the cavern, sounding weaker and more desperate than he would have liked.

"Knox! I'll do it! I'm in."

I'm in . . . I'm in . . . I'm in, the echo called back at him.

The skiff slowed, allowing Chase to catch up. He climbed into the boat, dripping wet, and hauled his fist back. He punched Knox in the face as hard as he could. Knox grunted, more in surprise than pain, and fell back against the gunwale, almost capsizing them. Chase grabbed the oars and sat down in Knox's place.

"Don't *ever* do that again!" he growled.

Knox stayed silent, huddled against the seat, hiding a grin.

Chase pulled the skiff up into the lee of the peninsula that separated the river and the bay. They waited. The moon rose, leaving a silver trail across the river. He wrung out the apron of his tunic and gazed at the stars. He tried to use Hesam's technique to chart their position and contemplated how soon it would be before he would stoop to speaking to Knox again. He gave his tunic another angry twist. After what seemed like hours, a rhythmic chopping broke the silence. Evelyn was coming toward them, rowing quickly.

Teddy signaled her with a soft Melorian owl hoot. *Hoo-hoo.*

Evelyn pulled alongside their skiff. She, too, was sopping wet.

"I got us something to trade," she panted, clearly pleased to see all three of them. She reached beneath the folds of her wet tunic. Rysta's necklace came tumbling out into her hands, its stone pendant swaying between her fingers.

"You stole it?" Chase gasped in disbelief.

"There's no time to explain now. We have to get moving," she said. Evelyn put her back into the oars and glided swiftly into the mouth of the bay. Her skiff moved rapidly ahead, as if drawn by some unseen current. It would quickly outpace the boys' skiff and their scant supplies if they didn't figure something out. Knox blew a low whistle to catch Evelyn's attention. She slowed and let them come alongside.

"I don't know what's going on; you're moving really fast," Knox said. "We can't keep up."

"Throw me the bowline," she whispered.

Knox threw it to her. She tied it to the stern of her skiff.

"Ted, get in the boat with Evelyn to even out the weight," said Knox.

When Teddy was settled in her boat, Evelyn passed him the necklace. She had tried to put it on before, but it resisted her. It suddenly got too heavy and her arms wouldn't move. Teddy had no problem, however. The necklace slipped easily over his head. Its stone pendant swung at his navel. Evelyn began to row again.

The boats slid in tandem toward the mouth of the bay. The sky above was clear, but the stars seemed small and distant. Except for the occasional drip of water from the oars, there was no sound.

"Chase! Knox!" Teddy called back to his brothers, his head hanging over the gunwale of Evelyn's skiff, the necklace dangling perilously close to the water. He pointed down into the depths. "Look!" The water rolled like oil past the skiff's bow. Chase couldn't see anything. Teddy jabbed his finger downwards again. "See?"

The smallest glimmer of movement caught Chase's eye, a foot or more below the bay's inky surface. The giant silhouette of a turtle, green and shimmering, swam up beside the boat, then surfaced. A wizened face protruded from the mottled shell; its flippers waved lazily just beneath the water, rotating in circles, easily keeping abreast of the skiff. As if called by some unseen command, several mounds of shells rose from the water, surrounding them like small mountains.

"What do you think?" whispered Knox. "Should we turn around?"

Chase hesitated. The skiff hadn't lost any momentum, and the turtles weren't slowing them down. Teddy reached out his hand to touch the turtle nearest his boat. His hand made contact with the top of the large, slippery shell. The stone at the end of the necklace broke the water's surface and then, suddenly, all the turtles submerged.

"Whoa? Where'd they go?" asked Knox.

"Where do you think?" Evelyn called back grimly. "We need to get moving!"

They rowed harder and the two skiffs sped across the river. A breeze picked up as they approached the middle; telltale ripples in the trail of moonlight showed that the current was flowing downstream, opposite of where they wanted to go, but again, it seemed to make little difference to the speed of Evelyn's skiff. They easily gained the river and made swift progress against the current, dragging Chase and Knox's boat behind them.

"Keep thinking you want to go upstream, Ted," called Chase, on a hunch. He could barely feel any resistance against his oars.

"Why?" Teddy yelled back.

"I think the necklace is helping us move—like an engine."

"Or magic."

"Or something." Chase sighed. He peered nervously across the river toward the bay. It didn't seem like they were being followed.

He stopped rowing, letting Evelyn's boat pull them for a minute, and turned around fully. Knox was crouched in the bow. Ahead, Evelyn was rowing hard. Beyond her, he saw Teddy with Rysta's necklace around his neck, a small, dark smudge against the immense, moonlit sky. The gravity of what they'd just done hit him. Like a dream, a vision came to him of an army of Exorians marching toward them, led by a flaming pillar of fire. He groaned inwardly. Even with the necklace, they would be no match for a half-immortal enemy hunting them. They had just handed Dankar the advantage.

Chapter 26

INITIATION

Louis lay in darkness, blindfolded and alone. The initiate's cell was a shallow indentation cut high in one of the rock spires that towered above the Dwellings, facing West. The ledge he was on was just wide enough to stretch out on and no more: One careless move would launch him several hundred feet down onto the desert basin below. He scratched cautiously at the sweaty blindfold that stuck to his face and resisted the urge to remove it. The scribe who brought him here had said only one thing: *The heart shares its secrets in the dark.*

He tried to lie quietly to preserve his body water for as long as possible. There had been no indication of how long he might be out here. His other senses had grown more keen to compensate for his lack of sight, and he was aware of the slightest shift in the air. If pressed, he could describe in detail every pebble that was sticking to his back. But there was no one to tell such things to and no one to guide him. All he knew for certain was that if he survived, there were only two possible places for him to go: to the arena to begin warrior training, or to the cliff encampments to become a scribe. The immediate goal was to survive. He thought of the countless others before him who had endured this test—and of those who didn't. What had happened to them? Did they give up and roll off the ledge to their deaths? How tempted might he be to do the same before the end? He licked his cracked lips and tried to ignore the growing hunger pains in his belly. As an outlier his fate was all the more uncertain; his daylights were unpredictable. Not even Dankar could foresee the outcome.

Louis tried to focus his attention by reviewing every detail of his trip back from Melor. An image came to him, unbidden, of Frankie riding a camel with her legs sticking straight out. He laughed out loud, breaking the tomblike silence. His throat ached with thirst. He stopped swallowing to collect saliva in a pool in his mouth, then let it trickle slowly down the back of his throat to ease the pain. He drifted in and out of sleep, growing more and more unsure of whether he was awake or asleep. Memories spun in his head as vividly as if he were seeing them with open, waking eyes, but they made no sense. One moment he was standing in the courtyard, watching Dankar with Frankie. The next, he and Frankie were walking together under the green canopy of the Melorian forest. She was singing.

Frère Jacques, Frère Jacques
Dormez-vous? Dormez-vous?
Sonnez-les-matines, Sonnez les matines
din-dan-don

Real bells tolled loudly as the song ended.

I must be dreaming, Louis thought to himself. He tried to wake up, but he was stuck in the dream. The tone of the bells deepened and stretched until they became the muted blast of a horn. He recognized the sound from somewhere. *Where was it?* He struggled to remember, the answer tantalizingly close, but couldn't.

A chill swept over him—unfamiliar, but welcome. The dappled light of the forest faded into a filmy gray, as if he were standing inside of a cloud. The horn bleated, persistent and mournful. Then, the ground shifted beneath him and began to sway. Above him, a sheet of fabric flapped aimlessly, making sharp cracking noises. A spray of water slapped his face. The cloud crowded in. A steady pounding sound took the place of the horn, and it felt like waves were tugging at his clothing. He felt their wet weight on his skin. Louis struggled to his knees, retching. A voice from somewhere in the fog called out to him. He turned in its direction. Frankie stood there, almost within arm's reach, her nut-brown eyes staring into his.

"You left me!" she said accusingly, pointing at him.

Louis tried to reply, but his throat was too raw to speak. The fog fell like a curtain over Frankie, obscuring her from his view. When it lifted again, a different little girl stood there pointing at him. This one had blonde pigtails and wore a yellow T-shirt. Her eyes were the color of the ocean. A searing pain erupted in Louis's head.

"You left me!" she said, just like Frankie.

The pain intensified. The sound of the surf crashed loudly in his ears. "*You left me!*" the girl in pigtails shouted. Her face crumpled into tears.

The pain in Louis's head pulsed, strobe-like, and shattered in an agonizing spasm that evaporated the fog and the little girl. Other fragments of memory came back to him, slowly at first, and then in a rushing stream: a house by the sea, a sailboat, a woman handing him a sweater. Then, from far away, he saw the girl in the pigtails waving to him from a beach.

"Grace," he moaned, not caring anymore what might happen to him. "I'm here! I'm right here!"

✢   ✢   ✢

Frankie stirred, jarred out of sleep by a sound. She opened her eyes and listened, but the sound didn't repeat. Silver-purple moonlight shone into her bedroom through the open window and lit on the bed, stool, and broom that were the room's only furnishings. She crossed over to the window and looked out, as she did almost every night. In the near distance she could make out the silhouettes of the pit-houses: mud-daubed huts where the women and children of Exor lived. Beyond them, dark shadows holding torches moved silently along the shoulders and steppes of the cliff. By day, Exor was a silent and seemingly abandoned place, but at night it came alive. The scent of cooking hung in the air, and people traveled back and forth, attending to their work in the comfort of the cooler night air.

Frankie spent hours watching the shadows roam the periphery of her vision, wondering if any of them were Louis. She hadn't seen him since the first day here, when he had brought her to this room. She tried to keep him from leaving, but he was impatient. He wanted to begin his initiation.

"I have to prepare," he told her, prowling the room and scowling at her like the first time she'd seen him. "Soon we'll know if I have the strength to become a warrior."

"I hope not," she said to him, pouting.

Louis sighed and knelt in front of her and looked her in the eye. "If I survive but am too weak to undergo the training, I will have to become a scribe—a personal attendant and guard of Dankar. Don't wish that fate on me, Frankie, please."

"Why not? Then you could come back and be with me."

"No," he replied, shaking his head. "No matter what happens, I will not live here again."

This made her cry. She knew it was true.

"I'm never going to see you again, am I?"

"No, but I may see you from time to time—from afar."

"But I won't recognize you if you're one of *them*."

He patted her shoulder and—this one time—didn't tell her not to cry. Then, he stood up to say good-bye.

"We have traveled the same path for many miles, Frankie, but our time together has ended, as all things must end. Be brave. Do not anger Dankar by being disobedient or unhappy in his presence. Do as he says and things will go well for you here."

"But what's going to happen to you?"

"That is for my daylights to decide. You are an Exorian now and, like me, you must learn to find strength in the least likely of places." He squeezed her shoulder and strode out of the room.

Since that day, she had only spoken to Dankar—and mostly only to answer his questions, which were unending and confusing. He wanted to know about things she had never thought about, such as: Who are the leaders of your country? To whom do they pay tribute? How many armies do they command? What weapons do they use? She couldn't tell him anything, which made him very angry. He told her she was lucky he had taken her in because there were many dangers in Ayda, including a kind of beast called a *tehuantl* that hunted little girls at night. He told her not to come out of her room until she could be more useful.

But, he also promised to bring her sister to her. For this reason, and because Louis had warned her to be good, she kept to herself and stayed out of Dankar's way, spending most of her time looking out her window, waiting for Evelyn, and hoping that Louis was still alive.

Chapter 27

UPSET

Evelyn's shoulders sagged over her oars. Teddy and Knox were sound asleep. Chase struggled to stay awake, splashing water on his face. They had traveled upstream for several hours, and now the sun was rising over the rocky cliffs like an eye opening. It lit upon the water with a painful glare, softened only by a white mist rising off the river. Chase shielded his eyes and looked toward the eastern shore. He saw a long, white plume of water falling from the top of one of the cliffs and yelled to Evelyn, pointing it out. Teddy woke up and Evelyn showed him the water chute. Her skiff began to tack right, toward the east. Chase suspected his hunch was correct: Rysta's necklace was helping Teddy steer their boat.

The line connecting the two skiffs suddenly stretched and tightened; the boats moved faster, creating larger wakes behind them. Chase thrust an oar straight down and felt the drag—they were definitely picking up speed. The skiffs, which had kept closer to the safety and camouflage of the western side of the river through the night, now glided quickly out into open water and the center of the river. A gust of northern wind blew down, which, combined with the current, created a lot of chop. The skiffs pitched up and down. Knox woke up with a yelp when his head smacked hard on the bottom of the boat. Waves were gaining in height and velocity, quickly turning into rapids and moving them downstream, back toward Metria.

Chase braced himself with his knees and dug the oar into the water again, trying to slow their speed, but it didn't work. A cold finger of fear tickled his insides. He looked downstream, half-expecting to see Rysta or a troupe of Metrians on their tail—but the river was empty. The skiffs hiked up and slammed down violently with each swell.

Teddy was laughing now, crashing up and down in the bow of his skiff, enjoying the bumps. The harder he laughed, the higher the waves seemed to rise. The skiffs were caught smack in the middle of the river at the height of the chop. Evelyn and Chase struggled to keep the boats straight and not crash into each other.

"Knox!" shouted Chase. "Untie the bowline!"

A moment later, he realized his mistake. Untethered, the trailing skiff spun wildly in the current. He couldn't maintain control. Knox wrestled with the other oar, and together they tried to straighten the boat and keep it from swamping. It was all they could do until the current exhausted itself somewhere farther south and released them. Chase examined the surroundings as best he could, wracking his brain to remember the topography of Ayda from Hesam's maps. The Hestredes flowed southeast of the mountains, bypassed the city of Metria, and emptied into the ocean. Would the current take them all the way south to the city, into Rysta's lap? His stomach turned over at the thought of what else might be there to greet them.

"Knox, we have to get out of the current!" he cried.

"I know! I'm trying!" Knox was on his knees, digging an oar deep into the river with all his strength, trying to keep them steady. Chase scanned the rapids for the boat carrying Evelyn and Teddy. They were surfing the chop less than thirty yards to the east. He could see Teddy's blond head bouncing in the bow when the skiff crested a wave. Rysta's necklace glittered in the sun briefly before they disappeared in a trough.

"Teddy!" Chase screamed, trying to be heard over the thrashing water. The waves were getting inexplicably bigger and the wind was blowing harder. He heard Evelyn shriek and whipped around in just enough time to fend off her bow as it came crashing down on top of his stern. No one was rowing now, they were just holding onto the gunwales, trying not to flip over. Teddy was beaming. He was having the time of his life. Chase's fear blossomed into panic.

"*Ted!*" Chase shouted again. He was desperate for Teddy to stop enjoying this so much. It was only making things worse. "Think about Melor, think about going back! We need to go upstream and out of the current!"

At that precise moment an enormous set of waves broadsided the skiffs, knocking them all overboard. The skiffs rolled over and over in the froth, the oars spinning wildly away. There was no time to rescue any of their supplies as they were all swept head over heels downstream.

Chase tried to swim close to Teddy, but the water going up his nose and in his mouth and eyes made it difficult to keep track of anything. Waves surged over his head. He coughed and spluttered, fighting to keep his head above the surface and not go under. A dark knob swept by him, to his right. Teddy's wet head. Chase zoned in and tried to follow. He had no idea where Evelyn and Knox were.

The river curved slightly and the chop quieted somewhat. Chase could see his little brother floating on his back toward the western shore, on the edge of the rapids. He swam sidestroke out of the main flush of the current so as to be in a better position to grab him. Chase was making good headway when a swarm of wrinkled heads and heavy-lidded eyes broke the surface of the water around Teddy: Rysta's turtles. He wasn't sure if he should be more relieved or frightened, and swam faster, trying to get close to his brother. The current fought him like a living thing, bent on stopping him, dragging him under. He struggled to see what was happening.

Teddy had climbed astride one of the turtle's shells and wrapped his skinny arms around the wrinkled head. He was smiling. The necklace shone like a star against his chest.

"NOOOO! TEDDY! DON'T!" cried Chase, flailing his arms and thrashing at the water. The turtles floated on the surface for a moment longer. The one with Teddy on its back turned to look at Chase. A heavy lid lowered over the turtle's enormous eye, and then it dove beneath the surface, taking Teddy down into the depths.

✛   ✛   ✛

Knox came ashore on the eastern banks of the river, his hair and eyes streaming. He scanned the surface, looking for heads, and saw one struggling toward him. It was Evelyn. She gained the shore in a few moments, breathing heavily. They had landed on a flat granite ledge that sloped gently into the river. To the right was an impassable cliff; to the left, a thicket of vegetation. There was no sign of Chase or Teddy. Knox and Evelyn said nothing, searching the river with their eyes. The rapids had subsided and the surface on this part of the river was calm, bubbling along as though nothing had ever disturbed it.

"Where are they?" Knox groaned, trying not to panic. He closed his eyes, unwilling to let his mind think the worst. He willed Chase and Teddy's heads to appear. He begged. Then he opened his eyes. Nothing. He collapsed on the rock. Evelyn sat next to him and patted his knee.

"Don't worry. They'll be okay. They're good swimmers. We've had a lot of practice lately."

Knox lay back on the rock and groaned.

"We shouldn't have done it, Evelyn. We shouldn't have stolen the necklace."

They sat together in silence for several more minutes. Knox pressed his ear to the rock, hoping it would pass on to him some kind of useful information. He jumped when Evelyn stood up and waded into the water.

"What are you doing?"

"Look!" Evelyn pointed to a small dark shape swimming against the current in their direction. She waved wildly. Within moments, they could make out Chase's head, his face contorted with effort. Knox waded in and together, he and Evelyn pulled him up onto the ledge. Chase was shaking, his breath whistling through his lips. His lips were blue from the cold water.

"It's okay, Chase," said Knox. "Just breathe."

"I lost him!" wheezed Chase, gasping for air. "I tried to stay close, but the current was too strong. The turtles came and . . . one pulled him under and I couldn't see anything and then"—Chase broke off, sobbing. "He didn't come back up. I tried to get him. I dove under again and again, but—"

Knox's knees buckled in shock. "Teddy?" he whispered.

Evelyn blanched beneath her copper skin.

Chase nodded, sobs ripping through him.

"I told you not to do it, Knox! I begged you. WHY DON'T YOU EVER LISTEN?" His body convulsed. He rolled over, spitting up water.

Knox dove off the ledge, swimming fast into the open water. He let himself drift downriver, scanning both shores and the surface for some sign of his little brother. The landscape was unchanged. He slapped at the water in frustration, tears streaming down his face.

"Rysta!" he howled. "GIVE HIM BACK!"

The river sped him along deftly. Knox stayed in the water, searching until he grew dangerously cold. He swam back toward Chase and Evelyn. They were sitting as far away from each other as they possibly could on the small ledge.

Knox pulled himself out of the water, his teeth chattering.

"Chase?" he asked.

Chase turned his head away.

Knox began to cry in earnest. "I'm sorry, Chase. I should have listened to you. You were right, okay. We shouldn't have—"

Chase cut him off by standing up, his expression dark.

"Shut up. I don't want to hear it."

Evelyn tried to intervene. "Chase, this is my fault. I stole the necklace."

"Do you think I don't know that, Evelyn? Are you happy now?" Chase glowered at her. "Does it feel more *even*?"

Evelyn's jaw dropped. "How can you say that? I . . . I never—"

Chase raised his hand. "Save it."

Knox's heart was racing. He didn't know which was more frightening: Chase crying, or this blunt hollowness.

"Rysta wouldn't hurt him," he squeaked. "He's her favorite."

"Even if that is true and he's alive," said Chase, through gritted teeth, "I'm sure she'll be happy to give him back after we stole her most *precious* possession, the thing she values most! You heard her, Knox. You heard what she said that night!"

Knox cowered. He had never seen Chase so angry before.

"There is *something* I would like to know," said Chase, turning a cold eye to Evelyn. "How did you take the necklace in the first place?"

It was Evelyn's turn to look frightened. She opened and shut her mouth a few times before answering.

"I tricked her into giving it to me," she confessed, speaking so low her voice was almost drowned by the rippling water. "I remembered that she took it off when she played that game with us, with Urza. I got to thinking about it, and I remembered a story my father told me about a cat that kills an ogre by getting him to turn into a mouse. I don't know—" She struggled for the right words. "I thought it was worth a try. I rowed out to the ship and asked for her to see me. I told her I wanted to know more about the daylights, that I was confused, that I didn't understand them." Evelyn took a shuddery breath. "I told her I was afraid that Dankar had killed my sister. I told her about my mother and my father, and the earthquake. About being an orphan, like her. She felt sorry for me! I used it." Evelyn's voice shrank even more.

"I asked her to show me again how the daylights of a Keeper transform. I told her it would be a great comfort for me to know that my parents' and my sister's daylights would live on as something else, but secretly, I remembered how weak it made her. She didn't want to do it, but I begged her. Finally she agreed . . . she wasn't happy about it."

"Yeah, well, *duh,* they know pretty much everything we're thinking. She probably knew what you were doing the whole time," Chase sneered.

Evelyn thought about this for a minute, then continued.

"Rysta took off her robe and the necklace and then . . . you know . . . did her fish thing. I grabbed the necklace and dove off the side of the boat and swam to the skiff and rowed as fast as I could to meet you."

"*You mean you just left her there?* She can't breathe air when she's a fish! You could have killed her!" Chase exploded.

A tear slid down Evelyn's cheek. "I was sure she'd be all right. She could just transform again. I never meant to hurt her. I just wanted to do something to save my sister."

"You did something; that's for sure," he growled. "Who needs Exorians when we have Evelyn."

"Chase, don't . . . please." Knox was still shivering. He had never felt more miserable in his life. "She's sorry. I'm sorry, too."

"You *always* say that. But this time, IT'S NOT GOOD ENOUGH!"

Knox began to sob again. Cold wind blew in from the north. Chase shivered and looked down at Knox, who was curled into a ball, and then over at Evelyn. He had never hated anyone as much as he hated them right now. It would serve them right if Dankar got them.

The sun on the river twinkled at him, hiding the dark depths that Teddy had descended into. A painful lump rose in Chase's lungs where the beast used to live, right below his heart. He could not let himself think about Teddy right now; if he did, he might never be able to move from this spot again. And he *had* to move. He could not stay here for another minute thinking that Teddy would not be following them like he always did, trying to keep up. Maybe Knox was right and Rysta had used the turtles to bring Teddy safely back to her. But what if she hadn't? What if she just wanted revenge? Or—worse—what if this had nothing to do with her, and he'd let Teddy drown all on his own? Tinator had made a mistake when he gave him the sword. He didn't deserve it. He wasn't strong enough. He couldn't bear to think about it. Chase buried his head in his knees and closed his eyes, wrapping up the pain in his chest tightly, like a bright, hard pebble, and pushing it down into a dark hole. After a long time, he opened his eyes.

"I'm headed east, away from the river, and then north," he announced.

Knox sat up.

"But that means going into the mountains, into Varuna."

Chase gave him a dark look. "That's where I'm going—I'm not asking you to come." His back was rigid as he walked away.

Evelyn and Knox hauled themselves to their feet. They cast one last look at the river that had stolen Teddy, liquid gold in the morning light, and followed Chase, wordlessly, into the brush.

Chapter 28

INTO THE MOUNTAINS

Chase allowed the other two to go ahead of him by several yards. He had no intention of speaking to either of them. Every now and then Evelyn bent down to scratch at the earth or pick something off the ground, storing her findings in a makeshift bag she'd tied together from her robe. Knox was up ahead. Evelyn bent down again. Chase saw the knobs of her spine poke through the thin fabric of her shirt. Flesh and bone. Fragile. The long trek had calmed him: He hadn't forgiven her, but he had stopped hating her.

The Hestredes lay to the southwest, a glimmering ribbon unspooling from the Voss; Chase knew the shortest way to the foothills of Varuna was straight north—away from the river. Knox was feeling unusually cautious and preferred to keep the river in sight, but they all knew they could not follow it the entire way. Soon they would be in unfamiliar territory.

The afternoon stretched slowly into evening; no one said a word except for Knox, who guessed out loud that they'd walked about twelve miles from where they'd started on the ledge. The terrain was uneven and slowly steepening. Orange-winged butterflies hovered and lit on spiky, flowered bushes growing alongside their trail. The air was warm and dry and buzzed with the industry of small insects. They walked on, seeing no sign of human habitation. When their shadows lengthened across the ground, Evelyn sat down, hungry and tired and unable to walk any farther. Chase broke his silence to agree to stay with her—albeit at a distance—while

Knox climbed to the summit of the hill to scout the surrounding area. He wasn't gone for long and and came jogging back.

"We're closer than we think," he reported. "When you get to the top, you can see the mountains and the lake. It's pretty rough going by the river—lots of up and down—but if we hike east about a mile, the land gets flatter and more open." He threw himself down on the ground. His face was flushed from running.

"Back in your element, huh?" asked Chase, not really caring if he answered. Knox looked at him hopefully, glad his brother was at least speaking again.

"What do you mean?"

Chase waved his hand, taking in the thick vegetation, the damp ground, the tall grasses and wildflowers bending in the wind. "You know, back on the trail. No food. Danger at every turn. Your daylights are happy."

"True that," Evelyn agreed, also eager to get back into Chase's good graces. "Melorians are easy to please."

Knox lay back, cradling his head in his folded arms. "So you agree with Rothermel? That I'm a Melorian? Do you think he's controlling my daylights right now?" He stretched out both arms, pretending to be a zombie. "Must walk. Must hunt."

"I wish you would hunt," grumbled Evelyn. "I can't stop thinking about food."

Chase grunted in agreement, still reluctant to begin speaking to her again. Evelyn withdrew a little bundle from her robe.

"I don't know if I'm a Melorian or not, but I did manage to pick some food on the trail." She untied the bundle. It contained a small pile of mushrooms and some kind of acorn-looking nut, which she offered to Chase first. "We'll have to make do with these."

Chase picked up one of the acorns and put it in his mouth and bit down. "Ow!" he cried, holding his jaw.

"You have to let them soften in your mouth first," said Evelyn. "If I wasn't so tired I'd go down to the river and get us some water so we could soak them, but—" She took another peek at him from under her eyelashes. He was frowning, but his eyes looked less hard. "Just suck on it for a while, like a candy. It will get soft pretty quickly."

Knox mimicked her. After a few moments, he made a face. "Sure doesn't taste like hard candy. Flo's never sold anything like this."

"Don't talk about Flo's! Just thinking about it makes me hungrier," groaned Chase. It also made him think of someone. The tight knob below his heart started knocking and a pressure built behind his eyes, but he was good at shoving beasts in his chest back underground. He cleared his throat. Knox stared at him hungrily.

"Tell me what you remember about Flo's," he said, eager to be back on Chase's good side. Everything was colder and emptier without his brothers.

Chase thought about not answering, but he had to admit, it was getting too hard to keep giving them the silent treatment.

"Dunno. I guess the soda fountain, the wall of pictures, some of the toys on the shelf, and those little red fish."

"Swedish fish," Knox volunteered.

"Yeah, those. And the chewy tan candies in the yellow wrapper." Chase tried to think of other kinds of candy he had liked, but found it hard to remember anything specific. One moment he could picture the inside of Flo's in vivid detail, but just as quickly, the image would vanish.

"Bit-O-Honeys," said Evelyn softly. "I liked those, too. And the chocolate bars with the coconut."

"Chase, remember my tree fort and that cave in the rocks?" asked Knox, with a wistful expression. "Man, I really loved that fort."

"Remember your stupid cap gun? I thought I'd gone deaf after you fired that thing!"

"Yeah, sorry about that."

Chase raised an eyebrow, surprised that Knox sounded genuinely remorseful. He looked out of the corner of his eye at Evelyn.

"That's the day we first met you."

Evelyn chewed her lip, thinking. When she answered it was as though she were pulling the words up from some great depth.

"On the beach. We found sand dollars."

Fragments of that first day at Summerledge came back to each of them. They took turns recalling pieces of it, weaving their memories together until the day was almost whole in their minds, and solid, like a blanket to ward off the chill that was descending as the sun set. Still, it seemed like a lifetime ago. No one said anything out loud, but they all knew how much they'd lost since then.

"Knox," asked Evelyn, taking a deep breath. "What does it feel like?"

"What does *what* feel like?" he replied, yawning. The sun was at its lowest point on the horizon, almost gone.

"The daylights. What does it feel like when they call you, like Seaborne told us?"

"I dunno, really." Knox shrugged. He frowned in concentration, trying to find words for the sensation he'd felt in the forest when they first met Rothermel. The feeling of belonging—no, he corrected himself—of *being* the forest.

"I guess if I had to describe it, I would say that it feels like everything you've ever wanted or ever missed is right there in front of you. But it's even better than you imagined. It is also a little scary, because it's like you aren't you anymore . . . or, maybe, you're more like you than you've ever been, but you are also everything else." He shook his head. "I'm explaining it badly. Chase—have you felt anything?"

"Me? No."

"Maybe you will when we get to Varuna," Evelyn suggested.

Chase pondered this for a minute. "That's convenient. I'm a Varunan, Knox is a Melorian, and Teddy's a Metrian. That leaves you and Frankie to Exor." He scowled. "That trick you played on Rysta could have been right out of Dankar's playbook."

Evelyn's face fell. She was quiet a moment.

"That's what I'm worried about," she admitted. "Don't you think it's weird . . . or at least one big coincidence that there are five of us, and five stones? It's almost like it was planned. One stone for each one of us—and if that's the case, then who planned it? And who is the Exorian? Me—or Frankie?"

Chase pointed his finger at her, as if it were completely obvious. Evelyn's hurt expression made him retract it. He pulled at his bangs.

"You're jumping to some big conclusions, anyway, Evelyn. We don't know if any of this is true, not even the part about the Fifth Stone. It could all be a mass hallucination—maybe they all ate some weird mushrooms or something, and made up all this stuff about the daylights and the stones to make everyone feel better about killing and kidnapping each other. Maybe there's nothing special about this place—or the Keepers, except that they're all insane." Even as he said, it didn't feel like the truth, but it felt good to say it for some reason.

"Do *you* think it's real, Evelyn?" asked Knox, confused. Chase cut in before she could answer.

"It doesn't matter whether or not it's real—the only thing that matters is the facts: Number one: We're stranded here. Number two: Frankie and Teddy have been kidnapped, at the very least. Number three: We're headed into the mountains with no map, no weapons, no warm clothing, and no food. We have no idea if Ratha will be friendly, and we know Dankar and the Exorians won't be. So, all in all, the facts pretty much stink."

Knox gulped. "But what if it *is* true? What if our daylights are stronger, and the power of the Fifth Stone is protecting the balance—and us?"

Chase pressed his lips together and looked at his feet. A strange mood had taken hold of him.

"Not likely, Knox. Tell me something: If Evelyn is right and it's all a plan, how do you explain the Fifth Stone? Which one of us is connected to it, and why aren't they feeling it? Don't you think one of us would be picking up signals from this all-powerful entity, or whatever it is? Wouldn't we have *some* inkling if it existed? Makes you wonder, doesn't it?" He leaned back with a satisfied smirk, perversely happy to be debunking the daylights.

"But I feel so different," Knox whispered.

Evelyn inched closer, saying, "I was raised among people who told me that much of what is true can never be seen. This is what it means to believe in something, whether it is a stone, or a person, or an idea. Sometimes belief is enough to *make* something true."

Chase exhaled a long sigh. "Maybe you're right, Evelyn—but where's the proof?"

"Chase," she said, "believing is always a choice, not a certainty." Her expression made her look far older than her age. "So, I think, the better question is: Do you or don't you."

"Do I or do I not what?"

"*Believe* in the daylights. In the Fifth Stone. Because if you don't, I don't understand why we are headed to Varuna."

Chase felt as if everything depended on his answer: their survival, Frankie's rescue, Teddy's life. Minutes stretched out as he considered what to say. He tried to think of a logical explanation for everything that had happened to them. A reason. Finally he lifted his gaze and met theirs.

Knox's peaked forehead was pink and sore-looking from the sun in Metria. His freckles stood out like constellations on his skin. Evelyn's dark eyes were troubled. Her skin was gray, and she had chewed her lower lip to shreds. The two of them looked cold and hungry. For the first time since the riverbank, his anger fell away completely and he saw them for who they really were: his brother and his friend.

"I do. I choose to believe," he said, truthfully. "I have to . . . for Teddy."

"I do, too," whispered Evelyn. "For Frankie."

"So do I," whispered Knox, squirming ever so slightly closer to Chase.

The darkness was now thick around them, the evening filled with the soft whirring sound of bat wings and the hooting of owls. Teddy's signal in Melor. The painful knob rose again in Chase's chest and knocked. He swallowed it. Together they watched as one by one, the stars appeared, high and remote in the vastness of space. The ground lay quiet and half-lit, the shadow of the mountains to the north just visible. In that moment, time seemed to stop, and they saw what the world might have been like when it was new and unpeopled: a perfect and absolute stillness, immense and eternal. Evelyn, Chase, and Knox huddled together, feeling very small.

☩   ☩   ☩

It was just past daybreak when Evelyn roused the boys to an overcast sky. The air was still and much cooler than the night before.

"The wind shifted again," said Chase.

"The top of this hill isn't far," said Knox. "I can show you what I told you about last night. I think if we move inland and walk on the flatlands, we'll get to the foothills of the mountains within a day or so; then we can turn west and head toward the Voss."

And then what? was the thought no one dared voice out loud. They also tried to avoid talking about their stabbing hunger pains. Evelyn's stomach growled loudly.

"We have to find some food," she whimpered to no one in particular.

By the middle of the following day, they reached the Varunan foothills. Peaks that had looked so peaceful and distant on the horizon were now at hand. Tall, rocky outcroppings undulated north, going from green to brown to white as they increased in height. The terrain once again sloped sharply uphill and the air was now quite cold. The children shivered in their Metrian dress, wrapping the long but far-too-thin robes around them as tightly as they could. Hunger, too, was taking a serious toll. Knox, who could almost always be counted on to make some kind of idle chatter, had grown sullen and silent. Evelyn was using all of her energy to put one foot in front of the other. Chase was the only one who was not tired at all. In fact, if it weren't for being cold and hungry, he would say that he'd never felt better. As he walked behind Evelyn, watching her weave and stumble, he considered what she had said about his daylights. Maybe they were tied to Varuna after all.

In front of him, Evelyn tripped on a small rock and fell. Chase stopped to help her up. When he looked at her he was alarmed. Her lips were blue and her teeth were chattering. He chastised himself for forgetting that as thin and ill-suited as his and Knox's clothing were, hers were even more so. She was out in the mountains wearing what amounted to pajamas. He unwrapped his robe and tied it over her.

"Here. You're freezing."

She looked at him gratefully, then pointed to her feet, clad only in sandals and thin socks.

"It's my feet. I don't think I can go on much farther without warming them up."

Chase yelled ahead to Knox, who turned around. They stood a discreet distance from Evelyn.

"We have to make a fire before she freezes to death, and we have to do it while we still have enough places to find tinder and fuel," said Chase.

"What about Dankar?" asked Knox, shivering.

"Death by Dankar or by freezing are pretty much even in my mind. I think we should risk it."

Knox nodded. "Let's make a fire here; we can warm up, then carry a coal with us. I think I can figure out how to make an ember chamber." He surveyed their immediate surroundings, stony and cold and silent. "It might not matter, anyway—we'll probably starve before we get much farther north."

"Perfect," said Chase sarcastically.

"Hey, the mountains were your idea—" Knox started to say, but cut himself short.

Evelyn offered to begin the fire-making process if they could find sticks and tinder. They brought her enough dry grass and small sticks for her to begin.

Using a sharp rock to gouge a narrow cup into a flat stick, she inserted a pinch of dry grass and poked another, longer stick into the cup. Then she chafed the end of the long stick between her palms, rubbing it back and forth as fast as she could. She was weak and tired and the effort quickly exhausted her, but she kept at it. Back in Melor, she had watched Mara make fire this way within minutes, but she had never tried to do it—or even thought she would need to. She remembered how they all had complained in Melor; how unfair it had seemed then that they would have to stay at Seaborne's cabin. Now, she would give anything to be back there, with Frankie and Teddy and Seaborne, forever. She was too cold and miserable to cry, but a tiny voice inside her began to chant: *Please, please, please.* She wasn't even sure who or what she was appealing to. It didn't occur to her to ask for anything more. A fire would be enough.

It didn't happen right away. Knox came back with an armful of dried grass and more twigs. They were having difficulty finding larger pieces of dry wood. She barely heard him through the sound of the chant in her head and the effort of rubbing her palms together. She was aware of the heat emanating from the tinder. Then, with a small crackle, the tinder began to smoke. Bending down, she blew gently over the flat stick, feeding the spark. It glowed with heat and she removed the friction stick. She cupped her treasure in both hands and transferred the starter to the nest of dried grass that Knox had built on one of the flat rock tables nearby.

She nursed the starter, feeding it with small twigs until a flame began to blaze. By the time the boys returned, laden down with wood, the fire was crackling along well. The sky grew darker and a dry mist descended in the valleys between the mountains, seeping slowly across the foothills.

Knox gave an appreciative bow. "Looks like we have a fire starter in the family."

Evelyn flushed a little; but it was true—they did feel like family. Broken and filled with gaps, but a family nonetheless. Knox held out his hands to warm them and snuck an expectant look at Chase. Evelyn caught it and eyed both boys suspiciously.

"What?" she said, wanting in on the secret.

"Should we tell her, Knox?" Chase asked.

"Well . . . I dunno." Knox pretended to stall. "Okay, I guess." Then he ran off. When he returned, he held three dead birds upside down by the feet.

"Dinner!" he crowed. "And it's not bugs! They were just sitting there, like they were waiting for us! I threw a few rocks and they keeled over, just like that." He began plucking feathers vigorously. When the birds were clean, they speared them and stuck them over the fire to cook. Their scent filled the air. They could barely wait for the meat to cook before tearing into them.

"I'm so happy, I don't even care if Dankar finds us," said Knox, licking his fingers.

"Well, you would, lad, if you had half a brain," said a deep, gravelly voice from down the hill. "I hope you've left me something!"

Seaborne's familiar shape came striding into view. He wore his long, tattered officer's jacket with the stained sleeves under a thick, fur-lined coat and leather boots. His eyes danced. Chase, Knox, and Evelyn were on him in a flash, tackling him to the ground.

"How did you find us?" Knox asked, a broad grin splitting his face.

"Well, I had some difficulty, I must admit, until you lit that fire—I smelled it right away and then, when you started roasting the birds, well, the hounds led me straight here in a dead run."

"The hounds?" cried Knox.

Seaborne whistled, and within seconds Axl and Tar were bounding into their midst, each pulling a small sled with wheels on the bottom.

Seaborne freed the dogs, and when they had been sufficiently hugged and patted, he unloaded the sleds.

"Mara and Calla thought you might be able to use these," he grunted, and threw each of them a pair of leather boots. Then he unpacked blankets, fur-lined clothing, ponchos, and, finally, two baskets of food. Chase, Knox, and Evelyn quickly donned the familiar Melorian clothing, not bothering to remove their Metrian garb. Evelyn sighed gratefully as she put on her boots.

Seaborne sat down by the fire and offered food from the baskets. He looked at the three of them in turn, slowly chewing a strip of smoked meat. Chase couldn't tell if he was annoyed or proud of them—maybe a little of both. Finally Seaborne spoke.

"Well, I'll hand it to the three of you. Not many on Ayda would disobey one Keeper, then steal from another. It's no wonder you ran away. I'm questioning the choice of the mountains, though. Not very well thought out. I thought we'd trained you better."

Knox protested; Seaborne waved him off.

"Good thing you're well-liked or you'd find yourself in a pretty pickle. When Rothermel heard what you did, he was half-ready to let Dankar have you."

An uncomfortable silence followed, lightened only by Axl, who groaned happily as she stretched her back to the fire. Evelyn was nestled deep inside the hood of her poncho.

"Why didn't he?" she asked quietly.

"Rysta intervened in your favor, and you had a few other—fans."

"*Rysta* intervened," Chase repeated, surprised. "Did you know about—"

"About your *brother?*" Seaborne finished, his voice rising. "Aye. Fine job that was, taking a small boy out on the river like that." He glared at each of them, then he stretched out his legs and yawned. "Well, I suppose he's better off than you are at the moment."

"We were headed back to Melor," blurted Knox, trying to explain.

Seaborne sniffed. "As if we'd have you."

"We didn't mean it to happen. We didn't mean for Teddy—"

"DIDN'T MEAN TO!" Seaborne yelled, with a force that made them all start. "What did you think would happen if you crossed a Keeper? You think she'd let you prance off with her necklace, right as rain, straight into the hands of the enemy? After everything she and Rothermel told you? You three have always been a little thick in the head."

"Is Teddy okay?" Chase whispered, looking at the ground.

"No thanks to you lot. Rysta didn't want him killed by your stupidity, so she sent the sea turtles to collect him."

"He's with Rysta, then? Alive? You're *sure*?" asked Chase, meeting Seaborne's eye.

Seaborne gave a quick nod. Chase felt the heavy knob in his chest break apart, replaced by a swooping sense of joy. *Teddy was alive!*

"Wait," said Knox. "I don't get it. Rysta let us go? With the necklace?"

"You really haven't learned anything, have you?" replied Seaborne. "The necklace is valuable, and not something she'd be pleased to tender, but the greater loss to her would have been the four of you. Did you really think she wouldn't know what you were up to? Do you think she couldn't guess?" He shot a severe look at Evelyn, then bit into his meat with an exasperated snort. "She's a mite older than you, for starters, and she's seen a thing or two. You thought you were being so tricky, sneaking off after that song and dance. The fact is—she *gave* you the necklace. She knew from your thoughts, particularly yours," said Seaborne, gesturing at Evelyn, "that you were determined to confront Dankar. She knew if you had the necklace she could protect you in some way. If you had it, she could use it to guide and advise you—did you not sense that? The necklace is of little use on its own without Rysta. She's connected to it."

Chase nodded vigorously. "The skiffs—it was like they steered themselves. I thought it was Teddy, you know, his thoughts, or something! He was wearing the necklace and I thought it followed his wishes."

"Yes, well, that was her error. She didn't plan on the little one wearing it. She thought Evelyn would keep it. Even so, she could not let you take Teddy to Dankar, so she stopped you." He glared at them again. "To the end of my days I will never understand what overcame the three of you. Taking a little boy on the river with nothing but the clothes on your back. Madness."

Seaborne shifted over and removed a large, wrapped bundle from one of the sleds. "But to your credit, you shook things up. Something has happened that has not happened in—" He began to count on his fingers with an absentminded expression, then shook his head. "Let's just say in a very long time." He cradled the bundle in his lap and whistled softly under his breath.

"What?" Knox cried, unable to bear Seaborne's attempt at suspense.

"There was a meeting," he said solemnly.

"What kind of meeting?" asked Evelyn.

"A secret meeting between Rothermel and Rysta—and a bittersweet reunion it was, I'm told. I was not there myself." His expression clouded over for a moment. "But not many were. It was brief."

"And it was about—us?" asked Evelyn.

Seaborne nodded. "Yes, to be sure, but not just you. Since Tinator's daylights were sent back to their source, there has been a growing restlessness in Melor. The scent of revenge lies thick in the Wold—it has led to some impetuous and foolish acts," his eyes darkened. "Not unlike your little adventure here. At the meeting, Rothermel and Rysta took brief counsel with one another. The idea of open war was dismissed, but your idea of using some precious gift as a negotiating tool was examined and determined to—ah—have merit—"

"—not a stone?" Evelyn gasped.

"Of course not," Seaborne scoffed. "But it was discussed that perhaps something else would do. Something Dankar wants very much." He grew quiet, allowing his words to sink in.

Chase understood immediately.

"You mean us."

Seaborne nodded. "I was told that your decision to abandon Rysta and the comfort and protection of Metria was seen as a declaration of willingness to expose yourself to the enemy. After much argument, it was decided that this could be used to Ayda's advantage: Rothermel would agree to turn you over to Dankar in exchange for a truce with Melor."

"But . . . but . . . he knows Dankar is a liar and a cheat!" Knox sputtered. "Why would Rothermel ever expect him to honor a truce?"

Seaborne's lips clenched into a tight line.

"There would be some guarantees: You would be given to him one by one. If the truce were broken, the exchanges would cease."

"That's slavery—no better than Dankar would do himself. I don't believe it! I thought the Keepers were under oath to protect us, not offer us up as live sacrifices!" objected Evelyn, flushed with outrage.

"That is the same argument Rysta used. But the case was made that you already accepted that fate—by your actions. You had been told of the danger, yet you chose to run away."

Evelyn stood up and stared down at him. "Is that what *you* think? We should be sacrificed to Dankar as . . . as punishment for trying to find my sister? Do you think that's justice?"

Seaborne shook his head. "Nay, Evelyn, calm yourself. I do not agree with the council. Nor do the few others who know of it. But there is great peril in Ayda, and some wonder if you were not sent to us for this very reason."

"To be offered to Dankar?" Evelyn sneered.

"Aye." Seaborne's voice was heavy with the truth. "I've been told to collect you and bring you back to the Wold. You are of no use to anyone if you are caught here in the wild."

Evelyn, Knox, and Chase stared at Seaborne disbelievingly. On instinct, they gravitated toward one another. Knox reached for one of the logs by the fire to use as a club.

"There's no need for that, Knox. I told you when I first met you, I'm not your enemy." Seaborne gave him a wan, exhausted smile.

"I'm beginning to wonder if there's much difference between a friend and an enemy here," said Knox.

"I was sent here to collect you, true, but I didn't say that was what I'm going to do." Seaborne stood and gave them a smile so familiar and endearing to the three of them that they almost dropped their guard. As he took a step forward, they stepped back as one, away from him.

"Come now. Have you lost all faith in your old friend, Seaborne?"

They did not respond.

"Maybe this will change your feelings." With a flourish he lifted one of the remaining bundles from the sleds and opened the flap. To their astonishment an assortment of weapons fell to the ground: Chase's sword, Knox's knives, Evelyn's dagger, and an assortment of slingshots. Then, Seaborne drew out Tinator's massive crossbow and a quiver full of sharpened bolts and hefted it onto his shoulder. "I'll be using this, if you please. The others, I think, belong to you."

"Wha—how did you get them?" cried Knox, squatting beside the pile and quickly stowing away his knives. "I looked everywhere for these! I thought they were gone forever. Rysta took them from us in Metria."

"Aye, Rysta does not believe young ones should be burdened with such things. She hates the thought of them being put to use. She returned them to Rothermel at the council. But it just so happens that Calla, ah, stumbled upon them, shall we say, and Mara packed them with the supplies."

Chase picked up his sword fondly, stroking the scabbard with his hand. The weight of it felt good in his grasp, like it belonged to him. Maybe he was being given a second chance to prove himself. He drew the blade from the scabbard and brandished it above his head. Now that he knew Teddy was safe, he would gladly admit that he had never felt so alive or so prepared to face whatever lay ahead.

"What's the plan?" he asked Seaborne.

"The plan, as much as there is one," replied Seaborne, "is to gain favor with the only person in Ayda who can give the three of you—and now me, since I've thrown my lot in with yours—a fighting chance." Seaborne threw a nervous glance over his shoulder at the gold-tipped mountains in the distance.

"Ratha?" asked Chase.

Seaborne responded with a curt nod.

Chapter 29

FALSE FOOTING

The temperature dropped violently the next day. By evening, a light snow had begun to fall. Evelyn snuggled deeply into her fur-lined poncho, silently saying another prayer of thanks for Seaborne's timely arrival. It was their fourth day out in the wild, and the mountains of Varuna were now before them. Scrubby, wheat-colored meadows and granite outlays had given way to tougher and more treacherous ground as they climbed, leading them up into a landscape devoid of color and definition but for the snow-tipped peaks towering over them. Depending on the time of day, the summits looked either tantalizingly close or fearfully remote.

Far below to the south and southwest, they caught a brief glimpse of the glittering waters of the Voss and the Hestredes river. They had skirted the banks of the lake the day before, but dared not stop out in the open. Seaborne was driving them hard, and as they trudged onward, everyone's hearts and footsteps grew heavier; each had to fight hard against the impulse to stop and gaze backwards, toward the warm waters and shaded groves of Metria and Melor. What lay ahead remained unknown, and, from the starkness that surrounded them, not very welcoming.

Seaborne called for a halt and busied himself with the bottom of the sleds. He planned to remove the wheels and replace them with metal runners for ice when the time came. The campsite for the evening was a wide sunken ledge at the edge of a rocky field. Evelyn was in charge of keeping their small fire burning. Knox fiddled with his throwing knives, unable to settle down. Chase had wandered off, as he had begun to do more often. Knox stooped beside Seaborne, watching him worry a wooden peg from its hole.

"How far do you think we need to go before Ratha finds us?" he asked.

Seaborne pounded the bottom of the wagon with his homemade mallet, ingeniously fashioned from a rock, twine, and a sturdy branch. "Don't know," he grunted. "Maybe we'll find her before she finds us."

"Rysta said she lives far up, on one of the tallest mountains."

"I've heard that, too, but no one knows. She's a solitary sort."

Knox smiled, thinking of Seaborne's remote cabin. "Takes one to know one, huh, Seaborne?" Seaborne didn't reply. Knox fussed impatiently with one of his knives.

"But what about her people, towns, villages, that sort of thing? Surely we'll come across somebody soon?"

"Not likely. I've never met a Varunan as long as I've lived on Ayda. They avoid contact with others. Most live on their own, hidden away in these mountains. For all we know, they may have us in their sights now," said Seaborne.

Knox surveyed the barren landscape. Who could possibly stay hidden here? But then again, this was Ayda—anything was possible. Of all the places that he'd been on Ayda, he liked Varuna the least. It was beautiful, which he'd come to expect. The sky was so blue it looked purple, and the views from the heights were magnificent—but there was also a hostile feeling about Varuna: empty and cold and bare except for rocks and moss and scrubby trees. Knox sniffed the air. It smelled like nothing, if nothing had a scent, and it filled him with dread. He picked up Seaborne's mallet and began striking the ground impatiently. Flint and snow spray flew up and dusted Seaborne's hands.

"Hey, lad, you're out of sorts, I know, but don't take it out on the mountain"—Seaborne grabbed the mallet back—"or me. It's your daylights; we Melorians are less at home with heights. Find something to occupy your mind and you'll feel better. Here." He passed Knox a thin metal blade and a honing stone. "Take this over there and sharpen it. Careful you don't cut your finger off." Grateful for a job, Knox took the blade and set to work.

Evelyn came back empty-handed from trying to gather firewood. Chase bounded up to the campsite a few minutes later. His cheeks were red with cold, but his eyes glittered in excitement.

"Over that ridge there's a huge snowbowl—and a glacier!" he panted, gesticulating wildly. "I saw the ice covering the mountain—a solid sheet of blue ice with green veins running through it!"

"Aye, and that's what you could see," said Seaborne with a worried expression. "You didn't walk near it, did you?"

Chase shook his head. "I thought I'd wait for you."

"Wise move," said Seaborne. "A glacier is frozen water—what you saw was just the curtain, the vertical ice. Glaciers will stretch vast distances covering the ground, only you don't know you're on ice because of the snow. It can be very perilous—I didn't think we'd meet up with one so soon."

"Did you run all the way back?" Knox asked, his eyebrow raised in disbelief. It seemed impossible that this was once the brother who could barely walk fast without wheezing.

"Yeah, I'm fine—" he answered. "It's easier for me to breathe up here."

"How odd," said Evelyn, catching Knox's eye with an "I-told-you-so" expression. "It's usually harder to breathe high up in the mountains—the air is thinner."

Chase was nonchalant. "Yeah, well, not for me, I guess." He lifted up his arms and let out a loud whoop. The hounds leapt up, ready for action.

"May I remind you that we are trying to be discreet in our actions here?" groused Seaborne. "We don't need to alert the whole blessed valley—and whoever is lurking there to find us—nor do we need to set off an avalanche. I don't fancy a meeting with anyone but Ratha up here."

"He can't help it," laughed Evelyn. "It's his daylights."

Chase shrugged. He was still hesitant about the idea of daylights, but it was hard to deny that his spirits and energy were responding to being in Varuna.

"What about you?" he asked her. "Do you feel any different?"

"No," she replied. "Colder, I guess." Her brow furrowed. "I guess that means I'm not Varunan. I'm definitely not Metrian—so I must either be Melorian, or Exorian, whatever that means."

Seaborne looked up from his work at the mention of Exor.

"Nay, girl. Don't be so hasty to put yourself in a box."

"Well, then, what am I?" she said impatiently. It was bothering her more than she cared to admit. Chase and Knox—and Teddy, for that matter—all knew more or less where they belonged. Why not her? She jabbed at the fire with a stick. "I don't feel anything."

Seaborne blew on his hands, coming over to the fire to warm them. He squatted beside her.

"I don't know much about the daylights and how they come to be divided or balanced within a person, but I do know that sometimes—in some creatures—there is more equality between them. I mean, it's not as easy to know which of the four is dominant, which makes it harder to discover one's true nature. Take me, for instance; I always thought of myself as a seafarer, borne and bound to water. 'Twas only after an age here that I came to know what really moved me, and I built my home in Melor. But even so, I'm still drawn to the sea."

"So, you can sometimes be both, or more than one?" asked Evelyn, trying to understand.

"Sometimes it isn't clear: All of us—even those beyond the fog—hear the call of the stones of Ayda, but for many of us, the calls are faint and confusing, even when one lives on Ayda where the stones are most powerful. These boys can consider themselves lucky to hear one that speaks louder to them than the other three, but just because you don't doesn't mean a thing. Don't go pigeonholing yourself in with Dankar—or anyone else, for that matter—and fretting. You'll only make it harder to hear the real call when it comes along."

"And what if it doesn't?" said Evelyn, not sure if she wanted to know the answer.

Seaborne leaned in to her with a conspiratorial gleam in his eye.

"It will. It always does. Trick is getting quiet enough in your head to hear it, because for some it's just a whisper." The wind gusted between them at that moment, blowing sparks up into the air.

Seaborne followed the glowing ash with his eyes as it rose, spiraling on a current of air, watching until it burnt out. Evelyn was quiet and pensive. He cleared his throat to continue, but before he could utter another word, an eight-legged missile of boy and dog knocked him flat: Knox and Tar roughhousing. He let out a deep grunt of surprise and grabbed Knox by the back of his shirt.

"You'll find that the *more* intelligent you are, Evelyn, the softer your daylights will speak," he roared. "And the simpler you are in the head—well, case in point." He shook Knox. Evelyn grinned. Seaborne released him with a gentle cuff.

"For that, Tar, you'll pull the heavier load tomorrow—and as for you"—he wagged his finger at Knox—"you'll sharpen all four sets of blades. If we must cross a glacier, it means we'll need them soon enough." He bent down and whispered into Knox's ear, "And you might as well set that stone to your own knives. Just in case."

⊹　⊹　⊹

On the very next day they found themselves navigating the fissures and seracs of the massive glacier. It spread before them like the cracked, snow-covered bottom of a bowl, its blue rim coating the surrounding mountainside. Up close, the glacier was frozen in blue-green serpentine cables of ice—ice that creaked and sang a ghostly chorus. Seaborne insisted they walk slowly, he and the dogs pulling the sleds, so as to better steer around any deep cracks. Chase knew very little about glaciers, but what he did know he was eager to share with the rest.

"Some of those big cracks can drop down for miles. You fall down one of those and you'll never be seen again," he said cheerily.

Evelyn froze mid-step. "But the ground is covered in snow—you can't see where you're going most of the time—"

"That's why you'd better look sharp!" barked Seaborne. He was testy and unsure of himself, trusting Axl and Tar to lead them. He grumbled under his breath. Knox tried to catch some of what he said, but only a few, unencouraging words were intelligible, like *mad* and *dangerous*. Knox tried to distract him.

"Rysta said that Ratha has no fear of Dankar. Is that true?" Knox yelled to be heard over a particularly loud groan from the glacier. Snowflakes spun and hovered lazily in the air.

"Well, ask yourself? Who in the blazes would be crazy enough to try and pass through here but you lot?"

Knox shrugged. "I dunno. Maybe Dankar would if he thought he could get the stone of Varuna. If Ratha lives on her own, she'd be an easy target."

Seaborne laughed. "I said she and the Varunans were a solitary sort, but they aren't unprotected. First off, they have this—" He gestured gruffly around him. "Not many Exorians would last long in these parts. Secondly, they have Ratha and her stone, both of which are not to be tangled with. Very powerful."

Chase caught up to them, listening intently. "How so?"

Seaborne stopped and shook the snow off his hood. He repositioned the basket on his back.

"I've been told that aside from—you know—the regular things, like changing the air and the wind and influencing those who are bound to it, the stone of Varuna can plant visions in your head—flights of fancy and imaginings, that sort of thing. You think you're acting by your own lights, but you're not. They're planted by her, Ratha." Seaborne's voice dropped. "'Tis a weapon."

"How do you know," Chase exhaled, watching his breath dissipate in the thin air, "whether your thoughts are yours or hers?"

Seaborne drew his lips together in a firm line. "Your guess is as good as mine."

"So what do you think? Are we here because we thought of it, or because she wants us to be here?" said Chase.

"I've been asking myself the same question, and the only way I can answer is this. It only matters if she *doesn't* want us here. If that's the case, I assume it won't be long before we know." He looked behind him. The snow was coming down harder and Evelyn had not yet reached them. The hounds were anxious to keep moving. The constant moaning of the ice unsettled everyone. "Where's the girl, now? I told you to stay together!" Seaborne grumbled. "I keep losing you, one by one. Soon there'll be none of you left."

Chase and Knox looked for Evelyn through the deepening veil of snow, but saw nothing. They called to her but couldn't hear a response—if there was one—over the eerie wailing of the ice.

"Wait here," Seaborne ordered. "I mean it—don't move."

They watched his back retreat into the snow toward the spot where they had last seen Evelyn, a dark smudge against the white flakes. When Seaborne was a couple of hundred yards away, he stopped. Chase shouted to him, but his voice was swallowed in the muffling snowfall. Seaborne took a few more cautious steps and then disappeared completely, like a magic trick. One minute he was standing there, the next he was gone. Just like Evelyn. Chase rubbed his eyes, trying to make sense of what he'd just seen.

"Seaborne!" Knox shouted, sprinting carelessly back toward the place Seaborne and Evelyn had vanished. The snow fell faster.

"Stop!" yelled Chase. "You'll fall through, too!"

Knox dropped to his hands and knees and crawled gingerly forward. He put his ear against the ground. Suddenly, he sat up and pantomimed wildly for Chase. Chase left the hounds, standing stock-still with their ears cocked, and crawled slowly over to Knox. He was sitting a few feet from the edge of a five-foot-wide crevasse that had been covered by snow when they had walked across it only minutes beforehand.

"Careful," Knox whispered. "I don't know what's under us."

To the right, they could see a gouge in the lip of the crevasse where Seaborne and Evelyn had gone in. Any big movements, and the same could happen to them.

Knox listened again with his ear close to the lip. When he straightened up, he said, "Here. Hold my feet, I need to get closer."

Chase's mouth dropped open. "You've got to be kidding."

Knox's face was white with cold except for his nose, which was bright red. "I don't think they fell far. I thought I heard something just now, but I need to get closer to be sure."

Chase's thoughts spun—crevasses could be miles deep. It was entirely possible Evelyn and Seaborne were lying dead at the bottom right now. Chase's mouth was dry with panic. He kept picturing Knox falling and falling, without end.

"They might be out of reach, Knox. It's too risky."

"So, you just want to leave them? Come on, Chase! It's Evelyn. And Seaborne. We have to do something. At least we have to try!" Knox was right, Chase knew, but he was afraid.

"Look," Knox argued. "You can sit here and think about it for the next ten minutes, but I'm going to crawl out there and take a look, whether you like it or not. I'd prefer it if you held on to me, but it's not a requirement." Knox lay on his stomach to flatten out his weight and slid his way slowly across the ice with his elbows.

Chase grabbed his ankles and pulled him back.

"Let's think about this first." He cast his eyes around in desperation. Axl and Tar were standing patiently, coated in snow and harnessed to the sleds—harnessed with rope!

"I have an idea. Just hold on a second."

He crawled over to the dogs and unfastened them from the sleds, taking up the rope, then crawled back several feet and sunk his sword deep into the snow, as far as it would go. He tied the two ropes together and fastened one end to the hilt of his sword. Then, he tied a loop around his waist and the other end around Knox's waist and stretched out on the ground, digging his feet into the snow. His hands were raw from the cold, but he grabbed onto Knox's ankles as tightly as he could.

"Okay. Now you can go," he said grimly.

Knox got ready to slither toward the opening of the crevasse. He paused and took a deep breath. "Chase," he said over his shoulder.

"Yeah?"

"Don't let go."

Chase tried to push out of his mind the image of Knox falling and refastened his grip.

"Never."

Knox punched his hands into the snow and dragged himself closer to the crevasse. When both he and Chase were fully extended over the ground, the rope straining to hold them back, he was still a good foot from the lip of the crevasse.

"I hear something!" Knox yelled. "I have to get closer! Get me closer!" He pawed at the ground.

Chase almost lost his grip.

"Wait, wait. I'll move the rope!"

Knox was shouting wildly. It was all Chase could do to hold onto him. He could hear faint cries for help now, too, as if they were coming from a distant tunnel. He hauled on Knox's legs, pulling him back.

"Both of them are down there. I can hear them yelling. I don't think they fell far, but there's a whole bunch of snow in the way!" cried Knox, diving back in.

Chase lurched forward; the rope cut into his skin. His hands were numb. Knox was jerking and thrashing, trying to dig some of the snow out of the mouth of the crevasse. Chase struggled to keep his grip. The rope around his waist grew slack. He was slipping. Panic rolled over him in waves. He whipped his head around and sure enough, the sword was almost parallel to the ground. It wouldn't hold much longer. He shouted to Knox, but Knox's lower half was already going over. In moments they would both be in the crevasse. Chase dug his toes and elbows into the snow. A sudden sharp pain bit into his calves like knives.

"*Aaargh!*" he yelled.

His body lurched backwards, slowly at first and then in one great heave as whatever was behind him gave a tremendous tug. He slid backwards to safer ground, pulling Knox with him.

Chase didn't loosen his grip until Knox had scooched backwards and was sitting up.

"It's okay. We're okay. You can let him go now!" Knox thumped Axl on her flank. She and Tar opened their jaws and released Chase's bleeding calves.

"That stings," winced Chase, examining the two large bite marks in both of his calves where the hounds had sunk their teeth into him. He patted them both gratefully.

The hounds sniffed the blood on his pants, then pawed the ground. Axl cocked her ear again and barked three piercing barks. Tar howled loudly. Knox covered his ears.

"I think they're telling Seaborne we're here."

"You heard both Evelyn and Seaborne? You're sure?" asked Chase.

Knox nodded his reply.

"Well, at least they're alive—for what that's worth." Chase pictured Seaborne and Evelyn slowly freezing to death just below the glacier's surface.

Knox faced his brother with a serious expression. Even his freckles looked pale and cold.

"Seaborne told us that Varunans live throughout these mountains. They may be watching right now. I'll stay here and mark the spot. You take the dogs and get help."

Chase shook his head. He couldn't just leave Knox—all of them—in the middle of nowhere. It was safer to stay together and let help come to them.

Knox's eyes flashed. Chase hadn't noticed until that moment that his brother's blue eyes were flecked with green.

"This is your country, Chase. Ratha is your Keeper. If anyone can find her or find help, it's you. Follow your daylights." He put his hand, gently for once, on Chase's shoulder.

"I trust you."

Chase looked at him for signs of sarcasm, but there were none.

"Tinator was right, Chase. You have the sword because you deserve it. I screw everything up." Knox turned his head away. "If it weren't for me, Frankie and Teddy would be with us, and now Evelyn and Seaborne—" He broke off, close to tears. "Please help me fix it."

Chase squatted beside Knox and scanned the surrounding mountainside. The snow had stopped falling and the sky had brightened. The sun hung to the west like a fuzzy, white coin; soon it would dip beyond the range and they would be in the dark.

"Seaborne also said that if Ratha didn't want us here, we would find out soon enough. I think we've found out," he said, standing; then he walked silently toward his sword. His calves had stopped hurting, the blood already congealed from where Axl and Tar had grabbed him. His body was able to heal itself more quickly. His daylights must be getting stronger. Chase resheathed his sword, squared his shoulders, coiled the rope, and hoisted his pack onto his back.

"It's not your fault, Knox," he said. "If you want to blame somebody, blame Dad's lab. But who's to say Mom and Dad wouldn't be lost out here, too, if they'd gone on the boat."

Knox raised his head. "Can you imagine Dad out here?"

"Can you hear me now?" Chase pretended he was holding a cell phone to his ear.

Knox cracked a little smile.

Chase chucked the knapsack up on his shoulder.

"Okay, I'll go find help—but don't do anything stupid like trying to dig them out of the crevasse. And the hounds stay here, with you. Just in case," said Chase.

Knox stared at him blankly. "In case what?"

Chase looked him in the eye.

"In case I don't come back."

Chapter 30

HEIGHTS

Chase's world was reduced to two colors: blue and white. He picked his way carefully across the remainder of the glacier and passed a raw night hunkered down in a depression in the belly of the mountain. Surprisingly, he wasn't cold. The thick boots and fur-lined clothing had done their job, and now that the sun had risen and he was moving, he was actually a bit too warm. His mind felt roomy and light in a way he had never experienced before, and his spirits rose with each step. It seemed entirely possible that help was right around the corner. Every now and then, he shaded his eyes against the blinding glare of the snow and searched the mountainside for signs of life.

But hours of walking failed to reveal even a hint of the existence of another creature. Occasionally, out of the corner of his eye, Chase thought he saw a slight flicker of movement, but when he turned his head to investigate, he saw nothing but snow and rock. Sometime after midday, his energy flagged. The blue sky that seemed so friendly through the morning was graying over again, threatening to snow. The light turned flat, and he had difficulty discerning humps and rises in the terrain. More than a few times he slipped and fell, but he kept walking. Thoughts filled his mind with vivid clarity: Frankie holding up her new knife; Teddy laughing at the bow of the skiff; Knox walking beside him in the forest; Evelyn's dark eyes peeking out from under her hood. Chase felt for the hilt of his sword. He remembered Knox's parting words: *Tinator was right*. Even now he wasn't sure he believed them. He hadn't protected his brothers and his friends very well. Tears pricked the corners of his eyes. He blinked them back and took another step, which sent him hurtling down a steep hill.

At the bottom he stayed on his back, like an upended seal, trying to stem his fear. He sat up and mentally went over the situation at hand. It seemed unlikely that Seaborne and Evelyn would survive for the days it might take before he found help—let alone Knox. Chase rubbed his eyes and shook the snow off his rucksack. Now was as good a time as any to eat. He pulled out a stick of dried meat and chewed on it thoughtfully.

Every Keeper had a realm, and that realm had a center or a city—Varuna should not be any different, Chase reminded himself. He just had to find it. He opened his canteen and took a drink; then, carefully, he funneled snow into the mouth of the canteen and stowed it under his coat. The warmth of his body would melt the snow. Chase shut his eyes.

In a flash, as if someone had dropped a slide into a projector, he saw a vision of a wide terrace set into a mountainside, surrounded by three sides of steep steps. At the center sat a large, square structure, several stories high, and an immense cauldron burning with purple flame. Mysterious carvings covered the walls of the building.

The image telescoped and Chase saw the scene as if he were standing before the cauldron, the towering building above him. A door opened. A rectangle of light poured from inside, and a woman with long black hair, dressed in a shimmering gown, stepped onto the terrace. She had eyes the color of ice. Then, as quickly as it came, the vision vanished; Chase was alone again in the middle of nowhere. Without warning, Chase's left hand suddenly exploded in pain. His eyes flew open. A large, tawny bird was perched beside him, snacking on a piece of his meat stick. It rotated its head around and stared sideways at him.

Chase tore off more meat and held it out. The bird hopped toward him, greedily nipping Chase's extended fingers.

"You'll need better aim if you want more," said Chase. The bird gazed back at him impassively. He moved closer. The bird launched into the air in a flurry of feathers and wings.

"Wait! Come back! I'm not going to hurt you!" he yelled. It felt extremely important that the bird not leave him.

The bird circled above his head several times and landed some forty feet away. Chase walked slowly toward it. When he got within arm's reach, it took off again. They repeated this several times, the bird never allowing Chase to get any closer.

"Forget it, I'm not playing," he said, after the third attempt. He took out his canteen again, ignoring the bird. It flew into a fury, shrieking and clawing at the canteen, attacking his face and beating his head with its wings.

"Back off!" shouted Chase, swinging wildly at the bird with his canteen. But it didn't stop until he started moving. Slowly it dawned on Chase that the bird might be there for a reason, to guide him, like the turtles in Metria. He stowed his canteen and kept his eyes on the bird. It began to snow.

The bird led him high along a mountain ridge. Snow fell heavily now and his progress was painfully slow. He had to stop frequently to stamp his feet and return feeling to his toes. There was no hint of a trail, and he had no way of knowing if he might accidentally wander off the side of the mountain. Every time he closed his eyes, he saw the vision of the celestial terrace. It must be nearby. Ratha must have sent the bird. Ratha would not let him die out here.

Or would she?

Seaborne said that Ratha could put dreams into people's heads—make them think they were acting on their own when they weren't. Could she be tricking him? Did she want him to find her, or was she leading him on some wild goose chase? Chase stumbled and fell flat on his face. He rolled onto his side, too tired to ward off the falling snowflakes.

"Ratha, help me," he pleaded into the white nothingness. No sign of the bird; it had vanished into the thick veil of snow, like everything else. Chase curled into a fetal position. Was there nothing on Ayda he could rely on? Rothermel had fought for them, and now he was ready to turn them over to Dankar. Rysta said she would protect them, but she had taken Teddy. And now there was Ratha. Who or what was she? And why should she bother to help him? If Chase hadn't been so cold he might have cried. Instead, he forced himself back up, using every ounce of concentration he possessed to put one foot in front of the other. Another few steps brought him around a corner and onto the open face of the mountain. He saw nothing but snow; a bitter wind shrieked through his hood, hurling ice fragments at his already stinging face. He used the last of his strength to retreat out of the wind and sit down. He was worn out. He needed to rest a little before going on. Snow fell around him in thick drifts. The roar of the wind lulled him to sleep.

He dreamt that he was plucked from the snow, like a dust mite from a blanket. The sensation of weightlessness washed through him as a steady, calm wind lifted him—impossibly high—over the top of the mountain and into the sky. He was drifting high above Ayda, her restless streams and grassy plains undulating below him, tinged gold by a setting sun. He saw the shining disk of Lake Voss, the pewter-colored fingers of the Vossbeck, and the green carpet of the Melorian forest that faded into smudges of browns and yellows and reds as his sight reached west and into a desert he presumed was Exor. He circled around to follow the Hestredes east into the jungle and down along the beaches of Metria, marked by the glittering blue domes of Rysta's city. He flew back along the river and north over the prickled spine of the Varunan mountain range, the blue of the glacier fields, and the white-hooded peaks that he had passed on foot. And then he flew higher.

The entirety of the island of Ayda showed itself to him, shaped like a heart and wrapped in a curtain of fog, endless and impenetrable, stretching farther than Chase's sight could reach. He flew higher still, until he saw the curve of the Earth against the blackness of space and the atmospheric halo that shimmered around it like a protective charm. An intense light coursed down on him, too bright to look at but also hot and pure and gentle on his face. He wanted to fly higher to meet it. His muscles strained, his heart burned, and the nerve endings at his skin pulsed with an all-consuming desire to fly into the light, to never again be divided from it. He sensed the movement of the Earth circling beneath him, slow and eternal, and felt a rush of gratitude for it and the light that held him with such grace—and then he felt no more.

Chapter 31

RATHA'S AERIE

Chase wasn't sure if he was dead or alive. Every nerve in his body hurt—a fair indication that he was alive—so he sat up and opened his eyes. To his surprise, he was perched on the edge of the terrace he'd seen before in his visions. Maybe he *was* dead after all, he thought; but then his nose started to bleed: real, warm spurting blood. He tilted his head back to stem the flow and scanned the terrace out of the corner of his eye. It was all exactly as he had seen it. The burning cauldron sat twenty paces from him in front of an oversized door leading into the towering structure; beyond the edge of the terrace, the sky pulsed in vivid, phosphorescent blues, greens, and purples, as if the furnace of the world had been lit. Below him, swirls of purple-black clouds whipped around in a terrifying whirlwind.

He got to his feet, head spinning, and drew close to the cauldron in search of some warmth. It burned a bright violet hue but gave off little heat. Pale light emanated from the door to the building, which was constructed of layers of white marble and covered in sculpted friezes and geometric forms. He could identify triangles, cubes, octahedrons, and another multifaceted form he did not know. Carved figures leered down at him from the corners, and cryptic markings that might have been letters were etched into the lintel above the door. He circumnavigated the entire structure, walking past three more identical doors before returning to the cauldron. The back of his neck tingled. He turned around and found himself looking into the gray eyes of the tall, dark-haired woman from his vision.

"Ratha?" he asked, his voice trembling.

The woman's face was blank. Her skin was very pale, and her eyes held none of the curiosity that those of her siblings possessed.

"It is I," she replied, though Chase was unsure whether she actually spoke out loud or just in his head. She moved, crossing the distance between them with astonishing speed. Her robe flashed and flickered in a multitude of colors as she moved. The effect was strobe-like. Chase put his head between his knees.

"My brother, my friends, they fell; the glacier—" He puffed from his inverted position. "You have to help them!"

"They are safe," said Ratha. "They were rescued soon after you left them." She stood a few feet away from him, perfectly still. "I have been watching you since you came to Ayda."

Chase raised his head. "You were watching us the whole time?"

Ratha did not break his gaze.

"Of course. Very little passes my regard in Varuna—or elsewhere."

"So you know we've been looking for you," said Chase, "and that Dankar and your brother and sister are after us."

Ratha nodded. "I also know you are unsure of whom to trust or whether you may trust me—not altogether unwise."

Chase felt for his sword and was relieved to find he was still wearing it. The knowledge gave him courage.

"What do you mean?"

Ratha shifted, and her robe changed colors. Chase found himself staring, transfixed by its hypnotic effect. She turned on her heel and glided to the edge of the terrace.

"It is a peculiar trait in humans to seek validation and direction from others and not from within," she mused. "It makes you vulnerable, deaf to your own daylights and ignorant of the power they possess. You become subject to the whims of those whom you presume to be more powerful than yourselves, always to your peril."

Ratha took a feather from the deep cuffs of her robe and tossed it over the edge of the platform. It bounced and fluttered like a buoy on an angry sea, catching each gust, floating back and forth, up and down, then, suddenly, banking into a steep dive and falling into the swirling, boiling mist. She turned toward him again and continued.

"But you have come far alone, farther than others might have expected of you—even if you did require assistance." She cocked her head to the side, reminding him of the bird she had sent.

"How did I get here?" Chase ventured.

"I brought you," answered Ratha.

"But I didn't see or speak with anyone the whole time since I left the glacier."

Ratha took a few steps toward him. Her eyes flashed, hungrily, with a purple light.

"Your brother is right, Chase, your daylights are bound to Varuna. It is this fact, and this fact alone, that allows you to stand before me, where few outliers have ever stood. But then, such is the way of our kind: to make our own way."

A stiff wind began to blow through the door closest to them, as if called by some unseen command. It mingled with a soft, warm breeze coming from the door on the opposite side of the building. The flames in the cauldron danced. Chase's bangs lifted off his forehead and the fabric of Ratha's robe billowed around her as she spoke.

"It is for Varunans to bring sight to the blind and strength to the weak. Like the wind that flattens the grass and stirs the seas and the trees, we give evidence of things unseen and kindle hope in the hearts of those who have none." The fire in the cauldron leapt higher and higher. The clouds pitched violently around the terrace. Her voice rose above the wind.

"I am Ratha, Keeper of the stone of Varuna, eldest daughter of Remiel and Rachel, mistress of wind and air, reader of stars and dreams, protector of all who heed my call. Your presence here is evidence of a dream that is now become real: a wish, barely spoken."

A tremendous gust of wind blew across the terrace and then seemed to suck back in on itself, snuffing the fire in the cauldron and leaving silence in its wake. Before Chase could register what was happening, Ratha was beside him again, her hand outstretched to his face. She cupped his chin in her hand and brought him nearer to her. Pursing her lips, she blew softly into Chase's mouth. His lips parted slightly and he inhaled. Her breath was icy and sweet; it filled his lungs completely and flowed through his chest and limbs. Any leftover weariness fell away and his mind turned blank, like a curtain closing across a stage. Slowly, an image materialized—he recognized it instantly: the granite rocks off of Summerledge. Waves pummeled the ledge with thundering booms. Cold, angry spray exploded into the air. At the very edge, a lone figure paced back and forth, drenched in frigid water. Wind buffeted the blanket she was wrapped in, trying to wrench it out of her clenched fingers.

"Mom!" he cried out.

The image changed. Chase now saw the house itself, another familiar face in a window, eyes blank and rimmed with red. His father's fists banged on the windowpane. Chase looked back to the rocks. The blanket lay crumpled on the ledge—empty.

"MOM!" he yelled again, caught in the vision. He sprinted to the place where she had jumped, but the ledge wasn't there. He was back on the terrace, kneeling before Ratha.

"Please," he begged, "my mom and dad. You have to tell me: Is it real, or is it something you've planted in my head?"

Ratha extended a long, pale arm and touched his brow. With only the barest hint of emotion, she replied, "That depends on you. On what you decide."

"What do you mean?"

"You continue to submit to what you have been told rather than what you know to be true," said Ratha. "Think! You are by right Varunan; consult your daylights."

Chase shook his head, hopelessly lost.

Ratha sighed. The colors of her robes shifted again and he heard her answer in his head.

"You and your companions have more than once questioned the idea of surrender, of resignation—a question that has led you here, and not in vain. I tell you that you have been brought to Ayda, through the fog of forgetting, to serve a purpose, and it is only by this service that you will be able to reunite with your family."

Chase groaned.

"Stand up!" commanded Ratha, and to his surprise, Chase's body obeyed. He heard a distant rumbling, like thunder. A flash of lightning cut across the swirling sky. Ratha was perched at the edge of the terrace, partially shrouded in mist and unearthly light. The shifting colors in her robes made his head hurt. He had to close his eyes.

"It has been a great mystery to my brother and sister why, after the fog of forgetting cut off Ayda from the rest of creation, certain outliers from your world have managed to land on our shores. It is a rare and ominous occurrence, but it is no mystery, for it is I who have seen what they cannot; I who brought you and your companions here."

"You! You did this?" Chase exclaimed, but the conversation seemed to be happening only in his mind, a mind that could not erase the image of his grieving father and mother.

Ratha nodded slowly.

"But why?"

"It is known to me that the Fifth Stone was not destroyed or lost after the Great Battle, but banished from Ayda, sent beyond the fog, beyond the reach of Dankar—and beyond the mindless folly of my brethren." Ratha spat the last few words into the wind.

"But I thought, I thought, the fog . . ." Chase's question trailed off, uncomprehending. Bile rose into his throat. He felt violently sick.

"You thought there was no way to pass through the fog," Ratha finished. "And yet, here you are, proof that it most certainly can be done. Indeed, it is not easy, nor is there any surety in how or where one will emerge from the fog—but it can be done. It *has* been done. I have brought others here and they have survived—"

"Seaborne," Chase mumbled, opening his eyes to slits.

Ratha's clear eyes darted to his. "And others."

Chase's eyes widened.

"More? How many? Where are they?" It seemed cruel beyond imagining that his brothers, Evelyn, Frankie, Seaborne, and countless other people were nothing but experiments for this terrifying creature.

"Child," she admonished. "Do not credit me with playacting the role of a god. That is the realm of your people. Is it not? Only the progeny of the Others could be so bold—so selfish—as to make a ruin of the delight that was once theirs, to treat the daylights and all they have wrought as if they were replaceable." When she returned her gaze to his, her clear eyes seemed to spark white, icy diamonds. They bore into him like knives. Her voice dropped to a low hiss.

"Human blood runs through my vessel, as well, but unlike my brother and sister, I have no love for it."

Chase cowered beneath her. If she had been holding a weapon, he thought she would have struck him. But Ratha needed no metal weapons to inflict pain. Instead, she sent him fast-forwarding through a nightmare, each vision in his head worse than the previous one: A man with a deep, bleeding wound in his chest lay dying on a sacrificial altar; a woman in rags groaned under the weight of carrying an enormous burden; a ship tossed on a rough sea, its cargo packed with people in chains; fallen soldiers in different-colored uniforms littered a battlefield, and then another, and another; a prisoner stared out at him from behind barbed wire. The vision expanded until he was seeing a vast slum-city, where people moved like ants through narrow alleys and garbage heaps. Then, the lens of his vision clicked back again and he was above the Earth, watching in dismay as acre after acre of trees fell and in their place grew concrete buildings, tracts of highways, and rows of houses. A darkness descended—not quite night, but nearly. The lens of his vision zoomed forward and he felt himself falling into the blurred darkness. He landed on his back, on the pavement, in the middle of a line of identical homes. Their silhouettes mirrored one another perfectly and their windows were lit with a matching, flickering, blue electronic light. In a flash of recognition, he knew exactly where he was: Elm Ridge Road.

Ratha spoke, her voice cold, dismissive.

"Who needs Dankar when you have already enslaved yourselves? The Others have taught you well." She stepped away. Chase's mind went suddenly, gratefully, blank.

"Few remain beyond the fog who can recall the light of their own making," said Ratha in a faraway voice. A final image dawned in Chase's head, like the sun rising over a shadowy mountain range. It was of a lobster boat with a blue hull, drifting quietly in the fog. A man sat at the helm, his gray-streaked hair and broad, sweatered shoulders unmistakable to anyone who had ever known him.

Captain Nate.

"What the—" said Chase, utterly confused.

"It is he whom I seek," Ratha interrupted. She retreated a few more steps.

"I don't understand," said Chase, still stuck with the image in his head.

She did not reply audibly. Instead he heard her voice in his head saying, again, "*Think.*"

He paused. The fog in the image crept lightly around in his head, as it had that day on the boat. The day they had come to Ayda. It grew thicker and engulfed him in its gauzy whiteness. He felt the peace at the center of it, the heavy weight of water held captive in the air. The pieces fell into place: The Fifth Stone still existed but was no longer on Ayda, which meant someone outside the fog must know about it—or have possession of it. *Ratha thought Captain Nate was that someone.*

"*He* has the Fifth Stone?" asked Chase, thunderstruck.

Ratha's eyes glittered.

"All that matters is that this man come to Ayda. I need your help to bring him here."

Chase exhaled. His lungs felt strong—purged and capable of breathing more deeply than he had ever been able to before, yet his knees still buckled under him and he was forced to sit on the steps. Clouds swirled below him in an eerie, more terrifying replay of the fog that had enveloped his mind, but, surprisingly, he could feel the same strange sense of peace. The dizzy feeling subsided. He spoke directly to Ratha, his eyes trained intently on her face.

"Let me see if I have this straight. You brought my brothers and me and my friends here, but you really want Captain Nate, because he may or may not have the Fifth Stone, which was banished from Ayda. You've brought other people from outside to Ayda for this same reason, but all this time you've been trying to get Captain Nate?"

Ratha nodded.

Chase shook his head in disbelief.

"I have searched long and erred many times in my effort to locate the Keeper of the Fifth Stone," she continued, pacing the edge of the terrace again, her hair and robes streaming behind her. "It is beyond even my sight to know whether this man is the one, but you must understand: He is known to me from another time, long passed. There is no explanation for the continued existence of his vessel than the one I have reasoned. At the very least, he is more than who you think he is—that I am sure of—as he has evaded my efforts to bring him here. Like a fisherman, I have caught others in my net, but never the one whom I seek."

"But—" Chase protested, his mind reeling with questions. "What makes you think I can convince Captain Nate to come here? And if he is the Keeper of the Fifth Stone, why can't he just come here whenever he wants—by himself?"

"If I knew the answer to your last question I would not need your assistance!" cried Ratha. "For five hundred years we have suffered Dankar's abuses, waiting for the return of the Fifth Stone. It is time for it to end. This man is the key. I know it. He has a debt to pay here and he will pay it—on my father's ashes he will make good!" Her eyes became less transparent and more human in her anger, but the expression on her face was monstrous. Chase recoiled. Here was a Keeper that would see them all dead to get what she wanted. Of *that,* he was sure.

"Okay, okay. It's just that it seems pretty impossible from where I am right now," he said, trying to placate her. "Plus, I'm just a kid, you know? Grown-ups don't listen to kids where I come from. Especially grown-ups like him. I've never even talked to him."

Ratha turned on him with a face that reminded him of her brother's in its weariness.

"It is true. You are young, Chase, and—as you have said—it is time for you to go home to your parents. You may think me cruel, but even I am moved by a mother's grief. If they had asked I might have tried to send the others back, as well." She hesitated, as if the words were stuck in her mouth. "Yet you—and your companions—have been the only ones to come to Ayda from beyond and question the things you were told. And only you, Chase Thompson, have come this far, to my very doorstep, in search of aid. All the others were too easily contented. They grew to love our lands more than their own." She paused a moment, then spoke quietly, almost to herself. "I wonder, Chase, if that will be your fate? You do love Ayda, do you not?"

Chase said nothing for several minutes. He remembered flying over Ayda, its now-familiar shape nested in a pillow of fog. His own heart constricted. Ratha was right. He did love Ayda—but he loved his parents more.

"What do you want me to do?" he asked.

Ratha smiled, which startled Chase more than anything else she had done so far. She came close. He felt his emotions soar—his daylights responding to her proximity. If she could feel it, she did not react. He wondered if she wore a necklace too, like her sister. He doubted it. Ratha emanated the power of her stone in a way her siblings did not. She would need no intermediary.

"If you agree to help bring this man to me, the sea captain, I will see to it that Dankar frees the little girl and that you and your companions are sent home."

Chase raised his eyebrows in disbelief. "You can do that?"

"I would not say so unless I thought I could."

"But how? Everybody else around here is like—" Chase lifted his hands and shrugged.

Rysta gave him a queer half-smile.

"My brother was not entirely wrong to think that Dankar is open to negotiation—he was only mistaken in understanding what prize Dankar values. Long have I followed the Usurper's thoughts, and to what ends you need not worry. If you agree to shoulder the task set before you, I shall ensure the release of your friend and assist you and your fellow outliers back through the fog. If you decide *not* to do as I ask, you shall be reunited with the friends who remain at large and left to your own fates here on Ayda. I shall not interfere with you again. It is not for any Keeper to control the actions of her people—and despite what you may think of me, I am bound by my vow. The choice is before you; I will leave you here to decide. But do not tarry."

Ratha's voice hung in the air long after she was gone. Chase stared into the ever-changing tumult of clouds around him, trying to sort it all out. He had no idea how to get off of Ayda, or how he would return, let alone with Captain Nate. And even if they could figure out a way to leave, if what Rysta had told them was true, none of them would remember anything about Ayda once they had passed back through the fog. And if by chance they did remember, like those who left Ayda in the ancient days before the fog, they would be driven crazy with the desire to find it again. Why should they be any different? Ratha must know that. He was doomed to fail.

Chase sighed. The clouds continued to roil around him, changing from deep lavenders to shades of apricot. He thought of the tube with the prisms and mirrors at the bottom that he used to love to look through when he was little. What was it called? The name was on the tip of his tongue. Already he was forgetting things. The longer they all stayed on Ayda, the more they would forget. If they were going to leave, they would have to do it soon. But what then? Spend the rest of his life trying to find a place no one believed in, and convince Captain Nate to go there? The whole plan was ridiculous. *Unless—!*

Chase sat bolt upright. Unless Captain Nate really *did* have the Fifth Stone! If he did, then he would *know* Chase wasn't crazy. And surely the Keeper of the Fifth Stone would be able to find his way back to Ayda. Chase felt like vaulting off the stairs. The Fifth Stone was the key. It was the answer to everything!

But what if Captain Nate *didn't* have the stone? Chase rubbed the hilt of his sword across his forehead. The cool weight of it was reassuring. He sighed, thinking of his mother and father and Ratha's vision. He thought about Teddy, far away in Metria, and Frankie imprisoned in Exor. If Ratha sent them all back through the fog, then everyone would be together again in Fells Harbor. Safe. It wouldn't really matter then whether or not Captain Nate had the Fifth Stone—or if he came back with it. *His* own family would be whole again. *But what about Ayda? What about Dankar?* asked a voice inside his head. Night grew close around him, pulling a blanket of dark over the colors at the edge of the sky. More stars emerged, flickering and close. Chase found the North Star, Polaris, aligned directly above the farthest corner of the terrace. His eyes traveled to each corner and then back to the center. Four corners. Four elements. Four winds. Four directions. Four stones—and one center.

He knew what he had to do.

TIME FLIES

When Ratha returned, she held a large fan in her hand. Her gray eyes were more tender. Chase could now see the resemblance between her and her sister.

"I'll do it," he said, "but you will have to show me how."

Ratha smiled her odd smile. "Of course. You didn't think I would send you back through the fog unguided?"

Chase shrugged. He didn't know what to think anymore.

"I . . . I have a couple of questions," he stammered. She gestured for him to continue with her fan.

"My mother, my father—what I saw. Has it happened already? Or will I get back in time to prevent it?"

Ratha gently opened and closed the fan, then used it as a pointer to draw an imaginary line in the air.

"The span of a life can be measured in many ways. Time appears to be one-dimensional and linear: one moment following the next, from beginning to end. But what if I were to tell you that time is more like the ridges of this fan?" She slowly opened the first section of the fan.

"Here you are born," she opened another. "Here you learned to read and to write," and another two, "and here you came to Ayda. The rest has yet to unfold. We can lay the time out flat"—she opened the fan—"or we can layer it, one event upon another, to create a plane where all things are occurring at once." She snapped the fan shut and handed it to Chase, who spread it out and closed it a few times, lost in thought.

"So you're saying that everything that is ever going to happen to me is actually happening right now, all at once, even though I can only experience it from one minute to the next?" he asked, his mind groping for understanding.

"Yes!" Ratha exclaimed, happy that his Varunan daylights had kicked in. "Past and future are nothing but visions to comfort the human mind—the only real time is now."

Chase tapped on the closed fan with his index finger. "And so, you can, sort of, drop us through the layers when we go back through the fog? Send us back to another time?"

She nodded. "It is an imperfect thing, but essentially, yes, I should be able to do so—I will try my best."

Chase mulled this over for a moment.

"I don't want my mother to worry. Or my father, or Mrs. Dellemere."

"Granted."

"And Frankie and Teddy leave with us."

"Of course."

"How will I convince Captain Nate to come back here? He won't believe me."

"You must tell him everything that you remember from your time on Ayda. If he is who I think he is, he will come."

"Why?"

"That does not concern you."

Chase rubbed his temple. "Okay, then. What's the plan?"

Ratha leaned forward and blew through his lips once more. Her breath snaked through his mind, settling in, and he saw it all play out. When she was finished, his heart was pounding.

"There has to be another way!" he cried.

"There is no other way." Ratha's face was next to his, her gaze intense and expectant. He realized that she needed him as much as he needed her.

"You must guard this plan with your daylights," she said. "Remember that your freedom—and that of your companions—depends on its success. Tell no one, not even the wayfarer, Seaborne. He will try to prevent it. He will not understand."

Overhead, a meteor trailed a shower of sparkling light. Chase had nothing left to say. He lifted the backpack at his feet, shouldered it, and strode to the edge of the terrace. The whirling vapors swirled ferociously around him. He turned back to Ratha.

"One last thing—how the heck do I get down from here?"

"The same way you arrived," answered Ratha. A man and a woman appeared at the open door of the tower, both dressed in white. One was dark-skinned, the other pale. Both had long white hair and clear eyes. They joined Chase on the stairs.

"Calyphor and Deruda are two of the last remaining ancients. They have lived on Ayda since its creation. It is by the efforts of their kin that my family was brought here so long ago. They will take you to your companions."

Chase mumbled a greeting. Ratha lifted Chase's chin and locked eyes with him once more.

"We may not meet again, Chase Thompson, but I will be watching you. When you are most alone, I will be with you." She paused to emphasize her point. "Bring back the sea captain and fulfill your purpose. Ayda will not survive without you." The wind picked up and the cauldron burst into flame again. With a swirl of her robe, she crossed the terrace. At the furthermost point, she stopped and uttered a single word:

"Kaleidoscope."

"What?"

"The toy you loved as a child, with the prisms. It's called a kaleidoscope." She left Chase with his mouth hanging open. Ratha had read his every thought. He eyed the two ancient Varunans next to him warily, wondering if they could do the same. Calyphor stepped behind him and wrapped his arms around Chase's chest. He heard a strange ruffling sound, then a flapping, and before Chase could determine where it came from, Calyphor vaulted off the stairs, launching them both straight into the void.

"*Aiiiyeeeeeeee!*" Chase yelled, his legs flailing wildly.

Calyphor kept him in a death grip, locking his arms against his sides. Chase closed his eyes and tried to stay conscious. They hurtled down,

down, down, diving through the whirlwind, the force of their descent causing his lips and cheeks to flutter uncontrollably. The rush of air quieted, and Chase heard a sloughing sound, like a sail catching in the wind. They broke through the clouds and glided swiftly over the dark silhouette of the mountains. It was not yet dawn. The world below lay hushed and sleeping, resting in the pause before the sun ushered in the rigors of the day. Deruda was beside them, her white hair streaming back as she banked into a turn, her wings stretching twelve feet across. Chase could only imagine how large Calyphor's wings were.

Soon they were skimming over the lower mountain ranges, past the glacier where Chase had left the others, over the stony ridges of the mountain pass, and down into the valley toward the glimmering waters of Lake Voss. Calyphor and Deruda landed softly on a wide, pebbly shore, folded their wings compactly beneath their robes, and stood calmly, looking very much the same as before. They pointed down the shallow stretch of beach and then rose again slowly, their wings beating the air. They hovered for a moment above Chase, and then, flew off into the brightening sky.

Chase watched in amazement as they disappeared, then sped across the bank of the lake in the direction they indicated he should go. He almost fell when he tripped over what he took to be a large log.

"Mind yourself, lad!" yelped a familiar, gruff voice. Seaborne sat up, sword in hand, one side of his face coated in sand and small pebbles. Evelyn and Knox were asleep a few feet away, wrapped in their ponchos. Something strong and furry thudded against Chase's back, flattening him.

"It's me . . . it's me!" he shouted. "Some watchdogs you are!" he joked.

Axl and Tar licked him in the face.

"Did you see me? I *flew* here."

"Lucky you," yawned Seaborne, "but don't go thinking you're something special. Evelyn and I had a little bit of the same treatment getting out of that blasted ice coffin."

"They told us you'd be here!" called Evelyn in a sleepy voice.

Knox launched himself at his brother. He was beaming.

"I knew you'd find her, Chase! I knew it!" he chortled. "How was it? Are you all right?"

"Better now!" replied Chase, happier than he could ever have imagined to see their faces. Just then the sun rose over the treetops, turning the lake a brilliant pink. Evelyn exhaled sharply.

"Chase—your eyes!"

"What?" he asked.

"Look," she said, and pointed him toward the lake. He knelt low to look at his reflection in the rose-tinted surface. His face looked back at him as clearly as if he had been staring into a mirror, although the image he saw was different than the one he remembered. His hair was longer now, and his face looked older and more angular; it took him several moments of close inspection to realize what Evelyn was talking about.

His blue eyes had turned purple.

✢   ✢   ✢

Seaborne, Evelyn, and the boys watched together in silence as the rising sun transformed the sky with soft colors that were perfectly reflected off the still surface of the lake. Only after the colors had faded into light blue did Chase speak again. He told them everything that had happened to him since he'd left them on the glacier, or *nearly* everything. He remembered Ratha's warning, and did not fill them in on the details of her plan, saying only that they were to travel back to Metria where they would be reunited with Frankie and Teddy, and sent home through the fog.

"She's been spending too much time up there in the clouds with the birdfolk," scoffed Seaborne. "No one's ever gone back through the fog." He turned his back to begin packing up the campsite. "But nonetheless, if she's willing to deal the devil with Dankar and get you back to your sister, that is no small thing, eh, Evelyn?" Seaborne smiled to himself. "And the little one is waiting for you in Metria. It will be good to have you all back where you belong."

"What about Rothermel and Rysta's meeting, and giving us to Dankar one by one?" asked Knox.

"Ratha said she knows more about what Dankar wants than either her brother or sister," said Chase. "She said not to worry about it."

Evelyn stared at the lake, her brow furrowed as if she was trying to work something out for herself.

"How is Ratha supposed to do all this?" she asked, her tone suspicious.

Chase frowned. He shoved some belongings into a bag to mask his nervousness.

"Ratha says we should go back to Metria right away and wait there for Frankie. She didn't tell me how she's going to get her there, just that she would."

"Then what?" challenged Evelyn.

Chase swallowed, buying some time to think. "Uh, it's kind of hard to explain. She said she's going to create a pocket or a window or something and send us through the fog. Back home."

"Just like that, huh?" Evelyn looked at Chase sideways. "She's going to do what nobody else has managed to do in the whole history of Ayda? Sounds fishy to me, Chase."

Seaborne snorted. "More than fishy; downright foolish, and not bloody likely, I'm sorry to say. Ratha thinks a little more highly of herself than she should. That fog was put there by forces more powerful than any one Keeper. She's mad to think of it. You'll end up lost, or worse."

"Worse?" said Knox.

"Worse," said Seaborne. "Washed ashore in some godforsaken pit in Exor or dashed on the straits off Varuna. If she thinks I've traveled hundreds of leagues on foot, fought my way through an army of Exorians trying to use me as a torch, and been stuck in a giant block of ice just to stand by and let you set sail in circles . . ." He lifted his head and shouted into the sky, toward the mountains. "Then she's daft!"

"You don't like her much, do you, Seaborne?" asked Knox, smiling.

Seaborne pulled at his beard. "Varunans aren't generally my sort, I will say that, but I like the lad well enough," he said, gesturing at Chase. He continued, gazing north toward the mountains again. "Still, if Ratha says we should go to Metria, then I think that's where we should go, and if she can get you back to your sister, then so much the better; but I don't believe a word she says about passing through the fog and going home. That was a cruel thing to put in your head. Don't think on it anymore, Chase, or any of you, for that matter. It's impossible. And even if it weren't, your minds would be so disordered when you came out the other side that you wouldn't recognize yourselves. It's another one of her visions, and a dangerous one at that."

"Do you think she meant what she said about Frankie?" Evelyn asked Chase.

"Ratha is the most powerful Keeper I've met," said Chase, shrugging. "She's helped us so far. So, yeah, I think she meant it."

He looked back at the mountains. Somewhere beyond his sight Ratha was watching. He shivered a little at the memory of her, as if a cold wind had crawled up his poncho. "I don't think we have a choice. We'll just have to trust her."

"Bad idea," harrumphed Seaborne. "But a bad idea is better than no idea, I'll wager."

☩   ☩   ☩

They mapped a route that would take them east along the shores of Lake Voss, then south toward the head of the Hestredes, where, if all went according to plan, a ship from Metria would be waiting. Huge boulders lined the immediate shore; beyond them the beach turned soft and shale-covered. Seaborne guessed that they would only be on foot for a few days at most. He hummed lightly under his breath as they set out.

"You're in a good mood," Evelyn noted.

"I like the idea of seeing the city of Metria again. 'Twas where I grew up, you know."

"Calla told us. She said you would take her there someday."

A misty look crossed Seaborne's rugged features.

"Aye, I plan to do that."

Chase was jumpy. To keep his mind off things, he asked Seaborne about the man they'd seen him with in Rysta's gazing pool. The one who owned the jacket he was now wearing. Seaborne scowled, tugging at the strap that held the sword to his back.

"He was an officer on the ship I served on as a boy—it was scuttled in battle. A cannon blew the center mast. I remember the sound of that, I'll tell you. Timber screaming. It's not a sound one soon forgets." Seaborne shook his head, then added, "He was a good man. He could have left me there, but he didn't."

"You're a good man, too, Seaborne," said Evelyn. "You saved us."

Seaborne bowed his head toward her, smiling.

They hadn't walked more than half a mile when Chase caught a flash out of the corner of his eye. He stopped, looking out across the silvery surface of the lake. Small ripples broke the otherwise crystal-clear mirror of the sky. He took another step and again saw a flash reflected on the lake. Knox caught Chase by the arm and pointed up. Long trails of light, like the tail of a comet, were shooting across the sky. The dogs barked an alarm.

"We have company!" shouted Knox.

"Here we go." Chase groaned inwardly, and unsheathed his sword. Backed up against the scree of boulders, they had two options: surrender or fight. If he surrendered right away, it would be too obvious. He said a silent prayer to Ratha, hoping Seaborne was wrong about her.

Within seconds, a host of Exorian warriors appeared around a bend in the beach. They raced toward them, bare feet churning the sand into dust clouds, their burning spears reflected ad infinitum on the surface of the lake. Chase counted twenty of them—too few for an all-out assault, but still too many for their small group to overpower; then again, that wasn't the point.

Knox balanced a blade between his thumb and forefinger. He gave Chase a wry smile.

"Team Thompson?"

Chase lifted his sword. The morning sun glinted off its sharp edges, illuminating the detailing on the blade. He squared his shoulders and took a fighting stance next to Knox. It wouldn't be the worst thing in the world to take a few Exorians out. A little justice for Tinator.

"Team Thompson."

The low *thwunk* of the crossbow resounded behind them. A large, iron-tipped bolt whizzed by their heads, finding its mark with a thud, quickly followed by another. Seaborne reloaded and fired into the oncoming Exorians as quickly as he could in hopes that he could buy some time. Evelyn was at his elbow, slingshot drawn. Chase and Knox attacked, darting between the unwieldy shields and dodging the flame-tipped spears. They had learned well from the previous battle and aimed for the unprotected knees and elbows of the Exorians and the tender seam between their tough patches of skin.

Chase's sword clashed with steel, locked in combat with the spear of an Exorian warrior. Knox extricated himself from the melee, circling from a distance, where his throwing knives could be most efficient. Axl and Tar dove in, savagely biting any exposed flesh they could find. An Exorian shouted in pain, then clobbered one of the hounds with his heavy shield. Tar yelped and retreated.

Seaborne quickly ran out of bolts; he dropped the crossbow and unslung his broadsword. The fighting escalated and a surge of battle fever passed through the Exorians as they realized their prey would not surrender without a fight. Chase felt it wash across him like a wave. His stomach lurched. Had Ratha planned on this? There was no way to know. He searched the face of an oncoming Exorian for any sign of complicity. There was none. Instead, the orange flecks in the Exorian's eyes danced like flames ignited by the heat of battle. Chase grunted in frustration, fighting in earnest now, slashing at whatever he could lay his sword on. Growls and yelps filled the air. Evelyn was down on one knee, scraping the ground for rocks to refill her slingshot. In the confusion she couldn't see two Exorians coming up behind her, their spears extended.

"Evelyn! Behind you!" Chase bellowed.

She looked up wildly, and drew her knife from the folds of her poncho. In an elegant pirouette, she sidestepped the first Exorian's spear tip, and drove her blade hard into the man's side, into the pink skin between the serpentine scales that protected his torso. She twisted her blade and yanked up, as Calla had taught her. His mouth opened and she felt the heat of his breath. His weight against the knife doubled. Evelyn quickly withdrew it and let him fall to the ground. She turned to face the next attacker, who had mysteriously abandoned her. She understood why a second later when the smell of burning poncho reached her nostrils. Without another thought, she sprinted into the lake and dove under.

The Exorians formed a semicircle around Seaborne and Chase, who fought back-to-back, their flank protected by the edge of the lake. The baked, hide-like skin of the warriors seemed out of place in the bright sunshine as it tensed and pulsed with their defensive movements. Seaborne was now fighting two-handed, his sword in one hand and knife in the other. Knox circled the periphery, throwing rocks, his knives used up.

The Exorians repositioned into a tight line, hemming Seaborne and Chase against the edge of the lake. They were no longer attacking and seemed uninterested in pressing their advantage.

"What's going on?" Knox shouted to Seaborne. "What are they doing?"

"I don't know; it's not like them at all," yelled Seaborne, smashing his sword into the closest Exorian shield. "Where's your fight gone?" he shouted.

The Exorian holding the shield looked at him blankly. Then, as a unit, he and the other Exorians advanced another step, pushing Seaborne and Chase back toward the lake. Water licked at their boots. The enemy took another step forward to force Seaborne and Chase into further retreat. The water now reached their knees. The Exorians stood at the edge and lowered their spears. A yell from Evelyn came from behind them. She was standing waist-high in water, blue-lipped and shivering.

"They won't come in!" she yelled.

"That's because they can't swim—the devils!" yelled Seaborne.

Chase let his sword arm fall.

"What are you doing there, lad? Didn't Tinator teach you not to quit?" barked Seaborne.

"This isn't a fight, Seaborne—it's a raiding party sent to capture us. They won't kill us."

"Doesn't feel that way to me!" shouted Evelyn.

Knox tried to create a distraction by whooping and running down the beach. Two Exorians separated from the rest to chase him. Out of habit, Chase advanced to help him, but he was roughly pushed back into the lake by the bulk of the enemy. Axl and a limping Tar prowled the semicircle of warriors, tearing at their ankles and calves. One large Exorian glared at Seaborne and jabbed toward their long, matted fur with his flaming spear.

"You'll be no help if you're roasted!" Seaborne yelled to the dogs, then let loose a long, piercing whistle. The hounds darted away.

Chase could no longer feel his feet. His ankles were numb, and the cold rose up through his bones in a nauseating ache. Evelyn was shivering violently. Seaborne growled at the Exorians and splashed them with water, trying to break the standoff.

"Damn you, you rot-ridden fireworms! At least make it a decent fight!"

Moments later, two Exorians returned with a kicking, struggling Knox. Another stepped forward, looking back and forth between Knox and the three others in the lake. He gestured with his spear for them to come out of the water.

"I'd rather not, thank you. It's quite nice in here. Refreshing!" replied Seaborne.

In response, the Exorian slammed the shaft of his spear into the back of Knox's knees, hard. Knox crumpled to the ground. The Exorian pinned him to the ground with his foot and slowly lowered the burning tip of his spear toward the back of Knox's head, pausing just above his neck. He turned and challenged Chase with his stare. The orange specks in his eyes were like sparks of flame.

"Don't do it, Chase!" gurgled Knox. The Exorian mashed his face into the ground with his foot.

Chase sheathed his sword and walked out of the lake, hands held above his head. Seaborne and Evelyn followed behind, their heads hung in defeat. Knox was yanked to his feet. The Exorians quickly stripped them of their weapons and shackled them together.

"You had to get caught, eh, laddie?" Seaborne groused at Knox.

"Where will they take us?" whispered Evelyn.

"Where do you think?" Seaborne replied, looking west.

Chase turned his eyes to the sky, looking for a sign. Surely Calyphor and Deruda were up there somewhere? He knew that part of the plan was to be caught by the Exorians on their way to Metria, but Ratha had led him to believe that she would intervene. With a sinking feeling, Chase realized he had never asked her *when*. How far was she willing to let this go?

Ratha, where are you? he begged silently.

Chapter 33

THE ENEMY

The Exorians kept them at a trot, heading due north. Soon the Voss was just a small silver disk in the background, the mountains of Varuna looming large to the east. Chase scanned their craggy surfaces for signs of life, but soon fatigue and thirst made it hard to concentrate on anything but moving forward. At dusk, they were allowed to stop. The prisoners were tied in a circle with their backs facing one another and moved a short distance away. Night was falling fast. They were too tired to speak, and fell into a fitful sleep leaning into one another. Evelyn was the first to be jolted awake by an Exorian unshackling her. She struggled, waking the others as he dragged her by the scruff of her poncho toward his company.

"Leave her alone, damn you!" shouted Seaborne, diving forward on his elbows after her.

A nearby guard bludgeoned him with the shaft of his spear and he slumped to the ground, bleeding from the forehead. Chase and Knox, still yoked to him, were slammed backwards. The guard made a menacing gesture. They watched helplessly as an Exorian circled Evelyn and then lowered her hood.

A tangled mass of dark hair spilled down in ropes between the jut of her shoulder blades. The Exorian grabbed it in his fist and pulled her head back, exposing her neck; then, he drew his knife. Its thin edge glinted in the dying light, sharp as a razor.

"STOP!" Chase cried out, struggling against his bonds.

The Exorian flicked his expressionless eyes at Chase and Knox, then locked them on Evelyn. She whimpered.

"If you touch her, I will end you all. By my daylights I will!" roared Seaborne. One of the guards kicked him in the gut, silencing him once more.

A rushing filled Evelyn's ears, the sound of her own blood circulating in her body. The gods of death—the Ghede—had been following her for so long; that they had finally caught up to her was less of a surprise than she thought it would be. She did not flinch when the Exorian raised the knife above her; she looked straight into his orange-flecked eyes.

The knife fell.

Chase and Knox shouted in dismay.

Dark curls floated to the ground. With a few more strokes, the Exorian sheared off all of Evelyn's hair, scraping her scalp bare, then released her. Watching her calmly pull up her hood over her bald and badly nicked scalp, Chase felt something inside him wrench free and knock against his rib cage. He swore to himself that he would never put Evelyn in danger again. She sat back down beside him. Beneath her hood, her eyes—now looking impossibly large—made it seem as if her baby self had suddenly emerged through her older skin.

Chase struggled to think of something to say that would comfort her, but before he did, the Exorian came for him, then Knox, and finally, Seaborne, whose hair was removed with particularly brutal strokes.

"You saved me a job, you devil! Thank you! It was high time I had a trim!" Seaborne sneered, wiping blood out of his eyes.

The rest of the journey was marked only by slogging weariness, which grew as the captives stumbled from the foothills of Varuna's western borderlands into Exor. The Exorians granted them only a few hours of sleep at a time, and very little to eat except for some dry bread and a clear liquid that was cool and strangely satisfying.

Their captors ate nothing, but sipped often from small gold flasks that each carried on their hip. The mountains passed farther and farther into the distance and the shift in climate was severe. Green scrub and low grasses slowly gave way to dust and thick-skinned plants covered with thorns. By nightfall on the third day, the exhausted sun cast small shadows across the same arid plains, rock hummocks, canyons, and spires of Exor that Frankie had seen on her journey. The prisoners moved slowly, trudging under the weight of the long trek, the heat, and their dogged refusal to take off their Melorian ponchos. The Exorians kept them shackled together and bound at the wrists so that when one stumbled or fell, the others were dragged down, too.

Any hope that Chase had in Ratha or the Varunans coming to their rescue had dried up with the scorching heat of the Exorian plain. Everything Ratha had said to him on the terrace had been a lie, he realized, a trick to further some plan of hers that had nothing to do with him, or any of them. She couldn't care less what happened to him or his family—hadn't she said as much? Chase wanted to kick himself for being such a sap. Seaborne was right about her and her visions. He had been a fool to trust her.

The sun lay flattened against the horizon when the Exorians and their captives were met by a caravan that included two wagons pulled by donkeys. The boys and Evelyn were bundled into one of the wagons, Seaborne into the other, and the donkeys whipped into moving forward. From the open wagon, Evelyn and the boys saw the moon rise above the barren straits, a sight made more ominous by the shadows of dark fingers of rock sticking up into the luminous sky, as if to point to their only way out. Rocked by the creaking movement of the wagon and totally spent from fear and exertion, they fell into a troubled sleep.

It was still dark when rough hands woke them and dragged them to their feet, pushing them forward. A heavy door clanked shut behind them and everything went black. A vague sense of space and chill suggested that they were underground again.

"I want to see my sister!" shouted Evelyn, to no one in particular.

"And you shall, very soon," said a voice from the shadows. They heard the sound of breaking twigs and saw a spark of fire. "You will find her very well."

A torch crackled into life and a pair of glittering eyes reflected its light. The face of a young man came into view—pink and healthy, not the scabbed ruin of an Exorian warrior. There was something boyish about him, though he was quite clearly a grown man. His head and chest were bare. He wore short white trousers and a webbed belt that held a small knife at his waist.

Chase used the firelight to study their prison. They were in a small, windowless cave.

"There is no escape, so I suggest you don't try," he said plainly, his eyes following Chase's gaze.

"Where's Seaborne?" demanded Knox, stepping toward the man aggressively. The man laughed lightly.

"Seaborne? So that is his name? I myself am known by many names, the most recent being 'Louis.'" He made a wry face. "Not my favorite, I'll admit, but since it was given to me by a friend, I will answer to it." He glanced at Evelyn with deep curiosity, then looked away.

"But we are talking of your friend. The wayfarer." The man blew on his torch gently, igniting the flames further. Light and shadow chased each other around the small confines of the room. "He is to receive special . . . ah . . . status considering his age and long tenure with the Melorians. There is much Dankar would like to learn from him."

Knox made fists with his hands.

"What does that mean? You'll torture him until he tells you about Melor? Their secret hiding places? Their stone? He'll never tell! He'll die first!"

The man smiled faintly. "I know little of such things. Clearly you—like someone else I know—have been confused by the trickery of the Keepers. This will change once you have spent time here and heard what Dankar has to say. In fact, I think that if you were to ask Frankie, she would tell you something quite different."

"Where is she?" said Evelyn growled.

"And, perhaps," Louis went on, ignoring her, "in a short while, when you know what she knows, you too will think less badly of Exor—and me."

"You're an Exorian?" Chase was puzzled. The man looked normal—bald, but all Exorians seemed to be bald. Maybe even—his eyes flitted across Evelyn's hooded head—the girls.

"Not by birth, no. I, like you, come from beyond the fog; but I have lived here a long time. It is my home."

Chase snapped to attention. So here was another of Ratha's unfortunate adventurers.

"What do you want with us?" said Knox through gritted teeth. "What have we done?"

"You have done nothing; that is the point."

Knox put his hands on his hips. "So, you're saying we haven't done anything and Dankar is this great guy, and we've been tricked by the Keepers—"

Chase shifted uneasily on his feet.

"And Frankie is fine . . . and we're just gonna *love* Exor once we get to know it better?"

Louis nodded encouragingly.

"Then tell me: Why have we been chased, attacked, kidnapped, scalped, and now locked in a dungeon? Sure seems like *someone* is mad at us." He yanked off his hood, then Evelyn's, then Chase's. Their three shaved heads glowed softly in the torch light. Louis sighed, a look of genuine concern darkening his eyes.

"I am sorry for this. I told my uncle that I should accompany the excursion so that this kind of thing would not happen. The warriors do not understand your kind. It is a fault brought on by their loyalty to Dankar." He stepped closer to Evelyn.

"You are otherwise unhurt?"

Evelyn nodded once.

The man hung his torch in an iron rung sticking out of the cave wall. Evelyn repeated the only thing she cared about:

"Where is Frankie?"

Louis paused, then replied, "Asleep in her room, I believe, or perhaps in the courtyard, playing."

"*Playing?*" cried Knox. He snorted in disbelief and sat against the wall. This was too much.

Louis smiled, amused. "You may join her soon enough, but first, Dankar would like to see you."

Chase gestured for Louis to come closer.

"Ratha said she would help us if we surrendered to you. Is she here?" he whispered.

Louis looked confused and then shook his head.

"What did you say?" seethed Knox, overhearing. "Ratha *told* you we should surrender? What else did she tell you that you conveniently forgot to share with us?" He looked at Chase as though he had never seen him before, then swore. "You sold us out, Chase. That's low, really low. If anything happens to Seaborne, I swear to God, I'll—"

"It's not like that, Knox," said Chase, cutting him off. "I knew we were going to get caught, but then Ratha said—" He sighed, realizing how stupid it sounded. "She promised she'd step in, and that no one would get hurt."

Louis laughed. "I see then that you are already wise to the lies of the Keepers. Perhaps Dankar will not have to do much to convince you. Come. He will see you now."

"No way," said Knox, crossing his arms in front of his chest and digging his heels in the dirt of the floor. "I have nothing to say until we see Seaborne."

The man shrugged as if they had all the time in the world.

"Then I will leave you here until you are ready." Louis's eyes searched the wounds on their skulls. "I will see to it that I alone attend you three. I will bring you food and"—His eyes flitted over their heavy, lined clothing—"other necessities. While I am gone, reconsider your audience with Dankar. You will find he is quite agreeable. The sooner you go, the sooner you may join Frankie." He addressed Evelyn directly. "Do not wait long; I'm told she has been pining for you."

The thought of Frankie alive, somewhere nearby, needing her, undid whatever reserve Evelyn had left.

"I'll go now!" she cried.

"Good," said Louis. "Then I'll be right back." He turned to leave and the light from the torch fell across his face, igniting the orange flecks in his eyes.

✝   ✝   ✝

Louis came back shortly with dampened rags for them to wash with and a long, gauzy white tunic for each of them. Once they had changed, he escorted them down a dark corridor and up several flights of stone stairs into a main hall, bare except for several large gold medallions that hung on the walls. They passed along the edge of the same fountained courtyard that had welcomed Frankie on her first day, and under an archway leading to a rectangular chamber adorned with tall, paneless windows. As it was late at night (or perhaps early morning), the windows were as black as yawning empty eyes. Overhead, rings of candles attached to long chains added some murky illumination. They approached a dais at the far end of the hall; it held a broad, cloth-covered chair, upon which sat a tall man, half-reclined, with a circlet of gold around his bare forehead. He rolled a gold scepter across his knees, the knob of which glowed slightly. Louis bowed and moved to the side, introducing the three children to the man's view.

"At long last, you have arrived." Dankar welcomed them with satisfaction.

Chase rubbed his newly shaved head, repulsed at the idea that it and the strange Exorian tunic made him look like a child in nightclothes coming for kisses before bed. He stood taller, determined to find out where Seaborne and Frankie were. He lifted his eyes in challenge to Dankar, but found his heart pounding in fear. Dankar's protruding eyes—cold and glittering—were so unlike the other Keepers. He wanted to warn Knox and Evelyn not to say anything. He glanced at them out of the corner of his eye. Knox stared straight at the floor. Evelyn hugged herself tightly, as if she was holding herself in. He breathed a small sigh of relief. They would not be fooled by gentle speech. Tinator would be proud.

Dankar smiled at them and twirled the scepter on his lap. Chase felt something leap in his chest and wondered if the others felt it too. He took a pointed look at the round ball at the top.

"It is beautiful, is it not?" said Dankar, following Chase's eye. "It is—I think the expression goes—just a chip off the old block, yet it is marvelous. I find I am much at a loss without it." He advanced the few steps from the dais toward the children, conveying his great height with ease. Their faces flushed in the wave of heat that preceded him.

"My cousins feel the same, I am told," he said, holding the scepter just inches from their noses. A surge of anger, then grief, then joy passed through them. Dankar stepped back and the feelings subsided somewhat. "But you three are no strangers to these trinkets, I think, having spent time in my cousins' company. I am told the water-hoarder carries hers in a necklace."

He glared at them, then forced his lips into a simpering smile. "We do so love our toys."

Knox bristled visibly.

"You have heard the same, I see," he said, arching a pale eyebrow at Knox. "But you must know that powerful as these offspring are, they are nothing compared to the might of their parent stones." Dankar's voice dropped to a hushed whisper. "Think of it! The ability to turn not only the tides of the sea, the purchase of seed, and the drift of the wind, but also the minds and actions of men. Is it any wonder the Keepers have always kept the stones of power locked away for themselves? And you think *me* ungenerous! My uncle Remiel was no fool when he crafted these stones. He knew he was leaving his children with a great advantage."

"I want to see my sister," Evelyn growled.

Dankar turned to face her. "Frances?" He took a few steps up the dais, and said distractedly, "Shall I have her woken and brought here? It matters little to me. She has served her purpose; she may join you again."

"Her purpose?" repeated Chase.

"She has proved more than sufficient in that sense, yes," Dankar mused. "It was always my intention to bring the five of you here where you could be—ah—useful."

"How so?" asked Chase through gritted teeth.

"Why, to flush my cousins from their hidey-holes, of course. I've done what I can with Exor. I desire a new challenge." He bared his white teeth. They glistened with saliva. "And for this I need a larger canvas to work with—*much* larger."

"And Seaborne?" demanded Knox.

Dankar glanced at Louis, twirling his scepter, then spoke softly.

"A tenderness for your kind is a fault of my brethren—a corruption of blood—that, until recently, I never had the misfortune to feel; but, alas, I find that I am not immune to the long tenure on Ayda and its. . . influences." He turned away and began to pace. "I have decided upon a different fate for the wayfarer than was arranged. He can be of use to me . . . to *us*."

Louis's head shot up in confusion.

Chase watched the interchange closely. Whatever was happening did not seem good for Seaborne.

"I'll kill you if you hurt him," hissed Knox, his mouth curling with insolence.

Dankar's towering form came toward him, forearms flexing in the flickering candlelight. He stopped a pace away. Chase checked his impulse to duck.

"I see your time with my cousins has given you a share of their false pride. But you will soon see that power is not bequeathed in Exor, it is *earned,* with sacrifice." Dankar searched Knox's face to see if his words were making an impact. Knox remained stonily silent. Dankar turned on his heel.

"It has been said that no outlier can withstand the presence of a stone of power for long—the daylights riot and the vessel cannot contain them. But, I have worked these many years to unleash the power of the stone of Exor and bend it to my will. I can bring the daylights of my people to the very edge of endurance and hold them, igniting their strength while ensuring their obedience: My warriors are the proof of my success." His chest swelled. "But they are born Aydans; their vessels are stronger than those who come from beyond the fog. The wayfarer is of use to me because he is an outlier, like you, yet he has long been on Ayda in the house of Rothermel, and his daylights have strengthened. He is human—only stronger. He is the next logical step in my—uh—experiment, shall we say."

"What experiment?" gasped Evelyn.

Dankar grinned and threw himself on his throne.

"Long have I waited to see if my efforts would prevail in vessels who are weaker." His eyes flitted across Louis's face, then back to the orb at the top of his scepter. "After all, there are so many *more* of you. When I am master of Ayda and Keeper of all four stones of power, I shall take my army of Aydan warriors across the sea, back to the lands of my father; there, I shall command the hearts of your kind, as is my due."

The skin on the children's arms bristled despite the heat radiating off the dais.

"But first I must make certain that your vessels will survive my mastery. I have no wish to rule over ash heaps."

Knox, who had been shifting nervously throughout Dankar's speech, began to shout.

"You're talking about brainwashing! Body-snatching! Or worse! Burning people alive!" He glared at Louis. "And you said we should trust this guy? You want us to be a part of this?"

Dankar replied for him. "My adopted son longs to see his native shore as—perhaps—you do. He is honored to do my bidding so that he may return from whence he came." Dankar gave Louis a small, remote smile. "Though he is hardy, he has not lived long enough in these lands. His daylights are not strong enough yet to endure the warrior transformation, though he did manage to survive his initiation—barely." Dankar twirled his scepter, breezily. "We shall see how strong the wayfarer is. He will do for now." His smile became a clear smirk.

"Poor Seaborne," Evelyn groaned.

Chase scowled. Ratha had betrayed all of them, and Seaborne worst of all. He wondered what she was getting in return.

"What are you going to do with us?" he demanded.

Dankar waved his scepter again. "*That* depends on *you*."

"How so?" asked Knox, moving closer to Chase.

"I value loyalty above all else. Should you wish to remain here as my vassals, you shall be treated much like the girl, Frances, and," with a nod to Louis, "her predecessor. If you do not, well, there is always the other alternative. You may join Seaborne. We shall see how your daylights fare against the stone of Exor."

Louis gave a visible start, his eyes clouded.

Knox snarled. "Great. Some choice you give us; either we're made prisoners or you turn us into barbecue."

"It's not us, or even Ayda, that he wants," Evelyn cried in a flash of understanding. "It's the Fifth Stone! It's always been the Fifth Stone. Of course! Rysta told us!" She glowered at Dankar. "You want to be able to leave Ayda so you can hunt for the Fifth Stone. That's what all this is about. The Keepers and their stones are in your way—they are the only ones stopping you!"

"And that pesky fog problem," muttered Knox.

"They won't do it, you know," cried Evelyn. "They won't take the bait and come after us."

"Hmmm, I wonder?" replied Dankar. He brought the scepter lightly to his lips, then stood and stretched with cat-like grace. His lips spread into a slow, evil grin.

"I think you'll find my luck has changed of late."

A gust of cold wind blew into the hall, sputtering and crackling the torches, quickly followed by the sound of water trickling in the courtyard fountain. The wind picked up and extinguished the candles. The room plunged into darkness. Outside the windows, the sky turned a rosy violet; then, the wind ceased abruptly and all was quiet except for the tinkling of water falling lightly over stone. Dankar laughed and waved his scepter in an arc. Torches and candles burst into flame anew and a line of Exorian soldiers entered the room leading a group of captives. At the center of a phalanx of guards stood the shining helmets of several Metrian soldiers, and between them, Rysta, holding Teddy's hand.

Chase, Knox, and Evelyn groaned.

Dankar beckoned for his quarry to approach.

Rysta came slowly, her bare feet gliding smoothly and silently over the floor. The Metrians followed. She knelt and whispered to Teddy. He scrambled across the tile floor to throw himself at his brothers.

"Tedders, you're okay!" whooped Chase, hugging him fiercely.

"You look weird. What happened to your hair?" asked Teddy, staring at the three of them. His own hair had grown past his shoulders. He looked taller and more grown-up in his Metrian robes.

"It's a long story, Tedders," said Knox. "We'll tell it to you sometime."

"No we won't," chided Evelyn, touching her scalp. "We missed you, Teddy."

"I missed you, too, but Metria is so cool. You can swim everywhere, and they have ice cream! Rysta says we're all going back there."

"She did, did she?" interrupted Dankar. His cold stare locked onto Rysta. He moved from the dais to walk a full circle around her, relishing the moment. "Tut, tut, cousin . . . more lies?" he said in his slippery voice.

Rysta stood motionless, a statue of herself.

"I see you have brought me a gift." Dankar tossed his head in Teddy's direction and then waved a silent command. Three Exorians disappeared behind the dais. Moments later, they returned with Frankie, bleary and half-asleep. Evelyn shrieked at the sight of her.

"You're finally here!" Frankie said happily, but without surprise.

Evelyn ran across the dais and threw her arms around her. Dankar leaned in closer to Rysta, bringing his face nose to nose with hers.

"Tell me, cousin, will you give me your little human if I give you mine?"

Rysta said nothing but her eyes filled with pity.

Dankar's expression hardened. He flattened his lips and snarled.

"Do not condescend to me, water-hoarder!" He grabbed the folds of Rysta's robe and yanked the collar back to reveal her necklace, its stone resting at heart level. His eyes widened. With a tenuous finger, he traced the outline of the chain across Rysta's collarbones, then lifted the necklace so he could touch the stone itself. The Metrian soldiers shuddered. Teddy shivered, too. Even Chase, Knox, and Evelyn felt a tremor—as though someone had put an ice cube down their backs.

"I have waited a very, very long time for this moment," he whispered.

"You will free the children, *now*," was Rysta's firm reply. "And Seaborne. That was the arrangement."

Dankar was transfixed by the necklace. "Oh yes, that. Of course," he replied, "they will be free to go—once you have done as I ask. Free to go *where*, I wonder, but it is no matter to me. I have what I desire at present. The rest shall come."

Rysta removed his hand.

"You must know that I shall never reveal the location of the stone of Metria. You may do as you wish to me. I am but its Keeper. The power of Metria may be curtailed by the doing, but you will never attain its possession. You have always been too bold, Dankar, in your understanding of the stones. They do not belong to anyone."

Dankar slapped Rysta hard across the face. The Metrian guards roared. Rysta calmed them with a look. Her skin was red and blistered where his hand had touched her.

"This—and the necklace—will do for now." Dankar waved his hand and commanded, "Take the prisoners to the canyon's edge!" He strode from the hall just as the sun sent its first streaks of color across the dim, gray pallor of the sky.

Chapter 34

THE FLOOD

The great Exorian desert lay before them in a magnificent striation of red, brown, and orange. Dankar led them down the stairs from the Dwellings and under the vine-covered trellis along the road toward the canyon. He marched quickly, his gaze fixed straight ahead. The stone pyramids that lined the road burst into flame as he passed. Rysta and the children followed behind him at spearpoint. Louis walked beside the prisoners, pacing his gait so that he moved evenly with Rysta, if at a distance. Rysta held Teddy's hand again. She moved fluidly, her brow smooth, her expression inscrutable. Evelyn, Chase, and Knox tried to query her as they walked, but received no answers. She did, however, grant them a smile when Evelyn apologized for the theft of the necklace.

Frankie walked beside her sister, looking confused. Evelyn watched her closely. On the surface Frankie looked fine, but there was something strange about her, unfocused and distant. Her attention wavered whenever Dankar's shining head became visible on the path before them. She also couldn't stop throwing searching glances up at Louis, who was too distracted by Rysta to notice.

Halfway down the road, the parade of prisoners and guards was met by a wagon and donkey, recognizable to Chase, Evelyn, and Knox as their own transport. The back was thrown open and Seaborne fell to the ground, bound at ankle and wrist. Black and purple bruises bloomed across his chest and face. He stumbled to right himself. Chase and Knox helped him to his feet. Rysta lifted his bowed head, which looked skeletal without its ragged mop of hair. Seaborne's swollen eyes widened as he recognized her. He tried to speak but Rysta silenced him with an embrace; when he was released, his countenance had changed from joy to anger.

"What are you doing?" he shouted. "She can't be here, you idiots. You know that! I'm gone for one blessed night and the whole world falls apart. What did Rothermel tell you? If Dankar has her, it's only a matter of time before he gains Melor, too. You've doomed us all! I thought you understood that part!"

Rysta smiled at Seaborne.

"Do not trouble these three with me, Seaborne. I have come on my own accord."

Seaborne hobbled on for some moments in stunned silence.

"I don't understand," he said, exhaling slowly.

"Dankar is going to let us go," Knox whispered, "in exchange for her—and the necklace. It was probably Ratha's big idea. You were so right about her, Seaborne."

"Over my dead body!" Seaborne roared.

"Ask Chase—he knew all about it," said Knox coldly.

"I didn't know about Rysta, I swear!" Chase protested. "Ratha told me we'd be captured on the way to Metria. That's it! She didn't say anything about Rysta or anyone else. You have to believe me, Seaborne; if I'd known about this, I'd never have agreed to it!"

Seaborne shook his head.

"Dankar can do no worse than this. We will not be free. None of us will be free ever again. All Aydans will suffer for this." A strange, anguished gurgle came out of his mouth. "It makes me curse the day you came ashore, the five of you."

Rysta shushed him.

"Seaborne, child, you have lived long on Ayda—do you still see only with the eyes of an outlier? Do you not understand that there are unseen powers at work here? Trust in them."

Seaborne bowed his head, chagrined, but his expression remained grim. Rysta nodded in the direction of the canyon less than a half-mile beyond.

"Beyond the canyon is the Broomwash. When we reach the edge, you will be free to cross over. There are camels waiting on the other side to take you to the border of Exor where my brother has sent his people to meet you. Once you are safe, more will be revealed to you." Even though her eyes never moved, Chase felt her watching him from under her hood.

"The plan remains the same."

"But what about you?" Evelyn interrupted, feeling sorry for any hard thoughts she'd ever had about Rysta.

Rysta threw back her shoulders, as if to remove a heavy burden.

"I come now to repay a debt: a debt that has been long overdue. Do not tax yourself with grief for me."

The road ended abruptly at the edge of the steep canyon that Frankie had crossed on her journey to Exor. A thin ribbon of water snaked through the canyon floor a hundred feet below. The pillars marking the end of the road burst into flame. Dankar stood between them and faced the captives, the orb on his scepter throwing off rays of heat and fire that made the air around it quaver. The sun beat down on the bare heads of the outliers and their faces were shiny with sweat. The distinctive, yowling rattle-cry of a *tehuantl* reverberated through the canyon like a warning.

Exorian soldiers stood at attention along either side of the road. All of the guards save for Louis joined their ranks and left the prisoners to take the final steps alone. Seaborne hovered near Rysta. She held him back with a look and joined Dankar at the edge. They were the same height and build exactly: two columns of shimmering strength and beauty—one blue and silver, the other white and gleaming. For a moment, it seemed obvious to the humans beholding them that they belonged together, moon and sun, and that the most natural thing would be to fall on their knees and worship them.

"You will let the outliers go now, Dankar," Rysta insisted, breaking the spell with her familiar, calm tones. Her gaze fell momentarily on Louis. "*All* of them."

Dankar pressed his lips together.

"Yeeesss, that *was* the agreement," he said slowly. "But, you see, the walk has cleared my head and—" He grabbed Rysta's wrist. "I have changed my mind."

"Don't you touch her!" shouted Seaborne, shaking his bound fists. "You coward! You twisted, sun-baked coward! Cut me loose and deal with the likes of me!"

Louis grabbed Seaborne's shoulder.

"Do not make it worse for her, wayfarer. It will go badly for the children."

"Who in the blazes are you?" asked Seaborne, shrugging him off.

"He's my friend," croaked Frankie from somewhere by his hip. "His name is Louis."

"When this is over, Frankie, you and I are going to have a long talk about friends—a very long talk," said Seaborne.

Dankar's oily voice interrupted them.

"I find these outliers to be rather effective tools of persuasion. I may still find a use for them here in Exor. They will prove helpful in solving, what was it?" He cocked an ear at Knox. "Ah, yes, that *pesky* fog problem."

Louis moved closer to Dankar, frowning.

"Listen to me, Dankar," said Rysta. "You persist in thinking that you are greater than what has come before you—or what may come after. Your blindness shall be your undoing. If you let the outliers go as you agreed, I shall bring the waters from the mountains to refill your river and relieve Exor of her perpetual thirst. With me by your side, your power will double from what it once was. Is that not enough? Is that not a fair trade?"

"No," growled Dankar. "Not nearly enough."

"Then I will not help you and you shall be doomed," said Rysta.

A shudder of fury rippled through Dankar's body, strong enough to shake his robe.

"How dare you say such things to me? As if you are better than me? If Ayda is cursed, you have no one but yourself to blame! *You* betrayed your kin, as your father did before you, all for these . . . these *lesser* beings." Dankar dropped her wrist in disgust. He began to circle Rysta, his voice rising. "It is a family trait, this habit of disloyalty. It has been our undoing since the beginning of time, and I am going to end it. *Forever.*" He glared suddenly at Seaborne and the children with such menace that Teddy burst into frightened tears.

"You will soon see, my dear cousin, that I am not to be trifled with. The outliers will *not* be released, and I shall not rest until you and your kin lie in piles of ashes, as mine once did. As for the wayfarer . . ." He snapped his fingers. Two Exorian soldiers broke ranks and wrestled a struggling Seaborne up to the canyon's edge. One kicked the back of his knees. The other brought the shaft of his spear down hard across Seaborne's already battered back. He grunted with the impact. Seaborne's bent neck looked white and vulnerable below his abused scalp. Dankar surveyed the figure kneeling before him as if he were nothing more than a beetle on the ground.

Louis drew closer.

"I had thought to use the wayfarer for another purpose, but since I will now have five other outliers to work with, I think I prefer to kill him here, so that you may bear witness. He was like a child to you, was he not?" Dankar asked, coldly.

Rysta did not move or speak.

"It matters not," he continued. "He will be the first example I set." Dankar leveled his gaze at her and hissed. "I will see to it that you lose everything you love."

Something in Rysta seemed to break. She folded into herself, her face disappearing beneath her hood. Dankar laughed maliciously and withdrew a curved golden blade from beneath his robe. He raised it high. It caught the sun and blazed with a painful white light. The blade plummeted through the air toward Seaborne's exposed neck, but was intercepted in a clash of metal. Louis had held back the blade with a spear. Dankar's eyes widened in surprise.

"Because you are dear to me, I will forgive this act of disobedience once. Step back and do not meddle in things you do not understand." Dankar yanked the spear from Louis's grip and nodded to a guard to restrain him. The tip of the spear burst into flame.

"Now where was I?" Dankar leered at Rysta, clearly enjoying himself. He circled Seaborne. "Tell me, cousin, how should this boy of yours die—by blade, poison, or flame?"

"STOP IT!" cried a small shrieking voice. Teddy flung himself in between Seaborne and Dankar. He threw his small arms protectively around Seaborne's back. "Rysta, don't let the bad man get my Seaborne!"

Dankar's smile widened. He twirled the spear in his hands and sneered. "It makes no difference to me—one or two."

The sight of Teddy and Seaborne together brought Rysta back to life. She threw her hood back and her pale, shining hair unspooled in waves. The stone at her breast burst into a vivid shade of blue.

"Try and touch them, fiend!" she snarled.

Light from the orb in Dankar's scepter leapt across the air to join the glint from Rysta's stone, and, briefly, it was as if the gate between the burning pillars filled with dappled light moving across water. Incensed, Dankar flew at Rysta, crashing her into the pillar behind them. The light from her stone grew stronger; she flowed from his grasp again and again.

The Metrian soldiers rallied and hurled themselves against the Exorian line. Seizing the opportunity, Evelyn launched herself onto Dankar's back. Chase and Knox sprang to help Seaborne and Teddy. Only Frankie and Louis stood frozen, immobilized by the fracas.

A blast of wind blew in from the northeast, throwing up a cloud of dust and sand that obscured the sun and extinguished the flames of Dankar's spear. Overhead, black storm clouds massed, heavy with rain. Lightning streaked across the darkened sky and the wind blew hard and bitterly cold. From the snow-tipped mountains on the horizon came the distant rushing of oncoming water. Lightning broke again across the sky and a thunder clap unleashed a torrent of rain. It pelted the earth in great stinging drops. The river at the bottom of the canyon boiled red with muddied water, gorging itself on rain and the sudden surge of meltwater. It quickly overtook its banks.

The Exorians broke off fighting, distracted by the downpour. They dropped their spears and cupped their hands to catch the precious water.

Louis and Frankie joined the others at the canyon's edge. The river was rising. The air filled with a delicious, wet scent.

"This changes nothing!" seethed Dankar, rain beading off his extinguished spear. He cast his eyes around wildly for support, but his soldiers stood mesmerized, their ruined faces lifted to the sky, their scarred lips open to reveal tender-looking mouths that guzzled down the rain. Dankar's gaze fell on Louis.

"Round up the prisoners!" he ordered. A note of desperation had crept into his voice. He sluiced rain off his cheeks with the back of his hand. "Now!"

Louis hesitated, eyes on Rysta. She was magnificent in her fury, her countenance pale and fierce in the mixed light of the two stones—mere shards of the true stones of power, but awesome nonetheless. His gaze traveled to Dankar's bulging eyes, then back to the red marks on Rysta's skin where Dankar had abused her. She reached out with slender, cool fingers and brushed his cheek.

"Outlier, do not listen to him. He does not understand."

Louis's face darkened in confusion.

She broke his gaze to look down at Frankie, who stood as close to Louis as she could without touching him. His eyes followed hers. Frankie turned her wet, round face to meet his. She smiled hopefully at him.

"You're a scribe, then?" she asked. "Are you sad?"

Louis shook his head.

Frankie grabbed his hand and tugged on it.

"I'm glad, Louis. I like you much better the way you are."

Louis leveled his gaze at Rysta.

"We are who we love," she said, smiling gently.

Her words pierced the strange remove that had come over him since his initiation—as if he was above himself, watching his actions but not connected to them, not caring one way or another. He gave Frankie's hand a squeeze and whispered to her.

"I like you the way you are, too," he said. And he meant it. He *wanted* Frankie to be the person who her daylights meant her to be—not like him. Dankar's pet. It was suddenly the most important thing in the world. He turned to Rysta for direction.

"I will stay," she murmured, "but you must go and take the outliers with you." She gestured toward the river. It had risen almost halfway up the canyon walls. The clouds opened in a fresh deluge. Within seconds the river swelled even higher.

Louis nodded and knelt next to Frankie. The bangle on her upper arm caught his eye. He snatched it off. It left a bloody scarlet indentation.

"Time to go," he said to her. "I hope you're a good swimmer." Then he grabbed the back of her collar and launched her over the canyon's edge into the river. She came up shouting, moving quickly with the current. Evelyn jumped in after her. Louis swooped down and cut Seaborne's bonds, positioning himself between Dankar and the remaining prisoners.

"You! YOU! Ungrateful human!" screamed Dankar. He seized Louis by the throat. Another peal of thunder boomed across the sky. The wind blew harder. Rain became hail. Dankar was momentarily stunned.

"Let him go, Dankar," Rysta commanded, her voice rising above the storm.

Dankar refused and tightened his hold on Louis with one hand. He brandished his blade with the other.

"Never," he snarled. "He's mine."

"I would get moving if I were you," Louis shouted to Seaborne and the boys. He wrestled himself out of Dankar's grip and took out his own knife. The two men circled each other, glaring. Thunder boomed across the canyon.

"You said you'd let them go," Louis yelled. "Now let them go!"

Dankar pounced.

Louis parried and yelled to Seaborne. "You are out of time!"

Seaborne maneuvered himself next to Rysta. He grabbed Teddy. "He's right! In you go, ma'am."

Rysta shook her head. "What has been put into motion cannot be stopped, Seaborne. It is my fate to stay. I have little hope for myself—but perhaps I may gain some for others." Rysta looked pointedly at Louis, fighting feverishly to keep Dankar at bay and buy them time.

"Then it is my fate, as well," said Seaborne, setting Teddy on the ground. "I will not leave you to this."

Rysta shook her head again.

"You must stay with the outliers. It is your appointed duty." She cast her eyes over the three boys standing at the lip of the canyon, lingering longest over Teddy's blond head. "Be most careful with them, Seaborne, for they are very dear to me." She leaned in. "As are you. Do not fear for me, my child; our vessels are impermanent things, but the daylights will endure."

"He wouldn't dare!"

"It is not for me to know what will happen—but you must go, NOW!" The light from the stone in her necklace grew blindingly bright. "I send with you the benediction of the stone of Metria! May your daylights protect you and guide you to peace!"

Seaborne picked up Teddy again, cast one reluctant look at Rysta, and threw himself into the roiling river. Knox grabbed Chase by the tunic and jumped after him. They all looked back in time to see Dankar whip Louis in the side of the face with the hilt of his knife, knocking him to the ground. Rysta's hair blew wildly in the wind as she bent down to shield him. Dankar walked once to the gate to look down the river, his scepter glowing with renewed vigor. Then, as the river bent south, the rain and hail eased and they were carried swiftly out of sight.

Chapter 35

CAST OFF

They had not drifted far when the swell of the river calmed and Chase and Knox met up with Teddy and the rest of their group, who had been waiting for them, treading water. They floated all together for a while, wondering how long this new river was and where it was taking them.

"Let's go a bit farther, then see if we can swim ashore," said Seaborne tonelessly.

"I don't understand why Rysta would stay there," said Knox. "After everything she told us about the balance of the daylights on Ayda—why would she just give hers up to Dankar?"

"He still doesn't have the stone of Metria," said Chase.

"Yeah, but he has her, and the necklace! That's good enough to do a lot of damage." Knox's voice broke. "The Melorians don't stand a chance."

"You don't know that," said Chase, thinking back to what Rysta had said on the way to the canyon. *The plan remains the same.*

"What do you mean to say, lad?" asked Seaborne, swimming closer. "What else have you not told us?"

Before Chase could answer, two light canoes came paddling toward them from the underbrush. They were constructed of bark and moved silently across the water. One was paddled by Mara and Calla, the other by Sarn and Duor.

"Melorians!" whooped Knox.

One by one the swimmers were pulled aboard, shivering. Calla passed out warm ponchos and then set her paddle back into the river. The canoes took to the middle where the current drew swiftly.

Evelyn pulled the poncho over her head and yanked up the hood.

"Are we going to the Wold?"

Mara shook her head.

"To the cabin, then?"

Again no. The canoes sped down the river, which began to broaden. A familiar mist crept along the boats, growing thicker and more chill. In the distance there was a strange rhythmic sound. It took Knox a minute to figure out what it was: waves, pounding a beach. They were at the mouth of the river, where it met the sea. Overhead, a few invisible gulls cried out a welcome.

The canoes glided gently to the left side of the river, their hulls scraping softly on the sandy bottom. Together, they pulled the canoes onto the beach. The fog curled and drifted around them.

"Everybody stay together," barked Knox.

"You sound like my father," Calla laughed. Knox went red.

The fog lifted enough for them to see the wide mouth of the river emptying its ruddy waters into the flat gray depths of the sea. Along each bank was a broad sand beach. Calla and Sarn led the way toward a twisted, surf-blasted tree trunk at the edge of some tangled vegetation that scrawled inland. Duor whistled one loud blast.

"With caution now; you are still in Exor," intoned a deep voice from the brush. It was immediately followed by Rothermel himself, his green eyes muted in the fog. Chase, Knox, and Evelyn stiffened. They had not forgotten what Seaborne had told them about Rothermel's anger and his willingness to trade them to Dankar. Rothermel stopped only feet from them. Evelyn noticed that the lines on his face had deepened, yet his expression remained kind, if careworn.

"It would seem that I still have not answered the riddle of your presence here on Ayda," he said. "I know not whether it is for ill or for good."

"Feels pretty 'for ill' right now," said Knox in a low voice.

Rothermel smiled sadly.

"Yes, that is true—but it may not turn out to be so in the end." Rothermel nodded to Chase. "Is that not so, eldest?"

Chase looked down at the sand.

"Chase? What's going on?" asked Knox.

"He means that I'm, I mean, *we're* still going to follow Ratha's plan. We're going home—through the fog, like she said, and then I . . ." He trailed off.

"What?" demanded Knox. "C'mon, Chase. Enough with the secrets!"

Rothermel came to Chase's defense.

"Your brother has made a vow to find the Keeper of the Fifth Stone and send him back to Ayda."

"Right," said Knox, exchanging a mystified glance with Evelyn.

"You know who it is?" she asked. "The Keeper of the Fifth Stone? And you didn't tell us?"

Chase squirmed uncomfortably.

"Better 'fess up, lad," Seaborne admonished. "You left a lot for the explaining, and it was a sorry thing for me to leave Rysta in that blasted oven; my heart is sore with the doing."

"Okay, okay. I didn't tell you because Ratha told me I should keep it to myself. She said you wouldn't believe me—especially you, Seaborne."

"Rightly so; she's not to be trusted," Seaborne huffed, then caught himself. "All due respect, Rothermel."

"Anyway," Chase continued. "You already know that Ratha said she was going to rescue Frankie, but I didn't know *how* she would do it. I swear. All I knew was that we were supposed to set out for Metria and that we'd get captured—"

"That sure worked out great," said Knox sarcastically, emphasizing his point by rubbing his bald head.

Chase ignored him.

"If I got you all to go along, she promised to bring us all back together and send us home—just like I told you." Chase hesitated again, aware of how crazy his next words would sound. "What I didn't tell you is that when we get there, I'm supposed to take a message to Captain Nate."

"WHEN you get there?" Seaborne scowled. "That's a laugh! And who in the skies' great thunder is Captain Nate? Why would Rysta take part in a fool's errand? It's impossible to get through the fog. It was a lie. All of it!" He glared at Chase. "And you let it happen! If you'd only told me everything I could have stopped all this nonsense."

"The plan for Rysta to go to Exor was devised without the eldest boy's knowledge—or mine," Rothermel interjected. "But Seaborne, you are right on one account: It is like my sister to tell the boy just enough to secure his promise. Though she, too, was deceived. Despite her wisdom, her plan did not proceed as she anticipated. Ratha did not think Dankar would go back on his word to free you in exchange for Rysta. Fortunately, I have more experience with the enemy."

Evelyn collapsed on the sand in a state of confusion.

"Chase, start from the beginning! The sea captain? How is he a part of this?"

This time, Chase left nothing out of his explanation of his visitation with Ratha at the the temple of Varuna, and her belief that Captain Nate was the Keeper of the Fifth Stone. As he spoke, a large flock of gulls circled overhead and amassed along the tide's edge. They craned their beaks and swiveled their heads as if they were listening.

Evelyn continued to shake her head in disbelief.

"I'm supposed to tell Captain Nate about Ayda and what happened to us here," Chase concluded. "That's the deal."

"But why should he come?" she asked in annoyance. "If he has the stone, he could have come anytime. Why now?"

"I may hold that answer," replied Rothermel. "My sister Rysta has told you about our parents and the events that preceded the Great Battle of Ayda, but she did not tell you the very important role she had to play in our misfortunes. She avoided this out of sadness and shame, I warrant. It is a wound that will not heal." Rothermel looked out into the fog, as if he could see the ocean behind it. One of the gulls cawed mournfully. Another answered.

"Of all the travelers that once came to Ayda, none managed to return to us but one—a great adventurer and explorer. He was known to us then as Caspar. He came to Ayda in my father's time, in the peace before the Great Battle. I still recall the sight of his ship sailing up the Hestredes: it was a broad ship laden with cargo"—Rothermel's brow furrowed—"and people taken as prizes for his king."

"Slaves?" asked Evelyn, shocked.

Rothermel considered her for a moment, then answered.

"It was not uncommon in those days for such ships to come ashore here, bearing souls stolen from one land to do the work of another, not unlike how the Exorians now treat my people. But in the days of my father and the Fifth Stone, such evil intentions were unknown to Ayda—and soon forgotten by any who set foot here. All who stayed were free to live where their daylights dictated. Most Aydans, with the exception of my family and the ancients, are descended from these lines. What happened to those who did not stay I cannot say, for they sailed out of my knowing."

"And Caspar?" prompted Knox. "What did he do?"

"He lived long on Ayda and fought bravely against Dankar's forces in the Great Battle, until his daylights were fragmented by the enemy. We believed him lost forever; I grieved for him as I grieved for my own brother." Rothermel's voice grew more and more sorrowful as he spoke. "And I was not the only one; for there was a woman on Ayda who, in the days before the Great Battle, came to love Caspar above all things. But to love someone, truly, is to love the nature of their daylights, and Caspar was not content to stay on Ayda indefinitely. His daylights longed for the sea, for distant horizons and stranger shores. It was a torment to the woman to see him suffer, becalmed and landlocked, and so she went behind my father's back and found a way for Caspar—alone among men—to come and go to Ayda at will."

"How?" asked Chase, Evelyn, and Knox in unison.

"I am told she gave him some kind of map, but I do not know for certain how she did this, only that she did."

"Who was the woman?" asked Evelyn.

Rothermel's eyes wavered and fell to the sand.

"My sister, Rysta," he admitted.

"The man in her pool," gasped Evelyn. "The one she got so upset about. It must have been Caspar."

Rothermel sighed. "The blessing my family received—our life on Ayda—relied on no further mingling of Watcher, or even half-Watcher, and humankind. My sister knew this, and yet she loved the man Caspar as my father loved my mother. It was her love that betrayed us and led Dankar to our shores."

Chase sat back on his heels. Everything Rysta had said in Exor fell into place. This was the debt she needed to repay.

"But I don't understand," he ventured. "If this guy Caspar was the only one who knew how to come and go, how did Dankar discover his secret?"

"Dankar had many spies then," answered Rothermel. "He was once as powerful a king in your lands as he is here. He was vigilant and cunning, and, eventually, had Caspar watched. It was not long before Caspar—unwittingly—led him here. You will remember that Dankar had been looking for Ayda since he first heard tell of such a place. We did not guard our island well enough before the fog. We have since learned better."

The gulls suddenly screeched into the air as if frightened. A dry wind began to blow down the beach, stirring the sand into eddies.

"That doesn't explain why Ratha thinks Captain Nate has the Fifth Stone," said Knox, looking at Chase, then at Rothermel.

Rothermel's green eyes glittered. "Does it not?"

Chase clapped his hand to his forehead, thunderstruck.

"Ratha thinks Captain Nate *is* Caspar!" he exclaimed.

Rothermel nodded.

"Wait," said Knox, braking the air with his hands. "I thought Caspar died in the Great Battle. Besides, they can't be the same guy. It would mean Captain Nate is, like, five hundred years, which he's not. I've seen him. He's old, but he's not that old."

"Not if he has the Fifth Stone," Evelyn cut in, thinking back to what Rysta had said about her parents. "As long as he stays with it, he won't die. Remember Rachel?" She turned to face Rothermel, who shifted uneasily at the sound of his mother's name.

"You think Caspar escaped from Ayda with the stone and that he's Captain Nate, or Captain Nate is him, or whatever. That's why Rysta let herself be captured! Ratha told her about Chase, and now Rysta wants Captain Nate to come back and bring the stone with him!"

The wind blew harder. Sand stung at their ankles and clung to Rothermel's long, grizzled hair. He nodded.

"You speak the truth, eldest girl. Time is short. Dankar has the stone of Exor and my sister. He may soon gain another stone. I do not know how long my sister's daylights will last so far from her home, and Melor is now in even greater peril. Our greatest challenge lies before us. If this captain is the voyager, Caspar, there is hope that the Fifth Stone will return to Ayda. "

"Dankar said that if it weren't for you, there wouldn't be any fog," said Frankie, finally breaking her dazed silence. "He told me we could go home whenever we wanted if it weren't for you."

Rothermel spoke to her gently.

"Little one, you have long been in the halls of the Usurper. He has told you many things, much of it lies. For that is his way. He will talk to you of friendship and loyalty when he knows not what they are."

"He said that *you* were the liar," Frankie insisted.

Rothermel frowned. "I have no doubt that he would prefer you to think that, but let me ask you this: Why would he not let you go as Rysta requested? Is this the manner of a friend?"

"But, he—and Louis—" she objected.

Rothermel looked to Evelyn for an explanation as to who Louis was. When he was told of the man who had saved them and protected Rysta, the creases on his brow thickened.

"I knew not of this outlier. I am thankful that my sister has at least one ally in her midst. Dankar may hold her and the necklace captive, but we must remember that she, too, is closer than ever before to the stone of Exor. Things may not proceed entirely in his favor. We will do what we can to aid her, and you must do the same." He motioned to the Melorians. "It is time."

Sarn and Duor retreated into the brush. Rothermel beckoned to Mara. She dug into the canoe and returned with a large basket, which she unpacked before them. It was the clothing they had arrived in, washed and mended.

"Something is about to happen in Ayda that has not taken place since my father's time," said Rothermel. "Ratha has promised to send you through the fog to the other side, as she brought you here, in the hope that you will persuade the man you call Captain Nate to return to us. She is confident that this man is the same man we knew as Caspar; that he lives on and will know how to find his way back. Pray to the *atar* that he loves Ayda and my sister still." Rothermel laid a heavy hand on Chase's shoulder. "As for my kin, we will prepare for all-out war with Exor—for we know not when or if you will succeed in your task."

Evelyn, Frankie, and the boys pulled on their old clothes, which felt tight and uncomfortable after so many weeks dressed in Aydan garments. When they were done changing, they looked much as they had on their arrival, except, in Chase, Evelyn, and Knox's case, bald and sunburned. Mara and Calla tied a wooden bead strung on a woven cord around each of their necks.

"These are made from trees that grow strong in the Melorian forest," said Mara. "They withstand much hardship and abuse and continue to prosper. Wear them with our friendship, and so that you may never forget Melor or the peril of Ayda even when you are beyond the fog." She tied Evelyn's necklace on last, and withdrew from her poncho a small, hollowed-out gourd containing a pine-scented oil. She massaged the oil onto Evelyn's scalp. When she finished, Rothermel put his hands on Evelyn's head and sang a low, unintelligible chant. Evelyn felt a tingling sensation.

"Evelyn—your hair! It's growing!" Frankie gasped.

Evelyn's hands shot to her head. It was true: Sprouts of thick, chestnut-colored hair were shooting out of her head.

Mara smiled faintly.

"Some things are easier to heal than others," she said, and repeated the action on the two older boys. When she had finished, it was as if the damage done to them in Exor had never occurred.

Calla and Seaborne crossed over to say good-bye to them. Seaborne swooped up Teddy in an enormous bear hug.

"Don't you want to come back with us?" Teddy asked.

"Yeah, Seaborne, we could show you everything that's been invented since you left," added Knox.

Seaborne shook his head.

"My vessel would not long withstand a separation from Ayda—nor my heart," he said, looking at Calla and releasing Teddy.

Calla's eyes swept over them, landing on Knox.

"Melorians do not say good-bye," she said.

"It is not our way," he replied.

Calla smiled proudly. "May your daylights keep you strong, child of Melor, wherever they lead you." Then, she leaned in to whisper ugently in his ear. "Do not forget all that I have taught you."

Knox nodded.

Rothermel beckoned for the children to follow him. He led them across the beach, to the shore where the mouth of the river met the sea. The gulls began to screech loudly overhead. Fog licked the banks of the river. Suddenly—silently—a boat came toward them out of the mist like an apparition.

"No way," said Knox.

It was the Whaler, being poled across the water by Sarn and Duor.

"I have come to give you back your boat," said Rothermel; then, lowering his voice so that only Chase, Evelyn, and Knox could hear, he added: "I do not know what you will find on the other side. Be prepared, and know that your memory will suffer. Ratha will be watching you, but even she has little knowledge of what might occur on your journey through the fog. Should you make it beyond, remember that our stones have little sway there. Whatever happens, you must trust your daylights. They have grown strong on Ayda and will not forget so easily." He stepped back. "We will look for your return, but we will not hope for it."

The boat crunched on the sand and the children exchanged places with Sarn and Duor.

Seaborne, Mara, and Calla joined Rothermel at the river's edge. Rothermel reached across the gunwale and touched each of the beads on their necklaces. The scent of the forest filled their nostrils and, for a moment, their spirits rose. They slipped on the life vests returned from Seaborne's cabin and watched the sand swirl at the Melorians' feet, tendrils of fog ebbing and flowing with each wave. The boat drifted easily away from shore and out into the open sea. Seaborne lifted his hand to chest level, his fingers splayed. All five returned the salute before the fog enveloped them.

"Chase?" Evelyn said softly.

"Yeah?"

"I take back what I said before—I'm glad I met you."

Chase pressed his lips together in a tight, little smile.

"Me too, Ev. Really glad."

Evelyn brushed her fingers against his. He gave them a quick squeeze. She leaned into him, so lightly he almost didn't notice it.

"Get ready," she whispered.

A flock of gulls roared past their heads, squawking and flying in a V just ahead of the drifting boat. The wind blew hard at their backs. The current picked up speed. The Whaler surged ahead as the wind propelled them forward. The fog took on the bruised colors that Chase recognized from his time with Ratha. It started to swirl, then it stretched and telescoped.

"IT'S A TUNNEL!" yelled Evelyn.

The gulls flew faster; the wind gusted, and the current shot the boat into the vortex of spinning fog. It bucked and shuddered.

"HOLD ON!" cried Knox, falling back onto the deck of the boat.

Light and shadow flickered in the fog with dizzying speed.

Find the sea captain . . . Do not forget! screamed the wind, in Ratha's voice.

Frankie moaned. Evelyn threw an arm around her. Chase and Knox huddled next to Teddy. The wind lifted the boat off the water and into the air.

And they were gone

Coming in 2015

CHANTARELLE

THE FIVE STONES TRILOGY

GA-MORGAN.COM